D1025636

T. DAVIS BUNN

ONE FALSE MOVE

A
JANET
THOMA
BOOK

THOMAS NELSON PUBLISHERS
Nashville • Atlanta • London • Vancouver
Printed in the United States of America

Publisher's Note: The characters, companies, and products named in this
book are fictitious, and no parallel to any real persons, companies, or products is intended.

Published in Nashville, Tennessee, by Thomas Nelson, Inc., Publishers, and
distributed in Canada by Word Communications, Ltd., Richmond, British
Columbia.

The Bible version used in this publication is THE NEW KING JAMES VER-
SION. Copyright © 1979, 1980, 1982, 1990 Thomas Nelson, Inc.,
Publishers.

Library of Congress Cataloging-in-Publication Data
Bunn, T. Davis, 1952–
    One false move : a novel / T. Davis Bunn.
        p.   cm.
    ISBN 0-7852-7368-9
    I. Title.
PS3552.U4718054   1997
813'.54—dc20

                                                        96-38695
                                                        CIP

Printed in the United States of America.

1 2 3 4 5 6 — 01 00 99 98 97 96

This book is dedicated to
Paul and Jan Sunderland
Whose wonderful friendship put the game in play

*"Where there is no law
there is no transgression."*
Romans 4:15

FEDERAL DISTRICT COURT FOR COLORADO

Docket Number: CF10284

United States v. Styx Enterprises, et al.

Deposition of Claire Kingsbury: Day One

Offices of Mr. Josiah R. Holloway,

Attorney for the Defense

MR. HOLLOWAY: Is it correct, Miss Kingsbury, that you have been nominated for a Pulitzer Prize in connection with this story?

MISS KINGSBURY: I haven't heard anything for sure, but I understand that is correct, yes.

MR. HOLLOWAY: Would it be fair to say that this prize would have a powerful effect on your career?

MISS KINGSBURY: Yes, I suppose it would. But I don't know for certain—

MR. HOLLOWAY: Miss Kingsbury, are you familiar with the Washington reporter who made up a story in order to win the Pulitzer Prize and thus further her career?

MISS KINGSBURY: Yes, I have heard of it.

MR. HOLLOWAY: Is it not true, Miss Kingsbury, that you have done the exact same thing with this story?

MISS KINGSBURY: No. Not at all.

MR. HOLLOWAY: Isn't it true, Miss Kingsbury, that this entire story is a charade, fabricated in an attempt to bolster your career with a Pulitzer Prize of your own, and that there is no substantiation whatsoever for the charges which you have leveled against Styx Enterprises?

MISS KINGSBURY: Everything I wrote was both carefully researched and well-documented.

MR. HOLLOWAY: We'll come to those documents of yours later, and I remind you that you are under oath. Miss Kingsbury, are you not very new to your job as reporter for the *Denver Herald*? Was this not, in fact, one of your first assignments?

MISS KINGSBURY: I was a stringer for the paper for almost four years. Following that, I was given a part-time assignment with the paper's western bureau.

MR. HOLLOWAY: A stringer. That sounds like a fairly menial position from which to research and write a story which has catapulted you to national attention. Miss Kingsbury, did you not become intimate with one of the Styx Enterprises senior consultants, a Mr. Donovan Stone? Don't look at the District Attorney, Miss Kingsbury. Answer the question, did you have an affair with Donovan Stone?

MISS KINGSBURY: I knew him, yes. But we didn't have—

MR. HOLLOWAY: Did he not then break off the affair against your wishes, leaving you high and dry?

MISS KINGSBURY: No. I mean, he didn't break it off, I did. And there wasn't any—

MR. HOLLOWAY: Were you not then fueled with bitter- ness, Miss Kingsbury, which led you to fabricate this story, a story fashioned from whole cloth, one which is a lie from beginning to end, the only true portion being that you wanted revenge?
MISS KINGSBURY: No, none of that is true.

MR. HOLLOWAY: Did you not then use this desire for vengeance to make up all the comments which you

have attributed to a certain director of Styx
Enterprises, when in truth not one word was true,
and in fact you have misconstrued, misstated, and dis-
torted his responses?

MISS KINGSBURY: No. Not at all. I wrote my story—

MR. HOLLOWAY: Your story. Yes, we'll come back to
what you actually wrote in a few minutes. Now then,
Miss Kingsbury, are you not a volunteer member of
the Colorado Rocky Mountain Firefighters, a position
you have held for some time?

MISS KINGSBURY: Yes, but I don't see what that has—

MR. HOLLOWAY: The purpose of that volunteer organization is to chase across mountain wilderness areas,
putting out fires in areas most people could not even
reach at the best of times. Is that not correct?

MISS KINGSBURY: Yes, I guess it is.

MR. HOLLOWAY: So you have volunteered for an organization that takes wild risks for the sake of a little
thrill, is that not true, Miss Kingsbury?

MISS KINGSBURY: We do it because we love the mountains and the forests, and we want to protect our national heritage.

MR. HOLLOWAY: That all sounds very noble, Miss Kingsbury, but let us return to what it shows about your character. Didn't you fabricate this wild series of accusations from this same base motive of enjoying a little thrill, wanting to bask in the limelight, regardless of what harm you might do to others? Did you not scheme to incriminate Styx Enterprises and its management for your own reasons of thrill-seeking and revenge?

DISTRICT ATTORNEY: Objection. Mr. Holloway, you are not asking questions, you are seeking to testify yourself.

MR. HOLLOWAY: That is the basest untruth.

DISTRICT ATTORNEY: You are turning every direct denial which my witness gives into a misleading positive suggestion. Miss Kingsbury, you are hereby instructed not to answer any further such questions.

MR. HOLLOWAY: I object to your instructions. You are interfering with a legitimate line of inquiry.

DISTRICT ATTORNEY: You are not soliciting informa-

tion. You are seeking to intimidate the witness. I

object to your manner. I hereby instruct the witness

to ignore all further such questions. And if you con-

tinue in this manner, we will close this session and

allow the judge to instruct you as to how to question

a state witness. His comments will be on the record,

and I will have them read to the jury as an example of

your methods of intimidation.

MR. HOLLOWAY: Very well. Miss Kingsbury, how on

earth did you ever have the idea for this story?

MISS KINGSBURY: It wasn't my idea, it was Harry

Mitchum's. The first I heard of it was through a

phone call . . .

OURAY AND
DENVER, COLORADO

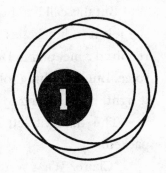

■ The day the revival came to town, Claire knew it was time to leave home.

Claire heard the departure bell sound the minute she set down the phone. It rang through her like a lonely highland wind, chilling her with an indifferent power. The internal arguments were over. She was leaving.

The letter from her mother lay unopened beside the phone. These brief notes came so seldom, they always threatened to stop her heart. Claire carried it back into her bedroom and stuffed it into her purse. The letter would have to wait. The day was already too full as it was.

The call had been from Harry Mitchum, Business and Features editor for the *Denver Herald*. The call had been nothing more than another assignment. For four years she had worked as a stringer before finally being given a part-time position with the *Herald*'s western bureau. A stringer was lowest of the low when it came to newspaper reporters, a dogsbody called in for small-time local assignments, or to fill gaps when the others were too busy. A part-timer with the paper's most far-flung office was hardly much of an improvement.

But this call had been different. Why, she wasn't sure, but she felt it in her bones. Maybe it was because the assignment required a meeting in Denver. Maybe it was the tone of Harry's voice. But something told her this was the one. If she handled it right, he was going to offer her a job.

The thought left her so scared she trembled as she packed.

"Claire? What you doing, girl?" Miss Emma, the woman who took care of both their office and their home, was standing in the doorway, peering over her shoulder. "That call you got this morning put a bee in your bonnet, did it?"

Claire squeezed the case shut. "There aren't any secrets in this town."

"Not when you get off the phone and skip into breakfast, especially after you come dragging in here after midnight last night." She stumped to the bathroom and wrinkled her nose over the dirty clothes hamper. "Heard the fire had you way up high this time."

"That's not such a bad thing." Claire popped open her last empty case, began filling it with books and papers. She couldn't let Miss Emma know how tired she still felt. And stiff. "We were able to take trails up above the tree line, then go back down when we got near the burn."

"Ain't ladylike, you hiking all over the back of beyond with goodness knows what kind of rascals for company." The grey head bent over, using two fingers to pluck out soot-charred shirt and trousers, only to drop them back in. "Come home so black not even Nathan will admit to knowing you. If I've told you once, I've told you a thousand times, fighting forest fires is not a proper hobby for a lady."

"You and Pop sure agree on that one."

The old lady walked over, peered down at Claire's packing, and said more quietly, "You going for good this time?"

Claire did not try to deny it. "I'll be back weekends."

"Shame the best and the brightest got to go off to find themselves proper work these days." Her voice was flat, the fight out of her now. "Well, I ain't one to hold the young back. But I sure to goodness won't be telling you good-bye. My old heart couldn't stand that." She started to turn away, then tried to hold Claire at the last with, "Your daddy will sure be sorry to hear you'll be missing the revival."

Claire forced the zipper closed, found herself suddenly without the breath to speak, and made do with a nod and a bright smile as she hefted the bags and started for the door.

The revival had been her father's idea. Claire wasn't sure how she felt about it, or about the scrutiny turned her way. The whole town was talking about nothing else. Most of those she met seemed genuinely excited by the event. A few viewed it as tomfoolery from a by-gone age. Back when many of their forefathers had been hard-rock miners, up in the hills six days a week and streaming into town Saturday nights with loot burning a hole in their pockets, revivals had been the way. Big and noisy and exciting enough to pull the miners away from the bars and the houses back on Third Street. Some of them, anyway. But there had not been one in Ouray for as long as anyone could remember.

Claire popped up the Blazer's back door, careful to avoid touching the outer surface as it swung open. The eight-year-old Chevy was probably still blue under its coating of dirt and road salt, but a stranger would be hard-pressed to tell. She settled two cases into the back. As she straightened up, Claire decided how she felt most of all right then was *pressured.*

Everybody seemed to be watching her these days, expecting her to live up to the example set by her father. And that made her angry. Religion was fine, as far as she was concerned, so long as it was kept in its proper place. Right now she just wanted to get on with her life.

But people weren't satisfied with that any more. They expected her to shine with her father's quiet fervor. Claire shoved the last case into place, knowing the only way she would ever be her own person was to leave. Wrenching as that thought might be, it was time to go. And not come back. Either Harry Mitchum was going to give her a job, a real job for a real reporter, or she was going to look elsewhere, and keep searching until her money ran out.

Claire stopped and looked around. Most locals did so at least once or twice each day, just pause in their work or their talk and take in the surrounding peaks.

Ouray sat at the base of a steep-sided bowl, the mountains too tight and constricting ever to permit much development. People who came and stayed took great pride in this natural barrier to all the hustle and building that filled other high valleys.

The bowl's western side contained the towering Twin

Peaks, and directly behind them rose Whitehouse. Over the years since her arrival, she had come to know each of these hills as she would an old friend, watching them change with weather and daylight and cloud and storm. She knew their moods. She appreciated them for their strength and silent steadfastness.

She continued her slow turning. To the southwest was Hayden Peak. Below that ran Canyon Creek, which entered Ouray at Box Canyon Falls. The vertical-sided canyon cut a shaft twenty feet in diameter and one hundred-and-fifty feet deep; the creek barreled through that internal waterfall with the sound of an endless cannon barrage. In the wintertime the icicles at the opening could be thirty feet long and as thick as her waist.

The Uncompahgre River entered Ouray through the same steep-sided canyon as Highway 550. That road was their only connection to Durango and the south. The entire eastern side of the valley was given over to the Amphitheater Range, with the National Forest Campground rising to meet the snow-covered peaks. In the summertime Claire loved to hike the hogback ridge, which wound its way along the peaks, the trails about six feet wide with drops of two thousand feet to either side. The trail, known as the Bridge of Heaven, looked eastward over the American Flats, an uninhabited emptiness extending for almost thirty miles. Claire stood in her driveway and traced her way along the ridgeline, yearning for the simple silent freedom that surrounded her whenever she was up there.

She heard a voice behind her say, "The revival starts in a half-hour. Since I'm giving the opening prayer, I guess we better be off." Claire dropped her gaze and watched her father move cautiously down the icy sidewalk. Offices for the *Ouray Star* were situated in a small wood-frame house near where Fourth met Main, about two hundred yards from their home. Claire braced her shoulders determinedly and waited for the coming storm. Her father caught her off guard by simply asking, "How do I look?"

She took in the dark suit, the carefully knotted tie, the starched shirt. "More like a preacher than a newspaper editor."

"Not necessarily a bad thing." He examined her in turn. She knew what he found only made the coming confrontation clearer—her high cowboy boots, her jeans, her flannel shirt showing beneath the goosedown vest. His gaze rose to her face, and she knew he recognized both the resolve in her clear green eyes and the promise of another argument. It seemed like every time they talked these days, they argued.

Which was probably why he swung around and started down towards Main Street. "I gather you're not staying around for the first sermon."

She caught up to him and tried to match his neutral tone. "I told you, Harry Mitchum is expecting me in Denver. With the snow last night, there's no telling how the passes are going to be."

"Whatever you say." Their footsteps crunched softly in the new-fallen snow. Claire shortened her stride and matched her father's step, an action she had been doing for so long she rarely gave it any thought. No more thought than she did to his silence; her father had always been a quiet man, but following his stroke twelve years earlier, Nathan had learned to do without words for hours at a time.

As she walked, Claire thought back to those early days. After his return from the hospital, each word had required tremendous effort, and he was forever dabbing at the moisture which dribbled from his mouth's left side. Back then, almost no one could understand him, not even the doctors. But she had never had difficulty, rarely even needing to ask him to repeat himself. They had all used her as the interpreter—the doctors and physiotherapists and nurses and lawyers from the bank. She had not minded. It had helped shield him from more of the pressure and pain which had caused the stroke in the first place.

She was drawn back to the present when he said, "I can still smell the smoke."

"It's my hair." She swept an impatient hand through her thick red tresses. Her hair was almost as bright as a forest fire and twice as unruly. "I washed it twice, but you'd never know it."

Nathan took another couple of steps before asking, "Was it bad?"

"Forest fires are always bad, Pop. But I wasn't in any danger."

November was far too late for a forest fire. But this had been an uncommon season all around. The driest September and October on record had all the locals predicting a hard winter, but the snows never arrived. Instead, winter seemed determined not to come at all. The days remained dry and warm, the nights balmy. The plains south of Denver, on the Rockies' eastern side, stayed dusty brown and parched.

Then, two nights earlier, she had been awakened by the chilling sound of thunder. Claire had slept the remainder of the night with one ear open, waiting for the call which had finally come at dawn.

"I worry about you when you're up there," Nathan was saying. "Especially when it's so high."

"You're the one who's always going on about how we need to give something back to our community." They had been through this so often her reply came automatically. "I help put out fires."

"I only wish my daughter would find a service that doesn't threaten her life."

She waved at a friend she scarcely saw, knowing she was just putting off the inevitable. But still she could not find a way to say what had to be spoken. "I love the highlands and the forests. All the volunteers do. We're doing it because it has to be done. We're careful."

Nathan gave in, saying, "They say it was a small fire."

"We caught it early. And the snows arrived just in time.' The words came hard, her chest tight and breathless, as though she had been running. She knew it had to be said, but did not know how. She opened her mouth, but couldn't speak. The air felt trapped in her chest.

His voice was quiet, his tone calm, as he spoke for her. "You're not coming back this time, are you?"

The air came out then, as though punched from her chest, the frustration turning to sudden anger. "I hate it when you do that. Read me like an open book. I hate it."

"It wasn't all that hard," he replied. "You received a phone call this morning, you started packing, you've been quiet the whole time."

She stopped, took a deep breath, and said, "Harry Mitchum has another story for me."

"Keep walking with me. My joints tend to stiffen if I stand still in the cold."

Again she matched her pace to his. "He didn't actually say it, but I think he's going to offer me a job."

"Then you should take it."

"What about you?"

"You want to go, go."

"Just like that?" She could not stop the welling up of anger, the same anger that had them quarreling almost every time they spoke these days. "Not even, 'I'll miss you'?"

"Of course I'll miss you," Nathan replied. That was one of the things that drove her around the bend, how nothing seemed to faze him at all. "I just hope you will carry your Lord and your faith with you."

"And I just wish," she shot back, "that for once, just once, you would tell me something without bringing God into it."

He looked over at her, his gaze calm and penetrating. "I am only trying to give to you from the best of what I have," he answered. "The very best."

They walked the rest of the way to the revival tent in silence. The snow scrunching under their feet made do for conversation. The closer they came to the revival, the louder grew the tumult. Nathan stopped away from the chattering throng and asked, "Why don't you come in just for a moment?"

"I told you, I have an appointment in Denver." She glanced towards where the crowd was warming up with a hand-waving hymn. "Besides, I really don't like all that noise."

"If you're listening to the noise, you're not hearing our

Lord," Nathan replied. He reached forward, hugged her hard to his chest, and then said into her ear, "Go in the peace and love that is only God's to give. Know I will be praying for you each and every day."

Claire stood and watched him walk over and join the throng, the people gladly making room for him with smiles and back-slaps of welcome. She turned away, the strength of his arms replaced by a sudden burning void.

Troy was not a thief. He crouched in the darkened alcove at the end of the tenement hallway and wished the guy would just disappear.

That was the trouble with reality. People couldn't be handled so easily.

His legs trembled from the worry and the need to remain utterly still. The guy had been standing there forever.

Now the guy glanced at his watch another time, sighed, and leaned against the side wall. His eyes remained fastened on the ground floor entrance. He had to be a cop. Nobody else could stay so quiet for so long. So intent. The thought left Troy so frazzled he was ready to blow right through the roof.

Troy hated this. But he had to have the gear. He had to. His Second Skin unit was so patched and worn it threatened to short out every time he moved, toasting him like a crispy fritter. And his headgear. The images were getting so scattered they gave him headaches. But his credit was stretched to the max and beyond. He was two months behind on his rent, and the phone company was on its third threatening letter. He had no choice but to play vulture and pick over the remains of another victim.

His gut wrenched at how close he had come to getting caught.

He had been busy straining around the yellow police sticky-tape, picking the apartment lock, when the guy had pushed through the outer doorway. Crazy, these tenements were almost always empty in the middle of the day, before the kids got home from school and the parents from work. But what happens? In comes this guy looking like an off-duty cop, stops at the same door, fishes out a key, unlocks it, then stations himself at the top of the stairs, keeping Troy away from the gear, blocking his exit, trapping him in this stinking corner.

He breathed with his mouth open, stifling the desire to groan. The guy checked his watch again, sighed, but stayed put. Troy raised a trembling hand to wipe the sweat. He had to get out of there.

Claire stopped outside the *Denver Herald*'s entrance to check her reflection in the glass doors. She was gratified to see that her nerves did not show. Coming back to Denver always required a reentry period, but this time was especially hard. The air had a thick metallic tang; it always tasted strange the first few days back. After that she stopped noticing. The people passing her looked less healthy than the ones at home, their faces pinched, their eyes worried. It usually took her a couple of days to get used to the people as well. She took a deep breath and pushed through the doors.

Inside the *Herald* building, all was granite and brass and modern efficiency. Anyone smelling newsprint and drying ink sported an incredible imagination, for all production was housed a good six miles away. Claire started for the bank of elevators, almost colliding with Harry Mitchum as he came sprinting out towards her.

"You're here, great. I was about to leave without you."

Claire fell into step beside him. "You didn't say anything about a time, so—"

"Just got a call. Come on, we're late. I promised him I'd be there almost an hour ago, but I was hanging around hoping you'd make it." Harry Mitchum punched the button for the underground parking garage, then sniffed the air and said, "I smell smoke."

"My hair. I washed it twice, but it holds smells like they were glued in place." She followed him into the elevator, wondering what to do with her hands. Harry always had that effect on her, but today was worse than ever. "I've been out on the line. There was a forest fire yesterday."

"Sounds like a good story. But for later." Harry possessed a remarkable combination of strength and intelligence. It would be easy to glance at his face and think him weak, for his features were fine-boned, his carefully trimmed hair prematurely grey. But a closer look revealed tightly focused determination and a quiet reserve of strength. A man of many levels and great depth. If truth be known, Claire had always been a little in awe of Harry Mitchum. Youngest editor on the *Herald* staff, only six years older than herself, yet already Harry had a national reputation. Claire had wanted to work for Harry Mitchum long before they had even met. "This one can't wait."

Harry said little as he drove, his attention focused on the road and a map spread out between them. He sped through a section of town that grew steadily worse. Claire tried to hide her mounting alarm, wondering if this were some kind of test.

Maybe reporters were not supposed to show they were scared by their surroundings.

Harry checked the address on the handwritten card attached to his map, pointed to a tenement, and announced, "That's the place. Now I need to find a lot where we can leave the car. Wouldn't want to have to walk home from here."

The rubble-strewn street was lined with ancient brownstone tenements. "Where are we?"

"Crown Heights." He pulled into a guarded lot, accepted the ticket, and parked beside a purple Mercedes with chrome wheel-guards and yellow leather interior. "Not exactly the sort of place you'd expect a banker to live, is it?"

She stepped from the car, watching a pair of quarreling drunks stumble by. "A banker?"

"Come on, hanging around isn't going to make it any better." Together they skirted around a trio of Latino homeboys and a boom box blasting gangsta rap. They crossed the street, pushed through a grimy outer door, and climbed a flight of rickety stairs. Feeble light was cast by a single naked bulb from the ceiling. Claire was careful to keep from rubbing against the mildewed wall. The air was fetid with damp and ancient weary grime. A distant television blared false laughter, and a baby squalled from the floor above.

The second-story landing was covered by a strip of frayed carpet. A man stood leaning against the wall. He pushed himself erect as they approached and announced, "You're late."

"Sorry." Harry accepted the man's handshake, then stepped back. "Claire Kingsbury, this is Phil Flagler. He's an engineer with the phone company. Claire is the staffer I told you about."

Phil's features held the story of Colorado—part Indian, part Mexican, part Anglo. His face was strong and sharp and timeless. Only the streaks of grey in his black hair suggested his advancing years. "You didn't say she was just a girl."

"Woman," Harry corrected. "And reporter. Good one. Very good."

Claire confronted the dark steady gaze straight on. She had met a number of such men up on the Western Slope, especially among the highland hunters. They were very cautious with their friendship, but once given, it was for life. Phil was dressed in navy trousers, white shirt, dark tie with the telephone company's logo, dark blue zip-up jacket. On his lapel was pinned a small silver cross.

Phil Flagler accepted her watchful patience with a nod and then pointed at a door along the hallway. "It's all in there." He walked over and peeled off the yellow police tape.

Harry interjected, "I thought you said the police weren't involved."

"A buddy put this up so the landlord wouldn't touch anything until after you saw what we had." Phil pushed hard on the flimsy door, which grated and shuddered across scarred floorboards. He motioned them inside. "They call them muscle machines, the kids do. Can't get enough of that high-powered stuff. Like the way we were about cars, I guess."

It was not until Claire stepped through the doorway that she realized he was talking about a computer. The machine was set up beneath the single grit-covered window, and dominated the apartment's only room.

"I don't understand," Claire said, turning to look at Harry. "This is a story about stolen computer gear?"

"Not stolen," Phil said. "I already checked. The kid went into debt up to his eyeballs for this equipment, but all of it is legit." He leaned in the doorway. "No, what we have here is a kid who's disappeared without a trace. Vanished into thin air. Young man, actually. Just took off, leaving behind all this gear."

She started to protest that this was not a story, but Harry gave his head a tiny shake. Claire sighed, rummaged through her purse, took out her pen and notebook, asked, "What was his name?"

"Clay Conway. Worked at some bank, the landlord couldn't remember which one." Phil's eyes remained on the computer. "What you see there is not your basic consumer set-up. He's running a series of stacked Alpha-TI microprocessors set in RISC motherboards—they're the newest thing, fully digitalized."

Claire looked up from her pad, saw nothing but a normal computer, maybe slightly larger than most. She fought down a taste of bitter disappointment. Being called to Denver for a new story had seemed so promising. "What's this system worth?"

"Hard to say, prices change so fast. My guess is within shouting distance of fifty big ones."

She scanned the room again. The mattress in the corner was covered by crumpled dirty sheets. The sink in the kitchenette opposite was stained and aged. There was a portable burner propped on top of the waist-high fridge, the door wedged shut with a folded card. "Fifty thousand dollars?"

"There's more." Phil pointed towards the cables snaking across the floor. The bundle was as thick as Claire's thigh. "Not one, but four ISDN hook-ups. Integrated services digital networkings. Grants him direct internet access. My guess is he had both incoming and outgoing lines running simultaneously, hook-ups for video, audio, the works." He examined her. "You don't know what that means, do you?"

The banked-up fatigue from the firefight and the drive and the tension turned her voice flat. She had been so *certain.* "No idea whatsoever."

Flagler turned his attention to Harry, who defended her by saying, "Neither will most of the people who read her story."

"That doesn't wash," Phil replied. "You don't send a sports writer out to cover politics."

"The problem with computer writers is they write for other computer geeks. We're going for a larger audience, especially if what you say about this story is true," Harry countered. "Claire is one of our sharpest reporters. She's got a great eye for facts and knows how to write. If anyone can take this story through to the end, it's her."

"Thanks, Harry," Claire said quietly. But if that was the case, then why couldn't she land a real job?

Phil Flagler explained to her, "The guy had a Web server, which means he was handling a *lot* of lines into the internet at once. The computer's been wiped clean as a whistle. But from the phone records I'd guess it was a Unix server running a fractional T-1 or better." He caught her baffled look and changed gears. "It's an operating system, allowing him to work simultaneously on as many as ten internet lines at once."

"Any idea what for?"

"Not a clue. There isn't a CD-ROM disk in the place, no floppies, and the hard drive's been totally erased. Doesn't even have the operating system. Whoever erased this system wasn't after finesse, they were after speed."

Despite her weary disappointment, Claire searched for a handle, something to hang a story on. "Money laundering? Drugs? Numbers racket?"

"No way to tell for certain, but my guess is no. If it were just one guy, sure. But this is not an isolated case."

Claire looked from one to the other. "Case of what?"

"Disappearances," Harry reminded her. "A lot of them."

"I know of a dozen cases in the metro area, maybe more," Flagler said.

"A dozen kids disappeared from Denver? Why aren't the police screaming about this?"

"They aren't minors," Phil replied. "Most are your typical computer geeks. Few friends, families scattered. Maybe somebody put out a missing persons, but if they don't have a spouse or family searching and pressing for answers, the police have more important things to go after. On paper it doesn't look like much. Young people in their twenties and thirties are restless. They get up and go all the time."

Claire walked over to the side wall where a single bundle of bright color lay amidst the grey squalor. She picked it up and realized she was holding a red superhero suit, right down to the silver lightning slashes on the shoulders and across the chest. Only this one had a tightly coiled electric cable attached to the back. She held it out. "What's this thing?"

"They call it a Second Skin," Phil said, barely glancing around. "Mainline Computer product, like the hardware. All these missing kids use Mainline products, don't ask me why."

Harry spun around. "You never told me that."

The sharpness of Harry's tone brought Phil up short. "Sure I did."

Harry gave his head an emphatic shake. "All you said was, the missing kids had nothing in common except they were all computer geeks."

"That's right. Geeks who used Mainline products."

"You never mentioned Mainline, Phil. Not once."

"Is that a problem?"

"At this point, anything that ties these disappearances together is worth a closer look." Harry mulled it over, then shrugged. "Anyway, you were saying something about that getup she's holding."

"Right." Phil cast a worried glance Harry's way, then went on. "Second Skins are made of the same stretch material they use for Speedos, you know, those tight-fitting swimsuits. There's a mesh of wires and sensors between two layers of cloth. It feeds data on body placement and movement into the computer."

Claire hefted the suit in her hands. It weighed almost nothing. "But what is it *for*?"

"Any number of things. Sometimes professional designers use them to place 3-D figures inside drawings or programs they're working on. But mostly they're used in games."

"I remember reading something about Mainline Computers going into the game racket." Harry's brow had furrowed down to a single intense line. "Did every missing kid have a suit like this?"

"I couldn't say. By the time we get there, everything they owned has usually been repossessed. Most of these kids were heavily in debt. The police see that as the perfect excuse for the kids to have taken off. So they're listed as bankruptcy and fraud cases, and nothing happens except they get a bad credit rating."

Claire bent over and picked up the hood that had been hidden beneath the skin. It looked like a fighter-pilot helmet, colored to match the suit, with bulbous eye patches descending down to cover almost half the face. There were also earphones and a flexible mike. "What about this?"

"Virtual reality headgear. Two small video screens set before each eye make any image look like it's in three dimensions." Phil watched Harry pace around the room. "I must have told you about Mainline."

"You didn't. Believe me, I would have remembered something like that." Harry turned to Claire. "Seen enough?"

"I guess so." She set the Second Skin and headgear back down. "Wish I knew what he was doing with that gear."

"Tell me what was wiped off the hard drive," Phil replied, "and maybe we can get somewhere."

Claire moved up close to Harry. "I wonder why these kids all go for the Mainline stuff."

"That may be worth checking on." Harry agreed, and motioned them towards the door. "There's a big computer trade show starting tomorrow at the convention center. We ought to get over there early and check this out."

"Sure," Phil said. "Interacta 2000. Heard it's supposed to be amazing."

"I'll swing by and pick you up," Harry told her. "Say about nine. Where are you staying?"

"I have a place over on Franklin." Claire stopped in mid-flow, her attention caught by an extremely nervous kid trying to ease towards the stairwell. She raised one hand, and called, "Hey, wait just a—"

The guy leaped for the stairs, took the steps four at a time, bolted across the foyer, slammed back the door, and was gone.

Phil Flagler stood dumbfounded, the keys dangling from one hand, and stared at the empty space. "What was that all about?"

"I don't know." Harry started for the stairs. "The kid looked terrified. Could that have been Clay Conway?"

"No." Flagler was definite about that. "Clay was blond and slender. That guy was dark-headed, right? I was busy with the door."

"Black hair," Claire confirmed. And truly fearful eyes.

DENVER

■ Donovan Stone entered the Denver airport and watched his girlfriend's high heels beat a staccato warning across the tiled floor. Trish was like that when she was angry, forging ahead with focused precision. For once, Donovan found himself not caring at all.

When it was their turn at the counter, the cute airline attendant gave Donovan her number one smile. He was confident enough in his looks to know what was behind it, and replied with a grin of his own. Trish, though, was having none of it. She slapped her ticket down hard enough to make them both start. Then she wheeled back to him and snapped out, "Hollywood. That's where you belong, not buried up to your eyeballs in this overblown cow town."

"Take a look around," he said, as quietly as he could manage. "Denver is growing up."

"It's the middle of nowhere and always will be. I can't

believe you keep dragging me back here, especially after I fought so hard to get away."

Donovan smiled grimly, wondering if she could see in his gaze how much he wanted a future where Trish did not belong. "I've been to Hollywood."

"Once," she snapped. "For what, two days?"

"A week." The longest six days of his entire life. He had been just another beggar in the land of Gucci-clad sponges, going hat-in-hand around the studios, hoping for crumbs. Not ever again. He had learned the hard way that wanting it was not enough. Not in Hollywood. There had to be an opening, something that brought the dream within reach. "Soon as this exhibition closes, I'll make some calls."

Trish tapped her fingernails impatiently on the counter. Every male eye within fifty paces was on her, and for good reason. Even when she was fuming, she possessed killer looks. "I mean it, Donovan, this nonsense has gone on too long."

The attendant stared at him, watching him like she would an actor on the stage. He hated public scenes. Always had. Which was why Trish had waited until now to start on this.

He leaned on the counter, drawing his face down close to Trish, and grated softly, "Playing beggar to the star-makers doesn't interest me."

This dark-haired pixie with the beautiful unlined face inspected him carefully. The freckles and the pert little nose were offset by impossibly bright eyes. A complexion the color of autumn—that was what he had thought the first time he had seen her—dark hair and eyes with the faintest flecks of warm glowing gold. Her gaze was far too open to have seen everything and done everything that it had. Trish had fled school and home at fifteen to escape a life that didn't fit—her way of describing a mother who ran around and a father who wasn't much of a father. She had found herself falling into the trap of learning to expect nothing more for herself, she had once explained to Donovan, so she left. She had moved with the wind for almost a year, working at Burger Kings and refusing to give in to the easy drugs and the easy people. Then she had taken a job in a Red Cross thrift shop, met women from good families, learned to dress and talk and smile and act. At seventeen Trish had been pretty enough in a very mature way to pass for twenty-one.

She also had obtained the dresses and the manner to land a job as hostess in one of the city's finest restaurants. She had worked there for three years, taking night courses at the local college. Now Trish was a cosmetician, a specialist at making women look beautiful. Nowadays she traveled almost constantly—today it was San Francisco—working for two of the country's top modeling agencies. But her goal was to work in film. Which was another thing drawing them together, this shared passion for the Hollywood dream.

She accepted her boarding pass from the attendant, then returned her stare to him, and declared, "If you don't move while you still can, somebody else will."

As Trish turned away from the counter, Donovan caught sight of the attendant giving him a frankly inviting look. He managed to respond with a wry smile before following Trish towards the departure gates. Their time together was definitely drawing to a close, he decided. Why put up with such nonsense when there were so many other possibilities waiting for him?

As she waited to pass through the security check-point,

she demanded, "Do you still think there's a chance of actually landing this deal?"

"More than a chance."

She studied his face. "Are you sure, after all this time?"

"There has to be." His reply was hardened by new irritations and old worry.

"Well, all I can say is, I hope you're right." The warning tone was clear in her voice. "For all our sakes."

He remained silent, but inside he agreed with Trish completely, though he hated to admit it. At thirty-one years of age, Donovan Stone had never known an instant's contentment. He had always been in pursuit, and never known what of. Until now.

Up to this moment, the race had always been for more. Better. New. Another. Women were treated like jobs, and jobs like cars, to be cast aside as soon as something superior appeared on the horizon. But now, finally, he had found a quest big enough to slake even his unending thirst for money and power and status.

She was watching him with a gaze that seemed to reach inside and feed on his hunger. "I still can't understand how a major Hollywood player would want to set up in the middle of nowhere."

"The computer company they're teaming up with is based here. And Denver's a city on the move."

Trish set her shoulder bag on the conveyor belt. "You sound as though you actually like this place."

"What I like is this deal." Donovan wanted this chance more than anything he had ever wanted in his entire life. All the desires and hungers he had ever known were focused down to this one tiny instant, a bundle so taut it threatened to explode at any minute, shattering him into a billion pieces of unresolved craving. His only hope, the only chance he had of making it through whole, was to land this deal.

Trish started towards the gate. "How long have you been working on this now, a year?"

"Fourteen months." Over a year since he had thrown away a promising career with a major consulting firm, going for the dream and starting his own company. Nothing but a single contract, a willingness to work, and a lot of drive going for him. But now the contract was drawing to a close, and his money was running out. And his time. For over a year this major deal had hovered just beyond his reach. If it did not come soon, he would have to give up.

The thought left him cold. He had nothing to fall back on. Everything he had, every last cent, had gone into his company. If it went under, he wouldn't even have a place to sleep. Desperate did not even begin to describe how he felt. And to have Trish pick on him now, at the point when he was already stretched as thin as he could go, was like sliding needles under his fingernails. He turned to her, the tension and the anger and the drive brimming up to the point where he was going to do it. Tell her it was over, here and now.

Trish chose that moment to look up, sense his mood, and draw him back with the alluring smile that was hers and hers alone. "It's going to be fine."

He felt himself slowly pulled from the brink. She could do that, even when they shared the tactic of playing other people's emotions like violins. She handled him with a master's touch. "You're sure about that?"

Her hand slid around his back, and she hugged him close. "Count on it. I only bet on winners."

And if they aren't winners, he amended for her, they were not kept around. "When are you back from San Francisco?" She made a game of checking her watch. "Five days and three hours and ten minutes." The sigh, the little grin, the pixie glance from those two golden-autumn eyes. "Whatever will you do while I'm gone?"

He started to answer with a flip remark, then noticed something new on her neck. "Turn around for a second."

"Why?" But she did as he asked, and when he lifted her hair, he saw that he had not been mistaken.

"A tattoo?" He leaned back so that he could see her face. "You've got a tattoo?"

She seemed proud of the new addition and shook her head so that the single star-shaped earring flickered in the afternoon light. The tattoo was the exact same size and shape as the five-pointed gold earring. "A sign of the times."

"What are you talking about?"

"Tell you when I'm back." The cold edge crept back into her voice. "You concentrate on proving you're a winner."

Before he could respond, she stood on her tiptoes, a signal that she wanted to be kissed. Then she walked through the gate, turning once to offer him a cheery wave. She mouthed the single word, *winner*—both a promise and a warning. Then she was gone.

Donovan returned the wave, reflecting as she disappeared that it was definitely time to be moving on. He needed the contract, and he needed another Miss Right to share the glory. Somebody a little easier to control.

DENVER

■ Claire started down the steps of the Franklin Street house as soon as she spotted Harry's car rounding the corner. He smiled in welcome and examined the house as she settled in. "Nice place. Is it yours?"

"Hardly." She ran a nervous hand through her unruly hair, then gave it up to a bad hair decade. "I rent the top floor."

He took a side road down to Speer, then glanced approvingly at her outfit. "Good to see you in a dress for a change."

"All Lillian's doing." Lillian Stockton Fletcher wrote the paper's society column and was fast becoming Claire's best friend on the staff.

"I didn't even know you owned anything but jeans." Another glance. "It suits you."

"Thanks." Claire had carefully scouted the paper's other women, but found little guidance there. Their choice in office wear ranged from grunge and spiked orange hair—a favorite among the photogs—to conservative knit suits and lace-up pumps. So she had asked Lillian's advice, then spent more than she could afford on two good outfits in neutral tones which could be easily swapped around. Low heels and a big shoulder bag completed the outfit.

Traffic enclosed them and slowed their progress to a crawl. Harry let out a pent-up sigh. Claire glanced over, noticed a faint greyness to his features, and started to ask if everything was all right. But there was still the uncertainty of her position, the unsolved mystery of her job hanging in the air between them. She turned back to the front with a sigh of her own. The air seemed frantic here. The longer she stayed in the city and the more she breathed the air, the more stressed her own life seemed to become. There was a constant push to do more and do it faster.

Claire checked her purse to ensure she had remembered her pad and tape recorder, and her hand touched her mother's still-unopened letter. She knew what it would say; her infrequent letters were always the same, chattering about Bel Air parties and all the famous people she socialized with, and then criticizing Claire for hiding away in a paltry mountain town.

Harry cut into her thoughts with, "It was nice to see you ready on time. Not many reporters can tell you what a watch is for."

"I've inherited that from early days with Pop," she replied, wishing she had the nerve to bring up the matter of her job. The fear of not being offered a real post left her weak. "He couldn't get started without me there to help, and it was hard on him to wait around. I learned to time my mornings to his schedule."

The rush-hour flow relented, allowing Harry to increase his speed. "He had a stroke, I remember you mentioning it before. Must have been a bad one."

"The doctors said he'd never walk again. They couldn't believe how fast he recovered, or so they said. It seemed slow as watching concrete harden to me. They said it was a miracle when he started moving around on his own." She thought about her departure the day before, and shook her head.

"What's the matter?"

"Nothing. It's just that Pop and I fought yesterday. We've been doing a lot of that recently. Fighting with him always leaves me uncomfortable."

"I talked with him, you know." Harry drove as he did most things, with verve and precision. "It was when we wanted to pick up that second piece of yours. He struck me as a solid down-to-earth type."

"He is." The response seemed lacking, so she added, "Pop doesn't talk a whole lot. When he does, it's usually about something religious. It gets to me, how he always seems to have an answer to everything."

"Are they right? His answers, I mean."

"I don't know. Sometimes, maybe." A long pause, then more quietly, "More than that."

"Must be nice, having answers to the hard questions."

The chink in Harry's armor caused her to look over. "Are you looking for answers?"

"More and more every day," he said quietly.

Claire waited, and when nothing was forthcoming, she asked, "Is there a problem?"

"Another time, okay?" He turned into the exhibition

center's parking lot, took the ticket, pulled into a space, and turned off the motor. "Right now, we've got a story to cover."

The Mainline Computers display dominated the hall, which was quite a feat, since everything from roaring dinosaurs to a miniature hot-air balloon were on show at other stands. But the Mainline scene outshone them all.

Mock fortress walls surrounded the entire stand. Turrets at each corner bore flags with the Mainline logo—a wizard holding a staff tipped by a shining jewel. At the display's center rose a metal tower, slightly conical in shape, its smooth surface a mirror of polished silver. A steel stairway wound its way around to the top. At the pinnacle rose a golden idol, a woman whose bearing was regal and ferocious. Under the flickering lasers the face seemed to snarl.

Along the fortress walls rose a glaring emblem, turned an angry red from internal lights. The script was ancient and spiked and as inflamed as the godlike statue. The caption's single word read: *BABYLON.*

Around the stand's entrance way were scrolled the words: *The Tower has been restored. Enter the kingdom and climb to the heavens. If you dare.*

Claire entered the stand, avoiding the crowd about the central display. When Harry joined her, she said, "I thought you said this company manufactured computers."

Harry surveyed the jammed central exhibit. Each of the stand's inner walls was decorated with a giant motif, a massive warrior's shield bearing the same ancient script as the flashing word overhead. Each shield bore a different caption: *All your hidden desires are hereby granted. The might of the universe is now yours. The dream of a hero's battle has now been found.* She turned to the shield behind her, which read, *The dark forces thought lost forever are now recovered.*

"Apparently they've come up with this new game," Harry told her, raising his voice to be heard over the clamor. "It's turned Mainline around. Eighteen months ago, this company was on the brink of going under. Now look at them."

He pointed to a bespectacled middle-aged man in the stand's other corner. The man had thinning blond hair and was bent like a bow. "That's Mainline's president, Russ Reynolds. He's the guy responsible for the turnaround."

But Claire's attention was caught by the man talking to Reynolds. He was the exact opposite of the computer guy, a young craggy-faced Marlboro man in a banker's suit. Electric blue eyes crossed the distance between them and fastened upon her. The lips pulled back, and he smiled. At her.

Claire realized Harry had said something. She forced herself to turn away and cover her temporary muddle with, "How do you know these things?"

"It's my business to know. They're a local employer, remember? Up until last year, they were looking for a buyer and hanging on by the skin of their teeth. They make great hardware. They were the first to bring a lot of new items to market. But the costs pushed them out of the reach of most consumers, and there were others in the next tier who were better established with the corporate buyers. A lot of their competitors were just waiting for them to fold so they could pick up their patents cheap."

Claire glanced back. She had to. The handsome man was still watching her, despite the fact that the computer guy had him by the arm, pulling him towards the center of the exhibit. He flashed her another smile, shrugged, and allowed himself to be pulled towards the small stage.

"Then up comes this game idea," Harry was saying. "And they make a film of it, you've probably seen the advertising."

"I don't think so," she said weakly. The guy was too good-looking to be real.

"*Babylon*'s become one of the year's top grossing films. Which fuels the game, which fuels Mainline's balance sheet."

Harry watched Reynolds glad-hand his way through a throng of admirers. "A lot of the movie was filmed at what they're calling the Airport Studios. When Denver's new airport was completed, they leased the old one to Swindley's group. They used the hangars as sound stages. Swindley Broadcasting of Hollywood is one of Mainline's new backers. That's Roger Swindley talking to the Mainline president now. Mainline has suddenly become a tremendous money-maker and job-creator for Denver, bringing film production to a defunct airport."

Claire tried hard to concentrate, knowing more than a story was on the line here. But that guy. Every time she caught sight of him through the crowd, her eyes were drawn like moths to a flame.

Donovan Stone allowed Russ Reynolds, Mainline's president, to pull him over to where people were fawning around the big squeeze from Los Angeles. Roger Swindley and Swindley Broadcasting were currently riding high on the crest of *Babylon*'s success, their first feature-length film, and were rumored to have a sequel currently in the works. Donovan knew all about him. Now that he was here, though, standing in line and waiting for a morsel of the big man's time, all he could feel was bitter rage. So much waiting around, and all for nothing.

He tried to focus on something else. Anything. He thought of the girl he had spotted and turned to Russ Reynolds. The head of the computer firm was bespectacled and harried and tremendously excited. Riding the same wave, barely believing it was happening to him. "Did you catch sight of the redhead?"

"What?"

"There was a stunner at the back of the exhibit. Tall, rangy, a real stand-out."

"Sorry." Russ had the ability to speak without moving his lips. "My wife had my vision surgically corrected when I got married."

"There she is. Against the back wall. She one of yours?"

"I don't think so. Maybe she's with Swindley's group."

"Can you check it out?"

"No problem." Russ Reynolds turned back as the crowd shifted. "Okay, Swindley's free. Time to focus on the game plan."

Russ Reynolds was a friend now, ever since Donovan had backed Russ and his reorganization plans. Donovan had been hired by First Colorado, the local bank who was one of Mainline's major new backers. The other backer was Swindley's group. Swindley and Mainline were cooking up something big over at the Airport Studios; the first Babylon film was only the tip of a future iceberg. Russ Reynolds wanted to bring Donovan in on that one as well. Which was fine with the bank, since they were rolling in the green from their

Mainline investment and saw this as partly Donovan's doing. The hold-up was this guy in front of Donovan, Roger Swindley. All three partners had to agree on any outside consultant, and Swindley had been dragging his heels for months. Fourteen, to be exact.

Russ Reynolds stepped forward and said, "Roger, you remember me telling you about Donovan Stone."

Pale laser-sharp eyes turned Donovan's way, and the show's clamor seemed to dim. The head of Swindley Broadcasting was rail thin. His blond hair was greying ever so carefully, his moustache as clipped and precise as his tone. "Several people have spoken to me about you. You're the consultant working with my colleagues, First Colorado."

Beneath the man's intense gaze, Donovan felt as though all his hunger for power was laid bare. "Nice of you to remember, Mr. Swindley."

"Call me Roger." His jaw's sharp angle was accented by the way he kept his features clenched. He spoke in monotones, his entire body barely containing some tightly bound energy. "My banker colleagues have spoken very highly of you, as has Russ here. I also understand you've done some useful work for one of our competitors."

Donovan smiled and remained silent, more than willing to let the guy do his own selling. His last deal for the consulting firm had been to help set up a North Carolina film studio for a nickel-and-dime producer. But the man had brought out a trio of major hits, and the work had spurred Donovan's drive to go it alone.

Bleached, almost colorless eyes kept him pinned like a

prey. "I've been led to understand you may be the man we've been looking for."

Donovan felt a surge so strong his bones seemed to hum. So what if the guy had the personality of a lizard? From what he'd heard, Hollywood was full of them. "I'd sure like to think so."

But Swindley had already turned away. His concentrated attention only permitted him to focus upon one item at a time.

Russ Reynolds pulled him away. "Isn't that guy amazing?"

"Swell." Donovan's excitement was like an electric current, zinging through him in tense little bursts.

"Yeah, I know, the guy's got the personality of a guided missile. But he sure saved our bacon." Russ pointed across the room to where a pair of dark-suited gentlemen were signaling. "Looks like your banker buddies want to bend your ear. I'll go check out the redhead."

"I won't forget this," Donovan said.

"You sure won't." The president of Mainline patted his arm. "I'm not going to let you."

Claire stood against the exhibit's back wall, surveying the scene. Harry had seen a contact and wandered off. She spotted the Mainline Computer president working his way through the crowd in her direction, and decided to try for a quote.

He seemed totally surprised when she headed straight up to him, and said, "I'm Claire Kingsbury, reporter for the *Denver Herald.*" Just saying the words gave her a thrill. "Can I ask you a few questions?"

"You're a reporter?" The news brought a worried frown.

"The *Denver Herald*," she repeated. "Do you have a minute?"

"I'm not sure I should be talking with you," he replied, backing off a notch.

But Claire already had her recorder ready. "Isn't it unusual, a company known for its computer hardware going into the games market?"

"This is more than just another game. It's another universe entirely." Russ Reynolds glanced nervously at the recorder jutting towards his face. "Babylon is the first truly made-for-DSVD game on the market. DSVD, or digital simultaneous voice and data disks, brings real-time network-gaming to reality. We have achieved incredibly successful simulation, as well as super-high fidelity. System performance factors are up in the stratosphere. We have achieved constant interactivity and full human sensory perception, with multiple players, for the first time in history. It is a total immersion package. This game has it all."

Useless. The words told her nothing, and the quote would read like techno-gobbledygook. But she kept up the ploy because the man's fear factor seemed to be increasing with every second he stayed around her. Which she could not understand. Not at all. "How has this been achieved?"

"A number of factors." He craned, scouted, took a relieved step towards the entrance. "You'll have to excuse me, the mayor has just arrived and I have to go greet him." When Claire continued to dog his steps, he backpedaled over to a pair of young people wearing Mainline nametags. "Here's our game designer and his assistant, Al and Gwendolyn. Why don't you have a chat with them?"

"Claire Kingsbury, *Denver Herald*," she said absently, watching as Russ Reynolds moved off like he was fleeing the scene of a crime. She asked the first question that came to her mind. "How long have you worked for the company?"

The designer was a skinny unkempt guy, his clip-on polyester tie attached to a flannel work-shirt. He smirked and replied, "Time doesn't matter in virtuality."

She dragged her gaze around. "Come again?"

His assistant had dressed for the occasion in a green miniskirt, orange stockings, and one orange glove, probably meant to match the color of her spiked hair. She said to the guy, "Another techno-dweeb."

"Virtuality," the guy repeated. "Virtual reality. Like virtuosity, only immersed."

"Interiority," the girl announced. "That's another new buzz word for your little recorder. It means being inside somebody else's head. That's what they're doing here. Growing new worlds inside people's minds, sharing a dream and a buzz with a thousand other plugged-in brains all at once. A super oversoul in the making."

The guy nodded in time to her words. "No question. We're making the gods of the nineties."

"Excuse me," Claire said. "I thought we were talking about a game here."

The pair exchanged smirks. As their heads turned, Claire noticed matching star tattoos on their necks. The guy replied, "Games is another word that's taken on new meanings."

Useless gibberish, she decided, and cut off her recorder. "You don't seem very comfortable here," Claire probed.

"I don't go much for face-time," the guy replied. "Useless

waste of energy, meeting in the flesh. Whatever needs doing gets done faster and better at the speed of Net."

"Better?"

"You know. Without all the hang-ups. Personalities set aside, strict information flow. Not to mention the fact that it's a world for the plugged in. Illiterates not allowed."

Like me, Claire finished for him. She asked, "So what happens when you win? The game, I mean."

"Like Al said," the girl replied smugly. "Then you're a god."

Claire spotted Harry waving to her from the entrance. "Excuse me," she said thankfully. "Got to run. Appreciate your time."

Harry demanded, "Who were you talking with over there?"

"A pair of game designers."

"The girl looks like a Christmas tree on fire." He motioned towards the podium. "Looks like Mr. Mayor's about to speak."

Denver's mayor looked like a ruddy-faced ex-football player. He pulled some notecards from his pocket and waved them over his bald head for silence. When the crowd was quiet, he held them out at arm's length, squinted, and read, "Mainline Entertainment Systems brings you the next generation today. Your destination, a world beyond time. Your speed, as fast as you dare travel. Your appointment is made, your transport waiting. Beyond earth, beyond reality as you know it, lies *Babylon*."

The mayor dropped his notecards to his side and gave a little chuckle. "Shoot, I don't understand a word of what I just said. But that advertisement wasn't designed for me, so I guess it doesn't matter. All I know for certain is that the Mainline group and this Babylon game are responsible for bringing in four hundred new jobs to the Denver Metro area." He flipped to the next card and read, "Software designers, application specialists, telephone access coordinators, plus a Cray super-computer and a whole passel of engineers. Not to mention the film production that's suddenly sprouting in our old airport complex."

He paused to beam out over the audience, then waved towards where Reynolds waited on the podium steps. "So let's give a big welcome to the man responsible for this economic boom, a genuine visionary for the twenty-first century—Mr. Russ Reynolds!"

The mayor backed away from the podium, cards fluttering as he clapped his hands over his head. The crowd joined in as Reynolds stepped forward. Nervous eyes scanned the group below him, fastened momentarily upon a person Claire could not see, then lifted to the pages held by his trembling hands. He began without preamble, "This is not merely another computer game. This is a new field entirely. This is entertainment redefined. The viewer does not simply empathize with some character acted out before him. In Babylon, there is no viewer. This is your world. The player experiences it all. The *player* makes it all happen."

"He's reading the speech like he's never seen it before in his life," Claire observed.

"He's president of a computer company, not a paid speaker," Harry quietly responded.

"Maybe so, but he sounds like a drone."

Reynolds went on, "The key to modern entertainment is escapism. Our intention is to provide the ultimate opportunity. Babylon is a city with its own rules. It takes the participants completely out of themselves. Before this, people remained stuck in their little chairs, in their little cinemas, in front of their little televisions. Chained to another's vision of escapism, held by events beyond their control. At last, we are delivering what all the others have merely promised. Technology has now become the means of human evolution. How can we tell the difference any longer between what is man and what is machine? We have machine pumps replacing hearts, we are pushing ever closer to where machines begin to think for themselves. We are evolving into a new mankind, half-flesh, half-godlike computerized oversoul."

He glanced down, again searching for someone Claire could not identify. His voice was so nervous it trembled as he continued, "You may not understand it. Few people over the age of thirty ever do recognize the transitions of history when they arrive. But change is here. My company's performance over the past two years is evidence enough. Believe me, ladies and gentlemen, the future is *Babylon.*"

Harry joined half-heartedly into the clapping, turned to Claire, and said, "Is this guy for real?"

"Look at the others," Claire observed. "They love it."

"Sure they do. This guy is connected to pockets deeper than Fort Knox." Harry's tone was bitter. "A visionary? Did I actually hear the mayor call him that?"

Harry Mitchum was both somber and silent during most of the trip back to the paper. Claire remained too unsure of herself to start a conversation. So she waited. And worried about the job.

Harry pulled into the basement lot and cut the motor. He sat and listened to it ping for a moment before saying, "I think this story may wind up being something big."

A sudden wrenching in her gut, and she found herself dreading the next words: It's too big to hand to a part-timer from our most distant bureau. Harry was now going to tell her that he had made a mistake. Of course. That was why he had been so quiet on the way back. Claire pressed a hand to her stomach, pushing away the sudden sick feeling.

"At times like this," Harry went on, almost talking to himself, "journalism encourages ecstatic mistakes. Reporters can spend years gathering facts, sifting through hot air. It teaches cynicism, because most people tell you only what they want you to know, shading the truth every color you can imagine."

Claire swallowed and managed, "What are you getting at?"

"Not only that," he continued, refusing to be hurried, "but stories are often trivial. Especially for a local paper like ours. A lot of what we need to report on just isn't all that exciting. So when something big comes up, there is a sudden adrenaline charge, and that can lead to big errors."

He opened his door and slid out. Claire pushed her own door open and forced her legs to stand. She started to speak, but he was already headed for the elevator, saying as he walked, "A journalist finally snags a hot one, but the shreds of evidence don't fit together. The pressure builds and along with it the fear that he or she will be pulled off before it's put together, and the big chance will be lost. So finally the journalist just plugs together what he or she has, regardless of accuracy."

He punched the button, examined her, and said, "What's the matter with you? You're pale as a ghost."

"I can't stand this!" She had to lean one hand on the wall. "Do I have a job or not?"

He showed genuine astonishment. "Do you think I'd waste all this perfectly good advice on you if you didn't?"

"Good grief, Harry." She was so weak she stumbled into the elevator. "How was I supposed to know? You didn't even give me a proper interview."

They stopped on the lobby level, and the elevator filled. "You want an interview? No problem." The doors clanged shut, sealing them in with six or seven others. All other conversation died as Harry demanded, "Why didn't you want to go into television?"

"I want to write, and not for someone else to mouth my words." She felt her cheeks grow red at the open attention, but kept on. "Plus I want to cover issues in-depth. Television news is lost to the thirty-second story and the ten-second sound bite."

"Sounds good to me," murmured a woman's voice beside her. "She after your job, Harry?"

"Not yet." He cleared his throat. "Claire Kingsbury, I am most impressed with your journalistic qualities and the way you have handled this interview. Could I perhaps interest you in a full-time position?"

"Take it, sister," intoned a deep voice from up front. "I got a couple of buddies that'd kill for the chance."

The doors opened on their floor. She followed Harry away from the chuckles. "Thanks a lot."

His grin finally surfaced. "I guess that means yes."

DENVER

4

■ The *Denver Herald*'s downtown operations stood at the end of the Sixteenth Street Mall, which was in fact not a mall at all, rather a thoroughfare closed to all traffic save buses. This pedestrian street had been a lifesaver for downtown Denver, and a project pushed steadily by the *Herald*. In eight years, the Mall had completely reversed three decades of steady decline. Now the bars and cow-town strip joints were relegated to a few blocks between the civic center and the new Coors Stadium. It was only a matter of time before they were bought and cleared up as well.

The Herald Tower was a building of beige Colorado sandstone, sharp cornered so that it could fit into a prime triangular lot. To one side rose the state capitol's gleaming dome, covered in hammered sheets of Colorado gold. Across Civic Square rose the Victorian clock tower of the City and County

Building. Straight ahead were a trio of modern structures, headquarters to the three largest Colorado banks.

Upstairs, the *Herald*'s office space was open-floored, with chest-high partitions granting reporters privacy only so long as they were seated. The Features section shared the narrow side of the fourth floor with Business and Society. On the other side of the central elevator shafts was the second newsroom, housing the larger staffs of City and Metro and Sports. They did not even have partitions, and the closer it came to the three o'clock deadline the more that room resembled total bedlam. Editorial offices lined the perimeter, observing inward through walls of glass. On good days, natural light bathed both pressrooms, and the air conditioners worked overtime, even in winter. On bad days, the clouds and smog closed in, leaving the rooms stuck in the gloom of a reporter chasing a useless lead.

After four years working first as a stringer and then as a part-timer with the western bureau, Claire had come to know almost everyone in Harry's sections—at least well enough to nod their way. She had covered seven regional stories, a couple of minor fires, two rescue operations, nine local elections, and more social events than she would care to count.

"He's busy," a bell-toned voice announced as she passed.

Claire allowed her momentum to carry her around and into the free chair by Lillian's desk. "Thank goodness."

The *Herald*'s society columnist was a mystery to most of the staff, but for some reason she had welcomed Claire's arrival and always brightened at her approach. Lillian shook her head over Claire's slender blue-jean-clad form. "Such incredible natural beauty going to waste. Just give me a chance, dearie, and I could remake you into a man-killer."

"Thanks, but men are already hard enough to find as it is."

In her early fifties, Lillian Stockton Fletcher's eyes were great and dark and set in a face that extended back in exaggerated angles from an aggressive nose. She possessed a delightful sense of the ridiculous, and was enormously rich. She was also persistently lonely.

Claire cast another quick glance towards Harry's closed door. "He offered me a real job yesterday," she said, hardly able to believe the news herself.

"Well, it's about time." Lillian was heir to the Stockton Soup fortune, the only child of one of Denver's richest scions and an English duke. That she viewed both her wealth and her position with amusement endeared her mightily to Claire. She also happened to be one of the *Herald*'s top prizes, a reporter who covered the Colorado society scene from within. Lillian had estates in Denver, Vail, and Beverly Hills, collected invitations like other people did porcelain figurines, and was addicted to parties and gossip. She asked, "When are you going to let me set you up with a nice young man?"

Claire felt the habitual hardening creep into her voice.

"I don't want a nice young man, Lillian."

"So I've noticed. Well, how about a rich young man who is not so nice? That would be even easier."

"No thanks. No man at all will do me just fine."

"Do I detect a hidden past lurking behind those beautiful eyes?" Lillian's gaze probed deep. "Some dark and obscure secret you haven't shared with your friend? There must be something, a lovely girl like you, never dating, never interested in a man."

"I'm just happy with my own company." Claire hid her tension by craning and searching the room. "Do you think I should check in before I leave for my first appointment?"

"If Harry trusts you enough to offer you a job, he trusts you to get on with your work." Lillian settled back, her gaze as calmly watchful as a cat's. "That would be a nice match for you, my dear."

"Who, Harry?" The thought was so ridiculous she had to laugh. "I want him to be my boss, not my boyfriend."

"There is no rule which says one must necessarily exclude the other. And you two certainly have a great deal in common. Looks, intelligence, talent. Not to mention a propensity for spending too much time alone. I would enjoy playing match-maker." She glanced around, then added, "Just so long as you keep the romance a clandestine operation. Newsroom rumor mills feed upon in-house romances, and the pressure is usually enough to kill them off."

Claire rose to her feet, suddenly eager to be off. "Well, thank goodness I don't have to worry about that one. When Harry's free, tell him I'm off to interview the bank staff where Conway worked. And give that other matter a permanent rest, okay?"

"It was just a thought, my dear," she said, turning back to her keyboard. "Just a thought."

Claire hurried towards the First Colorado Bank entrance. The wind was harsh and uncaring, pushing at her with a force that rocked her on her feet. In the summer it was often full of dust, biting and so dry it would suck her skin until it cracked and wrinkled like the desert floor. Now it was bitter cold, with a tight metallic city taste. Out of habit, she sniffed the air. But there would be no snow here. Not now. The sky was so clear as to appear without color. Claire pushed through the bank entrance and entered the marble-tiled foyer.

"Miss Kingsbury?" A harried balding man in dark suit and matching tie rushed over. "Hal Brooklands, manager of data processing."

"Thanks for seeing me, Mr. Brooklands."

"I wish I could say it's no problem, but we've got the auditors in next week, and there's a lot still to get done."

"This shouldn't take long."

"It can't," he said, trying for a humorous tone, but not quite making it. "You mind if we talk in the cafeteria? I've been at it since six, and this will be my only break."

"Not at all. I'm very grateful that you would see me." She allowed herself to be led into a crowded elevator and said nothing more until they were deposited in a large basement room. The cafeteria's food stations lined one wall. Most of the tables were already occupied; clearly there were a number of others who had gotten an early start.

He led her down the line. "Sure you won't let me get you something?"

"I'm fine, thanks."

"I don't see a free table." He pointed to the corner. "There are some of the others from my department. They were Clay's colleagues. Let's go join them."

The pair already seated at the table were young, bright, and eager. After the manager announced who she was, the young man greeted her with, "Strange to think the *Denver Herald* considers Clay to be news."

Claire seated herself. "An employee vanishes, one of your own colleagues is missing, and that isn't important?"

"You don't understand," the girl beside him said. "Clay had almost no personality at all."

"More than shy," the guy agreed. "A genuine recluse."

"But he was very good at his job," the manager interjected. "A real whiz on the computers."

"Iceman," the guy offered.

"If he is truly gone, we will miss him," the manager continued, trying for a sincere tone. "I can't believe he would allow his overdraft to grow to such a level he couldn't handle it."

Claire ignored the manager's comment and looked at the young guy. "What did you say?"

"Iceman," the guy repeated. "It was Clay's nickname."

"He had these little toys he kept on his computer," the girl added. "There was a warrior-type with these crazy swords, let's see, and a wizard and a little green dragon."

"And a tower," the guy added. "Don't forget that one."

The girl laughed. "That's right, a little silver cone with stairs circling it like a corkscrew. Crazy."

"We allow our employees to personalize their workspaces," the manager said. "It helps keep morale high."

"Those plastic figures were all from a game," the young guy offered. "At least I think they were."

"A game?" Claire looked from one to the other. "A computer game?"

"Babylon, sure, no question," the girl agreed.

"He was crazy about this video game called Babylon," the guy went on. "That was the only thing that ever lit him up."

"The only time he'd ever talk about anything," the girl agreed. "Start him on that and it was like hitting the switch on a wind-up toy."

The manager ate with the impatient motions of someone who did not have time to taste. He wiped his mouth, shot an impatient look at the pair, and said, "Clay was in our fund transfers section. It required a meticulous attention to detail and a strong sense of self-motivation. He always received high marks on his quarterly assessments."

But the pair were not that easily dampened. The guy laughed and added, "Sure, he was perfect. Come in, hit the time clock, and go hide like a mole in his little corner."

"Then go home and play Babylon all night," the girl finished. "He was totally wired to that game."

"I believe that's enough about the game nonsense," the manager said icily. "This reporter clearly has more important things in mind."

Claire pretended to make notes, trying to make sense of what she was hearing. "Was there ever any sign of drug connections or perhaps money laundering?"

The young pair laughed out loud. The guy asked, "Are we talking about the same guy?"

"Clay was afraid of his own shadow," the girl agreed.

But the manager had chilled. He demanded, "Is that what you think?"

"No, that is—"

"Because if your paper prints one word of this, even the smallest hint of scandal, our lawyers will sue you for libel."

"We don't think that and neither do the police, from what we've—"

"If I had known there was even a chance this would be your line of questioning," the manager said, his voice tight, "I would have refused to see you outright."

"We have no idea why Clay Conway vanished," Claire persisted.

"First Colorado is the top-rated bank in the state," the manager snapped. He shoved his tray to one side. The pair had melted back into their chairs, while all the nearby tables were now listening in. "We've been in business for over a century. The bank did not even close our doors during the Depression. There has never been a whiff of scandal associated with our establishment."

Claire stood. "Like I said, your bank is not suspected of any wrongdoing as far as I know. Thanks very much for your time."

"Donovan? Russ Reynolds here."

Donovan waved out the temporary secretary the bank had assigned him. His office was on the tenth floor of the First Colorado Bank. He had almost completed his final report for their board and now faced the desolation of an empty desk, with no prospect of further work—except for Russ and this new Airport Studios project. Which was still being held up by that character Swindley and his continual foot-dragging. "Russ. Any word from the Hollywood mogul?"

"Don't even joke like that."

"Sorry." The Mainline president always talked about his Hollywood investor with a trace of awe to his voice. Which was strange, given the fact that Reynolds was now the star of the hour. Donovan stifled his frustration and tried for a cheerful tone. "So what can I do for you?"

"It's what I'm doing for *you*. Remember that girl at the exhibit?"

"The redhead, sure, how can I forget?"

"She's off limits. Definitely a non-starter. That is, if you want to keep trying with Swindley."

Donovan felt a renewed surge of anger at the man who continually stood in his way. "What, she's one of Swindley's private stock?"

Reynolds laughed. "Hardly. She's a journalist with the *Denver Herald.*"

"A reporter? So?"

"That's a major problem with Swindley. I've never seen anybody who's got it in as much as he does for the press."

"What business is it of his?"

"Listen, you're new here. Believe me, I'm doing you a big favor. You want to get this consulting deal off the ground, you stay away from all reporters. Especially this one. She asks the wrong kind of questions."

OURAY AND DENVER

5

■ Nathan Kingsbury sat in his padded swivel chair, the roll-top desk dominating his cramped office. The back room of the *Ouray Star* was scarcely nine feet by nine. But the oversized picture window and its spectacular view of the Amphitheater Range prevented him from ever feeling confined.

Nathan held a sheaf of papers, in case someone happened to glance through the glassed-in door and noticed him sitting there. He had never imagined that it would hurt so when Claire left home. He had known for years that the time would come, sooner rather than later, when his little girl would depart to set her own life's course. Well, little no longer. She stood an inch and a half taller than he did now. But in his mind's eye she would remain the tiny child who learned to walk by grasping one finger in each little fist and screaming with delight at each tottering step.

He looked at the hands holding the unseen papers, pleased at his ability to make fists again. The flaccid slackness was almost totally gone from his left side. He lifted his gaze to the framed portrait on the desk's top, a photograph of his daughter at thirteen. Her copper curls looked ready to burst from beneath her Easter bonnet. Her smile reached across the distance of time, twisting his heart as it had when he had taken that picture their first Easter in Ouray. That week had been the first time he had felt movement returning to his left side since the stroke. And it had heralded her first smile in what had seemed like years.

All of Claire's pain had been set aside in that moment. All the heartache caused by the mistakes of two careless adults, all the worry from watching her father keel over with a crippling stroke. All was gone then, when she had opened her Easter box—the gift far too large for any basket.

Claire had been too old to receive a teddy bear, especially one almost as large as her young frame. But she had seen it in the window of the shop their first weekend in Ouray, pushing him along in his wheelchair. She had stopped and stared but not said a word, because money had been very tight after the move and buying the paper. So he had sent the office girl out to buy it, which meant the whole paper and then the whole town had known about his surprise. And he had discovered that it was not altogether a bad thing, sharing his secret, because already the town had been full of people who yearned to see the little girl smile.

So Claire had opened the box, with him balancing the camera in his one good hand, trying to be ready without making it too obvious. And in that first squeal of delight, he had seen the little child return, the one who had almost vanished in the pain and sadness of the previous eighteen months. Then she had raised the pink-and-yellow teddy to her cheek and hugged it close, and given him the first smile since her mother had announced that she was leaving. And Nathan's eyes had clouded over, so full of joy that when he had snapped the picture he had not been able to see anything at all.

There was a knock on the door. Nathan looked up to find the housekeeper, Miss Emma, standing in the doorway. The angular woman eyed him with the wisdom of long friendship, then said, "Call her."

He did not try to deny his longing. "All we'd do is quarrel."

"Maybe so," she agreed. "But that's a long sight better than just sitting there pining away."

Nathan glanced back at the photograph, aching from the loss. "I wish there'd been some way to have kept her here."

"Well there ain't." Strong mountain wisdom rang from her voice. "And wishing don't never put wings on fishes, nor make wrong answers right."

"No, I suppose not." He rose to his feet with ease, still checking each joint in turn, an unconscious search for weakness. Done without thinking, and thankfully without real need any more.

"And just where do you think you're going?"

"Home. I'm not getting anything done here." He reached for his coat, and again there was the catch to his heart, as he remembered an earlier time. Back when he had first been able to stand again, Claire had not been tall enough to raise his coat up and onto his shoulders. But she had refused to let anyone else help. She had grown used to taking the coat and climbing on a stool, to settle it herself around his shoulders.

"You just sit yourself right back down," Miss Emma rapped out. "I've had just about enough of your walking around the house, getting under my feet, and sighing like the world's done ended." She pointed at the phone. "Now pick it up and call her. Goodness only knows, if she yells at you it won't be the first time."

The woman shut his door hard enough to rattle the pictures. Nathan sank back down, his gaze caught by the embroidery on the opposite wall. His mother had made it as a wedding present. The Holy Spirit rose as a dove with the sun in the background, the Cross stitched in red around them both, and the words from Philippians beneath them, "I can do all things through Christ who strengthens me."

Nathan reached for the phone and prayed as he dialed the *Herald* number, Give me the strength, Lord, to let my baby go.

"Denver Herald, Lillian Fletcher speaking."

"May I speak with Claire Kingsbury, please?"

"I'm sorry." Lillian did a quick scouting of the far desk to be sure. "She's out of the office just now."

There came a long sigh over the phone. "Well, maybe that's best."

"May I take a message?"

Another pause, then, "Just tell her that her father called."

The man sounded so resigned she could not help but ask, "I hope there's nothing the matter."

"No." The word was drawn out long and low. "I just miss her, is all."

The confession gave her heart a sudden surprising twist. "Does she know that?"

"I think so, yes, I suppose she does."

"Suppose is not good enough." This could not be happening, but it was. Speaking sharply to a total stranger about a woman who was only now becoming a friend. "My own father spent a lifetime trying to use money as a substitute for words. But there's only one way for any of us to know for certain, and that's if feelings are expressed outright."

The expected explosion did not arrive. Instead, Nathan's tone perceptively brightened. "Are you my daughter's friend?"

"I try to be."

"From the sound of things, you do more than that."

"I'm sorry, I shouldn't have—"

"Don't apologize. You can't imagine how reassuring it is to know she has people there who care for her as you must."

Despite his obvious sadness, the man had a very nice voice. Warm and kind and strong. "Claire is a very special young lady."

"She certainly is." The last word became another sigh. "My life has developed an enormous void since she's moved down to Denver."

It was Lillian's turn to hesitate, before offering, "Your wife must be finding it very hard as well."

"My wife left us when Claire was eleven." About this there was no regret whatsoever.

"I'm sorry," Lillian said and felt a sudden surge to her heartrate. "Claire never mentioned that."

"No, she wouldn't have. Claire and her mother seldom communicate. Her mother remarried a number of years ago and has moved to Beverly Hills."

Lillian picked up a pencil to give her nervous fingers something to play with. She started to mention her own house opposite the Bel Air Country Club, but something held her back. Instead, she said, "Well, perhaps you should come down to Denver for a visit, and see how Claire is settling in."

Claire entered the newsroom and headed for her new desk, placed in the journalistic sticks at the room's far corner, away from the editors and the center of action. She could not have cared less. She had a job. The rest was trivial.

Lillian Stockton Fletcher, alias the Bag Lady, gave a frantic wave as Claire passed. Lillian had earned her nickname because of her penchant for taking freebies from any shop that offered them, which was incredible, given the fact that she was one of the richest women in Colorado. Claire veered over to her and waited by the partition as Lillian parodied a rapid talker on the other end of her phone.

Finally she set down the phone and said in exasperation, "Tessa Swindley."

"Who?"

"Leader of Vail's society circuit. Her husband is a Hollywood mogul in the making. Loathes the camera. Which makes it tough on Tessa. She's about what you'd expect, a failed actress who loves money and power and the big time. They have a huge place up in Vail. They're having a party this weekend and she wants me to come. Tessa lives for the chance to make a social splash. Hard to do with a husband who shuns the spotlight."

"I saw him yesterday."

"Who, Roger Swindley? Where?"

"At the computer show. Harry pointed him out. He's invested in this local company, Mainline Computers."

"That's right, they're partners in the new Airport Studios venture. Well, that's about as close as you're ever going to get to Swindley. He absolutely loathes the press." She waved it aside. "Never mind all that. You won't believe who I've been talking to. Nathan."

"My father?" Claire dropped her bag on the chair. "Pop called you?"

"He called *you*, but settled for me when you weren't around." She had the shining face of an excited teenager. "He's the nicest man."

"Yeah, he's great." Claire leaned on the partition. "What did you talk about?"

"All kinds of things. We were on the phone almost an hour."

"With Pop?"

"I asked him about Ouray. He told me nothing could make him happier than to live, die, and be laid to rest within sight of his dear and timeless friends. I thought that was so nice."

"Yeah, Pop really loves the hills." She inspected her friend. "You're blushing!"

"He invited me out. He's coming up. That was why he called, to see if you could meet him. Then he asked me out for lunch tomorrow, and I said yes. That is, if you don't mind."

"Why should I mind?"

Lillian seemed excited as a schoolgirl. "Now if only we could find somebody for you."

"No thanks," Claire replied. "I'm most lonely when I'm with a guy."

"Then what you need is to meet a different kind of fellow." She paused, suggested, "There's still Harry."

"I told you. Bosses don't count."

Lillian snapped her fingers. "Speaking of which, he stopped by on his way out and left you a note."

Claire accepted the paper and read silently, "The movie of that game, Babylon, is playing tonight. Might be worth checking out. I should be back around five. Want to go from here?"

"Personally, I never objected to mixing business with pleasure," Lillian was saying. "Especially with someone like Harry. The only reason he's not running this paper is because he's got the wrong motives. He loves journalism, but he also has a heart of gold. The two don't mix. He's married to his job until he sees a motive to do otherwise. But there've been cracks in the walls recently."

Despite herself, Claire was intrigued. "What do you mean?"

"I'm not sure. But our Harry has been looking a little down lately, as though he's missing something in his life." Lillian gave her a solid look. "Something big."

Claire's concerns over doing an evening thing with Harry subsided as they carried their talk of the day's news events with them out to the car. He listened with his focused attentiveness as she described the interview at the bank, giving her a hard look as the computer game-playing came up.

As they entered the cinema, he did a long slow sweep of the foyer, then said quietly, "Notice the people."

"What about them?"

"Some investigative journalist." He motioned to the crowd filling the lobby. "There's an almost total lack of young kids."

"This isn't an old crowd."

"I mean *kids*. Seven, eight, nine years old. The kind you'd expect to find watching this kind of film." He handed their tickets to the attendant and entered the hall. "Most of these people look college-age."

"It's six o'clock. They were probably at the afternoon show."

"And the movie's full," Harry persisted. "Look at this. Absolutely full. And silent. Notice the lack of chatter."

"So?"

"I see the occasional action movie. I've got five teenage nieces and nephews. There's always a lot of chatter. Here, nothing. And full. This is no Schwarzenegger movie."

He took the seat beside her and continued. "I checked the billboard. These actors are total unknowns."

As usual, Claire was left feeling that Harry Mitchum's mind scoped the situation at a level far above her own, leaving her racing just to keep up. "Yeah, but they spent a bomb on special effects."

"So? Special effect movies are a dime a dozen these days. It's not enough to attract this crowd."

After the movie ended, Harry remained oddly silent as they exited the cinema. Quick repartee and fast opinionated chatter was his trademark. This evening he quietly watched the crowd and strolled slowly through the cinema lobby. Finally he asked, "Notice anything?"

"I'm not sure," she said, but felt that she might be closing in. "There's something about this crowd."

"Like a club. Like they were all initiated into some secret society, with hand signals and their own language," he agreed. "So what did you think of the film?"

She shook her head. "Just as you said, all action and special effects. The world looked weird, though. No, not just weird." She searched for the word.

"Dark," Harry supplied grimly. "No goodness anywhere. Even the heros were bad guys."

"Wizards, warlocks, demons, magic everywhere," Claire went on. "And those warriors. Like the greatest thing anybody could ever wish for was either to control the powers of darkness or be invincible in battle."

"Evil," Harry said quietly. "A world and a story meant to glorify rage, violence, magic, and darkness."

"What do you—" Claire drew up sharply. A dark head by the exit arrested her attention. She darted through the crowd.

"Claire!"

At the sound of Harry's surprised call, the dark-haired guy turned around and locked with Claire's eyes.

She pushed her way impatiently through the crowded foyer. That second glance had confirmed her suspicion. It was the kid she had spotted on the stairs of Clay Conway's apartment.

As soon as he recognized her, his eyes sparked with the

same terror she had seen in the hallway. He shoved through the group surrounding him and raced for the doors.

"Wait!" But the guy was already gone, hurtling past the tightly packed throng of people trying to leave or enter, ignoring the yells and curses in his wake.

Claire stopped, defeated by the crowd's thickness. She walked over to where the group of young people were still gaping at where the guy had once been. "Excuse me," she said. "Could you tell me who that was?"

A young guy trying desperately to grow a goatee said, "You mean Troy?"

One of the girls became wide-eyed. "That was *Troy?* Why didn't somebody tell me?"

"Who is Troy?" Claire demanded.

"Only a living legend," the girl replied, her gaze on the exit. "I can't believe I sat there the whole time and didn't know it was him."

"You don't need to be telling her a thing," a black guy warned. He went on to Claire, "You want to know something, you go ask him yourself."

"I'd like to, very much." She kept her eyes on the guy with the goatee. "Do you know Troy's last name?"

"We don't know a thing," the black guy snapped. "Hello and good-bye."

Claire took a couple of steps back but continued to observe them. They were a strange group, seeming to know each other and yet very nervous at the same time, like kids on a giant first date. A couple of the younger ones wore Metallica T-shirts. One wore a silver overshirt with back tails long enough to look like a cape, emblazoned with a gleaming tower and the word *Babylon* written as it had been at the display. She spotted the same star tattoos that had been on the necks of the two game designers.

Harry moved up beside her and said, "What was that all about?"

She waited until they were well away from the group before saying, "That was the same guy who bolted when he saw us at the apartment."

His gaze turned keen. "Are you sure?"

"It was him." Claire examined the young people around her, both those going in and coming out. "Harry, have you ever heard anything about a tattoo, one shaped like a star?"

He mulled it over as they entered the dark Denver night, then shook his head. "Not that I recall."

"It's probably nothing." But little fragments kept coming to her as they walked. When she was back in the car, she asked, "Do you think maybe all this is somehow connected?"

"With the kid's disappearance?" He started the car, then sat there, mulling it over. "My head says impossible, but my gut . . ." He turned a troubled gaze towards Claire. "I mean, it's only a game."

DENVER

6

■ Instead of displaying the usual collection of photographs with powerful officials and yellowing cartoons, Harry Mitchum had decorated his office with surprising flair. The desk was supposedly the same one that had once graced Edward R. Murrow's den. The ceiling lights had been taken out, replaced by two standing lamps of brass and smoked glass. His swivel chair was vintage thirties, as was the sofa, the desk lamp, and the flanking leather chairs. The trio of brass spittoons seeing duty as planters fit in perfectly with the threadbare hook rug. On the walls were framed clippings of great stories from the twenties and thirties.

"I love this place," Claire informed him the next morning. "Always have, always will. If I ever make it to where they start handing out perks, I want an office just like this."

Instead of responding with something cute, Harry leaned back and sighed to the ceiling. "Got anything to report?"

She went through her study of the computer information and finished with her lack of any tie-in between the kid's disappearance and the hardware, the game, anything. When she was done, and Harry remained motionless, her nerves started acting up again. She glanced around the room, wondering if she should say something more, when she noticed that the plaques were missing from his desk.

Harry had a collection of little wood-and-brass placards, the kind that usually had either the name and title of the guy behind the desk or some profound saying like, "Think." Harry's signs, on the other hand, had quips from Mae West. He had a drawerful of the things, done up for him by a buddy in the printing department. He changed them every day or so. Some of those Claire had seen included, "When women go wrong, men go right after them." Then there was, "I generally avoid temptation unless I can't resist it." And "When choosing between two evils, I always like to take the one I've never tried before," or "Too much of a good thing can be wonderful."

She ventured, "What happened to your desk quotes?"

Harry slowly brought his gaze back to the room, then needed a moment before he realized what she was talking about. "They stopped being funny."

Claire hesitated, then quietly asked, "What's the matter, Harry?"

"Been worried about some things." He tried for a smile. "It comes from not having a wife, I guess. Nobody to go home and talk things over with."

She could sense that he wanted to talk, but was unsure what to say. She settled on, "Why didn't you ever marry?"

"I'm determined to avoid badges of journalistic success

like an ulcer, a smoker's cough, a love of vodka, a divorce, and a kid I see on weekends." He was quiet another long moment, then said as much to himself as to her, "This paper is more than just work to me. It's a passion. But fighting the good fight isn't always enough to fill up my days. Or give meaning to my empty nights."

The searing honesty silenced them both. Claire heard the pain in his voice, saw it in his eyes, and had the sudden urge to reach over, take his hand, and offer her own brand of sympathy and comfort. But she held back. This was her *boss*. Still, she could not stop her heart from feeling for him.

He grimaced. "I shouldn't be talking this way to you, my newest reporter. It might tarnish the paper's glitter."

It hit her then, a thought so bizarre that she started to discount it, only to realize there was a sense of power behind it, a sense of message. So she said gingerly, "Maybe you're just tired."

"In my bones," Harry agreed. "Not just for today. I feel like it's a burden I'm carrying into all my tomorrows."

"So come home with me." Just like that. "Take a weekend off in the mountains."

He looked at her, the hollow point to his gaze steadily shrinking. "I'm duty editor Friday night."

"Then let's meet up on Saturday, come back first thing Monday."

"I'd like that," he said quietly, "very much."

Her father had less trouble with the steep stairs up to her apartment than she had expected. He stood on the tiny landing, took in her narrow room under the eaves, the minuscule bathroom, and said only, "I'm grateful you would show me where you live. It makes me feel a part of this new life of yours."

"I'll probably get something bigger, now that I'm down here full time." Claire followed him back downstairs. "But I really like this neighborhood. There's a communal kitchen on the second floor for all the tenants, and I'm still not here all that much."

"Then I'd wait and get my feet on the ground before I moved," Nathan offered. He pulled up his collar as they stepped back outside. The pewter sky gave off a mist so light it drifted as much up as down. The air tasted wet, cold, bitter in a citified way. "Strange how I am chilled faster here than up in the mountains."

"It's the air," Claire said, trying for Miss Emma's country accent. "Bad air down here."

"That reminds me. I have four quarts of homemade stew and two loaves of soda bread Miss Emma made for you. Better take them up before we forget again."

She crossed the street, accepted the load, and ventured, "I understand you're having lunch with Lillian today."

He nodded. "I certainly did enjoy talking with the lady."

"I like her too."

"I'm glad to hear that." He shut the trunk. "You'd be most welcome to join us."

"No thanks, I'd just be in the way." She hesitated a moment, then said, "I need your advice about something. About Harry Mitchum."

"The gentleman must think a lot about you, offering you that job."

"He's an amazing journalist and a great editor."

"You don't need to sell me any more on Harry Mitchum. Besides the fact that you've been bringing him up for years, I happen to know all about him."

"You do?"

"Just because I'm out on the western slope doesn't mean I don't keep up with things. Now why are we talking of him today?"

"He's having a rough time. I want to . . ." she sighed. "I don't know what I want exactly."

"I expect you want to bring him home."

Her irritation flared instantly. "I hate it when you do that. Read me like I was an open book. I just hate it."

Nathan walked around to his door, refusing to be touched by her anger. "Bring him home, daughter. I'll enjoy finally meeting the man."

Donovan Stone reached for the phone at least a dozen times that day.

It had not been hard to find out the name of the *Herald's* new redheaded journalist. Claire Kingsbury. The name and the number was on a slip of paper there beside the phone.

By lunchtime Donovan had grown furious with Roger Swindley. There was nothing he hated more than waiting. And that is exactly what Swindley had kept him doing. Fourteen months since he had first fielded the proposal to help organize their Airport Studios project. His gnawing hunger for the big venture was growing bitter, a chancre that ate at his gut. And now this. Warning him off this girl. It was just too much.

Yet what angered him most of all was his own hesitation. Sitting there, worrying over the warning from Russ Reynolds, knowing all along that the chance of making it happen with Swindley was growing steadily dimmer, yet unable to break the chain and stop holding his breath.

Only a week or so of winding up his work here at the bank, then nothing. No contract, no income, no prospect for anything else. He had put everything into working with Russ on this new deal, even refused two other projects just to keep his decks clear. It was killing him.

The phone's ringing temporarily pulled him from his musings. "Mr. Donovan Stone?"

The young female voice startled him. "Claire?"

"I'm sorry, who?"

He had to laugh. Crazy that she would call him just because he was thinking about her. "No, never mind. I thought I recognized your voice."

"Oh. This is Roger Swindley's personal secretary, Mr. Stone. I'm calling to inform you that he and his wife are having a few people over to their place in Vail tomorrow evening. They were wondering if you might join them."

Despite his suddenly racing heart, the woman's attitude irritated him. This was not an invitation and the woman knew it. The message was passed on with the frosty politeness of a royal command. So Donovan replied with, "Hang on, let me check my calendar."

"Excuse me?" The voice chilled even further.

"Amazing. I just had a cancellation. Sure, that would be great."

The woman gave him directions with a frigid tone, then hung up. Donovan replaced the receiver with a smile, leaned back, and caught sight of the slip of paper bearing Claire's number. He stowed it in his drawer. There would be time enough for that later.

Claire was busy at her desk, sorting through the confusion of information and guesses, when she caught sight of a very subdued Lillian Stockton Fletcher entering the newsroom.

Claire rose to her feet and walked over to Lillian's desk. The closer she came, the clearer she could see Lillian's glum demeanor. She should have known it would never have worked between that pair. "Got a minute?"

"What?" Lillian looked up. "Oh, hello."

Claire settled into the seat by her desk. "It's okay, you can tell me. You didn't have a good time with Pop."

Slowly Lillian shook her head. "I'm not ready to talk about it yet."

"Sure." Claire nodded her acceptance. It was to have been expected. They were as different as chalk and cheese. "Total change of subject, then. I was wondering if you could tell me something about Roger Swindley."

"Why?"

"There's a story I'm working on. I don't know if he has anything to do with it, but I haven't got much else to go on, and thought I'd just ask."

Lillian focused with an effort. "He's very big league, both here and L.A. Got his start in cable television, branched out into film. Now the word is he's interested in computer video games. He's gone from strength to strength. Very secretive."

"You told me something about his wife being a real society queen."

"Did I? Oh yes, I remember now. She telephoned this

week. Well, it's true. Tessa Swindley positively adores being in the spotlight. Which is a real laugh, if you know Roger. He abhors having questions put to him in public. Never given an interview in his entire life, as far as I know." She eyed the younger woman. "Why, did you want to try and approach him?"

"Doesn't sound like I'd have much of a chance."

Lillian thought it over, then mentioned, "They are having that party tomorrow night. That's why Tessa called me, to make sure I had it down."

Claire sat up straighter. "You've been invited?"

"Of course. Are you interested?"

She started to tell her about taking Harry to Ouray on Saturday, but decided it would only lead to unwanted questions. "I'm travelling home this weekend. Vail is halfway. Were you going to the party?"

"I hadn't planned to. But it actually wouldn't be a bad idea for you to cover the function. Be sure and take note of whoever's there and what they're wearing." She sorted through a pile of letters and engraved invitations and selected one. "Tessa adores seeing her name in print. She invites me because she can claim I'm society. It saves her having to beg for a mention in the *Herald*."

Lillian started to hand over the heavily embossed invitation, then hesitated. "Don't go barging up and stick your recorder in Roger's face."

"I'll be discreet," Claire promised.

"I want you to be more than that, my dear. I want you to take great care. Roger Swindley is a strange man. And definitely not one to be trifled with."

INTERIORITY

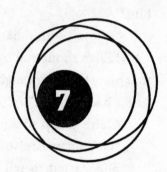

7

■ The new guy stumbled at the Gates of Oblivion and fell the entire ten-thousand feet down to the Drumming Sands. There was nothing Troy could do but laugh.

The new kid's warrior gear looked totally useless, despite the layers of steel-coated muscle he had chosen for himself. Troy powered down the sheer-sided cliffs, landed beyond the drum-sand border, and watched as the guy stood, dusted himself off, dropped his spear, picked it up, then almost stabbed himself when his sword-belt got tangled with his shield.

Drum sand was dangerous because it looked so normal, a shimmering yellow sea that stretched out from the Barrier Mountains all the way to the deadly pastures ringing the Tower of Babel. But the sand was hollow, merely a disguise for the Attack Tunnels underneath. There was no warning as to where or when the next assault would come. For that reason, only newbies and seasoned warriors came here any more. Newbies came because they failed to power up in time and got caught, warriors because the only way to earn their wings was to fight the dragons and win.

It was all part of the game.

The complexities meant nobody even started unless they *wanted* to spend years reaching the prize. The prize was achieved only after searching the Crystal Caves or climbing the Tower of Babel, both impossible without having won weapons and wings and battle honors beforehand. Even then, the prize—which was to become one of the elite Enforcer Princes or Princesses—only meant something to another gamer.

But Troy did not want the prize at all.

Troy stood on the last rock outcrop, a place he had used for many a successful attack, and watched as the new kid started across the sands. Ten steps later, the earth before him exploded in a billowing yellow storm. Flames erupted from the dragon's snout in a spume of murderous rage. The kid was saved by tripping over his spear again, and the flames shot out over his head.

The dragon climbed fully from the tunnel, shook himself off, and watched the would-be warrior scramble to his feet. When the dragon saw how the kid couldn't even get his sword clear of the scabbard, he sucked back the next fiery breath. Claws clicked open one by one, and the dragon took time to preen his scales. He was going to play this one like a cat with a mouse.

The kid tried to charge, which caught both the dragon and Troy by surprise. At least he had spunk. The dragon swiped both shield and sword away with one claw, then heaved itself up to full height and gave a hungry roar.

Troy decided he couldn't let the kid get toasted. He unfurled his wings and flew over, landing between them. He said to the dragon, "You might want to rethink this."

The dragon pulled up short. The roar died to a meek voice which asked, "Troy?"

"No way!" The newbie struggled to his feet. "You're *the* Troy?"

"I didn't know he was with you, Troy. Honest. I'd never try for a kill if you were—"

"Beat it," Troy replied.

"Sure. Yeah. Right. Thanks." The dragon gave a stiff-armed salute and melted back into the yellow sands.

When they were alone, Troy cut off the newbie's fluttering thanks with a sharp, "This is your first sortie, isn't it?"

The shoulders slumped until both sword and shield were dragging in the loose sand. "Yes sir."

"I'm not a sir. I'm just another gamer." He paused, then offered because he had to. "If you like, I could show you the lay of the land."

The kid popped back to full alert. "You mean it?"

"Sure. Give you a basic start-up package, show you around, keep you safe until you learn the ropes, all for one low price."

"Oh, you mean, I'd have to pay you." The kid's weapons drooped. "Thanks, I mean, that's really great. But I'm saving up to buy another—"

"Sure, sure. Forget it. Just stay out of Death Valley until you're ready to tango with the dragons."

Troy leaped skywards before the kid could reply, ashamed that he was forced to stoop to such levels. But he was beyond broke, and both his Second Skin and his headgear needed replacing badly.

He flew through the weapons chamber without acknowledging the salutes, dropped off his gear, and moved down the hallway toward the bulletin board. He searched the board for new queries, but found none. It was a frustrating and degrading task, this searching for the lost, but he had no choice. Discouraged, he started towards the outer gate.

"Troy, hey, what's the rush?"

Troy turned back with a sigh. That softly sibilant voice could only belong to one man. "I told you already. There's no way I'll work with you, Skate."

Standing before him was the only gamer not in proper garb. Instead he wore what he probably did on the outside, a double-breasted suit, but here it was cut too extreme, so it looked like a costume drawn for a Marx Brothers cartoon. "Thought I saw you log on," Skate rasped. He had a high, tin-like voice. Like an old-timey radio speaker with weak batteries.

"Didn't know you were interested in the comings and goings of peons."

"Now have I ever called you that?" The smile was a grimace painted onto his pretty-boy mask. Only Skate and the Tower Goddess could show facial changes, and on both of them the alterations were chilling. Skate went on, "Somebody wants to have a chat."

"No thanks."

"You should hear him out. He wants to make you an offer, clear up all those debts of yours, set you up for life. All in one fell swoop."

"Not interested."

"The news will disappoint him. And you know it's not wise to disappoint the big guy."

"He goes his way, I go mine."

Troy started to turn away, but was drawn back by the overly calm voice saying, "You know this means I'll be sent out after you."

"Anytime, Skate."

"Pity we won't have a chance to work together." The mask twisted into another smile. "Still, it might be nice to go up against some real competition for a change."

VAIL, COLORADO

■ The Swindleys' Vail home was a mock-Tudor manor set far back from the gates, a fact that Claire found genuinely amazing. Land prices in the Beaver Creek community kept even the richest from sporting that most ludicrous of extravagances—a lawn in snow-country. But the Swindley estate had one. Acres of it. All surrounded by a high stone wall.

Claire inched her way closer to the main entrance. In front of her was a Lexus four-wheel drive, this year's car of choice—a vital bit of information for people clawing their way up the Vail social ladder. The Lexus was preceded by a new Bentley convertible, no doubt belonging to the Aspen old-money crowd down for a night of slumming in the nouveau riche valley. Behind her rumbled a Lotus Elan, not exactly the most practical year-round car for a town that averaged seven feet of snow a winter. Claire's freelancing work had taken her to private estates in Vail and Telluride with ten-car garages. All this in the Colorado Rockies, where land and building costs gave downtown Manhattan a run for its money.

Vail and Beaver Creek were two communities wed by wealth, status, and a reverence for all things material. Together they formed a world apart, a fairy-tale land of year-round pleasure that catered to the super-rich.

Arriving at the front steps, Claire stepped from her Blazer, smiled at the scurrying valet, and tugged on the seam of Lillian's hand-me-down dress. All of Claire's va-va-voom suits were inherited from Lillian Stockton Fletcher, who had a habit of buying dresses by the gross and then discarding them after a couple of wears. Not that Claire was complaining, even though the fuchsia silk skirt with mother-of-pearl buttons up the slitted right side and a matching quilted silk jacket was a million miles from what she would have chosen for herself. What other newly hired reporter got to wear a two thousand dollar outfit, and had another four hanging in her closet? No question about it, there were definite advantages to having a rich friend.

The manor's interior was done in nouveau-Bavarian, Vail's current style of choice. Even for someone who had covered numerous such gatherings, this place was reason to gape. And not just Claire; all around her were murmurs of astonishment. The ceiling was a full three stories overhead, held in place by a rainbow-arc of redwood beams, each twice the width of a full-grown man. The floor was polished flagstone laced with an intricate granite-and-marble mosaic. Step-in fireplaces rose at either end, both burning man-size logs.

Claire allowed the crowd to sweep her down the stairs and out onto the main floor. She stood surrounded by a glittering, swirling throng, looking for she knew not what, and wondered if anyone else could feel as alone as she did at that moment.

A lot of the fun of film had disappeared when Donovan had started working in the game. And it really was a game, cut-throat as center-court Wimbledon, vicious as a backstreet knife fight, but still a game. Still entertainment.

The crowd slowly milling through Swindley's entrance hall was overdone in extremely quirky ways. The older guests, and those with the older money, stood around in their thousand dollar gowns and Sulka suits, talking in tones as cultured as the Queen of England, boring as mud. The younger ones clustered in louder throngs, all dolled up in four hundred dollar Rodeo-drive jeans and Armani tweed, rough silk ties, solid gold sportswatches, huge smiles, chatter as empty as the night air.

The actresses wore the most outrageous outfits, the biggest smiles, the brightest expressions. They were *on*.

Anyone who had made it to the top in the Hollywood game had learned to focus their hunger and ambition down tight as a cracking whip. Their male counterparts were only slightly more subdued. They stayed busy striking poses, standing where the adoring crowds and the sparkling lights showed them off best.

A night like this was crucial. The investors were here, the people with the power to set a project on go. This was not a party; it was a cauldron from which a deal could be struck, a new film started, a career launched or lifted or re-ignited. The scene sparkled and swirled and chimed with gay laughter. But a cauldron just the same.

Trish Owen gave Donovan's hand a tug. "Are we waiting for something, a cue maybe? Or do you want all eyes to turn our way for a grand entrance?"

"You go ahead," he said, only half kidding. "I don't think I'm up for this tonight."

"You need this as much as I do," she said, and took the great salon in with a sweep of her hand. "There could be a dozen new clients out there just waiting for you to come up and shake their hand."

"I never was good at mindless mingling," Donovan replied. "These parties give me hives."

"Then you're definitely in the wrong business," she said, sharply impatient with him now.

He started to answer, but was stopped when the crowd shifted like currents in a strong running tide, and there she was. Directly in front of him. The girl he had spotted before Reynolds had given his insane speech at the Interacta exhibition. His first thought was, This can't be happening. Not now.

She was tall, rangy, striking, the exact opposite of Trish. Nothing compact there. A shock of wavy red hair cascaded down her shoulders, as impatient and untamed as her walk. It was not the catlike pose of the city women he knew, practiced and polished until they used it like a lure. She walked like she had never had on a dress before, pushing the filmy silk to the limit with each stride, having a little trouble every now and then balancing on her heels. Then he realized Trish was watching him watch the girl, and he said the only thing he could come up with, which was, "What is that dress she's wearing?"

"De La Renta." Not needing to look back to reply. Her eyes steady on him. "Why?"

"I don't know, it just seems like she's a little too muscular to be wearing padded shoulders." Realizing this sounded awfully feeble, Donovan pressed ahead. "Do you know what I mean? Like she's just home from the range. Off with the boots and the jeans, into somebody else's dress."

Trish took his hand, gave him a look, something new, one he had not seen before. All she said was, "Let's go see."

Claire was standing by a trio of older women, pretending to sip from a glass she did not taste, listening to them carp about how an editor from *People* and another from *Cosmo* were getting the schmooze treatment from one of Hollywood's former hottest properties. How this very same actress had been too long without a decent script and was in serious danger of joining the over-the-hill gang, out of work and forgotten. It happened fast in Hollywood, especially with glamor girls pretending to have the thirty-ceiling still ahead of them. What a laugh. That woman was thirty-three if she was a day. Claire smiled with the others, saw their gazes track towards her, and turned away before they could ask who she was.

And there he stood. The man she had spotted at the Mainline computer exhibition.

Her first thought was, Incredible how a guy could be so good looking that it was hard to tell his age. She guessed at early to mid-thirties, and put the subtle lightening of his ruddy blond hair down to the premature coloration of a silver fox. And he certainly was that. A fox from head to toe.

Her attention turned to the other half of the pair, and Claire had to smile. The woman-child looked so perfect, so exquisitely beautiful that Claire wanted to walk over and punch her right in that perfectly formed snout. She was the kind of woman upon whom makeup looked so natural, it was hard to tell whether she was wearing any at all. She wore a little blue dressed-to-kill number that probably went for more than Claire had spent on clothes in her entire lifetime. Her knees formed a flawless joining for legs that looked far too long for someone as diminutive as she was. Her hair was pulled back to expose a neck like a Venetian vase.

And she held the arm of the best-looking guy in the room. No, that was not true. There were models and movie stars in abundance tonight, some over the top in the looks department. But he had something more, something which made it unnecessary for him to play the ego game. Claire realized she was staring, decided to turn away, but found herself held there by the thought of just how solid the guy looked.

Then her heart tripped up a frantic beat as she realized the pair were walking straight towards her.

She had eyes of broken glass. That was how Donovan always thought of eyes like hers, so full of some old pain that the look was fragmented. Hers were palest green, shattered emeralds of wary intelligence. He had to stop himself from asking what had brought her so much hurt.

Instead, he stopped there directly in front of her and said with a coolness that he did not feel, "You look about as out of place as I feel."

Which was definitely the wrong thing to say in front of Trish, who thrived on events like this. She found most of her clients here. Trish smiled her nasty cat's grimace and asked the girl, "Where ever did you find that dress?"

"In a friend's closet," she replied, without a hint of embarrassment. So straightforward and open about it all that he wanted to reach over, hug her, share a grand laugh. But the girl kept her gaze on Trish and went on, "Why, do I have it on inside out?"

Trish gave him the distant stare, the one signaling all kinds of caution, and said, "Why don't I leave you to console one another." Then she walked off. Wanting him to follow. Expecting him to run up and apologize.

Instead, he snagged two glasses from a passing tray and handed one to Claire, as though he had been doing it for years. "I've never really understood what I'm supposed to do at parties like this. But having a good time is definitely not on the list."

She smiled over the rim of her glass, a silent thanks for the simple gift, and said, "So what brings you to these lofty heights?"

He liked that. A swift turn of phrase, a way with words. Nice. "I'm a consultant. Mostly I work on startups, such as when a company is setting up a new line or division. I help them with headhunting the top executives and threading their way around the pitfalls."

"I know what a startup consultant does. You're the catalyst that makes everything come together."

He nodded acceptance, wondered at his desire to tell her anything more. But he did. "Up until recently I worked with a large group based in St. Louis. We dealt mostly with investment banks, overseeing new projects they financed. My last deal with them was a film production venture."

"Sounds interesting."

"Actually, it really was. I figured I'd never be in the film world again, so I might as well enjoy myself. And I had a ball. The studio was one of the new up-and-comers, setting up shop in North Carolina to ease out of the Hollywood cost spirals."

He liked the way she listened, green eyes focused so intently. She was clearly taking it all in deep. A lot of layers behind those beautiful eyes. A lot of mystery. He went on, "Anyway, I helped with the initial setting-up process. Then the company proceeded to make a trio of major box-office winners. So I went independent. I'm just finishing up a job, and I'm trying to get in on another film project."

"An American success story," she said.

He searched for a hint of derision, found none, only that sense of her words reflecting the truth as she saw it. Amazing. "And what about you?"

"Oh, I don't have any business being here at all." She had a way of bringing her glass to her lips, not tasting, a movement that was automatic, something done simply to grant her a chance to step back and think. "I'm a reporter for the *Denver Herald*."

He started to say something about already knowing, but held back. "I thought you people only traveled in packs."

"For events like this, that's generally the case," she agreed. "But a friend arranged for me to come tonight."

"What's your name?"

"Claire Kingsbury."

"I'm Donovan Stone." He reached into his pocket, handed her a card.

He watched her examine it, show surprise, and say, "You're based in Denver."

"We're neighbors. My client here is First Colorado Bank, just down the street from you. They gave me an office." He glanced around the swirling multicolored crowd. "Crazy that we had to come to Vail to meet."

"First Colorado?" She looked more keenly at him. "What did you do there?"

"I oversaw their investment in a local company called Mainline Computers." She showed a knife-edge interest now, a focus so tight it made him shiver, he liked it that much. "I'd like to stay and do more around here. You know about the game called Babylon?"

"I just heard about it for the first time at the Interacta exhibition."

"It's a major new money machine." He started to ask why she was interested in Mainline, then decided he cared more about making a move. "How'd you like to get together sometime? Maybe we could explore Denver's hot spots."

She laughed at that, a sound big and free enough to turn heads. "I didn't know there were any. But I'm just a newcomer."

Claire watched him share the smile. Dimples. The guy actually had dimples when he smiled. She tried to pull back, remind herself that this was not happening. Not to her. Guys like this did not walk in with a dreamtime date, then turn around and start hitting on her. Not a chance.

Then why was her heart racing?

"That makes two of us," Donovan said. "Maybe we should discuss things over . . ."

Claire did not need to turn around to know that he had just spotted his lady approaching. She spent an instant wondering about that, how she could even think that he might be interested in her when such a beauty hovered nearby.

"Sure," she said quietly, the word spoken to her heart's wish.

Donovan hesitated a moment before taking the woman's arm and drawing her close. "This is Trish Owen."

"Nice to meet you both," she lied. "Excuse me, I need to be mingling." Claire traded tight smiles with the woman and turned away.

She found herself immensely relieved to spot Russ Reynolds, president of Mainline Computers, standing to one side and by himself. She headed straight over. "Hello, Mr. Reynolds. Claire Kingsbury of the *Denver Herald.* I met you at the Interacta exhibition. Could I ask you a couple more questions?"

He was genuinely surprised. Almost panicked. "Am I supposed to be talking with you?"

The reaction helped her push aside Donovan's lingering impression. "I'm at Swindley's party, aren't I?"

"Yeah, I guess so." He drank from his highball. "It's just, Roger doesn't have much time for you media people."

She wanted to ask why Mainline's president was concerned about one particular investor's likes and dislikes, but something held her back. When Reynolds continued scanning the crowd, she covered with, "Does it ever bother you how negative and violent these interactive games are?"

"What's to bother? Violence sells. If the kids can't get what they want from us, they'll get it somewhere else. Look at where Babylon has brought us." Another heavy swig from his glass. "Swindley's people came up with a hook, a game high on the thrill-factor. They created something that made people go out and buy our hardware. Now we're rolling in the green."

This was new. "Roger Swindley's team developed the Babylon game?"

"The concept, sure. What, you thought a hardware company like ours could figure out a game concept and get it up and running, just like that?" He finished his glass, signaled a nearby waiter. "Swindley could have had anybody in the industry. He liked our equipment, liked sourcing his game directly to a computer manufacturer. It was the luckiest thing that's ever happened to us."

She watched him trade his empty glass for a fresh drink, take down half in one long gulp. If it was so great, why was he standing here by himself, looking so miserable? She probed, "Still, it must be tough, getting used to your new partners."

"What, you mean the Hollywood hype?" Another long swig, and the drink was almost gone. "Yeah, it gets under your skin sometimes. But that's the price you pay for success."

Donovan stood with Trish, looking down at a backgammon set redolent of eighties excess. The board was a solid slab of some semi-precious stone, palest blue with pink rivulets running like veins over the surface. Set into the face were triangles of inlaid ebony. Swindley's pieces were Canadian fifty dollar gold coins, his opponent's were antique Maria Theresa silver doubloons, the dice ivory.

Swindley fondled the dice as he watched his opponent move, the coins making a gentle chiming sound as they slid over the board's surface. Without looking up, the host said, "I understand you are the man to speak with when searching for talent and getting them settled in."

With all the attention turned his way, Donovan bit back the retort that this was the same conversation they had had at Interacta. "Mind if I ask who told you that?"

"It appears that the information is quite widely held," Swindley replied, tossing the dice, moving his pieces. Despite the languid tone, the man gave off an air of electric tension. "I've been most interested in what you had to say in your proposal to Mainline."

"Had I known you would read it yourself," Donovan replied, feeling Trish watch the two of them, knowing this was the perfect salve to dissolve the heat from having flirted with the redhead, "I would have sent you a personal copy."

"No matter. I very much liked how your proposal reflected my own thoughts when it came to expanding upon our success with Babylon." Swindley observed his opponent's move, then raised his eyes to Donovan's. There was the sense of coming under a laser-hard scrutiny. "I think we should consider doing some business together."

"I'm glad to hear it," Donovan replied. The smell of money coated every word.

"Perhaps you would be kind enough to come by my office next week, then."

"You mean, in Los Angeles?" Donovan was tremendously glad his voice remained steady. "Sure. Glad to."

"The earlier the better, as far as I am concerned." A moment's pause as Swindley rolled the dice and moved, then,

"I happened to notice you earlier, speaking with that young woman over there."

Donovan raised his gaze from the table, saw Claire standing near the entrance to the main salon, sipping at her glass, still talking with Mainline's president. "Hard to miss her."

"Indeed." Cold eyes of impenetrable smoke returned to him. "I was wondering if you could tell me who she is."

"A reporter. The *Denver Herald*, I think she said."

"That *stupid* secretary," hissed a voice from the table's other side. Donovan recognized Swindley's wife from the pictures she had starred in a decade or so earlier. Tessa Swindley's features were livid. "I will personally—"

"No harm done, my dear." The quiet words held a pointed warning.

"She had an invitation," Tessa Swindley said, her eyes boring into Claire's back. "I checked with the doorman."

"Indeed," replied Swindley. He turned back to Donovan and demanded, "What were you discussing?"

Donovan resisted the urge to tell him to mind his own business. "We talked about Denver."

"Fascinating." Swindley turned to his wife, and said, "Perhaps you should go have a word with Skate." Then back to Donovan. "Monday would work well for me."

"Monday's fine with me too," Donovan agreed, accepting the dismissal, giving a short bow, glad to be away.

Claire's next question to Russ Reynolds was cut off by someone snagging her arm, turning her around. "Okay, Miss, party's over."

A slender man with blond hair cut so short he looked

almost bald was there at her side. The man's skin was pale as a fish, and his eyes had no light in them at all. "I'm here to escort you to the front door."

"But I have my invitation right here." She started for her purse, only to have her hand snatched up and out, a pressure point touched, and suddenly her entire arm was on fire.

"Skate, she told me it was perfectly all right to talk with her," Reynolds insisted. He sounded genuinely scared.

"Sure, Mr. Reynolds, it's cool," the slender guy said, his voice at total odds with the rest of him. A breathless squeak, like dead treelimbs rubbing together. "Only Swindley wants you to go over, let him know how much you fed her."

"Skate, really, I said nothing that wasn't in our prospectus, I swear—"

Skate hissed for silence, his eyes darting to Reynolds, then back to Claire. "You're going to come peaceful, aren't you, Miss? It's nothing personal, but what the boss says, goes. And he says you go."

"She was just asking about Babylon, that's all," Reynolds said, his voice rising with the strain.

"Take it up with the man, sir," the guy snapped. Then to Claire, "The back door, right behind you. Move."

OURAY

■ Harry Mitchum was there at the Glenwood Springs turnoff when she arrived the next afternoon. His face had the pinched features of one who was not sleeping well. He slung his valise into the back, nodded a tight hello, climbed in, and settled back. He listened in silence as Claire outlined what had happened the night before at the Vail party. He spoke for the first time when she had finished, only to say, "What did he look like?"

"Who?"

"The muscle that threw you out."

"Like some guy with an awful childhood, worse past, and no future at all." She shivered at the memory. "He was called Skate. Isn't that a fish with a poisoned fang?"

"Strange how Reynolds reacted. For the president of a company riding the wave of success, you'd expect a little more spine." He mulled that over, then went on, "I worry about sending you into something you're not ready for yet."

She had a sudden memory of Donovan entering the room, staring at her, and she shivered a second time. "You think maybe I should write up what I've got?"

"And just exactly what is that, Claire?"

"Something's wrong here, Harry. I just know it."

"Okay, for the sake of discussion let's say there really is something tying Mainline and this Babylon game of theirs to these disappearances. Which, I have to tell you, is a hard one to swallow."

"But you think so too," she pressed.

He waved at the air between them. "That's beside the point. Anything this big would be on the story log for a major above-the-fold headline." His voice sounded drained of all energy, almost all life. "Which means we'd require double sourcing. Do you understand what I'm saying?"

"I think so," she replied. "Are you all right?"

"Just tired. I haven't been sleeping too well. Listen now. What we're talking about here is a story that is going to need rigorous documentation. The editors will demand it, and so will the lawyers. We need first-hand evidence, both on paper and on-the-record comments. Everything we use in building this story has to be attributed to a reliable source." He lay his head against the back rest and said, "Enough business."

"You relax," she agreed.

They drove on in silence, watching the western range rise around them, until Harry asked, "You sure it's all right with your father for me just to show up like this?"

"He loves newspapers and journalists and guests," Claire replied. "Don't worry about it."

"Can you tell me something about him?"

She thought that one over. "Somehow Pop's illness left him with the ability to look below the surface."

"You mean, of people?"

"Mostly, but maybe that's because people are what interest him most. Sometimes I find him watching me, and I get this feeling that he knows me better than I know myself."

Harry inspected her a moment before offering, "Must be hard to accept sometimes."

"It makes me furious," she agreed, but the heat was not there. All she felt at that moment was that she could tell this man anything and he would understand. Which was a very strange way to feel about her boss.

"I've met a few people like that," Harry said. "Not many. Two, maybe three. They seemed to have moved to a different level of awareness." He waited a moment, then asked, "What about your mother?"

The day seemed to chill slightly. "My mom?"

"You never talk about her. I was just wondering." Harry glanced over. "Have I said something wrong?"

"No." But the air was hard to come by. Weird. The unopened letter was still in her purse, and Harry had brought it up. The effort to draw breath hardened her tone. "Mom divorced us when I was eleven."

"You mean she divorced your father."

Claire shook her head in a violent arc. "She divorced *us*."

"You don't know that for certain."

"Being eleven doesn't make you blind. It just makes some

things hurt a lot worse." They slowed and entered the town of Silverton, but Claire remained caught in remembering another city, another time. "Like your mom taking off. And then your dad getting fired and having a stroke."

Harry sat there a long moment, then said quietly, "I'm sorry. I shouldn't have asked."

"You couldn't have known." Claire forced her chest to relax far enough to take a normal breath. "Anyway, we survived."

He gave her a long look. "You did more than that."

Beyond Silverton the peaks finally began to approach, old friends closing in on both sides. Claire found the tension easing. Harry was silent as they entered Ouray and drove down the main street, lined on both sides by turn-of-the-century buildings, well-tended monuments to the town's early mining days. Claire saw how involved he was with the scenery, so she drove all the way through town and up the hairpin turns leading along Box Canyon Falls.

She turned around at the top and started back. "Ouray needs a stoplight," she told him.

"You drive through and think, Wow, this is great," Harry agreed. "But swoosh, just blink one time and it's gone."

Again there was a flood of shared understanding. She turned down Third Street, the worst of the ruts now lost beneath the cover of snow. She pulled into an empty spot and cut the motor. "Mind if we walk from here?"

"Not at all." He was already clambering from the car, stretching, turning, gazing at the vast peaks. "This is magnificent."

"I'm glad you like it." A return home always started the

same, parking down by the paper, but not going in. Walking up the road, greeting neighbors and the surrounding mountain peaks, all her well-known friends. Nestling back into this valley, this world apart. Finding her roots again.

It seemed strange that she could share this so easily with Harry. He walked alongside her, silent and open to the experience, watching her and following her gaze as it rose to the peaks, taking them in as deep as his long breaths.

"Well, well, if you're not a sight for sore eyes."

Claire lowered her gaze from the mountains. "Hello, Miss Emma."

The old woman stumped down the front stairs of Claire's home, walked over, and gave her a quick fierce hug. "How is Denver treating you, child?"

"All right, I suppose."

"Pity you young folks've got to go down Denver way to chase your dreams. Flatlanders are a breed apart, I've always said. It's the air, you know. The plains breed bad air. Makes people funny." She nodded decisively. "Bad air."

"Miss Emma, I'd like you to meet Harry Mitchum."

"Young man." She treated Harry to a beady-eyed inspection, then demanded, "You treating my young lady like a gentleman should?"

"This is my boss, Miss Emma," she said, her cheeks reddening.

"Don't change things in my book." Her gaze remained defiant.

"Claire is a treasure," Harry said solemnly.

She nodded acceptance of that and of him. "You'll be staying the weekend, then?"

"If it's not too much trouble."

"Never a bother to host a gentleman with proper manners." She turned away. "I'll just go air out the extra room."

Claire felt as though her cheeks were on fire. "I'm sorry, Miss Emma is—"

"A prize," he finished for her. "I'm honored to have met her."

The words left her wanting to reach over and envelop his hand with hers. Claire covered by turning around and starting back down the road. "Come on, let's go see if Pop's around."

The newspaper was situated in a grey wood-shingle house near the corner of Main and Fourth. A brass sign dangled from a snow-covered post out front. As they approached, Claire saw it as she feared Harry would, a tiny shack at the edge of a no-account little town, and she wished she could somehow take back the invitation and make him go away.

But as they started down the walk Harry breathed, "This is great."

She turned to glance suspiciously in his direction, and confronted two shining eyes and a genuine smile. She let him open the door for her, and entered the familiar little office.

"Hey, pretty lady. How's the big city treating you?"

Claire pushed the door shut behind Harry and replied, "Awful."

"Now why aren't I surprised?" The woman occupying the paper-strewn desk was mountain born and bred, her strong features reddened by a lifetime of outdoor living. "You found out who's responsible for them paving Denver bicycle paths while all but our Main Street stays a dirt road?"

"Not yet."

"You do, you write it up, put it on the front page, call it the Denver Conspiracy." She gave Harry a flirtatious smile. "Who's your beau?"

"Annie Birdwell, this is Harry Mitchum." To Harry, she explained, "Annie is Pop's number one assistant."

"Number two, maybe. The top slot's yours and always will be." But Annie's tone had turned formal, and she was rising to her feet. "Harry Mitchum of the *Denver Herald?*"

Harry turned to Claire in surprise. She explained, "I guess I've talked about you."

"Just a minute, sir," Annie said, already moving for the door. "I'll go tell Nathan you're here."

When they were alone, Claire added, "I guess I talked about you a lot."

Harry did a slow circle. "I used to dream of working in a place like this."

It was her turn to show astonishment. "You did?"

"Be a great place to come after the rush loses its allure." His face took on that same look of tired sadness. "Which may be already happening."

"A small town newspaper is a grand place to get to know people," Nathan Kingsbury said, entering the room with Annie looking over his shoulder. "You learn who pays their bills and who doesn't and who can't. You learn who talks from spite and who talks from anger. You learn how to hide what should never be made public."

"I didn't know there was such a thing," Harry said, offering his hand. "Harry Mitchum."

"It's a genuine honor, Mr. Mitchum. Claire has told me so much about you I feel we're already friends." Nathan shook the hand and went on, "A small-town paper can't print what will hurt your neighbor, unless the town just has to know about it for its own good. The hurt would still be there long after the paper is thrown away and forgotten."

"A big city paper lets you be anonymous," Harry agreed quietly. "Which does not always breed the proper attitude among its reporters."

To Claire's surprise, the words brought a genuine smile to Nathan's features. "Heard a lot of good things about you, Mr. Mitchum, and not just from Claire. Consider it a privilege to meet you."

"That's not exactly what I was expecting. Most times, when I'm out on the western range, if I tell anybody I work for the *Herald*, I have to duck."

"Can't say I agree with all you folks write or all your paper stands for," Nathan replied. "But I admire quality workmanship, and you have always struck me as a quality kind of gentleman. And I am most grateful for the care and concern you're showing my daughter."

Harry glanced Claire's way, then responded quietly, "She is a treasure."

Nathan seemed surprised by the words, for he began nodding slowly, a motion that took in all of his upper body as he examined Harry more closely. As though he was seeing something, a secret still held from Claire. Then he smiled again and reached for Harry's shoulder. "Let's walk up to the house and see what Miss Emma's cooking for dinner tonight."

For Claire, the entire dinner was remarkable. Her father normally was not a talker. But tonight he held forth, competing with Harry to tell stories, the big-city editor and the small-town newspaper publisher comparing their worlds and clearly reveling in the chance to meet and talk. Claire found herself content to remain quiet and observe.

After dinner she rose and gathered the plates, signaling for Harry to stay where he was. But as she was turning towards the kitchen, she was halted by the sound of Harry saying, "Black noise."

Nathan tilted his head slightly. "I beg your pardon?"

"The opposite of white noise, which is a soothing collection of sounds, like waves on a beach. Black noise is cacophony. It incites fear, terror, anger, frustration. Recently I have started feeling as though that's what today's news is focusing on—creating more black noise."

Nathan leaned back in his seat, listening. Quietly Claire set her plates on the kitchen counter, then stood and watched from the doorway.

"Journalists look for crises," Harry went on. "We are pressed by competition and the tide of events to shout out dilemmas each day. They're coming so fast and furious we don't have time to talk about the resolutions." He gave a wry smile. "Or maybe we do. But a new crisis sells a lot more papers than solving an old one.

"Many of the people I work with," Harry went on, "they've never fit in. Not their entire lives. They were the outsiders in school, they graduated into the oddballs of life. Being on a newspaper staff is the outsider's ultimate power trip. They are paid to stand at a distance and observe. Which of course means most of them are flaming liberals to boot. Whoever heard of an outsider who was content with the status quo?" He fiddled with his spoon a long moment before concluding, "I wonder if that's why I'm increasingly feeling out of place in my own life."

Claire turned her attention to her father. There was a sense of Nathan weighing the atmosphere. Finally he spoke, his voice softer than it had been all night. "I hope you'll excuse me for speaking like this, but I have the impression that what you're saying is not really what is on your mind and heart just now."

Harry did not deny the observation. Instead, he dropped his gaze to his hands. The air seemed to pour out of him then, not just a sigh, but a total deflation. Claire glanced back to her father, and found him watching Harry with a focus so total it was as though she had disappeared.

"I feel like I've been brought face to face with my limits," Harry finally said, his voice almost broken. "Even that isn't strong enough to say what I mean. I can't seem to go where I want, do what I should, achieve what I set out to. I feel almost crippled, like everything I do is warped and tainted. As though I'm defeated even before I start. I'm surrounded by people who would just as soon see me fail, and battles I feel I've lost before I begin. Even when I win, I lose, because there's always the next one there waiting for me."

And then he stopped. His head remained bowed, as though the simple act of confessing to this stranger had robbed him of the powers of speech and vision.

Claire started forward, her mouth open to offer an assurance, but her father raised a single finger. Wait. Somehow that gesture was enough to halt her, as though behind his signal was an unseen power, a force so compelling that she could not fight against it. She watched as her father bowed his own head, but not in defeat as with Harry. Even though there was little visible difference between their positions, the feeling was entirely contrary. She could not explain how she knew, but she was certain. And somehow her father's act kept her immobile.

The very room seemed to gather together in a flood of unseen light, and Claire had the sense of standing at the verge of a miracle. A strange way of looking at her own dining room, but the sensation was so vivid it could not be denied. She was caught by a sudden insight, that her invitation to Harry, even the distress he himself had been feeling, had all been leading toward this very moment. Somehow the realization stripped away her ability to think, to move, to do anything more than observe.

Less than a dozen heartbeats passed before Nathan raised his head and spoke quietly, "If you will accept a new friend's advice, I think you might find some comfort in the book of Mark."

Slowly Harry looked up. "You mean the Bible?"

Nathan nodded. "In my mind, the author is focusing upon the message of Christ's ability to empower us, to meet our deepest needs, and to do so *now*."

He stopped then, as though offering Harry the chance to steer the conversation onto a more comfortable topic. But when Harry did not respond, he continued, "The word used most often in Mark is *immediate*. Used over forty times, in fact."

"Almost as though it was written for a journalist," Harry offered quietly.

"Written for everyone caught up in the pressures of today," Nathan agreed. "In the third chapter, we are told of a man who had a difficult life. He suffered from a crippled hand.

He was trapped by his own limitations. He needed someone to free him."

Nathan pushed back his chair so that he had room to stretch out his legs. He went on, "When I find a passage in the Scriptures that speaks to my heart, I like to stay with it for a time, until it talks to me on a number of levels. Let me show you what I mean. In this particular passage, we find that Jesus and the limited man were surrounded by cynics and legalists, who wanted both of them to *stay* limited. These cynical observers claimed to be there to uphold the law, but in truth they wanted to uphold the position with which they were comfortable. Their tightly controlled little world was far more important than either God's power or man's need."

Harry gradually straightened, as though the words he heard contained a power that fed both body and spirit, lifting him from his depression. His eyes fastened upon Nathan with the intensity of a drowning man clutching a life raft.

"The passage also tells us that Jesus recognized these worldly observers for exactly what they were. He realized they were dangerous, and would try to destroy Him if He did not act as they wanted. But it did not stop Him. Not at all. Instead, Christ turned back to the limited man, and He said just two words. He said, 'Come forward!'

"Those words were a call that speaks to all of us who have needs that leave us feeling as though we shall never be whole." Nathan's gaze matched Harry's for singular intensity. "Yet at a time when the invitation to come forward is made, it will feel as though our entire world is trying to stop us. Those who jealously guard their power and their position will be ready to pounce, to condemn us for heeding Christ's call. Yet if we have the courage to accept His invitation, God will take what is broken and deformed and limited, and make it into something beautiful. We will discover that His miraculous power of love and salvation will transform us into who we are *intended* to be."

Claire woke as she usually did when home, which was in the half-light of early dawn. She rose and dressed quietly, munching on an apple she had brought in the night before. She slipped from the house, and paused to enjoy the silence of a sleepy mountain town. It had snowed earlier in the night, and a fresh blanketing lay untouched over the streets. She strapped on her cross-country skis in the driveway, and pushed off, reveling in her instant solitude.

The sky still bore the last tendrils of the night's storm. Overhead the clouds were fine as thin gauze, with hints of blue shining through here and there. The rising sun was a faint golden shield beyond the eastern hills, not yet bright enough to cast even dim shadows.

She made it beyond the town's limits, followed the path leading from the road to the old railhead. When Ouray had been a mining town, the rails were used for carrying the ore to the outside world. Now it was a local secret, a perfect cross-country track, no grade steeper than six percent and never used by any outsider. She pressed on through breathless forests, the snow an undulating mystery of white and grey and softest silver. The air was still, taut, and eager with coming change.

She skied for a solid hour, not seeing another soul the entire time. She stopped, popped out of her skis, and took in the morning. The forest beckoned, a temple silent with secret reverence. The trees stood in respectful array, urging her to join with them, to be still, to listen.

Claire stepped off the path and into the forest. She leaned against a tree, heard the chatter of a squirrel, wondered at this strange restlessness within. For the first time that she could recall, the morning and the forest did not hold her. Her mind flickered from the evening with Harry to the meeting with Donovan, to work, to the story, and back to Harry. On and on, a swirling tide of choices and decisions and frustrations.

She looked about her, felt the forest and its silence become a mirror, urging her to go beyond the outer barrier of thoughts to see what lay at its center. It troubled her, this dawn and this silence, which had always before been a friend. She felt trapped there, unable to move away, knowing that wherever she went she would carry it with her still, the challenge and the call to look within.

With a shattering sense of being stripped to the bone, Claire felt herself enter a new realization. It held an impression of seeing what she had always known was there, yet never wanted to recognize; beneath her mantle of busyness lay an empty core. She had stood resolutely proud and determined, relying on her own strength, never even admitting that a choice was there to be made.

In that instant came a second shocking realization; all the arguments with her father had been a lie. She had been struggling to cover the simple fact that only in her father's eyes did Claire glimpse the truth. Each tiny flash of truth had been enough to infuriate her. Whenever Nathan had started to speak, whenever he had studied her with that steady gaze of his, she had felt threatened.

The years of lies lay exposed for what they were. Two forces heaved through her, opponents locked in eternal struggle. One shouted for her to turn away from these truths and their searing pain. The other offered an invitation, to do what she had pretended to do through years of churchgoing. And within her rang a message so powerful she thought for an instant that she had actually heard it with her ears.

Choose.

"*No!*" Her shout shattered the forest's peace. She rushed back from the trees, onto the path, and into the skis. Flying down the track, faster and faster, moving away from all that she did not want to face within herself.

FROM INTERIORITY
TO DENVER

■ "This is it, man! I told you, we don't need a Seer!"

Buddy Wiggins, alias Frostbyte, was a full-status Warrior who only two weeks ago had earned his wings. He took the thousand-foot cliff in a single ecstatic bound. He landed at the pinnacle beside his friend, the Wizard known as Lonewolf, and declared, "Totally awesome."

The plateau stretched out under rising dual moons, the signal they had been piloting by for almost a month of gaming. The plain was everything the fables and rumors had suggested, an undulating vista of rainbow crystal. Each rise was a different cave, each cave a crypt of hidden mysteries and powers.

Lonewolf started along the silver-flecked path. "Come on, let's get a move on it."

But the first hint of the climb-down hit him then, and Buddy said, "Hang on, I'm coming unglued."

"Tough." Lonewolf turned around long enough to taunt, "Don't tell me you've come this far just to give up and start over tomorrow."

"No," he said, reluctantly following along. "Guess not."

But by the time he reached the first grouping of caves, the edges of his self-made reality were becoming frazzled, and Buddy knew it was time to call it quits.

Yet the Wizard was already dancing in excited glee towards the first cavern. And it did look appealing. A rainbow kaleidoscope surrounded the opening, every glimmer of light turned into a tapestry of hues. Buddy sighed and started toward the next one. They had been struggling toward this moment for almost a year. He couldn't let his friend do it alone.

Inside, however, the shredded sensation increased, and he felt himself being pulled in two directions at once, which left him totally vulnerable and unready when it hit.

The diamond walls dissolved into a mass of violent tints. Red and orange and ochre clouds closed in and began to swirl, faster and faster, the patterns hypnotic. Part of him was held and pulled forward, sucked into the maelstrom. Another part began to awaken, feeling the weight on his head and the sweat inside his uniform. But he could not draw back. Not any more. He was trapped, and sucked farther and farther down.

At the center of the vortex appeared the golden mask of the Tower Goddess. She was cold and forbidding as ever. Her eyes opened and stared directly at him. He tried to pull away but could not. And the vortex drew him ever further downwards. The goddess grew larger and larger, until the merciless face was everything in his universe. And then she began to speak.

Buddy screamed. And screamed again, as his mind was torn in two.

Troy stopped by the bulletin board as soon as he had logged on that evening. It was a quick reflex now, a daily shot of futility. People coming and going avoided him, both because he was the reigning top warrior and because he was known to be looking for someone to take him on as a paid mercenary. There were no rules against having someone mark up kills for another gamer. In Babylon, there were very few rules at all. But it had not been done before.

"Troy, hey, hear you're looking for a trade." A wizard he knew vaguely, one called Shadowspawn, stopped alongside.

"Not a trade," Troy corrected, scanning the board. "Cash only."

"Sure, but look, I could work out something almost as good, you know, hot-wire your telephone system, give you unlimited time online, how does that sound?"

"No thanks." Making a swift illicit in-and-out was one thing. Stressing over having an illegal operation in his house every time he turned on his computer would be a breakdown in the making.

"Look around you, man. This is the land of barter and bargaining."

Troy started to brush him off, but stopped. He had heard about this guy, how he wanted to upgrade to warlock status but lacked the power-points. No need to antagonize a warlock in the making. "Tell you what. Let me find my way out from under this load, and I'll hunt you down, give you a hand. We'll work something out once you've upgraded."

"Hey, all right, a warrior after my own heart." Shadowspawn gave him the gametime version of a high-five, hands drifting together and through each other. The hiss of static from their contact served as confirmation. "Later, bro."

"Sure." Troy scanned the board for a final instant. He was actually into the first step down the corridor when he backtracked and examined the board more closely. Gamers were supposed to remain anonymous, but most came to know each other within a certain reality range.

A kid had gone missing, a no-show at some rendezvous point in the Mystic Mountains. That night he had also missed another contact in real time. Anyone heard anything, or maybe knew where he lived? Troy knew, he had made it his business to know. The label of Frostbyte belonged to a kid named Buddy Wiggins. He lived in Littleton, a bedroom community south of Denver.

Troy turned away from the board, utterly confused over what to do. He was hours away from coming down. Even so, he needed to hurry. Every minute counted now. The longer he waited, the greater the chance that someone would be there before him, scooping up the needed equipment to settle the kid's outstanding debts. If he was a full-on gamer, he had debts. The two went hand-in-hand. And nobody but Mainline gamers ever went missing. Troy knew that for a fact.

With a frustrated sigh, Troy reached up and worked the star-shaped patch off his neck. But it was too late to do much good. Hours and hours of the stuff was already into his system. Then he shut his eyes and prepared for the wrenching alteration. In truth, though, nothing could make him ready for what was to come.

Nothing.

He leaned against the walker's padded railing, bent over until his head was level with his knees, reached to the unseen keyboard, and typed in the log-out. His eyes still clenched shut, he waited for the peep, then lifted off the headgear.

It was even worse than he had expected.

Finding the kid's apartment while moving through the twilight zone would have been impossible, except for the fact that Troy had prepared for just such an emergency. Even so, it was still the hardest thing he had ever done.

The taxi number had been written on the wall beside the phone, but reading the numbers off a wall that kept dissolving with each random thought, then tapping them into a telephone that wanted to bite his fingers, was beyond tough.

He gave the driver the address, then slid down as far as he could. Reality was a problem for him at the best of times. Seeing cars melt into dragons and back again on the freeway threatened to push him over the edge.

When they arrived he told the driver to wait, got out, and made his way into the seedy red-brick building. He did not need a key. Dwellings for Mainline gamers were all alike, cheap and shabby.

The door to Buddy's apartment was tougher to handle. But he had been practicing with a credit card, and, despite his wandering mind, was able to slip it in and spring the latch. The apartment was just like he expected. The main room stank from unwashed dishes and dirty linens. The kid's computer was the only item of value in the whole place. Troy walked over, unplugged the Second Skin, and stuffed it as fast as he could into the headgear.

Then he heard the voices.

"I run a good home," a foreign-sounding woman was insisting. "I worry, of course I worry, Buddy not come back for two nights. But what can I do? He grown man. Boy on inside, but still grown man."

"Nobody's accusing you of anything, ma'am." The voice sounded hard and bored, and set off every alarm in Troy's mind that was still functioning.

"But the door is open!" The woman's voice rose a full octave. "How can that be?"

"Stay right there, ma'am."

Then reality reached into Troy's head, drew out the worst he could come up with, and suddenly sprang his most dreadful nightmare into full-blown life.

Two big men appeared in the doorway, blue uniforms with reality-type guns drawn, pointed straight at him. They shouted at him to set down the stuff, and stand there with his hands up. Troy did as he was told, although his strength had drained away and he was trembling so hard he couldn't speak. Not to mention the fact that the walls were still flowing like rainbow rivers.

As the policemen pinned him and patted him down, he couldn't help but wish he could just melt through the walls, stretch out his wings, and fly away.

He was spun about, and watched as the handcuffs came out and attached themselves to his wrists, ice cold and flaming silver. He tested them as he was led out of the apartment, the woman screaming for him to bring back that nice boy, Buddy Wiggins. The cuffs felt much harder than they looked, and the taste in his mouth was of prison.

That was the trouble with reality. He never could get it to do what he wanted.

DENVER

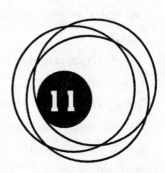

■ The early morning trip back from Ouray was made in almost complete silence. Claire found she did not mind at all. They traded off the driving, she taking them as far as Glenwood Springs and Harry continuing once they met the interstate. Few words were exchanged, but there was no tension or unease in the car. Instead, it seemed as though both had much to digest from their stay in the highlands.

From time to time she examined his face, both reassured and troubled to see that his distress and fatigue had faded. Glad for him, but troubled for herself, as though his own changes were a challenge.

They reached the outskirts of Denver before she finally broke the silence with, "It helped talking to Pop, didn't it?"

"A lot." Harry seemed to gather himself, as though taking her words as the signal to resume normal life. "Sorry to have unloaded on you like that."

"I didn't mind." But Claire felt something had to be said, which was very strange, since she rarely permitted herself even to think of such things, much less talk of them. Even so, she was not yet ready to let go of the intimacy. Or perhaps, the intimacy was not ready to let go of her. So she took a breath and offered the gift of openness. "On the way down you asked about my mother."

Harry straightened up behind the wheel. "You don't have to talk about that, Claire."

"When I was eleven, Mom announced that she did not love my father any more," Claire pressed on. "She told us that she detested Cincinnati, and always had. She was a big city girl, born and raised in Los Angeles, and she longed for a life of style. She hired a tough, abrasive lawyer and demanded almost everything."

Outside the front window, buildings and traffic began to close in around them. Even so, Claire looked through the dusty glass and saw there the memories of another time. "Mom went through hobbies like other moms went though Saran Wrap. She took singing lessons from an aging opera star. She started bonsai trees and rose bushes and origami sculptures and French sauces and left incredible messes for everybody else to clean up. Mom had no sense of humor but she laughed all the time. She had great teeth and she loved to show them off."

Harry moved into the slow lane, so that he could watch her occasionally. "I'm really sorry, Claire."

The genuine sympathy to his voice made it easier to keep going. And she wanted to. Which was very strange, because she rarely talked about her mother. Still, something about Harry and this moment made talking over the toughest things possible. "At the time, Pop was a banker in Cincinnati. He made it plain early on that she could have whatever she wanted, so long as he was granted custody of me. Mom used this lever to strip away everything she possibly could. She moved out to Beverly Hills and married a dentist. He caps a lot of teeth for the stars. Makes a bomb."

"Do you have contact with her?"

"She calls or writes these letters once or twice a year, telling me I need to get out of the Midwest and see the real world." Claire felt the same heat she did whenever her mother was on one of those tirades, putting Colorado down as just another Ohio with hills. "Around the time the trial started, Pop began to pay more attention to church. There was a new minister, and he had started a support group for people going through hard times. Before, church had basically been part of our social scene."

Claire stopped then, caught up in a sudden memory from several years before the divorce. Driving in another car, this one smelling new and shiny, her father taking them to the big church downtown. Her mother had turned around in her seat to talk to Claire, using her hands as much as her mouth, patting the back of her seat or Claire's knee in time to her words, wearing little grey Sunday gloves with pearl buttons at the wrists. Her lipstick was red, as red as her hair, and her eyes were all over the place, watching her husband, Claire, the scenery outside. Neither she nor Claire's daddy cared much for religion, Evelyn was saying. But churchgoing was an important part of Claire's heritage, and after all, she would meet some nice people there. So they were doing it for her. And it was important that she behave and pay attention to the Sunday school teacher and be a nice girl with proper manners and not run around in her fine Sunday dress. Evelyn had said nothing about God. Not one single word.

Claire took a breath and had to ask, "Where was I?"

"Church and the divorce." Harry gave her a look of genuine sympathy. "You don't have to talk about this."

But the memories kept flooding in. "After the divorce, Pop and I went to the front of the church to reaffirm our faith. Church has been important to us ever since."

"It must be nice," Harry said slowly, "having something like that to rely on in the hard times."

"Yes." Yet as she spoke, she was remembering something else. How she had gone up front to thank the families who had been so kind, and to bind herself to this new part of her father's life, and to show this publicly. Yet the day she and her father had stood before the Ohio congregation, there had been little faith at work, at least not in her. She had stood there because she knew her place in the world was beside her father—and joined the church. *Joined the church.* The words resounded through her. That was exactly what she had done. Joined with the church, not joined with God.

She tried to push that thought aside with, "That wasn't the end of it, though. Around the time the divorce became final, Pop's bank was acquired. He had been one of the three men responsible for the negotiations. He ended up fighting his own board and the other board simultaneously. He wanted assurances that there would be no massive lay-offs after the merger. But the purchasing bank decided it was cheaper to pay up front and fire at will. Pop's fellow board members united to make him the first senior executive to be axed."

"With this on top of the divorce," Harry murmured, "it must have been awful."

"Worse than that."

Harry's strong features were creased with concern. "That was when your father had his stroke, wasn't it?"

"The day the bank announced the first series of job cuts," she confirmed, as another flood of memories crowded in. "The left side of his body went totally numb. Pop's mouth sloped downwards. His face looked like partially melted wax. Swallowing became a major effort, his speech was slurred, and his eating hard to watch."

Harry turned on his blinker and slid onto the downtown exit. "And you helped him."

"I was the only one who could understand him. Even the nurses had to come get me to explain what he was saying. And I never had any trouble."

He stopped at a light, turned to examine her more closely. "You had to grow up in a hurry."

"I guess so. At the time, it didn't matter so much. Pop was getting better. That was all that mattered."

"And then you came here."

"It's home," she said, her voice matter-of-fact. "It has felt like that since almost the first day. As though Colorado was where I was intended to live all along."

She watched Harry pull into the *Herald*'s underground parking and reflected how this simple fact was something her mother would never accept nor understand. "Sorry to have unloaded all that old baggage on you."

"I like hearing about your past," Harry said, his tone soft, his features unreadable in the parking's shadowy half-light. "I like knowing what's made you who you are."

The companionable feeling bonded them tightly as they crossed the concrete cavern and entered the elevator. There was no need to say more. Not then.

But as soon as the doors opened upon the newsroom's clamor, the mood was shattered by a frantic Lillian racing over and demanding, "Why on earth did you turn off your phone?"

"It was my Sunday off, and I meant it to stay off." Harry's tone carried the same resentment Claire felt over their rude awakening. "I'm not the only editor in the place."

"Never mind that." She handed him a sheaf of messages. "Some guy called Phil has been phoning you every half hour and growing more frantic by the minute."

There was a side to city hall Claire had never seen before. And never wanted to again.

She stepped out of the elevator into a cramped lobby. Lawyers with suits and briefcases huddled in all the corners, mobile phones growing from their ears. The hall's single open door was flanked by a pair of hefty policewomen armed with metal detectors. A line of people shuffled through, raising their arms to be scanned, their expressions as downcast as their eyes. According to Harry, these would be the visitors for prisoners held here awaiting hearings, arraignments, and trial.

Following Harry's directions, Claire turned away from the crowd and crossed to the hall's only other door. It was metal and forbidding, with a single thick glass pane at head height.

She pressed the button in the wall alongside the door. A speaker beside the button crackled to life. "Yes?"

"I was told to ask for Officer Pendleton."

"Name?"

"Claire Kingsbury."

A moment's wait, then the door buzzed angrily. "Report to the desk."

Claire pulled it open and stepped inside. The officer's desk was set within a glass-lined cage, raised high enough that everyone was forced to look up and through the bulletproof panes to a trio of grim-faced guards on the other side. The voice that came through another speaker was as stony as the expressions. "Put your bag into the slot there, then pass through the metal detector." When she had done so, and her case had been carefully inspected, the metallic voice instructed, "Sign the clipboard and wait."

Claire did as she was told, struggling to hide her nerves. The chamber where she stood was narrow and long. At one end was the metal door through which she had entered. At the other stood a barred opening. From beyond the bars echoed shouts and bangs and curses and a disquieting smell.

Other than occasional glances shot her way, Claire was completely ignored. Guards came and went within the glass cage, which was banked with shelves of papers and rows of switches, flashing lights, and tiny security screens. Claire pressed her leather case to her chest, squeezing both arms around it, and studied the linoleum at her feet.

Finally the bars at the hall's far end clanged open. "You the reporter Phil Flagler called us about?"

"Yes." After ten minutes in the hallway, even the guard's stony expression looked inviting. "Officer Pendleton?"

"This way." He held the barred door open for her, waved to the guards in the cage, and then pointed her down a windowless corridor. The floor and walls were concrete, the fluorescent lighting grim and overly bright. The noise was stronger back here. And the smell.

He tossed a glance back her way. "So what's behind all this?"

"I'm not sure. Phil called and said we might want to talk with a guy you were holding." The policeman was massive, a foot taller and twice her girth. With each step his broad black belt shifted in a see-saw motion, causing his gun and riot stick and keys to slap against his legs. Claire had never felt so isolated. "That's all I know."

"Yeah, Phil's a good buddy, he goes to our church."

Claire glanced down a long side-corridor and saw several pairs of hands dangling through the line of metal bars. A guard leaned against the opposite wall, chatting with the prisoners in a voice as hard as the clanging metal.

"Anyway, this kid gets dropped on us yesterday, sorta fits with what Phil was asking me to watch for. Young, decent job, no priors. He's caught in the act, B&E in a bad section of town, only thing of value in the place is a buncha computer gear. So I run a check, find out the guy is carrying a load of bad debt."

Her interest started growing. "Does that make sense to you? A guy with a good job breaking into an apartment in a bad section of town, I mean."

He gave her a hard, humorous look. "Lady, you stay down

here long enough, nothing makes much sense any more except God."

She faltered, as though the power of hearing those words was amplified by the surroundings. Even here. The message was coming to her even here.

"But to answer your question, no, it doesn't. This kid is not a junkie, not a gang member, not anything much except scared. He was drunk, or maybe strung out on some designer drug, but nothing that you'd call addictive. We did a check for that too. Didn't come up with anything we recognize." He stopped at a barred gate, turned and stared at Claire. "The question is, does it mean something to you?"

"I don't know, maybe." Impatient now. Smelling a break in the making. "Did you find anything else?"

He gave his head an impatient shake. "You're not telling me any more than Phil did."

"I'm not telling because I don't know anything for sure," she replied. "Which was probably why Phil didn't want to say any more either."

He studied her a moment longer, then slipped his card through the electronic lock. A buzzer sounded, and the gate clanged open. "In here. Punch the button by the door when you're through."

She swung open the heavy steel door, stopped, stared, and finally managed, "Troy?"

"You've got to get me out of here," were his first words.

She forced herself to cross the whitewashed cement floor. Up close the guy looked even geekier: tousled dark curls, huge frightened eyes, a little heavyset, definitely not someone who knew his way around a gym. His wrist was manacled to a bar welded into the desk.

"Please," he said, his voice almost a whimper.

Claire scraped back the metal chair and sat down. "Your name is Troy, isn't that right?" She reached into her purse and brought out pad and pencil, all without taking her gaze from his face. "What's your last name?"

"Keeler. Listen, I don't have anybody else to turn to. You can't imagine what it's like in here."

She forced her mind to work. "You have to give me something."

That brought him up short. "What?"

"Something that shows you have the real stuff. Then we'll talk about maybe helping you."

He shook his head adamantly. The movement brought a tattoo into view, a star positioned just below his left ear. "First you get me out of here. If I tell you what I know, you won't have any reason to help."

He had a point. But she needed something to take back to Harry. She tried a shot in the dark. "There's some kind of conspiracy, isn't there? Something we're not catching."

A roar of anger exploded from the chamber next to theirs, so loud Claire leaped to her feet, the metal chair clanging over. The roar turned to a voice screaming curses. Feet ran down the outside corridor, the door next to theirs banged open, and a pair of hard voices shouted for quiet. When she picked up her chair, Claire discovered her hands were trembling badly.

"It's like that all the time in here. This place is a horror movie gone live," Troy said.

She forced herself to ignore the rage still pouring out of the next room and said, "Why were you there in that apartment building?"

Troy tried to calm down, but it was hard. Almost impossible. His eyes danced around the windowless cell. Jerking motions made the manacle rattle against the metal desk. "It's not what you said. A conspiracy. Nothing like that."

"Money laundering? Drug sales?"

He gave a humorless laugh. "Are you ever off the track."

She leaned across the table. "So tell me."

Harry listened to her report in absolute silence. When she finished, she sat cradling her cup with both hands, feeling comfort course through her with the coffee. Finally he said, "A game?"

"That's what he said."

Harry swivelled his chair around so as to prop his feet on the windowsill. "You mean to tell me these vanished kids are all tied into playing some video game?"

"Troy insists they are." Claire hesitated, then added, "I believe him. Almost despite myself, but I do."

Harry pursed his lips at the news. "Phil called while you were out."

"What did he say?"

"The kid's apartment where they picked Troy up, the police now officially have him down as missing." He fished through the papers on his desk. "I have the name here somewhere."

"Buddy Wiggins," she supplied. "Troy told me."

"Does this Troy have anything to do with the vanishings?"

"He says he was there to steal Buddy's headgear and that suit they call the Second Skin. He's too far in debt to buy another, and his own is falling apart."

Harry watched her gravely a long moment before saying, "All from playing that game?"

"Babylon," she confirmed. "There's more to this than what we're seeing, Harry."

"There's got to be," he agreed. "We're talking about computer gear that costs more than a new Porsche. These kids are going into debt up to their eyeballs, cutting off all normal contact with society, then disappearing as though they were pulled from the face of the earth, all because of a game?"

"No, I mean there was more than he was telling me. It was right there, but he stopped and said first I had to get him out of jail."

"Then do it," Harry said. "Has bail been set yet?"

"Five thousand dollars."

"Okay, I'll authorize payment to a bail bondsman through our lawyers. It'll let them feel like they're earning their retainer." He reached for the phone. "This may take an hour or so. Go pretend to be busy until I set this up."

Claire walked out of his office and saw Lillian Stockton Fletcher signaling to her.

"Call for you, Claire. Line one. Some man called Donovan Stone."

An electric current pushed away the stress and fatigue. "I'll take it at my desk."

Lillian gave her a wry look as she watched Claire race for the phone. "I guess he must be as handsome as he sounds."

BEVERLY HILLS

■ An executive from Swindley's office was there to meet Donovan at the Los Angeles airport. "Mr. Stone? My name is Chuckie. Mr. Swindley asked me to come out and meet you. Hey, you're as handsome as they said. You ever thought of going into the pictures?" A practiced laugh. The guy looked just like his voice sounded—a young dynamo on the way up, big smile for everybody who might give him a hand. Which included Donovan. "Here, let me take your case."

"I've got it."

"Right. Let me have your tags, I'll see to your luggage."

"Don't have any," Donovan replied. "I was planning on returning to Denver this evening."

"Right." Chuckie recovered with the ease of someone willing to adjust to everybody's requirements. "Let me have your ticket, I'll just make sure everything's okay with your reservation. Your driver's standing just outside."

"Come again?"

The skilled smile. "Looks like you're on the A-list now, Mr. Stone. Your limo's right out there, the white one."

"The one that looks like a boat on wheels?" But Chuckie had already turned away. Donovan passed through the exit doors, took in the stretch Cadillac, watched the uniformed driver open his door, and slid inside with a smile. The first of a long line of dreams was here in the making.

The Polo Lounge was located in the back right corner of the Beverly Hills Hotel. Newly renovated in a paroxysm of pink and green polka-dots, the famous curved banquette tables still lined the walls. They overlooked a rotunda of tables where the lesser mortals were forced to sit, and beyond that an enormous wall of glass. The outer courtyard was adorned with green wrought-iron tables and crisp pink linens and shaded by a grand old maple.

Donovan slid into the banquette and accepted the menu. The hostess gave him a stellar smile and pitched her voice loudly enough to carry. "Mr. Swindley just called from his limo, Mr. Stone." She waited long enough for nearby conversation to quieten. "He apologizes for making you wait, and says he shouldn't be more than another five minutes or so."

Donovan caught the scattering of glances cast his way.

Nearby conversation resumed at a muted level, so all could listen and learn who this new player was, the one with enough clout for Swindley himself to call, from his *limo*. Five minutes was nothing in this town. Some people had been waiting five years for a call from a man with that much clout. "No problem."

"He asked me to make sure you were comfortable and see if there was anything I could do for you." Another smile, this one with a stronger spark. A starlet on the make. No question.

"A phone and a Perrier would be nice," Donovan replied, glad he could make his voice sound that steady at such a pressure point.

"Certainly, I'll see to it personally," she assured him, and made it clear she was slightly disappointed by his requests.

Donovan returned the smile, slid his menu to one side, and glanced around. Younger women at the other tables were seriously beautiful, the older ones seriously thin. The men were tall and erect and dressed in hand-tailored suits or slacks and sweatshirts by Versace. Expressions were mobile, talk animated, eyes cautious. The looks kept coming his way.

"Here you are, Mr. Stone." A phone was set on the banquette's edge and plugged into the wall socket. From the same silver tray the hostess poured his Perrier over ice, set down the glass, and gave him a final smile. "My name is Kim. If you need anything, don't hesitate to ask."

There was no one he needed to speak with, but asking for the phone seemed the right thing to do. He started to call Trish, who was again working in San Francisco. But when he cradled the receiver, it came to him. He checked the numbers at the back of his pocket calendar and dialed the *Herald*. He was passed through an operator, then an older-sounding woman turned cautious when he asked for Claire, and put him on hold.

When Claire answered the phone, he turned his back to the room and said, "I hope you don't mind if I use you as my reality check."

"Donovan?"

"I'm in the Polo Lounge. As in the Beverly Hills Hotel. I'm drinking a ten-dollar water. I was met at the airport by a limo that had to be five feet longer than a city bus. Three televisions, a bar, and a guy named Chuckie to make sure I didn't get lonely."

Her smile lilted the edge of her words. "You're making this up."

"This is too good to do by myself. I need somebody to help me laugh at everything." He paused, then added from the depths of sudden honesty, "And help me get over my stage fright."

"You're scared? Why?"

"So much is riding on this meeting." He glanced out and over the room, the light sparkling from polished silverware and chandeliers and jewels and laughter. "I've been working all my life to get here, and now I'm terrified I'm going to blow it."

"You'll do fine."

He found himself breathless from the power of his own candor. Having told her something he had scarcely been able to admit to himself. "I hope you're right."

"Why is it so crucial?"

"Because I want this." Once the honesty was started, he could not cut it off. Feeling his gut clench with the desire and the closeness of success. Finally. "All of it. Right now."

"I'm not sure I understand what you're talking about, but I've always thought that it's good to know what you want."

"Come out here," the words almost leaping out. "Let me show you what it's like."

"Los Angeles?" Startled laughter rose again in her words. "Is that an invitation?"

"It is indeed."

"I can't. But thank you for asking."

"Why not?"

"Because I don't know you well enough." Her tone told him he should have realized that for himself.

"That's a matter for further negotiation. Say, dinner as soon as I'm back?"

"We'll see." She hesitated, then asked, "What's the Polo Lounge like?"

"Like sitting on the edge of a peppermint-colored stage. Only louder. Everybody in here is play-acting at life."

"You're not really complaining," she told him. "You love it. Just don't let it go to your head."

He started to say, It already has. Then he turned and saw Kim leading Roger Swindley towards his table. "I've got to go. I'll be back in a day or so. Can I call you?"

"I'd like that," she said, a softer tone to her voice.

Donovan Stone managed to hang up and rise to his feet before Roger Swindley made it to the table. The electric tension he had felt at their earlier meeting continued to surround the man. Swindley offered his hand and said, "Sorry to have made you wait."

"No problem." He waited for Swindley to seat himself before sliding back down. Now the glances from surrounding tables were lingering on him. The attention was disconcerting, but he resolved to ignore them as Swindley was doing. "There's a lot to entertain a newcomer here." Donovan felt Kim's smile as she turned away. "The ladies, for example. I don't see a single unattractive female in this room. The entire hotel, for that matter."

"There are no ugly women in this part of town." Swindley's voice was an odd mixture of blandness and iron control. "If you are rich enough to live here, you can afford to look good."

Swindley snapped the menu shut and set it to one side. He had yet to glance at the room. Another sign of power, Donovan decided—to be the one looked at, and know it, and know also that there was no need to either look back or respond to all those who would have given their eye teeth to be where he was right then. "Thanks for the loan of Chuckie and the limo."

"It's important that you make the right impression. Impressions are everything in this town, especially for a newcomer. I want people to recognize you for a mover and shaker if we're going to work together on something this big."

The electric bolt hit his gut again. "I didn't know the decision had been made."

"It hasn't been." Flat and cold and hard. "But my people are looking over your proposal. I understand there are a few questions."

"Anything I can clarify?"

"Later." Swindley inspected him. "Have you seen our movie, *Babylon?*"

"Yes." He had forced himself to sit through it. Twice, in fact. Bored to heavy-eyed yawning with the loud music, special effects, empty dialogue. Then he had gone to the library and read every review he could lay his hands on.

"What did you think?"

Donovan had prepped for this one. Decided to paraphrase *Entertainment Weekly*'s second review. The first one had panned the movie. The second had come out after *Babylon* had swept to the top of the weekly charts and stayed there like it was attached with superglue. "Frankly, I'm amazed you were able to make such a success out of an action thriller without a major star."

"Were you?" Swindley didn't appear the least bit displeased. "You and everybody else out there. Before the movie started performing, they were calling me just another loser. You know what they're calling me now?"

Donovan nodded. "The man with his finger on the pulse of America's youth." That one from *Variety*.

"They don't know the half of it. That's just the beginning. They haven't seen anything yet. Nothing at all." He stopped long enough to turn to the bowing waiter and say, "Caesar salad, hold the anchovies. Perrier. Dry toast."

"I'll have the same." It seemed safest. And wisest.

"Tell the chef we're in a hurry." Roger Swindley turned back, as though the man had suddenly disappeared, and went on, "I don't normally come here, but it is as good a place as any to make an initial public statement."

Donovan nodded, catching the emphasis on the word, *initial.* He saw the testing calculation within the man's hard gaze. "I understand." And he did. His voice sounded as tight to his ears as his gut felt.

"This is more than just a project to develop a film studio and more computer games. Whoever is brought in to help with the structuring needs to understand fully the scope at which I intend to operate. I chose the name Babylon for our first inter-active game to send the world a message."

"*You* chose the name?" This was news.

Swindley chose to ignore the interruption. "The internet grants us instantaneous worldwide communication. With this combination of web and game, we are rebuilding what was lost when the original Tower of Babel was destroyed. We are usurp-ing the powers of creation. We have a new world at our dis-posal, a new reality of our own making."

Swindley's features held a burning intensity, a single-minded driven quality. "In the ancient Arcadian language, Babylon meant 'Gate to the Gods.' I could think of nothing more appropriate for this first project and the ambitions that are now unfolding."

Donovan struggled hard to meet and hold the calculating gaze. "I can't think of anything I'd like more than to be a part of your undertaking."

"We'll see." Swindley turned away as the waiter reap-peared, this time accompanied by the maitre d', who person-ally supervised the careful placements of two small salads on two huge plates. The pantomine over, Swindley demanded, "Where are you planning to stay out here?"

"I, well, I wasn't sure how long—"

"Try the Bel Air. Tell Chuckie, he'll arrange things." The grey-blond head dipped down, the attention turned from Donovan to the salad. All discussion stopped. As though the man had room in his mind for only one thing at a time. Total focused concentration. Donovan sat and played with a salad his stomach absolutely refused to accept.

Scarcely five minutes later, the fork was dropped, the

head raised. The waiter was instantly there to recover Swindley's plate. "What are your plans for the rest of this week?"

"I've got some last minute details to iron out with the First Colorado project," Donovan replied. "I had planned to go back this afternoon. Then I'm free."

"Get back to L.A. as soon as you can. I want you to take my table for lunch at The Grill for a few days. Go at least one night to Ivey's, doesn't matter who with, have Chuckie set it up."

Donovan made hasty notes. "These are restaurants?"

Swindley nodded impatiently. He had no time for questions that could be directed elsewhere. "The issue is to be seen, not to eat."

Donovan managed to make it from his seat only a second behind Swindley, had his arm up in time to accept the handshake. Swindley went on, "I'm having some guests over for dinner tonight. Put your return off until tomorrow and join us."

Another royal summons. "Thanks, that would be great."

"Seven o'clock. And plan to stay afterwards, we'll be screening the rough cut of my second *Babylon* movie. Chuckie has the address." The concentrated gaze passed from him, the man turned away and left without another word.

Donovan dropped back into the banquet because his legs would no longer support him. The waiter returned, asked if he wanted anything else, showing him the same bowing respect. Donovan waved him away. The eyes were still on him, but it did not matter. He felt as though he had just moved from blazing sunlight to a cave, the man's power was that awesome.

He did not know whether to laugh or cry. With every step forward, it seemed that the goal moved another step away.

■ When Claire hung up the phone from talking with Donovan, she was startled to find Lillian Stockton Fletcher standing over her desk. The older woman demanded, "Who was that?"

"Donovan."

"I've already heard his name." Lillian came around and seated herself. "This is the man who's keeping you from being interested in Harry?"

Claire cringed, looked around, saw no one was within listening distance. Even so she lowered her voice and replied with quiet intensity, "Harry is my boss."

"Right." Lillian remained unmoved by the argument. "And who is Donovan?"

"I met him at Swindley's party." She had to smile. "He just called me from the Polo Lounge."

"He must be in the film trade, then. How thrilling." But

her tone said she was singularly unimpressed. "He must also be handsome."

Claire nodded. "Donovan is . . ."

"I know. I know all too well. He's dashing and he's gallant and he's ambitious. And it makes you quiver just to look at him."

Claire started to ask, How do you know, but then she saw Lillian's expression. She changed the question to, "Why does that make you sad?"

"Because there are a lot of Donovans out there. I've unfortunately known far too many of them," Lillian said. "And I'm afraid for you. That's all."

"I'm a big girl," Claire told her.

"Aren't we all." Lillian hesitated, then said quietly, "Nathan called last night."

This was news. "You talked with Pop?"

"For over an hour. He told me about your mother. The only reason I mention it is, I've been through something like that myself." She took a deep breath, gathered herself, and began, "I was an only child. When I was seven, my mother left me in every sense but on paper. She was too concerned with what all the right people might say if she divorced Father outright. She spent years living in whichever hotel or liner or family manor that kept her as far as possible from my father. And me. Father never bothered much about either of us. Which meant I was raised by nannies and boarding schools and people who were paid to care."

Lillian's dark eyes examined her a moment before concluding, "Such beginnings leave us very vulnerable to men like your Donovan. We do so want to believe that they can give us the strength and the caring we never knew at home."

Lillian's somber concern left her unable to respond with anything but honesty. "I've never had much luck with men. You've heard of the hearing impaired? I've always been one of the dating impaired. First I choose the wrong guy, then I manage to lose him."

Lillian gave a slow nod of understanding. "Well, let me tell you something about the ambitious Donovans of this world. He may like you a lot. He may even love you. But he'll only see you when it's convenient for him. You feel his focus upon you now, but that will change. Once he has you, he'll never consult you about anything. It will feel like it never even occurs to him that you have a brain or a will."

Claire tried to act indignant, but her curiosity was too strong. "How can you be so sure about someone you've never met?"

"Take it from someone who's been there. Men like this are a breed apart. They've learned to use their looks and their intelligence and everything else they have. Their drive is as focused as a laser, and when it's on you, it feels like the whole world has opened up at your feet. But what you don't see is how it will be when they are over the first infatuation. They never listen, and they become angry when it's necessary to learn something new about you. Like your own interests or your own needs."

"Maybe you're right," Claire said doubtfully. "But from where I'm sitting, Donovan seems like every guy I never had."

The older woman said quietly, "Let's hope he doesn't leave you wishing you never did."

"I'll be all right."

Lillian shook her head. "What in that little mountain town has prepared you for the Donovans of this world?"

"Thanks for your concern." She lifted the receiver, using the phone to end the uncomfortable discussion. She opened her directory and began searching out a number. "But I can handle this."

"Mainline Computers."

"Russ Reynolds, please."

A long pause, then, "May I ask who is calling?"

"This is Claire Kingsbury of the *Denver Herald*."

"I'm sorry, how do you spell your last name?"

A warning bell tingled in the back of her mind. "Is this Mr. Reynolds' secretary?"

"No, this is the central operator. What did—"

"May I speak with Mr. Reynolds, please?"

"I'm sorry, Mr. Reynolds is not available."

"Is he ill?"

A long pause, then, "I'm really not supposed to say anything."

The voice was young and nervous enough for Claire to risk, "You wouldn't want the paper to get it wrong, would you?"

"Well," the voice dropped a notch, then said, "Mr. Reynolds has left the company."

"What?"

"They say it's health—" The phone went silent for a moment, then a male voice broke in sharply. "Who is this?"

"Claire Kingsbury with the *Denver Herald*. Could you tell me what's—"

"The company will be issuing a statement shortly. Good-bye."

Claire was instantly on her feet and moving for Harry's office. She barged in, did a tense little two-step until he ended his own phone conversation. "Reynolds has been canned."

"Mainline's president?" He looked skeptical. "That's impossible."

"I just talked to the company operator. Claimed it was health reasons, but she didn't sound like she believed it herself."

"Why haven't I heard something about this?" He reached for the phone, pointed at the door. "Everything's set. You go spring this Troy Keeler and bring him straight back here. I'll check out what's happened to Reynolds."

The release gate for arraigned prisoners was at the back end of City Hall, as far from the Capitol as could be managed. Claire stepped into the winter sunlight, blinked, and wished she could go home and bathe off the smells. For once, the city noises were welcomed as they pushed away the clamor she had left inside.

The bondsman, lawyers, and paperwork had tied her up for over an hour. The day's stresses and strains were taking their toll. And Troy Keeler was no big help. He stood on the landing and squinted at the weak winter sun, looking like a big overgrown kid with nowhere to go.

"Come on," Claire said, tugging on his arm. "Harry's waiting for us over at the *Herald*."

"Who?" Now that he was out, he seemed reluctant to leave the safety of City Hall behind.

"Harry Mitchum. My boss. The guy who arranged to have you bailed out. You promised to talk with us, remember?"

"Sure. Yeah. Okay." He started down the stairs alongside her, still scouting in all directions, his gaze darting and fearful. "You came by yourself?"

"I'm a big girl." She was saying that a lot today. "What's got you so nervous."

"Nothing, only . . ." Troy Keeler froze on the bottom step. A look of sheer terror captured his face. "Oh *no!*"

"What's the matter?" She followed his gaze, now fastened upon a long dark limo cruising slowly around the distant corner. "Who're they?"

"I've got to get out of here!"

She made a frantic grab for his arm. "You're coming with me, bud."

His features were drawn into desperate lines. He ripped his arm from her grasp, scanned in both directions. "Sorry."

Then he sped down the street, whipped around the corner, and was gone.

Claire looked dumbfounded at the empty space where he had been, and muttered, "Sorry?"

The sound of tires scrunching along the road turned her back around. The limo picked up speed. The car's glass was smoked to a dark opaque, but she saw that the back side window was down. She walked forward, but as she did, the window began to power up. The limo passed her just as the window closed, granting her a meager glimpse of two very hard, very cold eyes.

"Wait!"

The limousine took the same corner as Troy and was gone.

Harry did not take the news well. "You let him get away?"

"What was I supposed to do?" The same question she had been asking herself the entire way back. "Join us at the hip?"

"If you thought it might come to this, it wouldn't have been a bad idea." He ran a hand through his hair. "Check out his apartment."

"I already did. Nothing."

"If he skips, we are going to have some hard questions to answer upstairs."

She nodded, but what she had focused upon was the one word, *we*. He was sticking with her. She was not facing this alone. "I'm really sorry, Harry."

"Not nearly as sorry as we may be in a couple of days." He sighed his way back into his seat. "Are you absolutely certain the guy in the limo was the same one who threw you out of the Vail party?"

"Yes." She would never forget that reptilian gaze. Never.

"Why would a computer geek know Swindley's bodyguard?"

"I don't know," she said slowly. "I don't know how he even saw more than the limo itself. I think maybe he just knew who was in it."

Harry waved her towards the seat. "Well, you were right about Mainline. Reynolds has been sacked. I've called around, the news has caught everybody flat-footed. And now the guy can't be found. I've tried every connection I know and come up with zip."

"What do you think is going on?"

"I have no idea." Harry mulled that one over, decided, "The game is our only possible connection."

"Looks that way to me." *Our* connection. "Could you ask Phil Flagler if the phone company would loan us some of that repossessed gear? I'd like to try out the game for myself."

Harry stared across the desk. "Okay, get back out there, cruise around the streets near Troy's home. I'll cover for you here, make some calls, see if anyone has anything more on the eruptions at Mainline." His tone stayed gloomy. "Long as I can, anyway. Shelling out five thousand dollars bail for a vanished lead is not going to make us a big hit with the people upstairs."

The toneless voice was slow in responding to Skate's news. "And you say this Troy has vanished?"

The hand holding the phone shook slightly. "I've got one guy on his apartment, another on his job, been all over the city myself. Nothing."

"This is not good." The words were spoken so somberly that they sent a chill through Skate's guts. The toneless voice went on, "And this young lady, you are sure she is not just a friend?"

"The bondsman showed me the check. It came straight from the *Herald*." He hesitated, then had to add, "I've seen her before, Mr. S. At your party. She was the redheaded reporter lady I threw out."

"Even worse. How much does she know?"

Skate found himself wiping at sweat. "Hard to say. I mean, they were just walking out the door when Troy spotted me and took off."

"But they might have spoken before. They must have had some suspicion, for the newspaper to put up bail. And you say she might have seen you."

"I didn't know what to do, Mr. S. I mean, you never told me anything about any—"

A soft sigh cut him off. "First things first. See to the young man."

"He's history," Skate agreed, awash with relief that his own end was not to be next in line. "Soon as he shows himself, it's over."

"The newspaper woman will take some consideration. Best leave that with me for a moment. And Skate."

"Sir?"

"Any further slip-ups will be extremely costly. Are we clear on that point?"

BEVERLY HILLS

14

■ That evening, the studio limo joined the long line of cars snaking their way towards the Swindley estate. Donovan struggled to keep a hold on his nerves and reflected over what that incredible day had already held.

After the lunch with Swindley, Chuckie had arrived with the limo. The bland-faced young man had given a simple nod when Donovan had related Swindley's instructions about the Bel Air Hotel. Donovan had ridden along in silence, watching the sunlight flicker through the orderly row of palms, wondering if any of this was ever going to pan out. Now that the lunch was over, his chances had felt as solid as smoke.

The limo had pulled through a pair of tall stone gates, and continued along a lane bordered by grand trees and manicured lawns. Donovan had glanced through the back window and asked, "A gated community in Beverly Hills?"

For once, Chuckie's amusement had been genuine. "You really don't know?"

"Know what?"

"This is *the* gated community. The term was invented here. This place is called Bel Air. The most exclusive section of the world's most exclusive town."

The limo turned into a parking lot far too small to justify a dozen valets, three of whom bounced forward before the wheels stopped moving. One for each door, another ready for when the driver popped the trunk. "Afternoon, sir. Welcome to the Bel Air Hotel."

Donovan looked out, saw several low-slung roofs amidst the trees, and did not move. "So tell me why we're here."

Chuckie waved the valets away and said, "Image is what's most important in Hollywood. Not who you are, but who you *appear* to be. This is what Roger pays me to do. Be there for you, anticipate the right moves." When Donovan held back, he went on, "This town is full of bottom feeders. They can't land a big one, so they go for the crumbs. Some do ads, others do gossip. You want to avoid both."

"That so?"

"If the big boys spot you hanging with the no-hopers, they'll class you as below their time limit. That's all it takes, one look and you're gone."

Donovan mulled it over, then decided it was worth the risk to ask, "Who's in charge here? I mean, who is really holding the keys to this project?"

If Chuckie found the question odd, his bland expression certainly did not reveal it. "In Hollywood-speak, you ask who it is that can sign off on a deal, place it on the fast track. And I can answer that very simply. The same guy who's picking up your tab."

Donovan nodded acceptance. "Lead on."

The hotel was reached via a stone bridge over a little swan lake. A single glance around the grounds was enough to know they were old; everything looked as though it had been growing there for centuries. Rosebushes with bases thick as his arm. Huge trees. Every blade of grass in its proper place.

The reception area was its own little house, done in Spanish colonial with stucco and beams and a working fireplace and broad-plank floors. Not to mention antique Persian carpets. Original oils on the walls. Two receptionists in designer wear, the bellhop in gabardine and alpaca. The place reeked of all the style that money could buy.

Everyone knew Chuckie, called him by name. The bellhop shook Donovan's hand and nodded gravely as Chuckie explained that he would now be coming and going on a steady basis. Always a pleasure to meet a new regular, the bellman said, no hint of derision at the game. Donovan thanked him and waited for Chuckie to pass over the required tip, but it did not happen. Instead, the prettier of the two receptionists came over, shook Donovan's hand, already knew his name, introduced herself as Connie or Tammie or something, Donovan unable to take it all in.

He allowed himself to be led out the side door, along one passageway after another, all of them open-air with delicate Grecian columns supporting high gabled roofs. Same for the restaurant area, where open gas-flame heaters flanked every table and offered warmth against the November chill, Bel Air style. The inner gardens were as lush and meticulous as everything else.

All the hotel buildings were set in their own private space, none more than two floors high. Donovan followed them around the pool, through a set of wrought-iron gates and into a private patio. Another outdoor heater waiting for him there, beside the table and chair and all-weather sofa.

He passed through the door and entered the Spanish tiled sitting room, equipped with a full kitchen behind hand-carved doors, ditto for the television and the fax and the stereo. The staff walked with him through the chamber and down a pair of steps, crossing the bedroom's Persian carpet and passing around the four-poster bed, checking out the huge bathroom, everything in marble and gilt. The bellman was there at his side with the receptionist, formal yet anxious that everything was to his liking.

Donovan held on to his grin for as long as he could, until they were showing him around the dressing area with its lighted mirror and second stereo and third television and fifth telephone. Then he had to let it go. He walked back out to the sitting room, chuckling and shaking his head.

Chuckie was at his elbow in a flash. "What's the matter, too small? Hey, no problem—"

Donovan stopped him with a hand on his shoulder. The move genuinely shocked Chuckie, which was why Donovan kept it there. "It's like somebody reached inside my head, drew out the plans, made it right the first go." He dropped the hand, did a slow circle, and said definitely, "This is home."

At least, it was home until he could afford a place like Swindley's. Donovan Stone presented his name to the butler and was bowed into a chandelier-lit foyer. He paused long enough to inform the man that Trish would be arriving later. He had called her from his suite, relating the day's events and the limo and the suite and the invitation. She had responded by insisting on flying out after she finished work, even if she could only catch the tail-end of the party. Just think of the contacts, she had told him, you could wait a lifetime for a chance like this. As Donovan had hung up the phone, he had reflected that he had already waited a lifetime, and still the contract remained where it had always been—dangling just out of reach.

Donovan walked slowly through Swindley's house, taking in the priceless artwork, the distant ceilings, the polished marble floors giving way to Oriental carpets big as half-acre lawns. And everywhere the glittering, swirling throngs. Everyone playing to the crowd, hoping for the break, the deal, the money, the power.

Ten-foot ice sculptures pierced by flashing lasers stood at the center of champagne fountains. The room could have housed the Rose Bowl, and it was one of several. A band played show tunes in one corner; Donovan recognized the conductor from one of the late-night talk shows. He grabbed a glass of champagne, accepted a shrimp concoction from a passing waitress, heard someone say the caterer had spent six thousand dollars on the mushrooms. Another responded with the news that Swindley had this place on the market, and was building another down on the Malibu cliffs. Something that made a little more of a statement.

Most of the voices he heard reminded him of jazz— smooth, polished, and totally unemotional. The sincerest words rang like lies. The faces saying them were blandly measured, as though everyone was busy reading lines from an invisible script.

He walked to the floor-to-ceiling windows, where a pair of truly beautiful women were conversing. The honey blond was vaguely familiar, a face seen on a couple of sitcoms, one of the super-lookers whose parts were added to keep male viewers glued through the commercial. Tiffany something. Sure. With remembering her name came a little thrill; he, Donovan Stone, standing next to a starlet. The other girl was darker and equally attractive, but unknown.

"I hear they got Mel Gibson for the project," the dark-haired one was saying as he approached.

"That was last week," Tiffany responded. "Manny says he talked to Ford's agent's secretary, the guy flipped and insisted the part is his."

"Maybe I should have my agent give his agent a call, see if there's a part in it for me." The dark-haired girl sipped at her glass and went on, "Did you hear about the one over at Tri-Star? The working title was 'Ten Years in Peking.' They've been sitting on it so long, the lawyers are calling it 'Eleven Years in Development.'"

"That's nothing. You know I've been seeing Brad. He was promised this part—"

"Brad Pitt?" The news rocked the dark-haired girl, but she recovered swiftly and played at bland boredom. "He's back in town?"

"Sure, you didn't know?" Tiffany chose that moment to turn around and size Donovan up. "Are we interrupting something?"

"I'm sorry," he said. "I didn't mean to intrude."

"Manners, hey, that's a novelty." Cat's eyes the tone of faded lust stared at him over the rim of her glass. "You must be new."

"The newest kid on the block."

"But you're here. Somebody must think you're something."

"I'm working with Roger on a project." A half-lie. This town was made of them.

"Roger Swindley?" Interest electrified. "He's got a new film going?"

"Not with me. I'm helping him set up a new operation. Interactive entertainment."

"Yeah, sure, I've heard of that. You, you're what's his name."

"Donovan Stone." Knowing she was lying, she had not heard a thing about him. Knowing she was beautiful enough and alluring enough to get away with it.

She did not bother to introduce herself. "The whole town is full of talk over this IE game thing."

"The whole world," her friend corrected.

"L.A. *is* the whole world." Tiffany was the star of the pair and not to be outdone. "So Roger brought you in to set it up. Wild. Where are you staying?"

"Denver most of the time. That's where the company and the studios are set up. I don't have my own place here yet. When I'm in town, I stay at the Bel Air."

"Of course, you're with those new studios going up in Denver. There *is* a film planned, isn't there, don't you dare deny it." A hand reached over, laced inch-long fingernails around his arm. "Come on, Donovan, let's go get something to eat. You have to be going places to stay at the Bel Air. I hear rooms there cost a fortune."

Donovan allowed himself to be guided into the dining room. "So do the suites."

Tiffany liked that. He could tell. "You must be tops at whatever you do if Roger Swindley likes you."

"Roger Swindley doesn't like anybody," the dark-headed girl agreed. "What is it you do?"

"I'm a consultant on start-ups."

"Sure, like an executive producer for the money side."

"Something like that."

"Tell you what," Tiffany said. "I'll tell you about this town if you'll tell me about the film. How does that sound?"

"*We'll* tell you about Hollywood," the second girl said, moving up close enough to rub him with her body as they entered the buffet line. "My name's Cynthia. But you can call me Cyn."

"I don't know anything about a film," Donovan insisted.

Tiffany chose not to let that faze her. "Have something to eat, we'll talk. Maybe that will stimulate your memory."

"Or something," Cyn said, breathing the words in his ear.

"Who's talking to who about which project, who's suing who," Tiffany was saying. "That's ninety percent of conversation in this town."

"They poach a lot here," Cyn agreed. "Talent, projects, directors, money. It's a very disloyal industry."

Donovan was dining on lobster and asparagus tips and champagne, their little trio cut off from the two other conversations swirling around their table of fifteen—one of twenty tables in a room so large there was space for a half-dozen more. Heads kept turning his way, wondering who this unknown was, what he had or did that was keeping this pair occupied. And why they didn't know him. "That's dangerous. Disloyalty has a way of returning to haunt people."

"Not in this town," Cyn retorted.

"Who cares what somebody's history is?" Tiffany agreed. "If their projects make money, they're up there with the angels and the producers. If the projects bust, they never existed."

"All that matters is twenty-four hours in each direction, at least until filming starts," Cyn told him. "There's a need to know the latest buzz, and know it quicker."

"Around here," Tiffany agreed, "you're either in the know or you're in Siberia."

"The laws of the magic kingdom," Donovan said, only half joking.

"Absolutely," Tiffany said. "Out here, the law of being in the know is bigger than gravity."

A bong sounded from out in the hallway. Instantly the tumultuous chatter subsided and people began rising from the tables. Tiffany was already on her feet. "Witching hour."

"Swindley likes his guests to come on time and leave on time," Cyn agreed. "It's a sign of his power that people do what they're told."

Donovan glanced at his watch and started feeling guilty when he realized he had forgotten all about Trish and her coming. "I, ah, Roger asked me to hang around."

All who heard turned towards him. Cyn's voice became awestruck. "You've been invited to a screening?"

"Something about the next *Babylon* movie," Donovan agreed.

The girls exchanged glances. Tiffany said, "You don't even know what that means, do you?"

"He invites like maybe a dozen people," Cyn said. "Whoever's slated for the top. There's every kind of rumor about what happens. You positively have to take notes and tell me everything." Cyn reached into her minuscule purse, came up with a pad and silver pencil, bent over at the waist, her dress sliding forward and open, giving Donovan the works as she wrote. The look she gave him as she handed him the paper was beyond steam. "Call me."

"He's mine," Tiffany said, her gaze matching Cyn's for heat as she pressed a card into his palm.

"Sorry, girls," Trish said, sliding in close, extracting the papers from his hand and tossing them on the table. She gave Donovan a hard look and demanded, "Watching the local fauna forage and feed?"

"Nice," Tiffany said, but her gaze remained on Donovan. "Call CAA. They'll know where to find me."

"Ask for Manny," Cyn said, ignoring Trish entirely. "He's *my* agent. I'll tell him to expect your call."

Trish was quiet only until they had moved beyond the nearest table. Then she let him have it, low and quiet. "You are unbelievable."

"I'm sorry," he started. "I just—"

But she did not come at him from the direction he expected. "You're here among the movers and shakers, you've got a chance to build on what you've got going, and what do you do but hang out with a couple of losers!"

Donovan glanced up in time to catch a little wave from Cyn. "They sort of attached themselves."

"And you didn't have any choice but go with the flow, is that it?" She was angry, he could see it, but the voice was icy quiet and the smile firmly in place. At times like this he realized how small she was, only a few inches taller standing than he was when seated, but with a power so tight it made her seem bigger. From between clenched teeth she whispered, "You've just let the chance of a lifetime slide by."

"You're jealous," he said, wanting to make light of it, ease out of the sudden flush of her rage.

"Oh, grow up." Her voice was a soft lash. "You think I care about which of these mindless bimbos you flirt with? I thought you were a keeper. But then you spend your time at the Vail party talking to that little redheaded flake, and now hang out here with a couple of bit actresses, it makes me wonder if maybe I've made a mistake. A big one."

The rage which flooded him was unexpected. He bit down on the retort, which was to correct her about Claire. Maybe he should just take this as his chance, suggest if that was the way she felt, she should leave. Claire would like that. No question.

But before he could make up his mind, Trish noticed his anger reaching danger-level and softened. Her tone eased as she murmured, "Hey, you." She brushed the hair from his forehead, traced a line down to the cleft in his chin. "I'm only thinking about your winning big, you know."

He nodded, still uncertain which way to go.

"We need to be moving, the guy at the door told me they were already gathering in the back."

He followed her through the double-doors, a little disappointed that the moment had slipped by. But it was too late now. Other people appeared, all headed in his direction. Together they entered a room styled after an Old English library. Everything was done in muted tones, leather, and low lighting. The crowd was about two dozen, the people intent on showing just how cool they were. Donovan allowed Trish to guide them over and join in an ongoing conversation, as though she had been doing this all her life. She scouted the room, asked, "Where's Roger?"

"He rarely comes to these events," said the man at her side, an older gentleman with grey hair pulled tightly back into a pony tail. He wore a silk turtleneck beneath his dinner jacket. "If he shows up at all, it's usually just to shake a few hands. He spends maybe a hundred thou on the party, then shows up for five minutes max."

The polished blond standing beside him, a young trophy wife by the look of the rock on her finger, added, "Some say he likes to sit behind the screen and observe. But I think that's just too sicko even for him."

Donovan was about to ask, Observe what? But the woman chose that moment to show a spark of genuine excitement. She pointed and squealed, "Oh, goodie, refreshments!"

Which caused Trish to turn around, catch sight of the young valet with the silver tray, and laugh out loud. "This is just too unreal."

"Roger always gives a good party," the jeweled blond agreed, picking up something from the offered tray. "Even if he rarely does show."

Donovan looked from the waiter to the tray and back. On it

were little squares of brightly colored cardboard. To each was attached a star, a shimmering holograph about the size of his thumbnail. Then Trish was at his elbow. "Here, let Mama help."

She took two, said to the others gathered around, "His first time."

Donovan demanded, "First time for what?"

"A surprise," Trish said, a look in her eyes saying that this was payback time.

The frosted woman peeled off the star, pushed up her sleeve, attached it to the star tattoo revealed upon her elbow. To Donovan she said, "This is so incredibly L.A."

"Welcome to the magic kingdom," the older guy said, brushing back his pompadour far enough to attach the star to his temple.

Then Trish had Donovan's arm at the wrist, pushing back his shirtsleeve, peeling off the star, and pressing it firmly in place. "There. All done."

He then watched her take the second and place it on the tattoo under her left ear, not needing a mirror to fit it on precisely. She smiled that cat's smile again and said, "Ready for fun and games?"

Polite applause broke out as two waiters brought out a tripod stand, upon which was a mock-up of the *Babylon Two* film poster art. Then they opened the double doors to the screen room, and one said, "Everyone is kindly invited to take their seats."

Even before the opening credits were finished, he was flying.

There was no lift-off sensation, not even the mild buzz he knew from alcohol. Instead, the reality of sitting in the darkened chamber with Trish there beside him was suddenly confused by the feeling of melting into the movie.

With the first scene, he was no longer watching. He was dragged into the screen. He *lived* the movie.

There was no sense of being separate, remaining himself and watching something at a distance. He was *part* of the film. Each thought was slowed and joined with a new reality that swept him up and carried him along.

Donovan's heart was hammering, his skin felt clammy. With a wrenching effort he spilled over the sofa's edge and fell on all fours. He heaved himself up and stumbled down the aisle. Trish might have called his name, he could not tell where the word came from, perhaps from the film or his own mind. There was no longer the ability to separate thought from reality.

He pushed through the doors and staggered into the brighter lights outside. Each thought became empowered to change reality. It did not matter where he looked. All he had to do was think, and it was real. The wall before him opened and spilled out a hundred babbling little people, all clamoring for him to shape up, because he was being watched by Roger.

He fumbled for the star, tore it off his skin, threw it aside.

"Donovan, dear, what are you doing out here?" Trish pushed through the doors and walked over, her gait a bit unsteady. She scanned the hall, saw they were alone, and allowed the mask of concern to fall away.

He found that he could not move. He was trapped by the power revealed in her eyes. She stood next to the poster mock-up for the new movie, the one with the Tower goddess rising from her throne, brought to life by the torch in her raised fist. Suddenly Trish took on the same countenance as the idol. A different face, but the same power.

"Don't you dare embarrass me in front of these people," she hissed, and with the words came fire. Flames shot out, encircling him, holding him fast. "This is as big a break for me as it is for you."

Donovan could not speak. The flames threatened to overwhelm him if he opened his mouth. He held perfectly still and watched as Trish split the flames by walking up to him, the goddess keeping her safe. The fire joined the two women together, Trish and the golden idol.

Trish's eyes were dark as night as they examined him. The cold face opened into a smile now, certain in their power. "Poor baby," she crooned, and the fire died to little flickers. "Did he get scared?"

Donovan nodded. Yes. He was definitely frightened.

"Don't worry." A hand reached over and stroked his arm, tracing a line of flames down his jacket. "Trish will take good care of you."

She tightened her grasp, and Donovan knew with utter certainty that there was no way he could escape from her power. Or the idol's. Every time he looked up, the goddess was there before him, warning him to behave. "Now come on back with me," Trish said, her soothing voice granted enormous power by the idol's unrelenting gaze.

Donovan did what he had to do, which was allow her to draw him back into the screening room, even though the door loomed before him like a pit of eternal darkness.

DENVER

15

■ The next afternoon, Claire opened the door from the cellar storeroom and called, "Is the coast clear?"

"What's the matter?"

"I'm not coming out unless we're alone."

"Wait, let me check." A pause, then, "Okay, all clear." The *Denver Herald*'s top computer technician did not try to hide his smile as he watched her step out. "You look like Superwoman."

"I never was much on comic books." She was dressed from neck to toe in an electric blue bodysuit, with lightning slashes across her chest, padded shoulders, and matching silver gloves. Claire covered her embarrassment with a frown. "How do I hook this thing up?"

"Easy. There's a plug right here, see?" He fitted the cable into the outlet at the small of her back. "Okay, now the head-gear." He handed her the plastic helmet, watched her fit it down and over her eyes. "All set?"

"I can't see a thing."

"You're not turned on yet. Tilt your head back so you can watch what I'm doing."

He grabbed her arm and led Claire through the slit in the padded walker. Through the soft slip-on boots, the rubber balls underfoot were springy as a trampoline.

The paper's computer technician was a young guy known as Casper, for his propensity to be elsewhere when needed. "Okay, I'm switching on the computer, putting in the game's CD-ROM, see? Now I'm typing in the code. Okay, we're booting up, and now I've got the signal to connect with the Net. Great, now I have to give your name. Done. See, it's reading off, 'Claire Kingsbury, you are now a gamer of Babylon.'"

The headgear was made of some ultralight plastic, the earpieces padded, and the mike at the end of a slender wire rested just before her mouth. She leaned her head back, resting the headgear's base on the back of her neck, and watched under the edge of the still-blank screens. "If the game is on the disk, why do we need the internet?"

"For the interactive bit, naturally." He was too excited about entering the game to be bothered by her low-level question. "Imaging has always been the tough part of anything sent over the net. It's great to see they've found a way to combine instructions with a CD-ROM base."

"Sorry, you missed me there."

He stopped long enough to glance over. "Internet pictures are slow going. Words are just a series of lightning blips, right? But for each pixel of color, you need a separate signal sent across the telephone wires. That takes a tremendous amount of time. So the game itself is stored on the CD-ROM disk and the computer's hard-drive."

Claire slipped the headgear off, so she could watch him more clearly. "But if that's all it takes, then why this expensive computer?"

"That's all, she says." He looked up from the screen. "The computer has to accept all the incoming data—from your suit and the Net and the disk and the hard-drive. And it has to constantly update the images you're seeing. Every time you shift position, what you see has to shift to match. Stacked mother-boards add to the speed and power; that's where the Alpha-TI chips come in. Incoming data is constantly being added to your hard-drive. This thing has five gigabytes of memory, and I'll bet the game takes almost all of it." Casper's fingers danced over the keys. "Okay, that should do it. Put your headgear back on and tell me what you see."

She did as she was told and replied, "Just static."

"Uh oh. The cyber elves are at work." He rose from the console and walked over behind her. "You mind if I give this thing a try when you're done?"

"Long as you get Harry's permission first, I guess it's okay."

"Thanks." He lifted the headgear up and off, fiddled with the connections. "Babylon is a major buzz. I hear about it everywhere I go. Hollywired is being born before our very eyes. Brings network gaming to reality."

"Reality?" The word jarred inside. "Is this supposed to be a substitute for life?"

"The world out there is safe only if taken in small doses." He caught her look and turned defensive. "Hey, what does the real world offer? A life of naked need and naked greed. Great big grey chunks of disillusionment."

Claire studied him, saw a hyper-intelligent young man with lonely eyes and the nervous movements of someone who had never learned to be comfortable around other people.

"I mean, sure, reality kicks in from time to time," he went on. "Sleep, eat, work, you know, the usual. But for pleasure, for *real* life, there's nothing you can't get more of faster and just like you want it, in virtuality."

"So you play games."

"Sure. In virtuality, I can be who and what I want. No hassle. No rejection. No ridicule." Casper handed back the headgear. "No desperation from being unwanted, unloved, weak, all that stuff the real world is so good at making you feel."

"But why do technofreaks let it go to such extremes that they get mired in debt, become addicted to a game?"

"Simple. Because we don't know any better." He turned back to the console, then asked, "Okay, get ready to try a dose of nineties reality."

"It was a game," she insisted, hurrying to keep up with Harry as he raced for the elevators. "Super fancy, but still just a game."

He glanced at his watch and sighed. "We need to talk, but I'm pressed for time today."

Lillian Stockton Fletcher chose that moment to rush over and say, "Would you—"

"Hang on to that thought," Harry interrupted, pulling a paper from his pocket and handing it to the older woman. "Call them for me, will you? Ask for Donna, tell her I'm running a few minutes late." Then back to Claire, crossing his arms, forcing himself to slow down. "I'm listening."

"The game's music is techno-rave, constant and driving," she told him. "Background noise is computer generated and eerie. The game's environment is locked to a higher tempo because of the sound. I started off in this grand chamber, like the foyer of a palace, but without walls, just these super-high pillars. The place is filled with exotic plants and storybook creatures. There are two different halls leading off, but one was barred to me."

His attention quickened. "You tried to get into the locked hallway?"

"Casper and I both. He thinks there's probably some kind of coding, like a password, that I have to earn or discover. He says a lot of games are played on different levels." She pushed her hair back, her hands and body still clammy from the suit. "So I walked towards the other hallway, the one that was open, and things got sort of eerie. I was actually walking, you know. That's what that padded platform is for. The little rubber balls imbedded in the floor make me feel like I'm on a trampoline, but I can walk around and still stay hooked up."

Harry waved at the air between them. "Save the technology for later. Just give me the gist."

"Okay. I passed through the entrance, and instantly there was this whispering voice that started saying stuff like 'You are great. You are all-powerful. This game will make you happy. You will want to play this game more and more.'"

"Subliminal messages," Harry supplied. "They've been banned from television and film, but games have a legal loophole." He shook his head. "We're still not any closer to having a story, though."

"A lot of threads," Claire agreed glumly. "But no way to weave them together."

"And no word from that kid who took off with our money?"

"None."

Harry sighed. "Claire, it seems to me that maybe it's time to pull the plug."

The dreaded words. "Not yet," she pleaded. "Something's there. I know it."

"A reporter faces a lot of these," he said patiently. "Stories that would be headlines if only we could track down the truth. But we're running a paper here, not a research institute. And this isn't coming together like I'd hoped."

Lillian rushed back over. "Call for you on line two."

"Take a message and I'll get back to them."

"Not for you, for Claire. He says it's urgent. Somebody called Troy."

"It's the guy!" Claire raced around the corner, almost tumbling over the nearest desk in her haste for the phone.

"Wait, wait!" Harry hustled to the next desk, punched the line, and said, "On three." And counted down.

They picked up together, and Claire said, "Troy?"

A soft voice said, "I owe you."

"Can we meet?"

"Not now."

Harry signaled, held up a sheet of paper on which he had printed one word. She read it and said, "We can arrange protection." She was answered with silence. "Where are you?"

Another silence, but just before she gave up, he replied, "Walisenberg. Can't say more."

Walisenberg was a slow-moving town south of Pueblo. "Would you let us help you?"

"I'll think about it." A pause, then, "Look, what you're after. It's not just the game."

"I understand that much. I played it, and—"

"You don't understand anything." Another pause. "Have you discovered the Starsign?"

"The what?"

"Time's up. Gotta go. Remember, Starsign."

"No wait—"

But he was gone.

Lillian looked from one face to the other, then demanded, "Mind telling me what that was all about?"

Claire ignored the question and pleaded to Harry, "You've got to let me go on with this."

Harry glanced at his watch again, then said, "Walk with me."

Harry guided her into an elevator they had to themselves. When the doors closed, he asked, "Was the game exciting enough to be addictive?"

"Not at all. Interesting, yes. I'd like to try it again. But definitely not addictive."

"Any idea what he meant about that thing, what did he call it, Starsign?"

The doors opened to the ground floor. Claire raced to keep up with his impatient stride. "None. But I'm going to find out."

"I don't know," Harry said, passing swiftly through the

lobby. "I'm still not convinced that we're going to be able to get a payback on this."

"Give me another couple of days," she pleaded. "I'm sure there's more to this."

He pushed through the outer doors, stopped, and examined her. "I'm glad to see you involved with a piece. I just hope your interest is not misplaced."

"Does that mean yes?"

Harry's response was halted by one of the cigarette crowd. On cold days they congregated just outside the downstairs card shop, where a buttressed corner offered both sunlight and protection from the wind. The heavy smokers were the ones who never bothered to put on a coat, no matter how bad the weather.

One of the regulars, bearing a paunch and a two-pack-per-day growl, walked over. "Heard you been stepping over the line with this stringer's assignment, Harry."

He swung around, his eyes widening. "Who told you that?"

The big man slid his bulk between Harry and the steps. "Dangerous tactics, giving a new schlepp the chance to step over the line. Especially with something this sensitive." His eyes were the color of frozen mud. "City news is covered by city reporters. Stringers assigned to features are good for hemlines and bake sales."

Harry took a step forward, demanded tightly, "I asked you, who's been talking out of turn."

"Somebody who doesn't like stringers any more than I do." He turned his attention to Claire, took his time scanning her from top to toe before saying, "That's why they invented dues, honey. So stringers like you have to pay them."

"Come on, Claire." Harry stepped around the big man, drawing Claire with him.

"Who was that?"

"Somebody on the way out." To her surprise, Harry did not seem overly upset by the encounter. "Did you hear what he said?"

"How could I have missed it?"

Patient now, drawing her attention beyond the obvious, playing the ace reporter. "He said somebody has been talking. Why? Because you were assigned to something sensitive."

"What does that mean?"

"Think about it. Giving us a warning before the first word has been printed."

He kept his back to the steps and the cigarette crew, the light in his eyes and the crouch to his shoulders adding intensity to his words. "Results, Claire. That's what you have to go after. We need it *now.* Something we can take upstairs and use to justify all the outlays. We're down to the make-or-break here."

Harry motioned to the people clustered behind them. "If they've heard something, so have the people upstairs. And that means pressure like you've never dreamed."

Skate felt a familiar apprehension while waiting for the man to come on the line, which was amazing, because he rarely felt nerves about anything at all. But something about this guy left him afraid for more than his life.

"Yes," the taut monotone said. "What is it?"

"You told me to call if the girl surfaced in the game, Mr. S.," Skate replied. He had learned that brevity and caution were the best way to play it with this guy. Fast and hard and finish. "The reporter."

"Ah yes. Good. How far did she get in?"

"Only the open level."

A quick burst of approval. "Which means that she did not obtain much information from the young man."

"Troy. No sir, looks that way."

"Excellent."

Skate hesitated, then added quietly, "Not yet, anyway."

"Yes, exactly." The monotone tightened. "Find him, Skate. And destroy the risk."

"I'm on it, Mr. S. He can't stay hidden for much longer."

She was back at her desk before Lillian Stockton Fletcher snagged her. "Claire, we've got to talk."

"Not now." She searched through the rising tide of paper on her desk for the telephone guy's number.

"Yes, now." Lillian seated herself, then said, "Even the paper's newest top reporter can spare me five minutes."

"If I don't get cracking, I won't be anything around here except fired." She found the slip with Phil Flagler's address and number and set it by the phone. "What is it?"

"Your father, that's what. He's coming in this afternoon. Flying up from Durango. He wants to take us out to dinner tonight."

"Pop?" Once again, the news that her father was interfering with her new life was both startling and unwelcome. "But I thought you didn't like him."

"That's not what I said at all. I said I wasn't ready to talk about it yet."

"Yeah, I can just imagine."

"No you can't."

"Pop can get really heavy with that religion stuff," Claire pressed on. "I better warn you, it only gets worse."

Lillian leaned forward in her chair and said quietly, "Your father is one of the finest men I have ever met."

She stared at her friend. "Is this Lillian Stockton Fletcher I'm hearing say that?"

"I'm not sure who I am any more," she replied gravely. "All I can tell you is your father's quiet ways have touched me very deeply. I'm falling in love with your father, Claire. And I want you to know this before it goes any further."

Claire sank slowly into her chair. "And his faith?"

"It has taken me a lot of lonely hours to come to grip with what that means, at least in part. I have found myself wondering if Nathan has a way of talking that is totally new to me, or if I have somehow become ready to listen for the very first time. I've decided that it really doesn't matter, so long as I can come to know some peace in my own life."

Lillian's smile was at odds with the sorrow in her eyes. "Anybody with as much money as I had can't be considered to have had a rough time. It's probably best to say that my early years were hollow. Full of travel and every material gift my little mind could come up with, but hollow. And I learned my lesson well. I have spent a lifetime coating my hollowness with possessions and movement from place to place. Running away from looking inside, and seeing the barren wasteland that was my inner life."

Claire turned and looked out over the newsroom. "I don't know what to say."

"Say you'll come to dinner with us tonight."

Then the elevator doors opened, and out he came. So handsome that every head in the room turned his way. Not just handsome. Dashing. Strong and focused and determined. And walking towards her.

Lillian touched her arm. "Claire?"

But she was no longer listening. Claire rose from her chair without even realizing she had moved, her full attention focused on the man approaching her. "What are you doing here?"

"I thought I'd surprise you." His gaze was only for her. The rugged features stretched into a smile, showing those two incredible dimples. "Hope I haven't broken too many rules."

Lillian turned to face the man, and said, "You must be Donovan."

Something in her tone erased the smile. He studied her a moment and said, "That's right."

"This is Lillian Stockton Fletcher," Claire said, covering the tension with a smile of her own. Wanting them to be friends, not understanding why the atmosphere had suddenly become so hostile. "She covers society."

"Must be exciting," he said and turned back to Claire, dismissing the older woman as cleanly as if he had shut an unseen door. "Can I take you away from all this?"

She waved at the mess of papers. "I really shouldn't."

"But you will. Excellent." He remained standing on the other side of her desk, his presence somehow filling the room. Dominating her vision. A camel-hair overcoat, dark pin-stripe city suit, muted silk tie, all of it worn with the ease of a model. "It's almost quitting time in any case, and I've got a bottle of champagne on ice at a restaurant just down the street."

Claire looked down at her own jeans and cowboy boots. "I'm afraid I didn't dress for dinner and champagne. I've been playing this computer game and—"

"Don't worry," he said, cutting in. "The place I have in mind is casual enough so it won't matter."

"But shouldn't I run home and change?"

"What for? I'm not concerned with the window dressing. I want to take you out. Now." Soulful concern creased his features. "Say you'll join me."

Lillian stepped into her line of sight and said dryly, "I'll tell Nathan you said hello."

Donovan did not even glance her way. "Nathan?"

"My father." She looked at Lillian. "I'd only be a third wheel."

"Of course." Lillian moved away, not even nodding towards Donovan.

DENVER

16

■ Donovan walked alongside Claire down the Sixteenth Street Mall, determined to put the day's scare behind him.

He had returned from Beverly Hills to find the First Colorado Bank's executive floors awash in rumors, each worse than the one before. Russ Reynolds had had a nervous breakdown. He had been carted off from work. He had gone blind. He had cancer. The bank's executives either were going quietly ballistic or were simply not available. For the first time since his arrival, his channels to the bank's top management had been cut off, which was as frightening as the rumors themselves.

Calls to the Mainline offices had produced nothing new. Yes, Russ Reynolds had taken a leave of absence. No, his successor had not yet been named. No, Reynolds' executive assistant was also not available—well, former assistant, actually, she had been dismissed. No, no reasons for the move were available. No one was available to see Mr. Stone that day, things were extremely busy. The Airport Studios project? Sorry, no word was available on that. The chairman's secretary would be back to him shortly.

Soon after, his phone rang. It was Reynolds. "Are you alone?"

"Yes." Picking up his phone, Donovan stood, walked around his desk, and slammed his door shut. "I prefer to pull my hair out in private."

"I got canned."

The words hit his gut like a stone from a slingshot. "I can't believe it. Mainline's profits have gone through the roof."

"Believe it. I do."

"You can fight this thing." Donovan tried to keep the frantic tone out of his voice. "You've got to."

"Forget it." Reynolds seemed oddly calm. "I've had all I could take of being a puppet."

"What are you talking about?"

Instead of replying, Russ asked, "How did it go in Hollywood?"

"With Swindley? He didn't say a thing about all this, not word one."

"That's not what I meant."

"Russ, you're not making any sense." Donovan paced the room as far as the phone's cord would allow. "Listen, let me go before the board. I can lay it all out, show how you're the one who's turned things around. They've got to offer you—"

"Forget it. My severance package is solid gold. And I've already fielded two other offers." A smile played down the wire. "Obviously some of our competitors aren't too worried about hiring a nutcase."

"I don't get you." What about me? Donovan wanted to scream. What about all the work he'd put into this? "Just when things were ready to hit the jackpot, you're going to walk away?"

"Like I said, I've had all I can take of being Swindley's front man."

"Swindley?" He stopped cold, staring blindly out of the window. "What's he got to do with this? He's just another investor."

"That's where you're wrong." For the first time, a trace of heat appeared in Reynolds' voice. "You think I'm the one who's been dragging my heels over offering you that second contract?"

Pieces of the puzzle began falling into place.

Swindley's claim to Babylon suddenly shot into tighter focus. "Who's in charge, Russ?"

There was a moment's pause, then, "Think about it. That's all I can say. Their severance package bought them a confidentiality clause. Just listen to what I'm saying. The guy who's always run things is still in place. You want the contract, go for it."

"Can we meet?"

"I'm not even supposed to be talking with you. But I owed you that much." A long pause, then, "A word to the wise, old buddy. Watch your step with Swindley. He's a menace."

Most of dinner was spent talking about Hollywood. Donovan made her laugh endlessly with his descriptions of Chuckie and the places and the people. But he said nothing about his work. Nothing of substance.

The only time they spoke of her work was when she used an early lapse in the conversation to ask, "Didn't you tell me you were working with Mainline Computers?"

He drew back slightly. "You don't really want to talk business tonight, do you?"

"Just one question. Can you tell me what's happened to Russ Reynolds?"

The distance was greater now. "How did you hear about that?"

"Strictly by chance. What happened?"

"I'm not allowed to say."

"Was he fired?"

He hesitated a moment, as though uncertain whether he would answer her at all. "Let's just say," he finally responded, "Russ is no longer in the picture."

Which was no help at all. But before she could say more, he leaned across the table and enveloped her hand with his own. "And that is all I have to say about the matter, on or off the record."

She smiled and accepted it, because she had no choice. Claire then listened to him go into great detail about the Bel Air Hotel, but nothing about the reasons behind his trip. Her questions were deftly turned aside. As were her own attempts to return to the story she was on. It was as though he had entered into the evening already certain where it would lead and how the conversation should go. Work or any other serious topic was not allowed to enter.

Because it was Donovan, and because the night was magical, she allowed him to control the flow.

When coffee arrived, he grew silent. She sensed what was

coming, yet was not sure what she wanted to do. His looks were a lure as strong as a flame. She saw the message in his eyes, and knew he was going to invite her back to his place. Claire did not want to hear the words yet, did not want to make a decision yet, so she said, "I couldn't do what you're doing. Go into a place like Los Angeles and start fitting in."

He settled back, the flame's intensity dimming slightly. "It's Beverly Hills, really, which is a world apart from downtown L.A. And why not?"

"I don't feel like I'll ever fit in, not even here."

Donovan showed alarm. "You should have said something. We can go someplace else."

"Not this restaurant. Here, in Denver." She played with her glass. "Underdressed, unsophisticated, undertrained. A hick from a mountain crossroads town."

"So why did you come?"

"Work. What else? Not much chance to cover the Middle East for the *Ouray Star.*"

"That's what you want to be, a foreign correspondent?"

His focus was so tight upon her, it was almost frightening. As though the rest of the world had vanished, and all there was room for was this table, their little candle, her face, her words. "A journalist. I want to become a first-rate reporter. It's just, I don't know, the price is sometimes a little high." She watched the hostess sashay past their table, the sequins in her cocktail dress sprinkling light everywhere. "City ways are strange to this girl."

Donovan made a pretense of checking under the table. "Yeah, not a lot of top executive ladies wearing cowboy boots around here."

"You were the one who didn't want to give me time to change."

"I'm not complaining. I just don't see many girls in that kind of footwear, is all."

"Cowboy boots are the most functional shoe ever made." She brought one defiant leg out from under the table and hoisted it a few inches off the floor. "Every part has a purpose."

He grinned enough to show dimples. "And you're going to tell me, right?"

"Look at the heel and tapered toe." She knew he was kidding, but for some reason it was suddenly important that he understand. "It's designed to slip easily into a stirrup, then keep you from sliding out. Plus a slightly stacked heel is more natural for walking."

"Do you ride?"

"Sure. Do you?"

"Never been close enough to a horse to find out." He pointed with his chin. "What about all that fancy sewing?"

"That's called the top stitch. Top leather is hard and tends to wrinkle over time. You throw a stitch into it to make it more pliable and give the leather a proper fold."

He propped his chin on one hand. "And the way it climbs your leg so far?"

She raised the leg of her jean. "That's the high shaft. It protects you from the saddle's abrasiveness on one side and from brush on the other." She settled her leg back under the table and examined his face. "Are you making fun of me?"

He laughed it away. "What gave you that idea?" Then before she could respond, he said, "Are you a skier?"

"I downhill and snowboard from time to time. But I prefer cross-country. My first love, though, is mountain hiking."

"A climber." Impressed.

"No." Patient with him now. She had spoken to other flatlanders who made the same mistake. "A hiker. There's a big difference. No pitons. I mostly stick to trails and seldom use my hands."

"I've seen pictures of people up on those trails of yours. Nothing to either side but a big drop."

"It's beautiful." She struggled as she always did when forced to describe how it felt up top. "There's nothing like walking a ridgeline with just the clouds and the wind for company. Sometimes I feel if I wasn't careful I'd leave the world completely, rise up and melt into the sky."

He smiled. "Fall down and melt with the rocks, more likely."

She wanted to tell him about her mountain world. Let him know where she had been formed. Yet there was the sense that he heard, but only with his head, not his heart. As though he was not giving the value she hoped for to what she said. "I'm a volunteer forest firefighter. My group covers the whole Western Slope."

Another of those rich laughs. "This is too much to take in one gulp." He signaled the waiter, asked for the check, and turned back around. "Would you like to walk?"

"All right." She watched him handle the waiter with ease, help her with her coat, flirt with the hostess as they passed, hold the door, grasp her arm, and move up close. Listened as he changed the subject back to Beverly Hills and the incredible hotel where he was staying. She walked alongside him, feeling the magnetism reach through the space between them, making her shiver from more than the night's chill. She wondered why she felt so incredibly attracted to him on one hand, yet frustrated on the other.

Then he stopped and smiled at her, and there was no longer room for disappointment. Only that incredibly handsome face, those confident eyes filled with humor and something more, a shared hunger, one that seemed to reach down inside her, making her hum with delicate tension, as though he was going to reach into her deepest being and play her like a finely tuned violin.

He pulled off one glove and ran a finger down the side of her face, and she felt a stream of fire rise in its passage. The hand continued along the line of her chin, pausing, pressing, raising her up, as he lowered his face and kissed her. Passion flooded her with the feel of his lips. A sudden thought rose unbidden, What about that other girl? But it melted with her resistance as she felt his arms go around her, drawing her close with possessive strength. She sighed away her concerns, knowing there was nothing else she wanted to do but give in.

DENVER

■ Claire arrived the next morning to the shock of finding her father in Harry's office. The sight welded her to the spot. The hollow point she had been carrying at her center since the night before suddenly grew and blossomed into flowers of shame.

Harry spotted her and waved, which turned Nathan around. He rose from his seat, and through the window Claire watched Harry take Nathan's hand with both of his own. Nathan then left the office, stopped long enough to share a smile with Lillian, then walked over towards her. "Good morning," he said, his voice as mild as ever. "Do you have time for a little walk with your father?"

"I'm really busy," she said weakly.

"Just down to the street," he said and turned toward the elevator.

They traveled back to the lobby in silence. Which was

good, as it gave her a chance to gather herself. Once outside the building, Claire said, "How long have you been waiting for me?"

"I was here to see Harry," Nathan replied, taking the steps carefully. "He has told me a little of your project. I am glad that electronic games are coming under scrutiny. They are the perfect avenue through which the forces of darkness could attack. Can you think of any other aspect of our society where anger and battle and hatred and darkness and wizardry are granted such total acceptance?"

When she did not answer, he went on, "Modern man is fashioning both new technology and a new society. These creators recognize no rules, no absolute power, no higher form of moral order. They build this void into everything they create. They have usurped God's position and set in His place the demon of anarchy. Such uses of technology urge our young people to live without rules, without order. They create new systems and programs at breakneck speed, rushing them out, pushed by profit and greed, urging our society closer and closer to chaos."

She sighed away the shame that made it hard to hear his words. "If I don't start seeing some real results quick, there's not going to be much scrutiny of anything."

"Harry said that as well," Nathan replied solemnly. "I will be praying for you."

They crossed the street. Overhead, the sky was jammed tight with clouds polished a uniform grey by the rising wind. Once they were walking along the Sixteenth Street Mall, Nathan went on, "Can you tell me why you brought Harry home?"

Claire continued to avoid meeting his eyes. "So you two could meet."

He walked alongside her in silence before repeating, more quietly this time, "Why did you bring him, Claire?"

The accustomed anger began to rise. "You tell me."

"I am only guessing. But perhaps it's because you care for him."

She feigned a shrug. "Sure. He's my boss."

He glanced her way, a slow look, then away. "So. You care for him. And perhaps more than just as a boss. Perhaps also you have noticed he is troubled."

She gave a single jerking nod of agreement.

"You care for him, he is troubled." A pause, then, "but you had no answers to offer him." Nathan granted her a chance to object. When Claire remained silent, he went on, "Answers in your head, yes. But answers of your heart?"

He spoke in a slow cadence, a challenge in itself. "Answers that carry the power of your entire being are there only when your entire being is committed." He stopped and turned to study her with eyes the color of winter smoke. "Being saved, going to church once a week, and keeping your faith tightly tied down inside your head is fine so long as your own strength remains enough. But when your strength proves inadequate to answer the needs of another, you need more. At such a time you are called to shine not as one who lives her own life, but rather as one who lives for a higher purpose. You can then respond only by showing in your life and in your heart and in your voice that you live for God."

Claire found that she could not hold his gaze and keep her anger at the same time. Which was bad, because all that was left in its place was a burning void at the center of her being.

"If this search does nothing more than bring the choice home to you," Nathan went on, "I give thanks."

"I've chosen," she said, her voice weak.

"You have gone through the motions, but you waver. You must make your choice with all you are. The Lord must be granted full entry. You vacillate because you know that in taking this step, He will reshape every last vestige of your life."

This time, there was no argument. All the heat and the frustration had been drained from her. "I'll think about it."

He faced her, the features she knew so well, shaped by years of determined struggle. "Do more than that," he said. "Pray for guidance. Ask for help."

When she returned to the office, she pushed aside the uncomfortable thoughts by diving into her work. She punched the number for the phone company man. "Mr. Flagler? Claire Kingsbury."

"Hey, good morning. And call me Phil."

"I hope I'm not bothering you."

"You kidding? These missing kids keep me up at night. How's the search going?"

"Slow," she replied, "and as confusing as calculus. But I feel like there's something big going on, if only we could find a way to nail it down."

"Don't give up," he urged her. "I've been working on this all by myself up to now. It means a lot to know I've finally gotten somebody else's attention."

"I'm hooked, all right." She hesitated, then decided that

if Harry trusted the man, she could as well. She told him what little she had found out, then finished with, "I can't seem to find something that will start pulling things together. I was just wondering, if I wanted to talk with some people who spend a lot of time playing Babylon, where would I go?"

"Wizard's Lair," he replied without hesitation. "It's a giant electronic arcade. Got a buddy who works an outreach program there. His name's Matt. Don't let his looks scare you, the guy is a genuine pushover. I'll call him and see if he can meet you this afternoon."

Matt was a giant six-feet-six, made bigger by steel-toed jackboots and legs like firmly planted oaks. His weight had to be cresting three hundred pounds. His burly chest stretched out the T-shirt's silkscreen design of a superhero planting a cross in the earth, with the caption underneath reading, "Powered By God."

The only fragile part about him were his eyes, which peered beneath unruly hair with a green so light that spring's first leaf would look ancient by comparison. "You Claire?"

"Yes." She allowed her hand to be swallowed up, marveling that someone so incredibly huge could be so gentle.

"Why don't you go on upstairs, have a look around. Then come back and we'll talk about what you've seen."

The Wizard's Lair spread over three floors, all of which were full. There were a few adults, but not many. Most of the gamers appeared to be in their late teens, their T-shirts declaring allegiance to one heavy metal group or another. The first floor held a huge cafe-style eating area; it was relatively quiet, the music somewhat muted with the volume turned down on the electronic games that lined the walls.

The second floor was a constant electronic racket, the rooms filled with various electronic games. Claire walked down the aisles, watched youngsters battle demons and karate experts and sword-wielding warriors or race along electronic highways with roaring sound effects and seats that swerved to match the road's twists and turns.

She climbed the stairs to the third floor, and entered bedlam. The entire floor was given over to one vast chamber. Floor, walls, and ceiling were all painted black. Over the entrance-way was the same angry red emblem she had seen at the computer show, and proclaiming the single word, *Babylon*.

The music was acid house, also known as rave. It pounded her ears with a relentless 4/4 beat at up to one hundred and eighty beats per minute—the maximum rate a normal heart can sustain and still survive. Lyrics, melody, and the human voice were stripped away. A non-stop, machine-generated beat drove endless computer generated patterns with the power of a drill. It hit her the moment she entered and did not let go.

The shrieks from the watchers were even louder. Lining every wall were giant video projection screens, and positioned from ceiling units were dozens and dozens of television monitors. All showed the same harsh terrain she had seen upon entering the game herself—a blazing orb overhead and battlelines of giants and gremlins and goblins forming upon the desert floor.

Interspersed through the room were chambers that resembled blackened flight simulators. Observers crammed around windows placed at the back of each chamber, allowing them to view the players. A barrage of flashing lights outlined oversized view-screens. The players each saw a perspective from slightly above the desert, looking down from what appeared to be a dragon in line with numerous others.

An announcer boomed, "Warriors, wizards, dragons, and goblins! Choose your weapons and prepare for combat!"

The loudspeaker then began relaying what sounded like coordinated battle lingo, as the players began picking electronic weaponry and moving into tighter formations.

"Tactics, see, that's why the Poltergeists've never been beaten. The Creek Gang don't stand a chance."

Claire turned to find herself staring into the leering face of a pimple-cheeked adolescent. "Who?"

"Cold Creek Gang. Out of Utah. That's who they're up against." He had to shout over the din. "Your first time?"

This guy, she realized, was trying to pick her up. Unbelievable. "Very first."

"My specialty is the drop zone. That's where the real action is." He gave another leer. "Want to watch an expert at work?"

"Maybe some other time." Claire started back for the entrance, but going was slowed by the crowds. In front of her, a kid wearing a Babylon cloak was shouting to a girl, "You have to translocate with total smoothness. A rough landing and you're open to the unseen attacker."

The girl nodded with her entire upper body. "This is just soooo cool. I never thought I'd understand how to get to the Tower."

"Use the Doom Gates," the guy said. "Just stay away from the River Styx when you're flying in."

Claire pushed her way past, climbed back down the stairs, and took a relieved sigh as she entered the relative calm of the street-level cafe. She walked over to Matt and said, "How can you stand this place?"

"Unfortunately, a lifetime's misuse of pharmacology has left me perfectly adapted to working with these kids." He closed his well-worn Bible and waved her to an empty chair. "When I came to the Lord, He called me to restore the years the locusts had eaten by being a beacon at places like this."

"But these kids are just playing games."

His gaze held depths of gentle sorrow, for himself, for those lost in the electronic maze. "In the first place, a lot of gamers are heavy into one drug or another. Second, few drugs are as addictive as the games themselves. High technology combined with violence and rage and pretended superpowers make for some very hooked junkies."

She held up her pad, requesting permission to make notes. When he responded with a shrug, she asked, "Why do they do it? Allow themselves to get addicted, I mean."

"It starts off as fun. They immerse themselves by degree. They discover the games allow themselves to become something bigger than they really are. More powerful. Invincible." He took in the entire arcade with a sweeping gesture. "This tidal wave is overwhelming our youth. They come from loveless, godless homes, where they feel powerless to alter their empty lives. They come down here, and they fill the inner vacuum with electronic gods. They come to prefer this new reality."

"They play Babylon?"

"Babylon is the flavor of the month for a lot of these users." He watched a crowd of a dozen or so excited kids troop past their table, then continued. "Interactive games are the wave of the future. The guys in marketing call them layered experiences. This means they go to arcades like this one and try out the game, then go to the shop and buy the home version. Which hooks them into buying increasingly expensive computer equipment. They shell out for the headgear and a modem so they can fight in their imaginary world from the comfort of their own homes."

Claire tried hard to keep up. "You're saying the companies encourage the kids to become addicted to these games?"

"Sure. The companies make money coming and going. They own the gear you find upstairs, they make money selling the homeware, and then they charge for every minute the kids play the game on-line."

Matt signaled to a pair that were passing by, and went on, "Have a listen to the kids who live for this, and see for yourself." He turned to the pair as they settled down and said, "Buzz, Chillian, meet Claire."

"Another real-timer," the guy sneered. He was rail thin, with blond hair in straight vertical spikes and the gaze of somebody staring back from the other side of the edge. A pair of stars were tattooed to his wrists.

"Claire's interested in talking with someone who knows their way around Babylon."

"Yeah? Then I'm her man." He fingered the thin gold chain around his neck and showed her the three-headed snake dangling from the end. "That's the emblem from the Tower Gate," he announced proudly. "I'm this close to earning the key."

"I spend more time on-line than just about anybody,"

Chillian declared, competing for Claire's attention. She wore the obligatory uniform of jeans and T-shirt, hers bearing the emblem of the great silver tower. There was a star tattooed to the inside of her elbow. She stared at Claire with manic eyes and proclaimed, "One day I'll get sucked in and never be heard from again."

Buzz was not impressed. "So how many people in real time hear from you now?"

Claire asked the girl, "Do you know of gamers who actually do disappear?"

"Happens all the time." Her gaze held the hopeless shadows of a darkened tunnel leading nowhere. "Games are major time suckers. Babylon's just the worst of a long line. They eat up lots of time, lots of life. Then one day, poof, there's just no life left."

The matter-of-fact tone was as chilling as the deadness of her eyes. Claire demanded, "So why do you keep playing?"

She mulled that one over. "I dunno. I guess because I have to."

"Gamers survive by concentrating on the moment at hand," Matt offered, his gaze on the pair. "It's the only way they can keep hold of what's left of reality."

Buzz seemed proud of the accusation. "Gamers are by definition wide-timers. We focus on everything happening now, with next week as much of the future as anybody wired can handle."

"The wide view focuses on now-time events," Chillian confirmed. "The past is dust. Dead and buried."

"The other day, my teacher asked us how many people would be wired in 2045," Buzz sneered. "Like she was totally with-it, getting us to extrapolate the internet users out fifty years. The answer is, Who cares? That's further away from me than Hiroshima."

"You want to keep up," Chillian added, "you got to focus on what's going down in the here and now."

Matt leaned forward, his voice quiet, his tone deceptively calm. "So there's nothing in the past that can offer you any answers?"

"Like what?"

"Like the Bible."

Their expressions turned pained. "Puleese," Chillian whined.

"Life is time on the wire," the guy agreed. "Cyberspace is today's reality. The rest is just paper hanging."

"The Bible has stood the test of time," Matt countered firmly. "Your cyberworld will come and go, but the Lord will remain forever."

Chillian's tone was mocking. "You're not gonna get anywhere around here with that turn the other cheek stuff."

"I'm into cyberjustice," Buzz announced proudly. "Don't get mad, get even."

"We're just doing our bit for anarchy," the girl agreed. "Working for a world where everybody gets what they deserve."

Matt was taking it all very easy. "I wouldn't wish that on anybody."

"Yeah, and that's your problem," the girl taunted, rising from her seat. "Cyberia requires a proper attitude, which you are definitely lacking."

Claire watched the pair walk away, then asked a second time, "How can you stand this?"

"Because the Lord has called me to help them find their way home," he said, his voice and gaze unfazed by their departure. "At least that pair is willing to listen. Sooner or later they'll find themselves lost and scared. Maybe they'll remember what I've said, and that I'm here to help them make the choice and take the turning."

The *choice.* Claire found herself propelled from her seat by the shock of Matt repeating her father's word. As she tucked her pad back into her purse, she asked, "One last question. A lot of those kids seem to have a tattoo, a small one shaped like a star."

"Sure. It's a sign they're regular users of a drug called Nova." Matt rose from his seat to tower over her. "Been nice meeting you."

She allowed him to swallow her hand again, feeling pushed by conflicting forces. On the one hand, there was the sensation that there was something important here, something she was not seeing. On the other, she simply wanted to be away from the noise and the weirdness and this man with his beaming faith. "Is there any connection between Babylon and this drug, what did you call it?"

"Nova. A lot of the kids are into both. New designer drugs are coming out all the time. This one has caught hold really fast, but that's all I can tell you." He gave his easy smile. "It's as easy to lose yourself on Nova as any other lure the darkness cares to use."

DENVER

18

■ By the time she arrived home that evening, Claire felt as though every nerve in her body was stretched taut by indecision. Then she cleared the top step, saw her door was open, and saw Donovan's coat draped over the hall chair. All the doubts and voices and tensions and confusion rose like a great wave and came crashing down, hurtling her across the landing and through the door and into his arms. All she could manage to say was, "You're here."

She heard the rich male voice say, "Your landlady said I looked honest enough and let me in. Shows how deceptive looks can be. Either that, or she likes surprises as much as I do." He pushed her back far enough to wave a hand at the meal set up on her little table. "I didn't know if you'd want to go out two evenings in a row, and I can't cook, so I had dinner catered."

"It's beautiful." And it was. There was a linen tablecloth

and matching napkins, two candles in silver stands, a single rose and a spray of white garland in a tiny crystal vase, and wine cooling in its stand.

"Breast of duck on wild rice, a nice chardonnay, I hope that's all right." He pulled back her chair, waited while she dropped purse and coat and scarf, and held it as she seated herself. "Shall I pour?"

"This is too much." She could not get over it, Donovan here in her room. Too tall for the low ceiling, too big for the small confines, yet managing to fit somehow. As much a mystery as he had been the first time they met, yet so magnetic and thrilling all she had to do was see him again and she was under his spell. "I just don't understand this attention."

"What do you mean?" He seated himself, poured their wine, settled his napkin in his lap. "You're a gorgeous girl, I like you, I want to see you every chance I get."

"I mean," she said, putting slow emphasis on each word, "you were with that other girl."

"Oh. Trish."

"Yes."

Donovan shook his head. "You don't understand. She's, well, Trish is something else. But being with her is like trying to hold mercury. You never can be sure it's actually in your grasp."

She waited, expecting more. When he did not continue, she asked, "So it's over?"

"Almost." He busied himself with his food.

"Almost." Not a very satisfying answer. "So where does that leave us?"

"Us?" He looked over at her, the dimples showing with his almost smile. "I like to hear you say that word."

"Where are we, Donovan?"

"I told you on the phone that day from the Polo Lounge. You're my reality check."

She could feel the direction shifting, knew she was unable to keep it where she wanted it to go. "I've never met anybody who looks like they need one less."

"Everybody does. Just like everybody needs something in their past that's so bad, they hate so much, they'll do anything never to have to do it again." He gestured with his fork towards her plate. "Aren't you going to eat something?"

She picked at the food. "You'll do anything to avoid something from your past?"

"Whatever it takes."

She studied the mystery who sat across from her, the craggy handsomeness, the shock of strawberry blond hair, the eyes, the smile, he had it all. "What is that for you, that bad thing?"

"My own personal living nightmare." He raised his glass and said, "Here's to keeping it where it belongs—behind me."

She clinked her glass, tasted, smiled her approval. They ate in silence for a time. "This is delicious."

"Glad you like it."

She watched him refill her glass and asked, "So you spend your life running away from the past?"

"No." He answered her reluctantly, the question and the direction from which it came leaving him uncomfortable. "I spend my life chasing the future. The past gives me speed."

So much was in that face, an amazing blend of stone

hardness and determination and desire. She leaned her elbows upon the table. "Tell me about your past."

He was silent a long moment, then reached across and took her hand. The touch was electric. His tone deepened as he said, "Let's talk about something else. Something more romantic."

For once she resisted the urge to let him lead her where he wanted. "I'd really like you to tell me."

He drew his hand away. "Why?"

"Because I don't feel I know anything about you. And I want to." It felt so strange, pleading with him to share something about who he was. As though she were pounding on a locked door. "I really do."

His voice was remote. "There is nothing romantic about making mistakes."

"I want to know," she persisted.

Donovan seemed to draw into himself. "I was wild. I don't know why. My folks raised two other children, they grew up normal, one is an insurance broker with my dad now, my sister is a paralegal and has two kids. I never could fit the mold. I was always in trouble. Got thrown out of school twice. While I was suspended that second time my buddy and I stole a car, tried to race the cops." He showed her a faint smile. "The cops won."

She reached across, took back his hand, just wanting him to know she was there, listening, accepting. "You went to jail?"

"Juvenile home. Awful. Unbelievably bad. I got into trouble a lot there as well. Then one day they gathered the ones they thought were not going to make it, couldn't straighten out, and took us to a federal pen. Showed us what it meant to do hard time."

His grip hardened with the clench to his jaw. She endured the discomfort, then said quietly, "It scared you."

The nod took hold of his entire upper body. "Enough to wake me up. I finished high school while I was still on probation. A kid's record is sealed, that was my one saving grace. It takes a court order to open it. I could go on to college, pretend nothing had happened."

"Start over again."

"Start for the first time," he corrected, his eyes on her face. "Before, I was just wasting my life."

"But look at you now. You're successful, you're going places. It's all behind you."

"Not up here," he said, pointing with his free hand to his head, then down to his heart. "Or here."

"So you use this memory to drive you forward."

"Keep in mind how far I can fall," he agreed. "Keep me cautious and tough and determined."

"Do you ever think about helping another kid who's trapped in the downward spiral?"

The question caught him totally off guard. He said doubtfully, "Maybe when things slow down a little, I might try to pull somebody up who has the guts and drive."

She examined him. "You've never thought of doing it though, have you?"

"Why should I? Nobody ever helped me."

She could feel herself being pulled in his direction, drawn by his focused ambition and the magnetic force of his personality. It robbed her next question of power. "Do you regret it?"

"What I did?" He pursed his lips. "I regret getting caught. A lot."

"I mean morally." Then, when he looked at her in amused contempt, she felt she had to justify the question. "You know, how what you did was wrong."

"I only did what everybody does. Everybody who wants to get ahead. My mistake was doing it for peanuts and cheap thrills." He stood up then, his power filling the room. He walked over, drew her up, and said, "Now how am I going to be rewarded for being your good little boy?"

"You're not little. And I'm not so sure about the good part either." Still, she held him close, her arms locked tightly to his chest. It was a struggle not with Donovan, but with all the other voices in her mind and heart. There was no response to them, except to hold on to him. To know him better. To find the answers that would show she was right and they were wrong. All of them.

He made a mock gasp, then said, "Mind if I take a breath?"

"Sorry." She loosened her grip and raised her head. "Would you like to come home with me sometime?"

He shrugged his lack of interest. "I'd rather get you out with me to L.A."

"Ouray is a lot closer," she said, pressing her case. "And a lot prettier. A beautiful town nestled in the heart of the Rockies. You'd love it."

"You think so?" He gave her his easy smile. "Personally, I'm not sure I could ever live in a place like that. The lack of change would kill me stone dead."

She struggled to hide her disappointment as she faced

him. "Small towns can be hard on some, I guess. On the bad days, it made me feel like the whole world was stuck in a rut."

"And the good days?"

"It was the finest place on earth," she replied, from the heart.

He laughed it off. "The best home I could think of is one where I don't have to stay too long." He reached up one hand to caress her face, her hair, her neck, his hand traveling down and across her shoulder, on and on. She felt her own desire mirrored in the heat of his breath as he whispered to her, "Care for a nightcap?"

"Sure," she said, returning his smile, wondering why something that felt so good could also feel so wrong.

DENVER AND PUEBLO

19

■ Claire's storm of emotions stayed with her through the night. The tumult threatened to split her mind and heart—desire on one hand, regret on the other. Angrily she fought back, silently telling the darkness that she had done nothing to be ashamed of, she was a woman in charge of her own destiny. Even so, she spent hours trying to find sleep.

When she arrived at the office, remorse tightened into choking guilt as Harry spotted her and waved her into his office.

Another staffer stood before his desk. She stopped in the doorway and watched him slap pages on the table, then snap at the reporter, "I want you to tell me who, what, when, where, why, and do it in seventy-five words, not seven hundred."

"But Harry—"

"No arguments. You've got five column-inches max for

the piece. And get it to me before the three o'clock story conference." Harry waited until the reporter had left, pointed her into the vacant seat, and said, "Some people around here think I'm running a course in remedial journalism."

She avoided his gaze by glancing around the office. The walls were bare. All the old stories had vanished, all the plaques remained off his desk. She wanted to ask what had happened, but could not find the strength.

"Some guy named Donovan's already called here a half-dozen times this morning. That something I need to know about?"

A sudden stab of guilt hardened her tone. "It's none of your business."

He observed her for a long moment, then asked, "Anything new on our little lost lead and the paper's investment in his bail?"

"I'm on it, Harry, okay?"

He continued his steady examination. "Are you angry over something I've done and don't know about?"

The words had a shattering effect. "It's not you. I'm mad at *me*."

"Want to talk about it?"

The genuineness of his sympathy left her feeling as though she had betrayed a friend. Which was crazy. Harry was her boss, nothing more. "Thanks, maybe another time."

"Right." He turned to business. "How was the arcade?"

"Scary. Loud."

"Think you've got a tie-in?"

"I'm not sure. A lot of the kids use it as a gathering point. You know, they play the game at home, then go out—"

"Well, now, ain't this cozy?" The man who had tried to stop them outside at the smokers' corner slid his bulk into Harry's doorway. "You two cooking up another secret story?"

"Stay out of this," Harry said, his voice flat.

The deep voice grated back, "You ought to be starting her out at municipals, Harry. You know that as well as I do. That's where rookies earn their stripes, municipals."

"She's been a stringer for four years and with our western bureau for eleven months more. And done good work. She's not a cub."

"She's too green to have that much time under her belt," the guy snorted. "And stringers still start on the bottom rung. I say she goes to municipal." He stared down at her, his face mottled by ancient acne scars. "Whattaya think of that, Miss Hot Shot Stringer?"

"The name is Claire." Municipal Court was the lowest of the low, where bookies, numbers runners, addicts, drunks, and homeless were processed through a judicial factory line. "Whatever Harry says is fine with me."

"There, see," Harry told him. "New to the job and already she knows more than you."

The guy's solid bulk blocked their only exit. "You've kept her on that story, haven't you?"

"Even better." Harry's gaze was level and cold as his voice. "I'm putting her on general assignment."

"That's not what I hear." The man's growl was a sibilant hiss. "I hear you're using her to tread through a minefield. One that might blow up in all our faces."

"Get out of my office." The force behind Harry's icy anger

turned the guy reluctantly around. He glowered at Claire one last time, then left.

"There's more than bluster behind that guy," Harry said, subsiding. "He's fishing for something."

"General assignment?"

"You write what I tell you to write. Same as before." He thought it over a moment longer, then focused back on her.

"Whenever you're stuck, go back to what you know. Follow the money. Check out your contacts another time, look for chinks in the story. See if old leads have anything new."

"I thought I'd try to talk to some more of the techno-freaks. Maybe try the game another time." Claire forced herself to her feet. Her mind remained held by the way he had stuck up for her. Again.

When she was at the doorway, Harry turned her around with, "One more thing. A key to success in investigative journalism is, learn to recognize the story within the story. Don't toss out something you find just because it doesn't seem to fit."

She could not drag her gaze away from him. "Thanks, Harry."

"You're welcome." He gave her his quick grin. "We're still friends, right?"

Her throat constricted so, the word had to be forced out. "Friends."

Claire was finally pulled from downward-spiraling thoughts by the ringing of the phone. "*Denver Herald*, Claire Kingsbury."

"Claire, hey, it's Phil Flagler. Been praying for you."

The unexpected words were a stab straight to her heart. "What?"

"You know, that you'd find what you need in time to keep this investigation alive."

"Oh." She leaned back with a heavy sigh. "Thanks."

But he was too excited to notice. "Got a pencil?"

"Sure."

"Take this down." He gave her an address in Pueblo, a nondescript city a hundred and fifty miles south.

"What is it?"

"Maybe nothing, maybe a miracle." His excitement almost danced across the wires. "Remember that guy they picked up, Troy something?"

"Troy Keeler?" She shot to her feet. "They've found him?"

"Not him, the guy whose apartment Troy was caught breaking into. Buddy Wiggins. When you get there, ask for Sandra, his sister. And be sure to let me know how it goes."

Pueblo was a worker's town. Claire turned off the interstate and joined a phalanx of pickups and grimy station wagons. The arid vista was flat and brown. Strong winds blew tan clouds of grit against her car. The mountains and the snows were lost somewhere on the other side of the dust-storm. Or the world.

She followed the directions to the city's eastern outskirts, where a tall stone fence bordered an estate a quarter-mile square. She pulled in at the gates, gave her name, then drove around stunted trees and a struggling lawn. The central building was old and stone and pretentious, with steep slate-tile roofs and gargoyles and peaked corners. The wings extending from either side were red-brick and functional-modern.

Claire entered the cavernous foyer and gave her name to the receptionist. Before she could take a seat, a young woman approached and said, "Miss Kingsbury? I'm Sandra Wiggins. Phil Flagler called and asked if I would talk with you about my brother."

"Nice of you to see me." She faced a lady perhaps a few years older than herself, it was hard to tell for certain. Fatigue and sadness had taken quite a toll. But strength was there as well, a solid centeredness that shone from the pale grey eyes.

Sandra asked quietly, "Are you going to expose the monsters responsible for destroying my brother's life?"

The sudden vehemence shocked her. "I'm afraid I don't—"

"Oh, nobody is as responsible for Buddy destroying his life as Buddy himself." She brushed an auburn lock from her forehead. The eyes dropped, the face started to crumple, but she caught herself and straightened. "I just want to know if you are going to expose the monsters before they have a chance to work their magic on anybody else."

"I want to," Claire said slowly. "But I need solid evidence before I can write the first word."

Sandra took the words in, then said, "Won't you sit down with me for a moment?"

"Thank you." Claire settled onto the hard wooden bench, and pulled out her pad and pencil. "Just what exactly happened to your brother, Miss Wiggins?"

"Call me Sandra. I'm not exactly sure. Buddy was a data processor with a big agricultural company in Colorado

Springs. That's where my family is from. Then one day he just vanished. Yesterday, the police found him wandering around the streets of Los Angeles."

"You think he was kidnapped?"

"I don't know what to think." This time the tears could not be held back. "Buddy hated to travel. He'd never been outside of Colorado in his life. When the police found him, he was in such a state he couldn't even tell them his own name."

Claire wrote swiftly, still not sure where the tie-in was. "What happened to him?"

Sandra Wiggins gathered herself, wiped her face with swift motions of both hands, turned back to Claire and asked, "Are you a Christian, Miss Kingsbury?"

Claire opened her mouth, but the words did not come. Simple honesty shone from Sandra's red-rimmed eyes, an appeal so strong she had to respond in kind. "I don't know how to answer that question. I've never been more unsure about anything in my entire life than I am right now."

For some reason, the reply granted Sandra the ability to regain control. "An honest and open answer. I like that." She took a shaky breath. "Buddy was captured by the dark forces. They can call it a game if they want. But I know. The powers of darkness were at work in my baby brother, and they took him."

"The game?" Claire tried to gather herself. "You mean Babylon?"

"Babylon is more than a game. At least it was to Buddy, and I think to a lot of other kids out there. It was all he ever talked about. All he ever did. Whether or not he was using drugs, Buddy's first addiction was to this evil."

"Drugs?" Claire wondered what it was about this

mild-voiced woman that was keeping her continually off balance. "He was taking drugs as well?"

Sandra rose to her feet, her quiet voice very determined. "I think I can trust you, Miss Kingsbury. I'll go and arrange things with Dr. Diaz."

"What is your interest in this patient, Miss Kingsbury?"

Dr. Ernesto Diaz was clear-eyed, darkly handsome, and focused. He gave the impression of being both perpetually in a hurry and immensely patient. Claire tried to ignore the sounds coming from further down the antiseptically clean hallway and replied, "This ties in with something else I've been researching." She hesitated, then added, "Maybe."

"Can you tell me what that is?"

"Soon," she promised, hoping aloud.

"The patient's family is very close." Dr. Diaz was in his early thirties, yet was aged far beyond his years. He hesitated by a pair of steel doors, observing her carefully. "They had the missing person documentation completed within twenty-four hours of his disappearance. That is what saved him."

"How can you be so sure of that?"

He punched a code into the electronic door-lock, pushed one open, and said, "Come with me."

Beyond the barrier, the noise was much louder, emanating from behind numerous solid-looking doors and from wheelchairs parked along the hall.

One patient screeched and offered the doctor a claw-shaped hand. Dr. Diaz unbent for the first time since her arrival, pausing to accept the hand and speak a few calm words

to the young man. The patient grimaced with genuine pleasure and settled back. The doctor led her on.

A well-muscled aide nodded an impassive greeting, as did
a pair of bustling nurses. Everyone seemed calm and easy with
the situation, except Claire.

Dr. Diaz stopped before a stout door, peered through the
reinforced window, then turned back to Claire. "Are you familiar with the term 'catatonic'?"

"I've heard of it, that's all."

"A catatonic patient is someone who holds a particular
position, often a very bizarre position, and often for a very long
time." Another glance through the small window, then,
"Buddy alternates between this and periods of manic activity."

He opened the door, and stepped in. Claire hesitated,
swallowed, then followed him inside. Or tried to. She could
not force herself past the doorway.

Dr. Diaz stepped over to the bed, looked down, and said,
"Catatonia, or catalepsy as it is often called, is usually related to
schizophrenia. That term refers to a serious loss of contact with
reality."

The young man lay on his side, his arms locked around
his chest. One leg lay flat. The other was cocked rigidly out-
ward, like a ballet dancer who had frozen and toppled over.
His face was clenched impossibly tight, with tension lines running from forehead to chin.

"Most of us have the ability to divert bizarre thoughts
when they arise," Dr. Diaz went on. "We do this by checking
our thoughts against reality, memories, what we know of the
world outside."

He looked down at the young man with a mixture of

clinical detachment and genuine concern. "With a schizophrenic, they lose this contact with reality. There is no longer the ability to tell thought from actuality. They experience hallucinations and delusions which are to them utterly, absolutely real. Abnormal beliefs are held with complete intensity."

Claire held up pad and pen, and when he nodded acceptance, forced herself to begin taking notes. "Why does this happen?"

"Any number of reasons. Shock, undue stress, emotional pain, genetic coding," he looked down at the patient and added, "or drugs. Especially some of the new compounds commonly referred to as designer drugs."

She looked up. "You think he was experimenting with drugs?"

"We have very little to go on here. But yes, that is my guess. There were lingering traces of some metabolized hallucinogens in his muscle tissue. But we can't tell how long ago he took whatever it was. These drugs may reside in the system for six months to a year after ingestion."

He motioned her back through the door. "Perhaps we would be more comfortable in my office."

"Just a minute. Please." Claire forced herself forward. Approaching the silent young man caused her entire body to ache, but there was something she had noticed on his arm. At closer inspection, she realized there was a star tattooed on his inner elbow.

"Buddy?" The word had almost no strength to it. She looked at the doctor and said, "Can he hear me?"

"Perhaps. We know very little about such states."

Claire found herself thinking of her father and his challenge, to have something to offer. Something to give in such a situation. The doctor stood patiently over her, watching. He had years of experience, watching and observing and waiting for a change.

Ashamed and unsettled within her own skin, yet driven by something she could not understand, she offered a silent prayer for the young man. Then she stood and allowed the doctor to lead her from the room.

The doctor's office was an oversized filing cabinet, with books and print-outs and forms and papers covering every surface. He hefted a pile from one chair, hesitated, then added to the pages on the windowsill. "Have a seat."

"Thanks," she said, liking the fact that no apology was made for the mess. Here was a man with few pretensions and no time for minor concerns.

With numb fingers, Claire pulled out her pad and flipped to a clean page. It took a moment to remember what it was she had intended to ask. "What did you mean when you said that these drugs are kept in the body for so long?"

"Like everything we ingest, hallucinogens are converted, or metabolized, by our bodies. Most of these metabolized drugs are neuro-toxic, and do not pass easily from the system. They are stored in fatty tissue, muscle tissue, or in the brain lining. As they are gradually released and flushed out over time, their effects are duplicated. Rarely is there enough to have a second hallucinogenic effect—what is typically referred to as a flashback. What is far more dangerous is that this gradual and undetected release kills brain cells very slowly, over a long period of time."

"Could you tell which drug he actually took?"

"Highly unlikely. These days there are new ones coming out all the time." He moved to the side table, lifted a pot from the burner, and asked, "Coffee?"

"Sure, thanks." More to have something warm to hold than because she was thirsty. The vision of that poor kid still lingered.

"The term designer drugs can mean two very different things. First of all, it can be an analogue, a compound similar to another already identified hallucinogen. Like LSD, only with minor alterations. One carbon or oxygen molecule might be shifted, for example. These variations on a known theme were quite popular for a time. As they were new, the drugs were not outlawed. But in 1986 Congress passed the Analogue Act, making all of these illegal as well." He poured her a cup, asked, "How do you take it?"

"Just milk, thanks."

"The other, more sophisticated, use of the term relates to a drug designed by a chemist."

"Thanks," she said, accepting the cup. "There are a lot of these?"

"Dozens. And growing more sophisticated all the time. These days, a drugmaker will select a desired effect and design his chemical with that end in mind. Others are taking pharmaceuticals already known to have neuro-transmission effects and altering them." He poured himself a cup, then walked behind his cluttered desk and settled into his seat. "The effects are amplified enormously. The problem is, of course, all side effects are exaggerated as well. Ecstasy, for example, was developed from an amphetamine, or speed. Increase the potency and you can raise the heartrate and blood pressure until the user's heart actually explodes. It and similar drugs also cause malignant hyperpyrexia, a condition where a perfectly healthy person simply gets too hot. The increased heartrate and rise in metabolic functions leads to liver and kidney failure."

She swallowed her queasiness. "That's what happened here?"

"No, not with Buddy. And this leads us to think he was using a non-amphetamine-based drug. This is an area of increased interest among the illegal chemists. People want longer highs, or trips, and they want to avoid the uncomfortable descent caused by speed-related drugs."

"You know a lot about this."

"Comes with the territory these days. Designer drug usage is skyrocketing at a rate not seen since the sixties. Party drugs are the new craze. MDMA, GBH, these are examples of drugs brought in from modern research in anesthesia. GBH is clinically known by the initials GHB, but the letters were switched around to stand for 'grievous bodily harm.' It actually separates the conscious mind from the more basic bodily functions. Ketamin is another, called Special-K on the street. The effect is similar, a detached euphoria."

She stared at him, seeing Buddy's rigid form silhouetted against the doctor's world-weary gaze. "Do you ever have nightmares?"

"Not any more." A sip from his cup, then, "Hardly ever."

She struggled to make sense of the jumble in her mind and heart. "Do you know anything about a drug called Nova?"

He nodded once, as though he had been waiting for the question. "You saw the Starsign on Buddy's arm?"

She bolted to full alert. "The what?"

"Starsign. That's what the kids call those star tattoos."

"Do you know how that's connected to the game?"

"Which game? Babylon?" He shook his head. "Only that a number of gamers use the drug. We know almost nothing about Nova. One day it was just another rumor. The next, talk of it was everywhere. You go to a nightclub these days, you'll see these tattoos on hundreds of kids."

"Or in one of the game arcades," she added.

"Those places are a menace. People who don't think games are addictive should take a look in our clinic. Drug usage and game playing are a vicious cycle, one drawing upon the other."

Claire made frantic notes. "You say the game playing and the drug usage go hand in hand?"

"They feed on each other." His tone had turned metallic. "We have outreach volunteers from a number of local churches, they go into the discos and arcades and try to talk with the kids. Our volunteers say they have never seen anything like this Nova, how closed up the kids become, as though they've been initiated into a secret sect. And we're seeing an increasing number of users in here. Or suspected users. We have not yet identified the metabolized compounds."

He glanced at his watch and rose swiftly to his feet. "I'm sorry, but I have another appointment that should have already started."

As they walked back down the hall, the sounds pierced to

her very soul. Most of the patients seemed so young. "Why do they take these drugs?"

"Energy, increased self-confidence, lack of inhibitions. The same reasons kids in the fifties drank liquor. And something more, especially with these newer, more sophisticated drugs. Being part of the scene has suddenly been pushed to the extreme. These drugs all have one thing in common—they release the person from ego-bound individuality. They actually perceive themselves becoming part of something bigger, greater, stronger than they would ever be on their own."

"It sounds like a religion," she observed quietly.

"Indeed, but a religion dedicated to what god?" His gaze looked ancient. "They become part of a new organism, one containing hundreds and hundreds of kindred spirits. They feel superior. They possess a knowledge lacking in the outside world. They claim allegiance to a new electronic oversoul."

He pushed the buttons to release the outer door, walked with her into the foyer, offered her his hand, and said, "Young people simply cannot survive on a diet of materialism. In a society that lacks a higher spiritual dimension, they will seek ways of their own to free the mind from the vicious material cycle. Drug-taking is just another symptom of an empty, godless culture."

Claire used the pay phone in the foyer to first call information, then a bar in Telluride where an acquaintance worked. Frankie was one of the odd collection of people Claire had befriended while fighting high-altitude fires. It was a risk calling her at all, much less making the request Claire had in mind, but something the doctor had mentioned had prompted an idea. Frankie heard her out in astonished silence, then promised to see what she could do. They made arrangements to talk later that evening, then Claire hung up and gratefully left the hospital. Although the foyer was silent, she felt as though the vast chamber echoed with what lay just beyond those reinforced doors.

Claire drove through the outer gates, then slowed and pulled to the curb when she spotted Buddy's sister standing under the bus-shelter. She rolled down her window and asked, "You came down from Colorado Springs by bus?"

"My car is in the shop," she replied simply. "And I needed to meet you."

"Hop in, I'll drive you home."

"Are you sure? I wouldn't want to be any bother."

Claire reached over and unlocked the passenger door. "I go right by Colorado Springs on the way back."

They drove for a time in silence before Sandra finally said, "Did you speak with Buddy?"

Hearing the quiet voice speak the name brought a sudden return to the hall and the room and the cries and the people and the body lying stiff on the mattress. Claire had to swallow the lump in her throat before she could reply, "I tried to."

"He was such a good kid, before he got involved in that game. I wish you could have met him."

"Dr. Diaz thinks it was a drug that has done this to your brother."

"Babylon *is* a drug. I watched it take hold of my brother and possess him. He was addicted. If he was taking some other drug, it was only to make the game stronger."

Claire shot a glance at the sister. "What did you say?"

"I said that Babylon is a drug." Her gaze remained locked tight upon the horror of her brother lying in an asylum. "Living in the material world doesn't have the answers. Buddy never accepted that. I tried to tell him about faith and Christ's gift of salvation. He treated it like a joke, something to push aside so he could get back to that evil game."

They drove on with their thoughts for noisy companions until Sandra began giving directions to her house. When they pulled up in front, Claire turned off the motor, hesitated, then confessed, "I said a prayer for your brother."

"It can only help," Sandra replied. "Would you like to come in?"

"I better be getting back. I still have to check by the office."

"I hope it was useful for you today."

"Very." Claire studied the woman beside her. "Thank you for arranging things."

Sandra's gaze was open and as direct as her words. "You mentioned back at the clinic that you were having doubts about your faith. Would you like to share them?"

Again there was a sudden swelling of her heart. This young woman had just returned from visiting her catatonic brother, yet was still able to show both interest and genuine concern for a total stranger. Claire pushed out a harsh breath in order to make room for the words, "I wouldn't even know where to begin."

"Then perhaps it would be a good idea if we were to pray together," Sandra replied. "Ask the Father to make your way straight for you."

This time Claire could only nod, the swelling matched by a pain of exquisite tenderness. She bowed her head and listened, and felt the words echoing deep inside.

"Heavenly Father, we thank You for this day. Despite its pain and sorrow, we give thanks for Your hand at work in our lives. We ask that You heal my brother." Sandra paused to gather herself and ease the tremor that rose in her voice. She swallowed, took a long breath, and continued, "Heal my brother, Lord. Make him well, both in body and mind and spirit. Use this as a lesson to draw him closer to You. Open his eyes and his ears to Your message. And Father, please find some way to get the example of my brother out, so that other young people will be warned away from this evil."

Another pause, then she continued, "My sister Claire has come to a hidden valley of her own, Father. You know her needs, You know her doubts and questions. Show her Your light, the brilliance that clears away all shadows and makes Your way known."

Claire felt herself flooded with a sense of peace so strong a sob escaped before she even realized she was crying. A stranger, a woman with pain and grief of her own, speaking with such calm assurance that her own heart was opened to receive. Sandra reached over, grasped her hand, held it tight for a moment, and continued, "Grant her the ability to discern what Your will is for her. Dear Jesus, bring her so tightly into Your blessed embrace that she can only know Your love, only know Your confident direction, only hear Your voice. Let her see with utter clarity that she is Yours, Father, Yours for all eternity. In Jesus' precious name do we pray, amen."

DENVER AND THE COLORADO HIGHLANDS

20

■ Donovan hung around his office far longer than needed, hoping that Claire would return in time for them to plan another evening together. When he did not hear from her, Donovan grew impatient, which surprised him as much as the fact that she was not there for him. He had a lifetime's experience of walking away from relationships that had grown uncomfortable. But here he was, hanging about, acting as though his evening could not begin until she arrived and took his arm.

This tall awkward redheaded girl held to an honesty and a sweetness which he hungered after. Her frankness was so straightforward he was left confronted by his own wiles. Claire was not strong in the sense of bulging muscles. She was strong in the sense of awareness and confidence. He liked that. There was nothing that excited him more than a challenge. The more he had her, the more he wanted, as if possessing her meant he could have this sweetness for himself.

It was her innocence that had kept Donovan from telling her about his drug experience in L.A. It had been there on his tongue to say, several times now, almost as though something beyond himself had been pressing him to speak about it. But confessions were not his way, and he had held back, not wanting to give her the wrong impression.

Twice during the night he tried her phone, letting it ring long enough to wake her up from a coma. But there had been no answer. And for some reason this had thrown him into a half-panic, which had surprised him even more. Jealousy was definitely not a part of his game plan.

The next morning he waited until he arrived at his office to call the newspaper. When she answered, impatience and disappointment turned his voice harsh. "Where have you been?"

"Yesterday I had to go to Pueblo," she said, and something in her voice said the day had cost her a lot.

He started to ask, What about last night? But he caught himself in time. He slowed down, tried for warmth. "I was worried. Can I see you today?"

"It wouldn't be a good idea."

"I really want to see you."

"Donovan," the word a long sigh. "I don't think—"

He lied, "I've arranged to take off today so we could be together."

"You did?"

"You said you wanted to know me better." He began

writing a list of people he needed to call, both to clear the day and to delay his L.A. trip. "This seemed like the perfect time."

Again the hesitation, then, "I've been able to arrange a contact through a friend. She's a . . . well, it has to do with work. I have to go up into the mountains today."

"I'll drive you up," he offered. "If that's the only way we can be together. But I'd rather take you somewhere skiing."

He expected her to come back with something like, Let's do that another time. Instead Claire told him flatly, "This is not a pleasure trip, Donovan. A friend of mine has arranged a contact with somebody who can talk about manufacturing illegal drugs."

But Donovan was too preoccupied with pressing his case to really hear what she was saying. "Well, at least this way we could enjoy the drive together. I'll be right over to pick you up."

"I don't understand what the motive is," Donovan was saying. "Hiking into the middle of nowhere to fight a forest fire. Where's the profit in that?"

Profit. The word rankled. It fit the clothes he was wearing and the car he was driving, but not the day's journey.

Donovan had come straight from the office, as though he had not wanted to give her time to change her mind. As she had settled in, he had stripped off his tie and coat, then donned a grey sweater that looked soft as a Himalayan's purr. Claire reached over, rubbed his sleeve, and had to smile. Going to meet a couple of illegal drug makers in his Armani slacks, polished shoes, and a cashmere sweater.

And the car. It was a Ford Explorer, one lined in leather

and polished as only a rental would be during a mountain winter. She asked, "Don't you have a car of your own?"

"Not any more." He seemed to take pride in the fact. "No house, no car, nothing but the clothes on my back, so to speak. The bank gives me an office, I rent my place in that downtown apart-hotel. It's all I need for the moment."

Despite herself, Claire was delighted to be with him again. Even so, the doubt and indecision remained a ball of tension that would not dissolve from her middle. Somehow praying with Sandra Wiggins yesterday made the disharmony she felt sitting there beside Donovan even sharper. "You're waiting for something?"

He glanced her way. "We were talking of this hobby of yours."

The day was pristine. A heavy snow had given over to a brilliant blue sky, and the mountains sparkled like gems. Claire turned from the scenery to plead, "Just answer this question, okay?"

"I know what I want," he replied tersely. "Until I can afford it, this will do just fine. Now tell me what's up there worth risking your life over."

She took him in, the strong cleft chin, clear blue eyes, ruddy blond hair. "Fighting a wildfire on a steep slope, not knowing what the wind is going to do from one minute to the next, not seeing anything beyond the next treeline, it's the toughest thing in the world."

Donovan shook his head emphatically. "Sorry. Starting a business from scratch with no money gets first prize."

"It was hard on you?" Claire asked, seeing the gritty determination weathered into his handsome face.

"Years beyond hard," he replied. "But let's save that for another day. I want to hear about the fires."

"Why? It's a world away from anything you know."

"That's part of it," he countered. "Plus I want to know how you've come to trust a drug dealer enough to put your life in his hands. That's what you're doing, you know."

"Her hands. The dealer is a girl," she said, mildly disappointed with his response. Knowing she had hoped to hear something like, *I want to know because I want to know what has made you who you are.* Feeling now that the words might never come.

She turned back to the day and the hills. "Fighting an out-of-control fire is the work of crazies. Either you're crazy in love with the hills or just pure crazy. There are a lot of both up there. You stay alive by knowing who is working to either side, and trusting your team with your life. It's that simple."

The memories began rushing back then, etched so clearly against the deep blue sky she could almost smell the smoke. "There are some truly funny moments, too. Not at the time, of course. There's no space for humor right then. No space for anything except racing to the next crisis. But afterwards. Sitting in the camp, everybody soot-smudged and bone-tired, even smiling is an effort. But laughing just the same, so full of the joy of living, of making it through, and doing something really meaningful at the same time."

"Risking your life to put out a fire on somebody else's land doesn't sound like joking material to me."

"I guess you have to be there." Sensing he did not really want to know what it was like, sitting there at night. And hurting because he seemed so focused upon himself and his own life that there was so little space for her. She glanced at him, and wondered if perhaps she had known this all along but simply had not wanted to see beyond his appeal.

She turned to her window and let the memories of the camps and the shared nights surge up. Times like that, the stories came out. Anything that could take away the danger-taste, the bile that spilled up sometimes in the exhaustion afterwards, when people slipped down inside themselves and realized just how close they had come to the final passage. Then the stories began, the teller so weary the words were slurred, but still people listening with a tight focus, searching for a reason to push the worry aside with a good laugh. Claire loved those moments, the sense of bonding so strong it brought tears to her eyes, there alongside the shaking laughter over the thought of what she had found coming around a corner in the trail.

She decided to try one more time. "The last time I went up was the week before I met you at Swindley's party. I was running along a ridgeline when the path did this jink and suddenly dropped down into the woods. No warning, nothing on the map, but suddenly I was slanting down three hundred feet and couldn't see anything up ahead except trees and the next curve. I could smell the smoke, but I couldn't find the fire.

"I was on point. There were six of us running in line, calling out to keep in touch when the smoke thickened and there was nothing on the radio but static. We kept jogging along, shouting back to the trio dragging the heavy equipment to hurry, when suddenly I spotted a burst of flames from a tree up ahead."

Donovan was silent and watchful, a straight stretch of

road permitting him to glance her way and observe the smile on her lips. His own expression remained unreadable.

The fact that he was finally listening made the memories more vivid. "Then I stopped cold. Wham! Straight in front of me, maybe fifty yards ahead, this full-grown elk came barreling around the next bend. I flattened myself to the side of the trail, and I think I shouted something to the team, but I'm really not sure, I was that shocked. I couldn't get far off the trail, the undergrowth was so thick I couldn't do anything but push it in some. Afterwards I found I had maybe a dozen thorn tears right through my coveralls, but at the moment I didn't feel a thing.

"That elk looked big as a mountain. And fast. It came thundering by on hooves like anvils. I could feel the earth shaking. But I couldn't spend much time watching the elk because about then I saw what was chasing it—a pair of full-grown black bears, running directly towards me fast. It was incredible to see something that big and ungainly move at that speed.

"About then, the earth under my feet just gave way, and suddenly I was sprawled halfway across the trail. I did my best imitation of a plow, pushing myself back further, but those bears just kept on moving, ran right past, and didn't even look my way. I looked back up the path, just in time to see about two dozen bunny rabbits come bounding around the bend, hot on the trail of those bears."

Donovan waited a minute, asked, "That was funny?"

She nodded, going no further. The memories were too pure, too good to be shared if he couldn't understand. Or wouldn't. It had not been funny then, with the smoke and the heat and the danger and the urgency of it all. But worth a shared grin later.

Or their team, that was another hoot. The wispy waiter from one of Telluride's hottest restaurants, probably weighed less than his fire gear, screeching like a wounded crane as he beat flames from the coat of the bulldoze operator. Then, when that didn't put out the fire, he catapulted onto the back of the burly man, throwing him to the ground, with the fire blanket wrapped around both of them, and rolled around in the dirt. Two guys who wouldn't normally have shared a word, much less a blanket, hugging each other for all it was worth, even when the fire was out, still too locked in panic to let go. Just laying there together in a ten-inch fire ditch, tighter than lovers, chests heaving with the strain.

He repeated his earlier question. "You're sure this contact of yours is trustworthy?"

"I've known Frankie for almost ten years," she replied and suddenly found herself thinking about the black doctor, Gary, another of her team. The last time up, Frankie had tripped over a fallen tree limb and badly sprained her knee. Gary had carried Frankie, this hard-eyed bargirl and part-time drug dealer, with her butch haircut and neo-Nazi tattoos, three miles over brush with the flames licking at their heels. It was totally crazy, what danger brought out in people.

On the back of that memory came another. It had been that same night, just two weeks ago. As they sprawled in exhaustion around the fire, Claire had watched Frankie limp over to where Gary sat reading his Bible, as he did every night. Frankie had sat down beside him and started talking softly. Gary had listened gravely, the fire turning his dark features into carvings of onyx, then lifted the Bible in his lap and began pointing out things to her. Frankie the drug dealer and serious party girl had just sat there quietly, a tear trickling down one smudged cheek. For some reason the scene had burned a hole into Claire's heart.

When Claire had called Frankie back after returning from Pueblo the night before, it had been a totally different woman on the line. One who informed her that she had stopped dealing and was planning to go back to school. Joyful. That was how she had sounded, though still willing to use old contacts to help Claire out. She was both joyful and excited over the changes in her life.

The word came to her again, as clear as the other morning when Nathan had spoken it aloud. *Choose.* Claire glanced over at Donovan, knew she was still too weak to tell him what she was thinking. Not yet. So she said quietly, "If Frankie says these people will treat me right, that's exactly what they'll do."

Their destination was one of a hundred such towns dotting the Colorado highlands. Their locations were marked by interstate signposts which tourists glimpsed and swiftly forgot. Such villages were ignored by the development scramble— either because of mountainsides too steep to use as ski runs, or valleys too narrow for development, or a dozen other reasons.

This particular town was marred by a series of high-altitude mines. From where she sat, they looked like giant worm-holes in the mountainside. The pit openings had long tongues of stone and debris falling alongside the rail-tracks used to bring down the ore. Further down, warehouses climbed the jagged cliff faces like giant metal staircases. The entire scene held a dismal, abandoned air.

They entered the town along a street so rutted that traffic meandered in weaving lines from sidewalk to sidewalk. There was no activity at the railheads, no smoke from the smelters. "The mines have played out," she told him. "Either the locals find work at one of the ski villages, or they go on welfare, or they leave."

"You've been here before?"

"There are towns like this all over Colorado. At least this one's within driving distance of Vail." She glanced at her notes, spotted a street sign, and said, "Silver Street, that's our right turn."

The sidewalks were empty, save for a few stragglers and a couple of winos. The cars parked near dirty snowdrifts were mostly of seventies vintage. More than half the storefronts were boarded over. For sale signs sprouted everywhere. "The locals shop at the big chain stores nowadays. Half the houses are rented out to kids working the slopes of luckier villages. They pack in, eight kids to a two-bedroom house, and build their lives in the towns where they can't afford to sleep. Villages like this have lost their heart."

"So let's leave."

"Soon." They passed a long line of dwellings hardly larger than shacks, each with a postage stamp lawn. Years ago these would have been occupied by families of hard-rock miners. Now they looked lonely and forlorn.

The houses ended, giving way to hard-scrabble earth and stumpy pines. Up ahead the road swerved towards a saddle-back pass between two cliffs, with a small lake at its base.

Again Claire checked her notes, then pointed ahead. "Turn in there."

"Here?" Donovan turned into the restaurant's rutted lot. "This is the place?"

Despite her own nerves, his tone made her smile. "You were expecting a rendezvous at the Hilton?"

"I don't know what I was expecting, but it sure wasn't this." The restaurant was a locals-only sort of place. Pickups sprouted heavy layers of grime, rifle-racks, CB antennas, and the occasional set of ten-point antlers instead of front bumpers. The sign said, "The Claim Jumper, breakfast all day."

"I'm out here to meet with illegal drug makers," Claire reminded him. She climbed from the car, striving to mask her own nerves with a lecture. "They don't pay to advertise. Or stick out, or show up where they're not known. They'll choose a spot somewhere in the back of beyond, then make their returns to civilization someplace where the locals don't particularly care for the law."

Together they entered the restaurant, ignored the stares cast their way, and settled into a corner booth. Claire studied her menu until Donovan leaned across the table, lowered his voice, and said, "Most of these guys look perpetually dazed."

"Probably coming off a major high. Makes mornings hard to face." She scanned the crowd and saw exactly what she expected to find. "These are the people who keep the tourist world running smoothly. They operate the snowplows, build the homes, dig the basements, pave the roads, lay the pipe. They can't live in the resorts they build and staff, so they travel up to twenty miles each way to work—remember, this is twenty miles of mountain road, come snow or fog or freezing rain. It's a tough life."

"So why do they do it?"

"The pay for some, for others because they love the mountains and didn't have the good sense to choose better parents." She returned her attention to the menu. "Folks in these towns develop an attitude, if they didn't have one to begin with."

The guy came in then. She knew it was her contact as soon as she raised her eyes. He was blond and scraggly bearded, with the weak raspy voice of a dedicated night-flyer. He knew everybody in the place, made his way over trading high-fives and comments about past flights. His face was beyond alert. His eyes held a manic intensity. He swept the room before focusing tight on her, then Donovan. He glanced back through the entrance, then walked over, sliding in beside her. He announced, "Jason didn't say nothing about no third party."

"It's okay. He's a friend."

"Hey, that's just grand and all. But Jason said a tall chick with red hair. Nothing about a guy."

"Okay." Seeing that arguing was futile, she turned to Donovan and said, "You'll have to wait for me."

He glanced around. "Here?"

"Besides," the guy added, "the scooter doesn't have room for no third party."

"You can wait in the car," she said to Donovan, then turned to the guy. "Excuse me?"

"I mean," the guy replied, "we coulda stuck him on the sled, but it's already full. And besides, Jason said just you."

"A scooter and a sled. How grand." Turning back to Donovan. "You want to stay. Believe me."

"I'm trying." A pause, a glance at the wild-eyed guy, then, "Will you be safe?"

"Relax," the guy said, sliding out and rising to his feet. "We're not gonna hurt the lady. We're just your basic pharmaceutical company on the rise."

She slid from the booth, patted Donovan's shoulder, and said, "Okay, let's get this over with."

To call the scooter modified would be like describing an Indy car as an automobile with wider tires. The hood had been stretched a full two feet, with a hole cut in the top to accommodate the chrome air intake. Instead of the maker's emblem on the front, there was a skull-and-crossbones. Claire took a long look and asked, "Chevy?"

"Naw." He swung one leg over with the proud action of a cowboy straddling an unbroke stallion. "Ford modified four. I was holding out for a straight six, but hey, this thing gets going, you're gonna think you're riding a solid fuel rocket."

"How reassuring," she said, but the guy didn't hear her, as he chose that moment to fire the scooter up. There was a pair of blasts, like a stubborn Harley chopper starting cold, then the sound of a rapid-fire cannon barrage.

The guy did not even bother to try and speak, just handed her a helmet and motioned for her to hang on and hold tight.

Uphill was bad. The saddleback was assaulted with a speed that threatened to pull her off, a g-force so strong her only hope lay in squeezing every shred of breath from the guy's body.

Downhill was awful. They crested the ridge and cleared it, their overloaded sled the only thing which kept them from flying into the treetops. Claire gave a good scream at that one, but was saved from embarrassment because the guy was whooping too, only he did it out of glee.

Claire could not even close her eyes because she needed to lean with him for the turns. They rammed through snowbanks at thirty miles an hour and more, the motor roaring and white exploding around them like it was hit by a mortar round. Snow struck her with the force of shotgun pellets. They hurtled around trees, the guy taking the forested slope like an obstacle course, sliding by so close the lower branches whipped at her face and shoulders.

By the second ridgeline she was growing used to the prospect that she might survive this after all. She even managed to breathe every once in a while. When they leapt over the third ridge, and she saw a bowl-shaped depression with cabins at the center, she cried out in relief. The guy took it as a challenge, whooped in reply, and opened the throttle up full. She buried her head in his shoulder, and prepared herself for oblivion.

Instead, a few moments later he cruised to a halt, cut the motor, and said, "Thank you for flying with Untied Airlines."

Claire released her death's grip from his chest, and on the second try found enough strength in her legs to stagger off the scooter.

It was only when she was standing that she realized she had been too scared to be cold. She walked around, trying to stomp feeling back into her feet and hands. Then she turned back and croaked, "I've spent all my life avoiding guys like you. Now I know why."

The grin did not shift a notch. "Better be quick. You don't want to make the return trip after dark."

The door opened behind her, and a voice from the bottom of a barrel said, "You Claire?"

"Yes." She turned to face a black bear in coveralls and a checked lumberjack shirt. "Jason?"

"Come on in." He turned and vanished into interior shadows.

Claire took a moment to catch her breath and look around. The circular bowl was perhaps a mile wide and lined by steep peaks save for two passes—the one through which they had come and another directly behind the cabins. The snow-covered expanse was treeless, except for a stand of pines decorating the run-up to the second pass. The cloudless sky was colored the spectacular blue-black found solely in such rarified reaches. The only sounds were those of several voices and a muffled generator somewhere out back.

The stillness was oppressive. She had never felt so far from the comfort of the known, even though she had often hiked such hidden highland valleys in the summer. She stared at the central cabin's open door, and felt her veneer of safety utterly shattered.

A voice from inside shouted, "You coming or what?"

"Be right there." As she mounted the porch steps, a stocky woman holding a high-powered rifle and a pair of Zeiss binoculars watched her with a hard gaze. Another guard, this one male, scrunched along a well-trod path to her right. Claire entered the cabin, waited for her eyes to adjust, and heard the deep voice say, "Frankie said she could vouch for you."

"We've been together on a fire-fighting team since we were teenagers."

"A hero."

"No, just a lover of the mountains and the woods."

The chair creaked complainingly as he shifted his weight. "Well, come on in and shut the door."

Light came from the front windows and a pair of open bulbs. The cabin was warm, comfortable, and spartan. The back wall served as a kitchen. Heat came from a central wood-burning stove. The cabin's far side was curtained off, but the curtain was flung back to reveal a half-dozen bunk beds. The unfinished floor was covered with an ancient Navajo rug. The table and chairs were scarred from much use. A battery-powered boom box and a multi-wave radio/transmitter sat on a shelf beneath a series of racks that climbed the nearest wall. The racks were all full and held a variety of armaments and bandoliers. Claire spotted the curved clip of a machine pistol and felt a queasiness gather in her middle. She hoped it did not show. "Who owns all this land?"

"What I heard was, you wanted to talk about drugs." The guy's dark beard was so scraggly his mouth was barely visible. "Why don't you just stick to that."

The rear door was flung back, and a spindly figure announced, "Hey, it's company of the female variety. Outstanding!"

The guy wore a filthy lab coat and an oversized sweater that hung almost to his knees. He crossed to the front window, peered through, and demanded, "Has Gretta made it back?"

"Not yet." Jason checked his watch. "She's not the most reliable courier I've ever had, not by any stretch. But she's never been this late before."

"She'll get here." The guy called Chef turned back, hiked over on too-long legs, peered down at Claire, and declared, "You're what's her name, Frankie's friend, the writer."

"Reporter. Claire." Every nerve in her body was screaming danger. There were no rules here. None. No safety net if something went wrong or this guy decided it was the proper moment to go off the wall.

"Wild. And look where it's got you to." The guy was a merry trickster, with the untamed eyes of a wizard. Or jester. It was hard to tell. "I'm Chef."

Claire tried hard to gather herself. She was here to do a job. But the sense of unleashed threat was almost overpowering. She asked the newcomer with his frizzy hair, "You're the scientist?"

The rail-thin guy puffed out with pride. He looked very strong, with muscles like taut wire cables. "Hear that? Recognition at last."

Claire fumbled for her pad and pen. "How did you wind up out here?"

"Jason's idea. We hole up here when winter shuts out the world. All the hunters know to stay away from this place. Summers," he paused and tossed a glance towards Jason, "we're elsewhere."

"Drugs," Jason said, still wary. "That's what Frankie said you wanted to know about."

Claire acknowledged the orders with a nod. "So what can you tell me about your operation?"

"We are exalted members of the original Kleptonian Neo-American Church," the wiry guy announced proudly. Jason leaned back in his chair, rolled his eyes, and sighed loudly. The chemist ignored him. "We have three basic principles. First, psychedelic substances are religious sacraments. Second, use of these is a basic religious right. And third, we encourage ingesting them in gradual stages."

Claire pretended to take notes. She had never felt more completely out of place. Never. "Interesting."

"The church is an absolute monarchy. It is also authoritarian, xenophobic, and indifferent to most social issues."

"Drugs," Jason repeated. "Talk about them."

Chef gave a happy sigh. "So much to cover, so little time."

"Start with the basics," Jason suggested. "Like LSD."

"A synthetic non-starter," Chef snorted. "About as natural a product as plutonium."

"I hate that," Jason growled, leaning forward with a force that threatened to topple the chair. "Oh, wow, it's harsh 'coz it's synthetic. Welcome to the nineties, man, the synthetic generation."

"You're too much." The wiry guy winked at Claire.

This was clearly old territory—two guys locked together for months at a time, with little to do except argue. To Claire he explained, "This guy stays stoned on 2CB. Talk about a mental expectorant."

"You're crazy." There was only mild heat to the response, which was good, since Jason was of a size that promised serious damage to anyone who got him riled. "You want to dive in, get it all the first go. 2CB is delicate. You take it, then learn to let it take you."

Chef's frame was perpetually taut, the muscles on his neck cording as he shot back, "I prefer the natural route. Natural foods, natural high. Anything the matter with that?"

"Not so long as you prefer to keep your highs in the last century."

"Oh, right." Chef turned back to Claire, and gathered himself as though preparing to leap into flight. "Okay, psilocybin, you've heard of that. It's the primary goody from 'shrooms. But there are other chemicals we're just getting a handle on. Baeostasin is a good example. Now we're taking a look at what happens to a drug after the body has ingested and metabolized it."

Claire struggled to keep up. "Where did you study?"

"Berkeley. Took me years to unlearn the stuff they wrap chemistry in these days." The over-bright eyes reminded Claire of a moth circling a flame, coming ever closer to the ultimate burn-out. "Look. When you take a psychedelic, your body changes the chemical. Purifies it into what can pass through the blood-brain barrier. This process is called metabolization. So what we're doing now is trying to identify these metabolized compounds and produce them ourselves. Send out these drugs of ultimate purity, weaving a new magic carpet for the nineties."

Jason crossed massive arms across his chest. "Great stuff, long as you like your drugs prechewed."

Claire hesitated, then decided it was time to ask, "What can you tell me about a drug called Nova?"

"Top of the list," Chef announced. "A major find."

"Listen to him now," Jason scoffed. "All of a sudden, synthetics are okay."

"There are exceptions to every good rule," Chef responded. "Nova has it all. Total shift on reality. Lets you loose to go where you want, how you want."

She felt herself tighten down, another sliver of the puzzle taking shape. The journey had been worthwhile after all. Maybe. If she got out of this in one piece. "You're producing it here?"

"Much as we can." Jason now, the business side of the partnership. "Got clients wanting everything we can make and more."

"I'm into making mental explosions, setting off total evolutions of the mind. Nova is the guided missile of designer drugs," Chef continued. "So powerful you can't even ingest it except in micro doses."

Claire nodded as she wrote, hoping it looked like she was staying up with them, understanding it all. "So this stuff is too strong to take in tablet form?"

They both laughed. Chef answered, "Put a drop on your tongue, they'd be peeling little bits of you off the ceiling."

"Permanent orbit," Jason agreed. "Out beyond Pluto, screaming through deep space with the comets for company."

"Is that normal?"

"Listen, this stuff redefines normal." Chef ran nervous hands through his grizzled scalp. "This is something totally new. You take it, you have the power to *create reality*. Actuality is yours to command, change, alter, all by the power of thought."

"Like the freaks have been saying all along," Jason agreed, his voice a metronome on slow gear compared to Chef. "The world is yours to command. You don't like it, change things around."

"All you need with Nova," Chef went on, "is some way to channel your thoughts. Focus your attention."

"You mean," Claire interrupted, "like with a video game?"

"Sure. Then whatever you see or think or want, it instantly becomes real. You know what that means?"

"Thoughts aren't trapped in your head any more," Jason told her. "Reality can't ever hold you down. Not ever again."

"All you need," Chef continued, "is to put a Starsign on your arm, or neck, or anywhere else that a vein comes close to the skin. Stay zoned for hours."

"A Starsign," Claire repeated. "That's the name for the little star tattoo, right?"

"The tattoo and the tab," Jason corrected her. "People who use the drug a lot like to get tattooed, it's like a badge that proclaims they're part of the newest thing. They're wearing star-shaped jewelry too, from what I hear."

"The tabs are little holograms, we get them with the chemicals." Chef shot a nervous glance at Jason, who had started to frown mightily, and changed course. "They're star-shaped because that's where you're headed. The next galaxy."

"The next reality, " Jason corrected.

"So all the Nova tabs are star-shaped, drug-saturated decals." Claire made swift notes. "Have you ever heard of a game called Babylon?"

"Sure. We . . ."

There was a snarling roar in the distance. Instantly the two men tensed, as though an electric current had been switched on. Chef said, "It's about time."

"That doesn't sound like her scooter," Jason muttered.

Shouts started from beyond the distant cabin. The snarling machines whined up into impossible revs, then there was a booming from outside; first close to the porch, then farther off in a series of echoes. And voices. Shouting and slicing through the silence so powerfully they were all on their feet before the first echoes ended.

The front door slammed back. A wild-eyed guardswoman shouted, "Visitors!"

"Out the back," Jason barked, more at the chemist than at Claire. "You know the drill."

She had been half-expecting something ever since her arrival. Now that the crisis had come, Claire could not respond. She watched the wiry scientist race through the back door, only to be replaced by two women and the guy from her scooter. Jason was already by the side cabinet, handing out guns and ammo. She managed, "What is—"

"Move!" He was all business, crisp and direct and steely. "Take cover out back. *Now!*"

Another pair of blasts, one close in, the second farther off, spurred her to flight. She reached the back door and crouched with the handle still in her grip, when it was abruptly slapped away. She knelt out of reflex, searched, saw no one near her. Then she spotted the splintered hole at the top of the door. A bullet had passed within ten inches of her head.

She dove off the porch and into the snow, scrambling for the meager protection of the cabin's rock support. Another boom, muffled and thumping the air, and Claire saw the nearest scooter go up in flames. The shots were coming fast and furious from the front of the cabin.

A skier flew by, headed out and away towards the stand of

trees and the closest ridgeline. Claire recognized the chemist. She raised one hand and screamed, "*Wait!*" He paid her no mind.

The air overhead was ripped apart. Again. The third machine-gun burst shattered the window directly above her, showering her with glass. She leapt to her feet and bolted in the direction from which the skier had come.

She rounded the corner, saw two overturned scooters lodged in the snow with gunmen using them for cover, and dove into a shed. She huddled on the dirt floor as two holes appeared overhead with a shower of splinters, followed by a pair of piercing booms.

Her panic gave the moment a timeless quality, granting her the space to think, That's what it sounds like to be on the receiving end of a shotgun. Claire used light from the new holes to sort through the cross-country boots scattered about the floor, picking out a pair meant for a woman's foot. She found it almost impossible to fit them on, her hands were shaking so hard. Trying to tie the laces almost had her weeping in frustration. But they had to be tied, and tight, or she would never make it.

Finally taut, she slipped the over-flap into place, scrambled to her knees, grabbed skis and poles, fitted her toes into the cross-country bindings, and when the guns paused for a brief moment, she pounced.

The depression sloped slightly downhill behind the cabins, granting her a chance to build up speed as she pushed hard for the trees. She followed the other tracks, fleeing with great gasping thrusts of her skis and poles. The treeline was a hundred yards ahead, an infinity of white distance. Another pair of bursts to her right showed they were still firing in her direction. She found more strength than she knew she had, her speed not decreasing a bit as the slope began to rise towards the trees and the ridge.

She passed the first tree with a cry of relief, only to be spurred to even greater effort when the second tree blew wood-splinters at her face. She ducked and weaved, racing up the steepening slope. Each sliding step was a grunt and a push and a slide, her muscles beginning to tremble with the strain.

Through the last stand of trees, the ridgeline became visible just ahead. Her chest heaved and sobbed in a desperate effort to draw in enough breath.

Out of the trees she surged, cresting the pass, not even trying to duck as more gunfire sounded behind her, afraid the move would unbalance her and send her sprawling, for the ridge's other side was a tremendously steep drop.

She did not even pause, just pulled back as far as she could, lifting the tips of her skis out of the dry powder, flying faster than she had ever gone on cross-country skis. Her heart felt ready to burst. The tears streaming from her eyes froze to her cheeks in the sudden wind. Bending the inside knee almost to where it met the ski, she leaned into impossible turns. Trees whipped by so fast they blurred into threatening green shields, the forward branches protruding like hungry lances.

Then she was at the slope's base, the ground rising before her towards the next ridge. She stopped by falling over, her limbs shaking so hard she could only collapse in a heap. Overhead and behind, thunder continued to echo in a deep blue sky. She lay there for several dozen breaths, until the first shreds of strength started to return and the sudden silence spurred her to move.

Standing up was a series of groans, testing each joint in turn, vastly amazed that everything appeared to be still intact. She brushed the snow from her jeans and sweater, her bare hands icy and rubbed raw by the pole straps. Claire checked the sky. Another half-hour before the sun went below the ridgeline. She checked the shadows, tremendously relieved to find she was headed in the right direction.

She started off, ignoring her body's protests. She had to hurry. She did not want to spend a night out in the open.

COLORADO HIGHLANDS

■ Claire settled deeper into the Explorer's leather seat, sipped from her cup, and sighed in genuine relief to be safe and headed home. But Donovan's presence offered no comfort. Instead, he radiated tension. She tried to break through to him with, "Who do you think was behind the attack?"

"Who knows?" Donovan's tone was clipped and tight. "The whole thing is crazy."

"What do you mean?" Donovan's reaction surprised and disturbed her. Something more than concern about her safety had surfaced as she had explained her story and her research. It had only intensified as she had described her escape from the lab. She probed with the thought, "A turf war between freako chemists is my guess. They sure didn't act like police. There wasn't any warning or rights or anything that I heard."

"That's not what I was talking about." He held the steering

wheel in a knuckle-white grip, and ground the leather back and forth. "I can't believe I let you go off like that."

Claire leaned against the Explorer's far door, his suit-coat wrapped around her shoulders. The heater was on high, and she had finally stopped shaking. Her hands were wrapped around a styrofoam cup of hot chocolate. They ached like the rest of her, and blisters were forming between thumb and forefinger where the ski-pole's strap had rubbed the skin raw. "It wasn't your decision."

He gave her an exasperated glance. "What did you find out there that was worth risking your life?"

"Maybe nothing." Headlights swept by on the interstate's far side, illuminating his creased forehead and angry gaze. "Maybe a lot. I've got to go over this more carefully."

"And what about me? My reputation is on the line in this mess too, you know. What was I supposed to say to the world if you hadn't come back?"

"But I came back, Donovan. I'm right here." And then, for some reason, she found herself smiling at the memory of her return.

She had skied into the cafe parking lot just before dusk, to find him sitting behind the wheel of the Explorer. Papers had been spread all over the place, and he was dictating into his little recorder. Like he was in a plane, or waiting for some appointment, the lumberjacks and hunters going in and out of the cafe staring at him, Donovan doing his best to ignore them entirely.

Claire had skied right up to his car, knowing she had to get the whole way before stopping. Her strength had given out then, and slowly she had sank to the wet and muddy pavement.

Which had brought a couple dozen faces to the restaurant's front window.

Donovan scrambled out, picked her up, and carried her around. He almost tripped over her skis, which were still attached to her feet. He had no idea how to get them off, and she couldn't explain it to him because suddenly she was giggling too hard. The poles remained attached to her hands, just dangling over his back as he lifted her and carried her around. He took off the skis by unlacing the shoes, then settled her into the car. She felt the softness of the leather seat, and the warmth of the car, and finally allowed herself to accept that she had made it out alive.

Now, as Donovan drove in grim silence back towards Denver, Claire watched him in the light of the passing headlights. It was strange, that anger of his. "What's the matter with you?"

"I get driven up on a wild goose chase, and you ask me that?"

"There's something going on here," she said, searching his face in the half light, wishing it was only concern for her well-being that had him so wound up. "I wish I knew what was going on in that head of yours."

"That's simple enough." Her words only seemed to increase his anxiety. "There I was, thinking we'd have a chance to get to know each other—"

"I told you what we were doing, and you said you wanted to go."

"And what happens, but I get left in this stinking hole of a mountain town, in a muddy parking lot, for six hours, while you go off to the back of beyond and get shot at." He glared at her. "Does that clear things up any?"

"Thank you for being so concerned about me," she said, her sarcasm muted by fatigue.

"Look," he snapped back. "I think you should stop it. This story is taking over your life."

For a moment she was so stunned she could not take it in. "Stop?"

"You heard me. What is there about a computer game and a couple of druggies that's worth getting killed over?"

The weight of his words gathered in her stomach like stones. "This is my story, Donovan."

"That's right. A *story*. One today, another tomorrow, another the day after that. The same day this one winds up on the bottom of a bird cage."

It was not that his words hurt so much. It was the message behind them. That he understood so little about her and her dreams. Or cared. "This is what I do."

"No it's not. This is just one story. Go find another."

"Just like that?" Her voice sounded drained, as grey as she felt inside. "I think this is really important."

"That's crazy." His words pushed at her, filled with his determination to drive her off the search. "You're so caught up in the thrill that you've lost sight of what's real."

"Not now, Donovan." The air felt so thin it would not fill her lungs. "I'm exhausted."

"Exactly. You're so tired you're slurring your words. And for what? You almost got yourself killed out there." When she remained silent, he shook his head and muttered, "You haven't heard a word I've said."

"Oh yes I have." She sighed, and closed her eyes against the world. "All too well."

They did not speak another word the entire trip back to Denver. Claire spent most of the time slipping in and out of quick dozes, waking up to the thunk of the tires over a rough spot, or bright lights coming around a curve towards them, or a horn, or her heart. Each time she glanced over at Donovan, and felt the pain anew.

She could watch him in safety now, as he was focused upon the driving and his own anger, which she still did not fully understand. Mainline Computers was partners with Swindley, and Swindley was partners with the bank where he worked. But she could not believe that some minor thread like this would cause such a reaction.

She started to ask him, then stopped, because there was another side to her reflection—one which said this was the perfect moment to stop it all, call it off, step back and away. And this was what hurt most of all. Not that she was losing him, but that in accepting this message, she was forced to realize she had never had him at all.

Donovan pulled up in front of her house and stopped, still staring out the front window. Claire slid from the seat and said quietly, "Thank you for driving me up today."

He looked at her long enough to say, "I'll call you once I get to Los Angeles."

She shut the door, then stood and watched the car speed away.

Claire entered the house, and forced her legs to climb to her floor. She unlocked her door, picked up the phone, and called Harry's number from memory. She let it ring a dozen times, shedding her coat and wrap. Finally she set down the receiver, leaned against the wall, and was struck by a different need. Another thought, one so surprising she was certain it had not come from herself. She picked up the phone and dialed another number.

When Nathan answered, she said, "I'm so tired I feel it down in my bones. If I slept a thousand years, I couldn't get rid of the weight."

Nathan was quiet a long moment before replying, "Your soul is tired."

"That's it." The tone of quiet understanding forced her to swallow the welling sadness. "That's it exactly."

"I discovered something when I was in that place," he said, his voice as gentle as she had ever heard it. "I found that if I was tired because I was trying to do what I felt the Lord wanted, it was all right. It still hurt. But it was okay to hurt."

Her first thought was not of what had tired her out, but rather of Donovan. And Harry. A tear leaked out from under her closed eyelids. "I've made a terrible mistake."

"We all have, at one time or another."

She swallowed again, and strained to breathe without sobbing. She slid down the wall to sit upon the floor. "Not like this."

"Is it your job?"

"No. Well, that's why I'm tired. Part of the reason." She felt the comfort of her father's silence, knew he was inviting her to continue. Not demanding. Not even asking. Just there, if she needed to talk. Which she did. "I think maybe I'm doing what God wants, but that's not been the main reason why I've been doing it."

Nathan sighed, then said, "You don't know how marvelous it is to hear you say those words."

"It doesn't feel marvelous to say them. It feels awful." She wiped at her cheek. "And then there's this other thing. A guy."

"Not Harry?"

"No." The tremors took her then, but she managed, "I feel like I've dirtied my soul."

"I understand."

His quiet strength, his listening without condemning, broke her down entirely. It was a long moment before she could go on. "What do I do?"

"Repent," he said, soft enough for the words not to scar. "Repent and ask the Savior's healing grace."

"I don't know if I've ever really prayed," she confessed, too disheartened to stand behind her pride.

"In the twelfth chapter of John, Jesus tells us to walk in the light while it is still shining." He paused a moment and then went on, "You see this as a hurt, a wounding so great you feel shattered by it."

"That's right," she whispered. "That's exactly right."

"See it also as what has brought you to the place where you can look beyond yourself," Nathan told her. "Respond to His call while you have a chance. Come home in prayer. Ask God to bind you closer. Seek to know him better."

She tried to control her trembling breath enough to ask, "You really think He still wants me?"

The sudden smile in his voice rang through as he said,

"My beloved daughter, the only whole heart is one which has been broken and then put back together by God."

Claire sat at her window in the tiny top-floor room, and watched night close in with the snow. And the wind. Time flew past in great fitful bursts of white, illuminated by the light from her window. All the thousands of swirling thoughts and questions, with no way to manage them, no way out. Except one.

She pushed back her chair, making room there at the window to go down on her knees. Feeling the sense of despair and defeat rise up, engulfing her with the frustration of finally giving in.

Then the feeling was gone, pushed aside with such tremendous force that it would have terrified her, had it not been so gentle. There in its place was a silence so complete she heard nothing, thought nothing beyond the snow's light tapping on her window, and her shallow breathing, and the single gifted realization.

At last she was doing what her Father wanted.

The power of that attainment was enough for her to bow her head. And begin to pray in peace. For the very first time.

■ "Can I help you?"

Claire stepped closer to the inquiries desk. "I was wondering if I could get some information on who owns a parcel of land."

"Depends." Beady eyes peered at her through half-moon spectacles. The man's white shirt was ancient and two sizes too big. His scrawny neck had a full inch of play inside the collar. "You got a location?"

"Sort of. It's up in the highlands."

"A sort of location." The man humphed a quick laugh. "Well, I guess I can give you a sort of answer. Towns are sectioned by lot and block number."

"It's not inside a town."

"You sure? Heaps easier looking inside a township. And it's hard to tell sometimes exactly where their lines ended. Amazing how big some of the mountain towns used to be. You see them now, you forget they mighta had ten times the population back when they were still mining the hills."

"I'm sure." Claire glanced around. The Assessor's Office was located in the basement of the oldest state government building in Colorado. The grand facades and luxurious marble foyer did not extend down here. Fluorescent lights marched into the distance, illuminating endless rows of metal shelves and bundled papers. The air smelled musty. "This is land out in the middle of nowhere."

"Well, that's different." He had the accent of the country-bred, and a quick light to his eyes. "Open range is listed according to the number of lines east or west of the New Mexico Line Meridian."

"You got me there." Claire smiled her thanks and started to turn away. "It was a long shot to begin with."

"Well hang on, don't go rushing off. Ain't exactly like we're on fire down here." He swept his arm around, taking in the pair of men in dark suits huddled in the far corner, pouring over a detailed map. Otherwise the cavernous basement was empty. "You see any other pretty gals wanting to waste my time?"

"I'm afraid that's exactly what I'm doing," Claire confessed.

"Well, least you ain't another pair of fly-by-nighters out for a quick buck on a land deal," he said, not caring if the two men overheard him. He leaned across the counter and said, "What you got?"

Claire took out her pad and pen, wrote down the town's name. Then she sketched out Silver Street leading to the restaurant's parking lot, the lake, the saddleback ridge, the pair of valleys they had traversed, the bowl where the cabins had been. "That's all pretty vague, I know."

The inspector studied the sketch. "You sure about the compass headings?"

"Yes." Definite. The sun had guided her home.

"Well, let's go see what we've got." He rapped knuckles on the counter, then turned and disappeared into the shelves.

Claire leaned on the counter and felt submerged in the sense that she was missing something. Some key element of the story was eluding her, something that would bring everything together, make all the pieces fit. She tried to push it away, but it only came back stronger.

The clerk returned so swiftly she was sure it was bad news. Instead, he grinned across the counter and announced, "If your headings are right, we're in luck."

He opened the file, unfolded weather-beaten maps, and swung them around. "Turns out one fellow owns that whole section of range, from the town limits right up to where it meets the national park."

Claire bent over, saw the squared-off segments each with a number, ran her finger down the list on the adjacent page, and saw that all contained one name. She breathed, "Incredible."

"Naw it ain't. You see a lot of that up in the hills. Folks with more money than sense decide they want to own a piece of paradise. They buy up these parcels, probably ain't never set foot up there if they can't reach it by car. But that don't matter. They own it." He shook his head. "Dang fools, if you ask me."

The map's drawings were similar to the topographic

charts she used when hiking. Claire traced her way over the first ridge, the second, seeing in her mind the forest and the slopes and the snow, hearing the gunfire. Going back to the ownership sheet. Then she said the name out loud: "Swindley."

"He's a moneybags, I take it," the guy suggested. "Got to have some serious bucks to own that much property."

"Yes, he's rich." For every question the information answered, a thousand new ones sprang to mind. Claire straightened. "I can't thank you enough."

She left the building, wondering at her lack of excitement over the news. Another piece to the puzzle, another thread exposed, and yet there was no satisfaction. Only a sensation that she was looking in the wrong direction, hunting for the wrong key.

She hurried across the central square and headed for the newspaper offices. Maybe Harry would know what she needed.

"I can't believe you were so stupid."

"What are you talking about?" She stared at Harry, a Harry she had never known before, one angry with a fierceness that wilted her. "This was important."

"Important enough to risk your life?" No longer able to sit still, he bounded up and began pacing. Each time his path took him over towards the door, she caught sight of other journalists observing them from outside. "No story is that important."

His office had continued its metamorphosis, and this too caught her off balance. There was a new plaque on his wall, one under which he passed with each circuit. It read,

Commit your way to the LORD,
Trust also in Him,
And He shall bring it to pass.
He shall bring forth your righteousness as the light,
And your justice as the noonday.
Psalm 37:5-6

"I expect my journalists to act like adults," he went on. "This means judging situations before they develop." He whirled about. "Am I getting through to you?"

"Loud and clear," she said faintly.

"This was something I would never have sanctioned," he said, resuming his pacing. "Which is exactly why you didn't tell me, I am absolutely certain."

She could only gulp and nod. She hated this. Hated the way she felt as though something had come between them. Hated having him angry at her. "I'm sorry, Harry. It won't happen again."

"Right." He deflated instantly, walked back, and seated himself behind the desk. "You can't get me angry, Claire. It wrecks my whole day."

"I said I was sorry." She tried for a trembling smile. "Friends?"

His gaze suddenly became open and revealing. Dark depths stared out at her, and he opened his mouth to speak, only to draw back and drop the cloak over his eyes.

He glanced at his watch, rose from his chair, and said hoarsely, "Come on, friend." As though coming so close to saying something had cost him dearly.

She followed him from the office, wondering what had gone unspoken. "Where are we headed?"

"Time for you to meet the resident dragon lady." He pointed to the corner office with its glass wall facing out over the newsroom. "Our managing editor wants to make your acquaintance."

Claire dug in her heels. "Not today, Harry. I'm not up to this."

"She decides the when, not you." Harry pulled her along. "Be forewarned. Britt Shaw generally looks like she just got off a cross-country Greyhound bus. Matted hair, dress skewed, stockings with a run in them."

The woman behind the desk had her back to them, and was leaning over talking intently with the two people sitting across from her. Their faces had the stricken look of people being given the lash. "But she has a heart of gold, right?"

"Actually, she's a pain in the neck." Harry grinned. "But she's also the boss."

They positioned themselves by the window and waited while the pair inside continued melting farther into their chairs. Harry asked, "You going home this weekend?"

"I hadn't planned on it." She started to say that her father had invited Lillian down, then decided now wasn't the time. "Why, did you want to come?"

"Can't. I'm duty editor Saturday night." He turned his back to the newsroom and said to the window, "I was just wondering if you'd like to come to church with me on Sunday."

Her internal tumult was instantly forgotten. "What?"

"I've started attending a great church not far from here." He turned to face her. "Would you like to join me?"

"Maybe." The power of his quiet words brought out a confession of her own. "I prayed with someone the day before yesterday. Then again by myself last night. First time in a long while."

His eyes lit up with something new. More than interest. Gladness. "Yeah? That's great, Claire."

She told him about Buddy's sister and what she had said. Then she stopped, remembering the night before, and found her chest beginning to swell again. She knew she could not speak of that without breaking down, so she returned to the previous day. "Sandra Wiggins really caught me off guard. This total stranger, talking as though the words were coming straight from my own heart."

"I'm beginning to believe that's how God works," Harry said quietly, his face aglow. "Using the unexpected to catch us when our barriers are weakest, and we're most likely to hear His voice."

Claire found herself comparing this to the feeling while driving back with Donovan. There had been no understanding whatsoever from him, not even the desire to know her dreams and goals. And now here she was, finding not just acceptance, but an invitation to be more open than she had ever been, and about things which had always gone unspoken. "I can't believe I'm hearing you say this."

"Me either." He glanced to the side, then said, "Heads up. We're on."

The two reporters entered Britt Shaw's office, their shoulders slumped in abject despair. The *Herald*'s managing editor took a moment to gather up the papers on her desk, then pointed a finger straight at Claire.

She forced her legs to carry her over. A journalist at a nearby desk gave her a grimace of sympathy. Claire could not find the strength to smile back.

"Claire Kingsbury, right? Britt Shaw." She shook hands with a solid grip, then waved them in. "Take a seat."

The managing editor's office was shaded a dull hospital green. Greyish-green felt carpet met wallpaper the color of cheap greeting card envelopes. The woman occupying the cluttered desk obviously gave the decor as little notice as she did her own appearance. Britt Shaw was lithe and so active it was hard to get a feel for her size. She leaned back in her chair, then demanded sharply, "Is this one of your new Christian mafia, Harry?"

The acid in her voice shocked them both. Harry recovered first. "What are you talking about?"

"It's her dad I'm seeing around here, isn't it?" She studied Claire. "I want to know what we have here, a journalist or a troublemaker?

Harry leaned forward and said with quiet intensity, "Are sides being taken, Britt?"

For some reason, the query shook her. She brushed at greying hair and changed the subject. "Why am I not seeing something across my desk on her story?"

Harry held to his quiet intensity. "Claire is working on a project that might make it to the front page, if we can overcome our sourcing problems."

She shot him a severe look. "You've set up a former stringer with a front page piece?"

"She's ready for it," Harry said firmly.

The managing editor showed bitter doubt. "I'm getting flak from upstairs about this."

"How interesting," Harry said softly, his gaze hard as nails, "since not a single word has been written."

"You're locking horns with me, Harry," she barked. "I don't like my editors locking horns with me."

"If you would stop and think for a minute," Harry said, not budging an inch, "you'd realize that something big must be coming down for the board to be getting rumbles even before we start writing."

"Not if this stringer of yours has been out stepping on toes and getting in the way," Britt snapped back. "What I want to know is, are we talking carnations or compost?"

"I think it's big," Harry replied instantly. "A major breaking sweep."

"You willing to bet your career on this?"

Harry settled back, his face giving nothing away. "That's what you'd like, isn't it? A chance to do away with me."

"What I see," she said, her voice so tight it was gravelly, "is you becoming infatuated with a troublemaker. One who's not performing."

Claire started to open her mouth to object, but Harry was there first. "And I tell you this is going to be a major story."

"It's your funeral." She waved her hand towards the door in dismissal. "No late-night insertions after I've gone home. I want to personally approve all the copy."

Claire forced her legs to carry her from the office. Harry matched his pace to hers. When they were away from all but watching eyes, he said quietly, "Attention from the people upstairs means this thing is going to be lawyered to death. The in-house attorneys will read everything you write. They will require iron-clad documentation, double sourcing of everything that refers to Swindley in any way, and attributable quotes."

"If this story ever goes anywhere at all," she responded shakily.

"Don't let Britt get to you," Harry said. "Anything this big was bound to attract some opposition."

She stopped and turned to him then, not caring who saw as she lay a hand on his arm. "I've never really understood what it meant to have someone show confidence in me, until now."

The gaze opened up again, but his voice retained its calm steadiness. "Go out there," he replied, "and make me proud."

Claire hunted Casper the friendly tekkie down, which was not all that easy, his habitual disappearing act magnified by the approaching three o'clock story-conference deadline. But she had no article to file, and he was delighted to have a reason to return to the game.

When she joined him after donning the Second Skin, Claire asked him if he had played the game yet.

"You kidding?" He slid into the chair and began switching on the computer with practiced motions. "I'm about ready to move in down here."

"Have you been able to get into the barred hallway?"

"Not yet, but I figure it's just a matter of time. You know, win enough points and, bingo, you're in."

She hesitated, then moved up closer. "Do you feel addicted to this game?"

He laughed. "I was addicted to Babylon before I played it."

"But why?"

"Because it's what I always wanted and never had."

"Have you ever done drugs?" As soft as she could, easing into it, not wanting to destroy his balance.

He gave her a slight nod in reply.

"Nova?" She set the headgear down on the stage's padded railing. "Ever tried that?"

"Sure." A shy smile. "It's great. Especially when you're gaming."

"Why?"

"Why is it great, or why do I take it?"

"Either. Both."

"The doctors call me mildly depressed. They gave me pills for years that were supposed to make me better. You know how they say that, 'Take this and you'll be better.' Only I never was. Just mild little buzzes, then I'd want to sleep. One day I got tired of sleeping, so I started trying out pills of my own."

"Nova isn't a pill," Claire pointed out.

"Same thing." He was growing easier with her in stages. "You know, for years I thought, 'Hey, I'm not normal. I have to try harder. I need to trust the doctors to give me that little boost into normalhood.' Then I took this drug Nova, and all of a sudden, normal doesn't matter so much any more. Or reality. If I don't like it, I can change it."

"Just like that."

"Sure. Why should I have to worry about the rules and neuroses of society? I should have the chance to chart my own course." He looked at her. "Babylon gives me that chance. Especially when I'm on Nova."

She felt an unseen door suddenly open within her mind

and heart. Claire examined his face, sensing a new ability to see beneath the surface. There before her was a lost and lonely spirit, confused by all the choices arrayed against him. Choices that clamored to suck him in and steal away who he had the chance of becoming.

"If you'd ask for help," she said quietly, easing down to sit upon the stage, looking up to him now. Not threatening, not pushing. Offering a gift. "You might find your cry of loneliness has meaning."

The words shook him deeply. "Who said anything about crying? I'm a big boy, remember?"

"I was talking about your heart," she replied.

"No you're not." His gaze hardened. "You're talking about God, aren't you?"

The power that filled her with the need to speak formed a shield, one so strong his coming rejection could not touch her. Not at all. "Prayer is a much stronger comfort than all the drugs and games this world will ever offer. And one that carries with it the gift of eternal salvation. Lasting peace. True healing."

But he was no longer listening. "Sure, I've heard about you and Harry. Lillian too. That's what the rumors say. It's spreading like a plague around here." He hit the computer's power switch, keyed in, then started for the door. "Everything's automatic now, just give it a chance to warm up."

Claire watched him leave, felt a sorrow that she knew was not her own. For herself, there was only peace, a gathering of solidity, a focus upon this new direction of hers. It was a wondrous moment.

She bent over the keyboard, answered the various questions and watched the game's portal come up on the screen.

She attached the cables to the connection at her back, then picked up the headset and fitted it down over her eyes.

"Claire?"

She felt her heart soar at the thought that Casper had returned. But when she lifted the headset from her eyes, she saw Harry walking towards her. "Oh, it's you."

"Thanks a lot." He stopped in the doorway. "Should I leave?"

"No, no, I'm glad to see you." And she was.

"I have to say, you look fantastic in that get-up."

"You're making fun."

"Not a chance." He gave his gentle smile. "It just hit me after you left, I've got a Bible study tonight. If you like, we could grab a bite and go together."

"I'd like that. A lot." She lifted the headset. "I just wanted to try out the game another time."

"Mind if I hang around and watch?"

"Be my guest." Claire pointed at the computer monitor. "You can follow along on the screen, but there's not a lot to see." She fitted on the headset. "All the action's in here."

It was much the same as the first time, the entry being a long ramp up and into a grand palace foyer. The pillars supporting the high room were of multicolored gemstone, sparkling in the electronic light. Two halls branched off, the smaller one open to her, the other gated shut. She had no desire to try the open hall again. It branched soon after the passage began, then branched again, and all of those she had tried led to a similar sort of game; people came in and grabbed weapons and started fighting. Only the battleground and weapons altered.

Claire stood before the closed and barred doors. They were four or five times as large as the others. She started forward, just to see if she could walk through. As soon as she passed the barrier, her headgear was filled with visual static and a grinding noise. She backed off hastily.

"Ouch."

"What's the matter?"

"The doors to the second hall are still locked." She pivoted, inspected the first hall, saw it was still open. Good. The trial had not cost her entry. Resigned to more battles, she entered the first hall. Once again, she passed through an invisible curtain of voices. She rocked back and forth on the springy stage, and heard the whispering throng.

Harry said, "It looks like you're dancing to music I can't hear."

"I'm listening to those subliminal messages again."

"Wait, let me get settled so I can write them out."

There was the sound of him shifting the terminal's chair around. "Okay, what are they saying?"

"'You are great. You are all powerful. You are utterly content. There is nothing you cannot do if you set your mind to it. You can conquer all. You are completely invincible. You are totally happy.' Then they repeat themselves." She started down the hall and then stopped short. "Hey, I missed that the first time."

"What's the matter?"

"There's a bulletin board here. The top notice says, 'Every effort is being made to avoid stranding our inbound warriors.' Does that make any sense to you?"

"I'm not sure."

"Here, take a look at this."

"All I see is the hallway extending down the screen."

"Oh, right. Another notice. It looks official, like it's written on sheepskin in some funny script. It says, 'Retrofit your armor using the new beta-upgrade. Available to all sorcerers and battle-proven warriors at your nearest weapons shop, upon presentation of credentials.' Are they talking the same language?"

"Every secret order has its own techno-speech."

"But this is a game we're playing, Harry."

She was silent long enough for Harry to ask, "What's wrong?"

"Nothing. I don't know." A pause, then, "There's something here, a scrap. It's crazy."

He was growing impatient. "Talk to me, Claire."

"It looks like somebody has tried to etch a message into the bulletin board. But this is electronic imagery. How is that possible?"

Harry thought it over, then suggested, "Maybe one of the whizzos got into the control code and altered it so he or she could leave something. What does it say?"

Claire read off: 'Carl, Carl, why don't you call me any more? Your seer languishes, your quest goes unfinished. Check the other board.'"

He waited, then, "So?"

"What other board?" She stripped off the headset, rubbed her head vigorously to fluff out the matted hair. "I have got to get behind those other doors. I wonder if there's something I have to earn, like those credentials they mentioned."

Disappointed and frustrated, Claire stepped off the stage.

"I don't understand. There's tremendous artwork and a lot of possibilities. But it's still just a *game*."

"Even so, we've got the makings of a good story," Harry told her. "A game that's tied to the rising use of designer drugs. This is something people have suspected for a long time, but we're talking about actual proof."

"No, that's not it. There's something more at work here."

"Like what?"

"I don't know. But I can't shake the feeling that we're missing something vital." She shook her head, trying to push it away.

Harry sat and watched her. "Maybe we should let it pass today, come back and try tomorrow."

She started to agree. Had almost set down the headgear. Then it hit her.

Her fingers fumbled with haste as she fitted the headgear back on.

Harry demanded, "What's going on?"

"Maybe nothing, I don't know." She walked over until she was standing in front of the great barred doors. She leaned over the stage's railings until she could reach the keyboard and typed in one word: *Starsign*.

Instantly there was a booming rush inside her head as the bar dropped away and the gates rolled back. A great voice resounded, "Claire Kingsbury, welcome to Babylon."

She whispered, "Oh, wow."

"What is it?"

"I'm in."

INTERIORITY

23

■ Claire took a few steps down the computer-generated passageway, this one lit by great flaming torches. "The images are totally different here."

"You mean better drawn?"

"I mean different. It's a totally new set-up, a higher level of quality." She continued to walk until her own passage joined with others, and she entered an emerald green forum. People came and went in the distance. "I can see other gamers. Wait, there's another bulletin board here. Listen to this. 'Lost crown of Barsoom! I have uncovered the authentic map, need gallant warrior and ultra-wise wizard, otherwise we're toast. Meet the Seer Alicia at Moonside Plateau. Be ready to vanquish all comers as a test of your genuine status. Only the strong need apply. Reward: All the jewels you can carry, and a free ride to rock-and-roll land.'"

"Claire? Miss Kingsbury?"

At first she thought it was Harry, then she realized the sound had come over her earphones. She turned around so fast she almost fell when her hip caught the stage's padded rail. Then she stumbled again trying to back away from the menacing beast.

The warrior was a full ten-feet high, helmeted in gleaming silver, the same mirror finish to his shield and to the chain-mail draped across his sword arm and to his multitude of blades. She righted herself. "Yes?"

Harry demanded, "Are you all right?"

"I've been hoping you'd figure it out," the warrior said, his timid voice sounding strange coming from such a massive knight. "Like the sign says, welcome to Babylon."

An impatient Harry demanded, "Tell me what's happening."

Claire swivelled her head up far enough to look under the visor and say, "It's Troy."

Harry was saying, "The guy who scarpered with five thousand dollars of the paper's money, is that right? Did you tell him we're expecting it back?"

Troy countered with, "Who said that?"

"My boss," Claire responded. "Harry."

"Tell him if he talks that loud I can hear him myself, and I'm not going anywhere." Troy read off a string of digits and numbers. "That's a safe address on the web. Not in my name. Anything left there is automatically anonymized. Don't let anybody else have that."

Harry scribbled as Claire dictated. He then lowered his

voice and said, "Tell him if he'll come in we'll arrange protection."

Claire did so. "He says he'll think about it."

"We'll run him upstairs." Harry spoke as quietly as he could manage, that close to a breaking story. "The publisher's secretary is a notary public and a lightning typist. We'll whip out his statement, have him sign the notarized document, and lead into the story with, 'According to a sworn deposition obtained by the *Herald*.' That'll get us by the lawyers."

Claire waved at him to be quiet, as Troy was saying, "I really am sorry to have left you in the lurch outside the prison."

"How did you know Skate was in the limo?"

"I didn't. It was just a hunch." A pause, then, "What did he look like?"

"You haven't seen him?"

"Only in the game, and all I see there is his mask."

Harry interrupted with, "Talk to me."

Claire tilted her head back. "I can't. You're just going to have to wait until we're done."

He started to argue, halted himself, signaled agreement, and settled back into the chair. "Just take care of yourself, all right?"

"Yes." Claire turned her attention back to the headgear's dual monitors and said, "Skate is scary."

"You're telling me."

"But what is Swindley's bodyguard doing inside a game?"

"I didn't know he was anybody's bodyguard, I don't know who any Swindley is, and Babylon is more than a game." Troy pointed down the corridor. "We can stand here and talk or I can show you. Which will it be?"

"I know, it's a kick, all this gear." Troy ambled alongside her as they continued down the corridor. "I'm glad you made it."

She examined him more closely. "Why do you look so much clearer than the other gamers I've seen?"

"They have to limit resolution when a lot of people are gaming. The higher your status, the more space you're given in the memory banks."

"So you're pretty high up the ladder."

"The highest independent warrior in the game." It was said without pride, almost beyond matter-of-fact, as though it had become a burden without value.

"What's an independent?"

"That's my word to explain certain things around here. It's easier to understand if I just show you."

They took a hallway leading off the forum, one with great crystal pillars overhead. Their passage was flanked by gleaming suits of armor, strange-bladed swords, crossed spears, and battle flags.

Claire asked, "Why does some of the setting have a sort of unfinished look?"

He glanced over his shoulder. "You're not flying?"

"You mean, using the Nova drug? No."

"Then we'll have to take it careful." He thought a minute, and decided, "Probably be best to sign you in as a seer. That'll cover any slips. Most of the seers are fairly scattered anyway."

"Are you on Nova?"

"'Course." He paused at a great portal bearing a grand golden shield embossed with the silver tower. "Hold your questions until we're through and out the other side."

"What is this?"

"The weapons room. Need to sign you up."

She entered behind him, and gasped aloud.

A raucous cheer greeted the sound. The room was enormous, the ceiling so high a small cloud drifted beneath the rafters. A half-dozen forms, they could not be called humans, sat around great wooden tables. Their weapons and shields lay piled at their feet. Several full-sized dragons spewed smoke from their nostrils. Wizards sparked clouds of lightning and power from their fingers. Witches wore black so complete they moved like liquid shadows. And there were many warriors. But that was not what held her fast.

The entire far wall was not there. Instead she looked out over a sweeping moonscape.

Apparently the chamber was a transporting stage, because as Claire watched, the moonscape blurred, shifted, and she was suddenly staring at a barren desert far below, ringed by cliffs so high they stabbed the dusky sky. The scene held for perhaps a minute, then shifted again. This time she was confronted with an alien landscape, where dust devils raced across a red plateau, and two great gleaming moons chased each other across the star-flecked sky.

Another slow transition, then she looked out over a river that steamed in grudging fury; beyond it spread a field of plants that raised and snapped in hungry delirium at everything. At the field's center rose a gigantic silver tower, a cone so lofty the idol at its pinnacle looked down upon the sun.

"A new kid," snarled one of the wizards, his vast silver robe crested by the signs of the zodiac. "Let me at her."

"A seer," Troy corrected. "And she's with me."

The jeers reduced to silence. Claire watched Troy step over to the vast side alcove, where another warrior stood guard. "Need to register a new seer."

"Sure, Troy." Respect tinted his bored tone. "Name?"

He dropped his voice, and murmured, "Claire Kingsbury."

"Sure, I've got her here."

"Change it to Clarity," Troy replied.

"Not a bad handle for a seer. Noted." The weapons master reached behind and said, "You want to check out anything in particular?"

"The Tower. No use wasting time."

The weapons master turned back. "You serious?"

"I can handle it."

"Yeah," the weapons master said. "But can she?"

"She's with me."

The weapons master shrugged, turned, searched, and said, "We haven't had much call for that since, you know, the last time. Wait, here it is." He passed over what appeared to be a shining chart and a crystal ball.

Claire accepted the parcels, then followed Troy over to the edge of the stage. As she watched the vistas continue to shift, she whispered, "What was that name thing all about?"

"No need to advertise you're here. The weapons master is a friend, but a lot of the others I don't know so well. Better to use a handle, in case someone decides to gossip." Troy stepped onto the perch, and as he did, great silver wings unfolded from his back. He reached for her. "Hang on."

Instead of heading toward the silver Tower, he dropped off the perch and slipped down and down and down, the cliffs spilling towards a yellow desert floor directly below. Claire gasped and tried to hang on tight, found herself holding on to nothing, which only made it worse.

Scarce inches before they were to plow into the desert, Troy evened out their flight. He hugged the sand, gliding at speeds that blurred dunes and driftwinds and oases. His sureness was so complete, his guidance so subtle, Claire found herself relaxing, giving herself over to his care.

"Isn't the Tower the other way?"

"We're not headed to the Tower. There's another couple of treasure troves that will do just as well." He swerved to miss a rock outcropping by inches. "I said the Tower just to throw them off the scent."

"Throw who?"

"Whoever comes after us." He gestured with the hand not holding her to the bundle clutched to her chest. "You can drop that stuff."

She released the ball but unfolded the sheet. "I'm looking at something. A horoscope wheel or something."

"That's the Seer's Chart. You learn to read it, steer people around. You're the guide, I'm the warrior. That's the way the game works. Or supposed to. But everybody wants weapons and powers and the chance to do battle. Wizards, warlocks, dragons, witches, and warriors—they're a dime a dozen. Most just wander around in little lost groups."

She decided now was not the time to confess she had enough trouble with a road map. "A seer can't have weapons? Why?"

"That's the rule. One of very few in Babylon." He landed then, bringing them to rest on a tall rock ledge which had sprouted from the desert floor. "Okay, are you ready?"

"Ready for what?"

"To see what's going on here." He started checking his arsenal—sword, lance with a brilliant blade, what looked like jeweled bombs around his middle, tiny daggers to the toes of his boots, a plumed helmet, and a shield of gold. He loosened his cloak, drew a sword, did a careful scouting. "We should be okay here, but you never can tell. This is the edge of the Badlands, and up ahead are the Crystal Caverns."

"Why are they called . . ." Claire followed the path around a jagged rise and stopped cold. "Oh my."

"It's amazing how they do these segments up." Troy was clearly not affected by what lay ahead. "I've seen most of them now, maybe all, at least from a distance. Never wanted to scale the Tower. The near edge of Snapping Dragon Fields is as close as I've ever been to that one."

"This is fabulous," Claire breathed, stepping forward. "I've never seen anything like this."

"Yeah, it's swell." He kept a pace or so behind her, constantly scouting in every direction. "Like I said, the treasure troves have the most incredible graphics. Like they were designed as lures."

"Lures for what?" But she was not really listening. The caves' entrances were made of carved gemstones, tall as houses. The light was a constantly shifting rainbow, cast by hundreds of giant polished prisms. Claire started towards the nearest entrance.

Troy leaped in front of her, blocking her way. "Don't go in there! Are you nuts?"

"But I thought that's why you brought me here."

"Just stand there, will you? And don't do anything." He shook his head disgustedly. "Totally nuts."

She stepped to one side, so she could see around him, and peered through the entrance. "Look, there's a jewel on a stick, a scepter. And a crown."

"I'm telling you. Don't go any closer."

"Why not, it's beautiful."

"It's a trap. I'm sure of it." Talking in a rush now. "This is the whole objective of the game, see, to arrive here. It can take years, and even then a lot of people never reach them. You've got to fight your way through all kinds of battles, picking up clues and powers along the way. Most of the time, the ones who get here, they go in and get these things, and they change."

She tried hard to listen, but the allure of the sparkling caves and their glorious booty was hypnotic. "You mean they win?"

"I mean they *change*. Once they come out, they've got these crowns and robes and stuff, and they win the title of Enforcer Prince and Princess. They get free access to the game, as much as they like, and discounts on any new Mainline hardware. A lot of stuff like that. But these aren't the things I'm talking about." His tone turned brooding. "I've lost too many of my friends. They start talking about getting close to one of these treasure troves, or that they've found a way through to the Tower, and then they're gone. Either that or they're changed. There's more at work here than you think."

Claire found it easier to concentrate if she looked at him and not the cave. But it was hard. "What are you talking about?"

"I don't know anything for sure. I've never gone in any of these places. But I've been around, and I've listened, and I've watched." Troy took a deep breath, as though the words were all pushing to get out, now that there was finally a chance. "Something happens to the people when they go in there. It's almost like the whole game is meant to get them really hooked, ready to face whatever it is they find inside these places."

Claire turned completely around, so that her back was now to the cave. The vista behind Troy looked dim in comparison. "You mean they disappear?"

"Some of them. Just a few. Maybe one in a hundred. Less. The others," he hesitated, as though unsure how she would take it, "they start going out, spending all their free time getting others hooked on the game. I've tried to talk with them in real time, people I've known since I started gaming. But they aren't really there any more. It's as though they've been reprogrammed."

Troy turned and glanced inside the cavern. "These aren't treasure troves. They're nightmares in the making."

Troy led her back away from the caverns. They stopped by a great crystal tree, its emerald leaves shimmering in the electronic sunlight. Claire probed, "You think they're assigned to go out and get other kids addicted to the game?"

"And the drug. Don't forget that. They go hand in hand, see."

"Just exactly what does Nova do?"

"You think the game is clear to you now, you should try it while flying. Every thought becomes its own reality. So when your thoughts are all caught up in the game, see, Babylon becomes the *only* real world. You aren't just *playing* at being a great warrior, you *are* one." Troy spent a long moment scanning in every direction, then returned to the point that concerned him most. "These Enforcers start hanging out in real time at game arcades, computer stores, software shops, places that carry those weird comic books. They talk to other kids. I've watched them. They sell them on the game, they brag about winning and what it means to become Tower royalty."

"Become what?"

"You know, work for the Tower. It's the big structure by the River Styx. The Tower of Babel. You can't miss it. It dominates the world."

"And it talks to you?"

"Not everybody. Only the Enforcers. They make it up to be some big thing, to be able to get stuff directly from the Tower. As though being mind slaves to the game is a good idea."

"But what does this have to do with the kids who go into meltdown and then vanish?"

"I don't know for certain, but they're connected. They have to be."

Claire studied the warrior image before her, wondering about the unseen young man. "You know all this evil's going on. Why do you still play?"

He was very long in replying. "It used to be fun. A lot."

She tried to keep it gentle. "And now you're addicted."

"Yeah. Oh yeah."

"Would you like to stop?"

"I don't know." He sounded so sad. "What else is there? I mean, reality's never held much attraction for me."

She had no answer. Nothing. And in the emptiness of having no way of helping this sad young man, she found herself bowing her head, shutting her eyes against the almost overpowering images, and praying.

And suddenly there in the midst of the electronic universe, she found herself drawing back into focus. Realizing with a clarity that what was real remained real even here. Real and in control. She looked at Troy. "Have you ever thought of giving faith a chance?"

"You mean, God?" But he did not draw away. Instead his tone turned wistful. "You think He'd want to have anything to do with me?"

"If Jesus will offer salvation to me," she replied, "He'll do it for anyone."

"You don't know," he said slowly.

"I don't need to," she replied. "I've got enough shame of my own."

He thought it over. "And you think it might free me up from all this?"

For some reason the question brought a burning to her eyes. "Free from the *need* for this. Freer than you've ever been in your life. I know. It's the truth."

He nodded slowly. "So what do I do?"

"We could pray together, if you like."

"What, you mean here?"

"God is everywhere," she said, knowing this with more certainty than her own name, feeling the power of this statement rearranging her world even as she spoke. "He's been waiting for this moment all your life, waiting for each of us to turn to Him in prayer."

His tone said he was almost afraid to hope. "How can you be so sure of that?"

"Because," she replied quietly, "He's showing it to me, even here, even now."

Claire took off the headset, sighed, and lowered herself to the edge of the walker. Harry watched her with grave eyes. "What you just said was beautiful."

"It felt clumsy." She stared into the calm depths of his grey eyes. "I wish I could have done it better."

Instead of disputing, Harry simply gave a slow nod. "I think moments like that bring up all the things we have left to resolve inside ourselves. We want to be the perfect servant, but since perfection isn't ours yet, we have to settle for the best we can do."

"Why is it," she said softly, "you can say what I feel even before I can find the words for myself?"

Harry's gaze deepened, but before he could respond, Lillian's head poked into the doorway. "Thank goodness, you're both here." She scurried over, started to speak, then realized what Claire was wearing. "Tell me that's not the coming thing."

"It's a Second Skin," Claire said, but her smile was for Harry.

"Yes, and that's exactly what it looks like." Lillian turned to Harry and said, "There's some pow-wow going on upstairs. Ron's been looking all over for you."

"The publisher?" Harry pushed himself to his feet. "What on earth does he want with me?"

"With both of you," Lillian corrected and gave Claire a nervous smile. "A word to the wise, my dear. Wear something a little more sedate for your first visit to the executive floor."

CENTURY CITY AND
BEVERLY HILLS

24

■ The Swindley Broadcasting Studios were located at the back side of Century City. They were as unimpressive as any film production unit, squat concrete pillboxes worn by weather and hard use. But the executive offices resided in an adjoining skyscraper and were another thing entirely.

Donovan entered the penthouse executive suite, and paused to look around. The entire back wall was solid glass, and the view down the Avenue of the Stars was stupendous. He did a slow sweep of the receptionist's pink marble desk, the white-silk Chinese carpets, the ultra-contemporary chandeliers. He had to smile. Hollywood was different from every other place on earth. They knew how to spend money. They knew how to *live*. Even walking into an office out here was a major high.

"Mr. Stone, good morning, sir." The receptionist was an

actress on the make, and she unleashed her full-wattage smile for him. "Mr. Swindley said you were to go right in. This way, please." She rose from her desk and did a walk just for him, back to the suede-and-chrome double doors. She opened one and smiled him through.

"Donnie, come in, come in." Swindley waved him into the office, then turned back to the wide-eyed geek seated opposite his desk. The guy was dressed in a floral print shirt and purple silk trousers, and looked to Donovan like a wilting orchid. Swindley's voice became flat, cold, and final. "Sorry. Not interested."

"But Mr. Swindley—"

He stopped the guy with an upraised hand, glanced up to where Donovan was still standing. The suite was an elongated L, a good hundred feet of glass looking out over the Los Angeles sprawl. "Have a seat over there, Donnie. I'll be right with you."

"Donovan," he corrected quietly, standing tall, still facing the desk.

Swindley was caught in the middle of turning back to the hothouse flower. "Come again?"

"Donovan," he repeated, not needing to raise his voice. Going with his gut reaction. Which was not to let himself be classed as just another Hollywood geek. All the waiting and hoping was drawing him down to a razorlike edge. "Not Don. And certainly not Donnie. Donovan."

Swindley came full around, his gaze rock hard. The wilting orchid gaped at Donovan in open-mouthed amazement. Daring to stand up to the money was definitely not part of the norm in Hollywood. The guy turned back to Swindley, waiting for the eruption.

But it never came. Instead, Swindley nodded and said, "Donovan, then. I've been out here too long. Take a seat."

"Thank you, Mr. Swindley." Respectful, keeping his voice calmer than he felt by a mile, not making a big deal of it.

Swindley directed his attention back to the other guy, and said coldly, "In the first place, Civil War films haven't made money since Gable and what's her name tangoed through a charbroiled Atlanta. In the second place, you've got so many settings and battles and crowd scenes, this film would cost more than the war did."

"But Mr. Swindley, we could—"

"Not interested. Good-bye."

Reluctantly the guy rose and made for the door, pausing there long enough to cast Donovan a look, equal parts astonishment and envy.

When the door had closed, Swindley walked over to the side bar, poured himself a designer water, and said, "I've got a dozen men out there, and all they're supposed to do is filter out the duds. And still I get hit daily with crazy ideas like these. It makes you wonder whether any of it's worthwhile. You want something to drink?"

"No thank you, Mr. Swindley."

"Roger will do." He walked over and seated himself. "So, Donovan." Stressing the name. Letting him know he had gotten away with it. Once. He drained his glass, and set it down on the chrome and glass table between them. "My sole concern is what is going to make the most money. How secure is my investment, and how fast is my return?"

Donovan was used to this by now, as used as he could be to a man whose vocabulary included neither hello nor good-bye. Swindley started with the point he wanted to make, left when it was completed. There was no room for what was nonessential, like friendship or courtesy. Which would be fine, if the guy would ever give him the contract. "You're a businessman," Donovan replied, going with the flow. "You want people who will respect your money like you do, keep your risk low and your gain high."

There was a microsecond of the laser-sharp focus upon him. A single nod. "Hollywood runs along two distinct tracks," Swindley told him. "One is the avant garde, and for them I have no time whatsoever. The other track is geared to the feeling of the moment. That is where the money is. My task is to anticipate the public's mood six months from now, and cater to their tastes."

"Or try to shape it according to your will," Donovan offered.

Swindley nodded slowly. "It is reassuring to know we think along similar lines."

"My business is built around understanding the desires of my clients," Donovan said, trying to unwrap the mystery. He felt as though there was a second conversation now, one which he was supposed to understand but didn't.

"Today's wave is the computer," Swindley went on. "Interactive entertainment. Virtual reality. Mix that with the required doses of violence and rage and sex, and you have the makings of a profitable venture."

Donovan leaned back, kept his face blank. The surge of excited hunger was so great, it felt like a ball of fury raging in his belly. Donovan knew it was time to speak his mind. "This is the kind of place I've been looking for all my life," he said, his voice matching Swindley's for quiet intent. "Deals spun out at lightning speed, everything riding on a nod. That's the kind of power to go after."

There was yet another nanosecond of total pinpoint power upon him, all the approval Swindley would probably ever give. "And what have you been doing up to now?"

"Hand-to-mouth action," Donovan replied, the answer there instantly, fueled by days and nights of frustrated waiting and hoping. "Bending over backwards to cater to some knee-jerk banker from Nowhere, Middle America."

Swindley studied him for a long moment, then said quietly, "Tell me, Donovan. How would you describe what rules you?"

There was the sense of time focusing down, the moment linked to all his dreams. "Hunger."

"You want wealth and power," Swindley said.

"So much," Donovan said quietly. "So bad."

"So do most people," Swindley replied. "What I want to know is whether you want it enough."

"Point me in the right direction," Donovan answered. "Watch me fly."

"No second thoughts when you find out which way?"

"You've made it. You know what it takes. That's enough of a guideline for me. I'll follow your lead." So close. So *close*. "Give me the chance, Mr. Swindley. Just one chance."

There passed the longest moment of his life, standing on the brink of arrival or cataclysm, all his hopes and dreams bundled together and held in the clinch of this peculiar man.

Then the outer doors banged open and Chuckie rushed in. "Mr. S—"

Before he could take a second step into the room, the gaze had shifted, the voice turned to an ice-cold knife. "I left instructions that we were not to be disturbed."

Chuckie blanched, but held his ground. "You told me to let you know the instant Skate called."

"Ah." Swindley waved the young man inside. "He found Troy?"

"No." Chuckie let the door close behind him, shot a swift glance at Donovan, then said, "It's the reporter."

Swindley gave a hiss of rage. "She made it in to Babylon?"

Chuckie nodded. "Skate says all the way. Traveling with Troy."

He slammed fists down on the chair arms. "They had their chance back on my property," Swindley muttered, "When they missed her there, I knew she was going to be trouble."

"They were headed for the Tower," Chuckie went on. "But they never made it."

"A ruse," Swindley said, his normally pale face mottled with rage. "That Troy is as much a menace as she is. Tell Skate to call out the Enforcers. Have them search the other troves." He waved Chuckie out, then sat and pondered in grim silence.

Donovan watched the man brood, knowing in utter certainty that they had been talking about Claire.

He knew as well that he had come to a fork in the road. Along the one passage stood Claire, and the honest integrity he had sensed in her. He could remain silent, and hope that what he had already said and done would grant him success. The other way meant forsaking her trust, doing what would rupture their relationship for good. That is, if she ever found out.

He sighed, and shifted in his seat. There was no choice. Not really. Or perhaps that choice had been made long ago.

The movement brought Swindley around. "Yes?"

Donovan took a breath. "That reporter you mentioned. It's Claire Kingsbury, isn't it?"

Swindley's gaze intensified. "How did you know?"

Donovan waved that aside, then added the lure, "You have every reason to be worried."

"Why is that?"

Amazing how natural it felt to play this card. As though all along he had been building this stonelike mask of ambition. "I think," Donovan said flatly, "it's time we started talking specifics."

"That reporter," Swindley pressed. "You talked with her at my house in Vail."

"And I've seen her several times since. She seemed worth keeping an eye on from the very start," Donovan confirmed. "She told me the details of her investigation two days ago."

Swindley was silent a long moment, then murmured, "I agree. It is indeed time for decisions and offers."

Donovan kept his voice steady, though it cost him. "And contracts."

"That as well." There was no blustering. No rage. Instead, Swindley smiled for the first time that Donovan had ever seen. "Your proposal dealt only with a possible short-term consultancy. My Denver Airport Studios shall oversee our push into interactive entertainment and production of more feature films. What if I were to offer you the position of president of this new venture?"

"I would say," Donovan replied, and this time could not entirely keep the tremor from his voice, "I am your man."

"I will need to speak with that young reporter," Swindley pressed. "Which means you must arrange for her to come out for a little visit."

Donovan fought down a welling sense of despondency. "I can arrange that. No problem."

His resolve faded, however, as Donovan went over the contractual details with Swindley's staff. When he reentered the lobby three hours later, remorse hit him full strength. The limo pulled around; Chuckie got out and held his door, but Donovan could not move forward. The force of what he had just done left him immobile.

Finally Chuckie walked over. "Everything all right?"

"Fine," he said, his tone wooden. "Just got hit by the downside of my decision."

Again, there was the sense of Chuckie understanding him before he even spoke. "Yeah, there's always that."

Donovan followed the younger man out to the limo, settled himself into the leather-lined luxury, and struggled to push away the hollow remorse. "So what do you do when you're not playing sidekick?"

"I watch over the projects given the go-ahead." Chuckie accompanied the words with his bland smile. "It looks like things are going ahead for you. Congratulations."

"Thanks." All this hope, all this preparation and scheming and dreaming, and he felt nothing now except empty. As though he had swallowed a vacuum big enough to draw in his entire world. "Where are we going now?"

"Swindley ordered his number one lawyer to draw up the papers. Sid Vetz and his brothers have a lock on a lot of the major deals in Hollywood. You're meeting him for the signing." Chuckie caught Donovan's grim expression and said, "Are you worried about it?"

"No, not about that." There was nothing to be gained by regret. Donovan struggled to push aside the silent accusations in his mind. "Know what Swindley asked me? He wanted to know if I was hungry enough."

Chuckie was not the least surprised. "Yeah, he'll throw stuff like that at you. It's his way of testing."

"He did that to you?"

"Basically the identical question. Wanted to know if I was determined enough to make it happen." Chuckie drummed two fingers on the smoked windowpane. "I told him I'd come into this world on the L.A. bus. Then I spent two years hustling mail rooms, and breaking my knuckles on all the closed doors in this town."

He swung around to face Donovan, gave him the polished smile, but the bland tone had gone flat and hard. "I told him the only two ways I was ever leaving here was the back of a limo or the back of a hearse. Then I asked if that was determined enough for him."

Hamilton's was called a cigar bar because upstairs from the wood-paneled saloon was a room-size humidor containing almost a million dollars worth of tobacco. The saloon opened into the city's most exclusive wine caterers, where a hundred thousand dollars for a case of wine was not unknown, nor the most expensive on offer.

Donovan walked in and spotted a heavy-set man waving him over. He passed through the crowd to the prize corner table. "Mr. Vetz?"

"Call me Sid. Use the last name, I could be one of five brothers, and we don't get along all that great." He offered a stubby hand with manicured fingernails and a huge golden ring. "Great to meet you, kid. Have a seat."

Donovan slid into the leather divan. "You and your brothers are partners, though, am I right?"

"Two of them. That's two too many. They're hotshot Harvard types, all polish and opera and lobster thermidor, you know what I mean? Me, I'm having too much fun in the trenches. Course, that ain't saying I don't enjoy the finer things in life."

Vetz unscrewed the top from a silver container, slid out a cigar the size of a hotdog, snipped the end with a gold-plated clipper. He used a match to light a long wooden wick, then used the wick to light the cigar. When it was going strong he blew out the taper, took another puff, and said, "That took some moxie, telling Swindley to skip the Donnie-boy hype."

"How did you hear about that?" Donovan glanced around. The saloon was filled to the brim with people and laughter and talk and smoke. "There wasn't anybody else in the room."

"It's my business to know." Sid Vetz was not fat, rather big-boned and bulky. His heavy frame was well hidden beneath a tailored double-breasted suit, white-on-white shirt with French cuffs, and a hundred-dollar tie. But nothing could be done about the bull neck or heavy jowls or balding pate. Sid let out a long stream of smoke, then said to the waiter, "Bring my pal here a glass of whatever's best."

"We just opened a bottle of Pol Roger '61, Mr. Vetz."

"That good enough for you?" At Donovan's nod, the waiter departed, and Sid continued, "You're probably wondering why I asked you here, instead of having the documents messengered over. Strange place to sign a contract, am I right?"

"The thought crossed my mind."

"Scenery's good. And the gossip's hotter. They see us sitting here, watch you sign on the dotted line, read about it tomorrow in *Variety*, the buzz starts getting louder. You're emerging in a singular fashion. That's the definition of a Hollywood launch."

Donovan shifted impatiently. Yammer, yammer, yammer. This town was full of words, most of them empty. "Can I take a look at the contract?"

"See, you're smart. I like that. Why I wanted to talk with you personally was to learn if you were smart enough to take some advice." He tapped the cigar on the ashtray. "You don't know what you're facing out here."

Donovan nodded his thanks as the waiter set down a tall crystal flute of champagne. "So tell me."

"Hey, put me on retainer and I'll open the floodgates, pal."

Donovan did not return the smile. "I never buy goods I haven't checked out."

A big laugh. "So look who can't take a joke. Seriously, pal, this place is misery on new kids. And getting tougher all the time. There's a major consolidation going on. I should know. I'm in on half the deals. All the power is shifting into the hands of a few big players." He waved a lofty hand at the door. "Exit the Japs, they're out but don't know it yet. Swindley, now, he's one to watch. He and his backers have pockets deeper than the Pacific Basin. Take it from me, in two years, three at the max, he's going to have a dead solid lock on entertainment in this country."

"The contract," Donovan said, his voice tightening. "Now."

Vetz responded with a smile as false as the gleam in his eyes. "A man of action. That's the kind to watch." He slid papers from his pocket and handed them over. "Long as he has the sense to let those in the know guard his back."

Donovan knew an instant's panic at the thought that the contract would not read as expected. But as he poured carefully over the document, his muscles relaxed. The salary was enormous, the benefits and bonus package even larger. The way it was structured, he could basically live off the expense account and bank his entire paycheck. The length of employment was as Swindley had promised, five years with no possibility of early dismissal. A dream contract for a dream job, a launching pad for the stratosphere of corporate stardom.

Donovan started as Vetz jabbed a gold-plated pen under his nose. "It's all there. Just like the man said."

He reached for the pen, struggling hard to push aside the sense of overwhelming regret. Claire would never know, and even if she did, he could make it up to her. Besides, and here the words were so overpowering he had to say them out loud, "I've waited all my life for this chance."

"So don't blow it." Sid responded. "That's why you need me."

"I'll think about it." But in truth his internal struggle left little room for anything else. He hesitated a moment longer, flipping through the pages one last time, ignoring Sid's impatience and the glances shot his way from all over the room. He had to be certain.

He unscrewed the pen and set the pages down flat on the table beside his untouched glass of champagne.

"Initial each page where it's marked and sign the last," Sid instructed him. "Both copies."

Donovan did as he was told. Halfway through the process, however, he stopped. The sensation was so strong he felt himself clench tight with renewed panic.

The sudden impression seemed to solidify into reality. Right there before his eyes, the pen stopped using ink. Instead, it began to draw from his own blood. The red fluid seeped from beneath his fingernails, tracing its way down the hand-scrolled gold pen and onto the page. The image was so overpowering he could not continue. His name remained half-finished.

"Something the matter?"

"No." But the image did not vanish. Instead, it began to expand, and to Donovan's horror the words on the page seemed to come alive. Letters grew long tails and serpents' tongues and hissed their malevolent fury at him.

A flashback. That's what it had to be, apparitions from that drug Trish had stuck on his skin at the party. Donovan looked up, struggling to draw reality back into focus, but it did not help.

"You're not going to get a better offer anywhere," Vetz pressed impatiently. "Sign while there's still time."

He nodded dumbly, as the scene before his eyes turned his gut to ice. The room's mantle of rich smoke changed until it was no longer the product of cigars. Instead, unseen fires raged just beyond his field of vision, their eternal smolderings pouring forth a dense effluvium. The people themselves altered to fit the scene. Their hands became talons, their faces grew blotched and scarred, their chattering laughter sounded like the raucous cry of ravens.

"I don't have all day," Sid barked. "You gonna sign or not?"

Donovan found his vision drawn back to the contract, for his hand had begun to move of its own volition. Which was not altogether a bad thing, since it meant he did not have to look at the man seated beside him. He was terrified of what he might find.

He sat and watched as the bright red color sprawled its course across the page, then another, and another, until all the pages had been signed and initialed.

When Sid reached across, Donovan found that the images continued to overpower his sense of reality, for talons grew from reptilian scales as one claw reached for the pen, and the other began flipping pages as Sid added his witness to the contract. Only Sid did not write his name with blood.

He wrote with fire.

■ "A paper is essentially split into two divisions," Harry was saying as he led Claire into the elevator and pushed the button for the top floor. "Before, the publisher was usually the owner, and acted like a CEO of a normal company. But now we're owned by a conglomerate. Radley Enterprises is up to twenty-five papers and counting. So we've got some high-flyer sent down from headquarters as top bean-counter. He's an accountant by training, never been near a newspaper before. He's out to win medals with the home office by paring us to the bone."

Harry ushered Claire from the elevator, and together they entered the plush surroundings of the publisher's outer office. "Under him and the board is a general manager, who handles presses, finance, and advertising," Harry went on. "Alongside the general manager is supposed to be the editor, who is chief executive of the newsroom. But the powers-that-be decided this was a wasted space, and when the old editor retired last year, they didn't fill the slot. Britt's wearing two hats now. Just like I've been assigned two editorial slots."

Claire followed Harry to the chamber's far corner and listened as well as she could. The sound of Harry's voice helped allay the unsettled feeling of being way out of her depth. Which was probably why he kept talking, his voice calming, assuring, solid. She tried to match his quiet tone as she asked, "Why do you think we've been called upstairs?"

"The story," Harry replied definitely. "We're closing in, and the opposition is worried enough to start applying the pressure. I can just imagine what's happened. They called the corporation, not here but the home office. They let them know they were going to withdraw all their advertisements from all the papers, unless we are forced to call it quits."

Claire found the receptionist staring at them. Hard. She looked away, asked quietly, "Who is *they*?"

Harry's voice was as soft as her own. "Who do you think?"

"Well, look who's here." Britt Shaw entered the lounge, smirked at Claire, then said to Harry, "You should feel honored. It's not often somebody gets to walk to their own funeral."

When Harry ignored the comment, Britt turned and stalked over to the receptionist. He sank into the corner chair and motioned for Claire to take the one beside him. He watched Claire twist her fingers into tight nervous little knots, then stretched out his legs, and said in a soothing tone, "I'll never forget that first piece we ran of yours. 'My Great Aunt Bertha's Radial Tire Dessert.' What a title."

Claire had to smile. "I can't believe you remember that."

"Never forget it. You'd dug up all these little-known facts about fruitcake. My favorite was, 'Fruitcake is the only dessert which is guaranteed to survive the U.S. Postal Service.'"

The receptionist chose that moment to say, "Mr. Hatteker will see you now."

Britt turned around long enough to offer another smirk and the words, "Nice knowing you, Harry." Then she walked into the office ahead of them.

Harry rose to his feet, waited until Britt had left the chamber, then turned to Claire and said quietly, "There is absolutely nothing about this that I would have changed."

She nodded slowly and said, "Friends."

Ron Hatteker, the publisher, was a youngish guy in a designer suit and tortoise-shell glasses. He sat behind his enormous desk, flanked by Britt on one side and the mayor's attorney on the other. His features were evenly handsome, his ambition glowing like an emblem stamped to his forehead. "We have a responsibility to the stockholders of Radley Enterprises," he intoned, trying to mask his relative youth with pompous gravity.

"Maybe so," Harry shot back, "But this doesn't mean you can run the paper like it was an appendage of the Denver Chamber of Commerce."

The mayor's attorney looked genuinely taken aback. "Why not?"

"Because we have a responsibility to the people," Harry snapped. "*All* of them. Not just the people of the Chamber. Nor those of any particular party."

"Harry, there's much more going on here than you

think." The publisher gave a nervous glance towards the pair flanking him. "The advertising budget represented by Mainline Computers and Swindley Broadcasting is enormous. We have heard from both groups. Unless we stop this harassment, they threaten to pull their advertising from our newspapers. All of them, Harry. The board has gone absolutely ballistic."

"Not to mention your potentially jeopardizing the jobs Swindley and the Airport Studios might bring into the region." The city attorney looked at Harry with genuine loathing. "Your hotheaded gung-ho attitude could cost us millions."

"You mean, cost the mayor his re-election," Harry replied acidly. "If we were to take a close look, how much would Swindley's companies have contributed to his campaign?"

The attorney blanched and looked to the publisher. "Ron, you've got to exercise some control here."

"Good luck," Britt sneered.

The publisher took that as an opportunity to pass the buck. He turned to his managing editor and said, "I believe that is your department, Britt."

"I tried and got nowhere," she replied angrily. "That's the trouble with these religious types. They've got God in their pockets, and an exclusive on the truth."

"Let's remember what it is we're supposed to be talking about," Harry insisted. "We've uncovered something major here."

"Correction. You've come up with insinuations," the mayor's attorney lashed back. "Half-truths and inconclusive evidence that might have a major effect on this city's economy if it were ever to come out."

"Not to mention on the revenues of this paper," Ron Hatteker added. "I have to say I am inclined to agree with the mayor. This story is simply not worth the trouble it could cause."

"What about the principles this paper was founded on?" Harry argued, and pointed to the motto enscrolled over the publisher's doorway. He read the words, "'Dedicated to the principles that no good cause shall lack a champion, and that evil shall never thrive unopposed.'"

Hatteker shrugged. "I'm not sure that fits any longer with our company policy."

"What about this one," Harry said, then paraphrased, "No one can serve two masters. Either he will hate the one and love the other, or he will be devoted to the one and despise the other. You cannot serve both truth and money."

The publisher bristled. "Since when does one of my employees get off quoting the Bible to me?"

"Since right now." Harry stabbed the air between them. "This story is big. Take it or leave it at your peril."

The lawyer demanded, "What's that supposed to mean?"

"Close us down," Harry shot back, "and we'll first go public with the story through the *Rocky Mountain Press*, then we'll follow up with another story about how the *Herald* and the mayor's office tried to quash it."

There was an instant's frigid silence, then, "Get out. Both of you. Now."

Back in the hallway, Britt sneered, "Way to go, Harry. Nothing like burning your last remaining bridges." She gave

Claire a thin smile. "Nice knowing you, Miss Kingsbury. Hope your next job lasts longer than this one."

Harry hung back, allowing Britt to take the first elevator by herself. When they were alone, Claire said, "I thought you were great in there."

"I'm no good at anger," he replied, his voice hollow with fatigue. "I never was."

"You could have fooled me." They stepped into the next elevator, waited for the doors to close, then she asked, "So what do we do now?"

He glanced at his watch. "Bible study starts in an hour. If you like, we could ask them to help us pray for guidance."

"It amazes me," Claire said slowly, "just how right that idea sounds."

They rode down in silence. When the doors opened to the parking garage, Harry looked at her and said, "I want you to stay on this story."

"Don't worry," Claire replied quietly.

"I mean, go all the way." He turned to face Claire straight on. "Whatever you need."

"But hurry, right?"

He nodded somberly. "Fast as you can."

BEVERLY HILLS
AND DENVER

26

■ When Donovan awoke to the familiar luxury of the Bel Air Hotel, his relief was so great he shouted out loud.

He slid from the four-poster bed and padded across the Persian carpet. He flung back the curtains, took in the sunlight and the blooming mimosa and the birdsong, and had to laugh. A flashback. That's all it had been. The stress and the worry and that awful drug Trish had given him, it had brought on a nightmarish flashback.

But it was all over now. Donovan rushed over to where he had thrown off his clothes the night before, frantically searched his pockets, and drew out the contract. He exclaimed with relief and joy when he saw that the contract was indeed signed and initialed—not with some supernatural force as he had imagined, but just in ink. Natural, normal, black ink.

He crushed the contract to his chest, and jigged a quick

two-step across the suite. Finally, finally, it was done. It was his. The money and the power and the status and the position.

Just one final piece needed to be set in place. Donovan allowed his momentum to carry him over to the phone. He dialed the *Denver Herald*'s number from memory. But clutching the contract to his chest as he did was not enough to sustain his elation. With each ring, he felt the joy and relief slipping away.

So when the operator finally came on the line, it was with a sigh that Donovan said, "Claire Kingsbury, please. This is Donovan Stone."

That morning, Claire walked straight from the elevators toward Harry's office. When she saw he had not yet arrived, she changed course for her desk. Eyes followed her progress across the newsroom. There was no place on earth, Claire reflected, where gossip traveled faster than here. No one approached or spoke. Nobody wanted to get too close to the condemned.

Except Lillian. She walked up, handed Claire a steaming mug, smiled as though the whole world was smiling with her. "You're not going to believe who's waiting for you on the phone."

"This is not a good day for surprises," Claire protested. She noticed the pair of suitcases camped out beside Lillian's desk. "Where are you going?"

"Los Angeles. Time to start ridding my life of some unwanted clutter." Lillian gave her head a tiny shake when Claire started to frown. "Smile, dear. The entire newsroom is looking for a scoop."

"Tell me something I don't know."

Lillian laughed gaily, as though Claire had just told a splendid joke. "You know the best way to make a gossip bleed? Act like you don't care."

Claire sipped at her coffee. Over the rim of her cup she happened to notice Britt Shaw watching her, the expression turning increasingly bitter. The sight gave her strength to smile back. "How's this?"

"You're learning." Lillian patted her arm. "I'll tell you a little secret, my dear. When it comes to predicting which way the wind is blowing, people don't know half as much as they think they do."

"What is that supposed to mean?"

"Just stay with Harry, trust him, and do your best."

"I will." This time, the smile had genuine strength behind it. "Thanks, Lillian. You're a pal."

"Now, that's better." Lillian's eyes glittered mischievously. "Ready for your little surprise?"

"No."

"Yes you are. Just hold to that wonderful poise you're showing."

For some reason, Claire's heart started hammering. "I've never been poised. Especially not now."

"Ah, that's where you're wrong."

"Tell me what it is, Lillian."

The great dark eyes willed her to be steady as she replied, "Evelyn is on the phone for you."

Claire felt as though she would have jumped out of her skin, except for Lillian's hand resting on her arm. "You're kidding."

"Steady now," Lillian soothed. "The eyes of the world are upon you."

"Not today, I can't handle it."

Lillian took a step back. "I'll be praying that you can."

Claire found great peace in the simple words, enough to walk over, turn her back to the room, and say in a quietly cheerful tone, "Mom, is that you?"

"When I heard the news that you had finally left that miserable little town, I jumped for joy. I really did."

"Ouray is a lot of things, Mom," Claire eased herself down into her chair, "but miserable is not one of them."

"Miserable I said and miserable I meant. Of course, Denver is hardly the focal point of the world, but it certainly is a step in the right direction."

Claire sipped thoughtfully from her coffee. It was not her mother's words which were the cause of this internal reflection, but rather her own calm. Usually Evelyn's tirades against everything to do with Colorado sent her through the roof. But not today. This day, she felt . . . Claire searched for the word to describe how she felt. Sheltered. Yes, that was it. She felt as though she was sheltered from the arrows of Evelyn's words, and from the storm of her own emotions.

"Claire, are you there?"

"I'm here, Mom."

"Well, you were so quiet, I was beginning to wonder." Clearly her mother was uncertain how to take the absence of defensive anger. "Never mind. Why I was actually calling was to tell you that you really must come out to Los Angeles. I mean, now that the traveling bug has finally bitten you, why stop halfway?"

"I have a job, Mom." As soon as the words were spoken, Claire sensed a subtle undercurrent, one that left her feeling as though she should not have spoken at all.

"Oh, nonsense." Now that there was opposition, Evelyn became far more spirited. "You haven't been out here since Ted and I were married. And as for that job of yours, I'm sure Ted could use his connections to land you something far better with the *L.A. Times*."

Claire opened her mouth to reply that if she ever got hired by one of the majors, it would be on her own merit. But again she felt the sense of wrongness, and she stopped herself. Confused, she drew the receiver an inch or so away from her ear. What was she missing?

"Claire?"

She brought the receiver back. "Just a second, Mom. I'm thinking."

"You're what?" Again, the reasoned response seemed to leave Evelyn floundering.

"Thinking." Something more was at work here. Claire could not explain why she could be so certain, but the feeling was as real as Evelyn's presence down the line. Claire closed her eyes and lofted a swift prayer for guidance upwards.

"Really, I can't see why you need to think about this at all. I wrote you in my last letter that we would pay for your trip. You should just trot on back home, pack your bags, and catch the next plane out."

"I'm a little busy right now, Mom. There's a big story

breaking." The words were a little hard to get around the sudden pang of guilt. Claire glanced at where her purse lay. Evelyn's last letter still sat there, unopened. "But thanks so much for the offer."

"I'm not letting you off the hook that easy, young lady. I am *ordering* you to come out here immediately, do you hear me?"

"I hear you." Claire glanced up to find Lillian signaling frantically and pointing at her own phone. Claire lowered the receiver, heard her friend say, "It's Donovan Stone, he's calling from Los Angeles."

An instant of unexpected insight flashed through her mind and heart. "Perfect."

"What?" Her mother showed a flash of irritation. "Claire, is there someone else in there with you?"

"Mom, I'm sitting in a newsroom, of course there is. Hang on just a second, please." Before her mother had time to respond, she turned back to Lillian. "Do you have room to put me up for a couple of nights?"

"In Los Angeles?" Lillian brightened immensely. "Are you kidding? We could play dueling bedrooms for weeks and still not use them all."

Claire lifted the phone. "Mom, how would you like me to come by for dinner tonight?"

"Tonight?" The sudden agreement left Evelyn speechless. "Well, I suppose—"

"I have to try and arrange a couple of things. I'll get back to you within the hour. Thanks for calling, good-bye."

Claire set down the receiver, took a deep breath, and nodded when Lillian raised fingers for line three. Another breath, another forced smile, then she lifted the receiver and said as cheerfully as she could manage, "Donovan, good morning, how nice of you to phone."

Claire intercepted Harry before he was halfway to his office. "I need to go to California."

"It is customary," Harry said, marching on, "to allow one's boss a moment's peace and at least a half-cup of coffee before dropping any bombs."

"I'm serious, Harry."

He allowed himself to be halted. "When?"

"This morning. I've already made the reservations."

"Given the present state of affairs, I doubt the paper would be willing to pay your taxi fare to the airport, much less fly you to L.A."

"That's taken care of as well." Claire flashed a smile as Lillian passed them on her way out, suitcases in each hand. "My flight leaves in two hours. Lillian's was already full."

Harry stared from one woman to the other. "Is there some conspiracy going on? It's not polite to plan intrigues behind your editor's back."

"I want to try and speak with Roger Swindley." Claire hesitated, then added, "And there's some unfinished business I have to take care of in person."

"You really think Swindley is going to see you?"

"I'd like to give it a try. There's something we're missing here. Something vital. Every time I start going over what we know, I feel as though we're lacking the key element, the one thing that will tie it all together."

Harry sighed his acceptance of the inevitable. "Well, at least let me drive you to the airport."

Donovan eased his way into the limo's leather luxury, and said in greeting, "I just spoke with the *Herald* reporter."

"Claire Kingsbury, right?" Chuckie's bland features turned his way. "What did she say?"

Donovan nodded his thanks as the driver shut his door. "It's all taken care of."

"This is fantastic." Chuckie reached in his jacket pocket, extracted the mobile phone. "Roger's going to want to thank you personally for this."

Claire had actually surprised him, how easily he had convinced her to come, almost as though she had already planned it. "She'll be arriving late this afternoon."

Donovan listened to Chuckie's polished enthusiasm, then accepted the phone and responded as best he could to Roger's praise and thanks.

When he switched off the phone, he suddenly felt as though he could not pull enough air into his lungs. He lowered the window, watched the palm trees cruise by, but still he felt as though he could not draw a decent breath. He pretended at calm and asked, "Mind dropping me off? I'd like to do a little shopping."

"No problem." Chuckie leaned forward to rap on the glass. When the driver had pulled over and Donovan had alighted, Chuckie leaned through the open window and pulled his masklike features into another smile. "Welcome to the magic kingdom, Mr. Stone. Hope you enjoy the ride."

Donovan stood there at the corner of Wiltshire and

Rodeo Drive, forcing himself to throw off the clutter of feel-ings. He was acting like a loser, he told himself repeatedly. It was time to fly. His dreams had finally become reality.

He stood there until the clamor in his mind and heart had eased to a silent whimper. Then he crossed the street and began taking long strides down the tree-lined drive. The weather was crisp and bright, which meant the furs were out with the sunglasses. Donovan strolled down Rodeo, savoring the feeling that he could finally afford to shop at a place like this without cringing.

In Beverly Hills, shopping was not an act or even an occu-pation. It was a way of life. And if Beverly Hills had a heart, it pumped the length of Rodeo Drive. Donovan stopped first by Battaglia's, already his favorite men's shop. The staid wood-lined elegance of a British men's club muted even the brashest client. Above the shelves and racks rose walls deco-rated with signed photographs of past customers, stars one and all. He sipped his espresso while ordering a sports coat with two matching slacks and a couple of ties.

He stepped back out into the sunlight, reveling in the feeling that he was finally over his funk, and paused to admire a couple of passing ladies. Beverly Hills was definitely a center of style. Maybe Europe had it, he'd heard it was another dimension entirely over there. It gave him a real kick to realize he could afford a trip now, first-class all the way. Anything and everything, all but the time, and he'd make that happen soon enough. For the moment, though, Beverly Hills was enough. People dressed and styled and walked and talked and drove and ate with class. What was more, they appreciated it in oth-ers.

Donovan walked across the street to Fred's, the most exclusive jeweler on the town's most exclusive street. He put a pair of ruby and diamond earrings on hold, thinking that would finally get around to melting Claire's heart. At seven thousand dollars it was an extravagance that deserved a good solid scream. But what the heck, he was only in love once that week.

DENVER TO
LOS ANGELES

27

■ Harry hesitated outside the entrance to the Denver Airport. "You're sure this is the right thing?"

"For the fifth time, yes." But she did not mind the question, nor the concern that fueled it. "Something's still missing from all this, Harry. I just know it."

"We've got the makings of a great story, Claire."

"Not yet. I've searched and searched, but I can't figure out what it is that's bugging me. Something about Swindley, something about the game, I don't know." She shook her head. "I just feel like we're missing the last vital piece."

Harry mulled that one over. "How do you intend to get in to see Swindley? He's got a reputation for loathing the press."

"Donovan managed to set up an appointment for me."

"Donovan." The word was scarcely a sigh. "That's your friend, right?"

She set down her case so she could reach out and touch his arm. "He's not my anything. And that's the truth."

Harry turned and looked back towards the city. From the new airport the Denver skyline looked like a Lego game set against the Rockies. The land surrounding the airport was utterly flat, dry, and dusty. Even at the onset of winter the region was held by the timeless grip of the plains.

"I've been so used to keeping an emotional distance," Harry finally said, "I don't even know how to stop."

Claire felt her heartrate surge at the words, as though she had been waiting for them without even knowing. "What do you mean?"

"It's crazy, isn't it, how what I thought was strength was really my own way of running away from the challenge of caring. And this hard cynical shell, when it shattered, left me more helpless than I've ever been in my entire life." He looked at her, the smile not quite making it to his eyes. "Who could imagine a tougher challenge for a newspaperman than to strip away his cynical nature and find the strength to care."

"No, that's not what I meant," she said, the words sticking down deep, as though she already knew the answer, had known it all along. "You've talked several times about something hitting you hard. Who hurt you, Harry?"

His throat was so tight the swallow was audible. He looked at her a long time, the gaze so open it did not leave her room to hide. "A beautiful young lady pops up one day, stands there in her cowboy boots and jeans, straight and tall as the mountains, and says she just wanted to thank me for publishing her article. You remember that, Claire?" He took her silence for an answer and said in a tone she had never heard before, "I've loved you from the first moment I laid eyes on you, Claire. I love you still."

She nodded, or tried to, but sudden tremors were tightening her muscles to where no movement came easy.

"You stood there in the doorway, and I felt my whole frozen know-it-all little universe come crashing down. Everything I had spent a lifetime using as ways to keep from caring, all of it vanished in the blink of an eye. In the days and weeks that followed, I couldn't put the pieces back in place. The lies were exposed, and nothing could make them appear to be truth any more. All I was left with was this hollow emptiness. Not just sorrow over loving someone who didn't love me. I tried to tell myself that was it, but honesty did not come to me in half-measures. I was seeing the void of a life unfulfilled, of a soul longing for its Maker."

He regarded her for a long silent moment, drinking her in, then said, "I'm glad knowing you has brought me first to my knees and then to Christ. Really glad. But I wish it could be different between us. I can't help that."

When she did not answer, or could not, he led her inside. Which was good, because at the moment she could not have managed walking on her own. He settled her into a chair by the window, took her ticket and her luggage over to the counter. Done with a minimum of discussion, as though the confession had robbed them both of the strength to speak.

Claire watched him stand in line for her and check her in. She waited and hoped that something would come to her. Some way of telling him that within her own heart, their friendship was ripening into something more. Something that probably had been intended since the beginning, but she had been too caught up in past hurts and selfish desires to understand.

But when he returned, she remained as far away from words as she had been when he left. As though something still stood in her way, something that needed doing before she could respond with words and feelings of her own.

Harry seemed to sense it even before he approached, because he preceded his arrival with a smile and a hefting of the shopping bag he had brought with him. "A little gift for your trip. I bought it a while back, been carrying it around in my trunk, wondering when would be the right time." He sat down beside her and put the bag in her lap. "Go on, open it, they're calling your flight."

She forced her hands to move, pulled out the paper, and looked inside. "Oh, Harry."

"All those boots you wear look completely worn out. How many pairs do you have, anyway?"

"I don't know. I get attached to them, and have trouble throwing any out."

"Well, a star reporter deserves better."

"It's too much." She pulled the boots out one at a time. The rich leather shimmered in the airport lighting. Pale golden ostrich rose to join finely stitched shafts the color of a well-worn saddle, all soft as silk. She turned one over, read out loud, "Luchese." She looked back at him. "Harry, I can't, these cost you a fortune."

"Take them," he said, his voice low but carrying such emotion she could not hold his gaze. "Please. If not for you, for me."

"Thank you," she whispered, thinking that these were words she often repeated to him. "Thank you for everything."

"Will you put them on? I'll carry the other ones back. I'd really like to see how they look on you."

So she did. Right there, pulled off the ones scarred and scratched from years of hard wear, then slipped into the others, and knew the instant they were on they had been special ordered. "How did you get my measurements?"

"I called Miss Emma. She mailed one of your old pairs. Do you like them?"

"We're already old friends." She stood up, pulled her jeans straight, and asked, "How do I look?"

"Great. You always look great." He stood with her, hugged her once quickly, so tight the breath caught in both of them. Then he released her and gave an over-bright smile. "They gave your flight's last call two minutes ago. You've got to run."

"Harry—"

"Go, Claire. Just go."

The flight took her directly over I-70. The air was brilliantly clear, the view spectacular. She watched the outskirts of Denver give way to brown foothills, and they to sparkling white highlands. Beyond Loveland Pass, Dillon Lake glimmered like a sun-dappled blade. Copper Valley gave way to Vail Pass, then on to Glenwood Springs with Aspen in the distance. Only when the snowy peaks were replaced by the scarred canyons and eerie forms of Monument Valley did her homesickness begin to fade away.

She sat wrapped in a silence that was more than just an absence of words. She turned her head towards the window, convinced that more than just her own heart and mind were at work.

Suddenly she saw with crystal clarity the three tasks of the trip arrayed before her. Donovan, her mother, Swindley—all awaiting her arrival. Taken together like that, the duties seemed insurmountable. Any one of them alone would be almost too much.

She sat there, and in the quiet internal mirror Claire saw her needs revealed, not as flaws, but rather as opportunities. Claire squeezed her eyes tight, found words there waiting for her. And something beyond words, a gift as gentle as the silent mirror. She said, *Fill me, Lord,* the words rising from far beyond herself. And with them came a love so powerful she could not help but release one hot tear.

She lay her forehead against the bulkhead, overwhelmed by the sense that her Father in heaven had been waiting all this time for her to turn and reveal her needs and ask His help. And comfort. And healing. And guidance. And love.

The taxi dropped her off on a broad Beverly Hills avenue, one lined by tall palms and stately homes. Lillian Stockton Fletcher had the door opened before Claire was halfway down the path. Claire gave her friend a hug, took a pair of steps across the old flagstone foyer, and declared, "I've seen factories smaller than this."

"I would imagine a lot of factories held more love than this house did as well." She led Claire around the double staircase with its sweeping balustrade, down a hallway strung with a trio of crystal chandeliers, and stopped before a pair of double doors. "You can sleep in Mother's room. I'm just along there in the humble abode of dear old Dad."

Timidly Claire walked through doors twice her height, took in a chamber larger than the newsroom and done in a pastel rainbow of raw silk. "Thanks for letting me stay with you."

"Are you kidding?" Lillian slipped one arm around her shoulders and gave her a vigorous hug. "I can't tell you how great it is to have some company here while I sort through the memories. Now I'll leave you to freshen up. When you're ready, come join me in the living room."

When Claire returned to the front of the house, she found Lillian surrounded by boxes, papers strewn haphazardly around the room. The older woman was sifting documents and books and old articles. Claire pulled over a chair. "What are you doing?"

"I'm going to try and straighten out my life," Lillian replied, without looking up. "Rid myself of things I have used to hold the world out. Starting with the sale of this old place."

Claire surveyed the room, its rich setting, the great bay windows overlooking a carefully cultivated lawn. "How does it feel?"

"Free," Lillian replied quietly. "For the first time in my life, I am cutting away the dross, making room inside myself for something greater."

"Do you know what that is?"

"Your father, for one thing. Beyond that, I don't feel much need to look just yet." She looked up then, her eyes filled with a lustrous joy. "I have prayed about it, and I feel at peace. What future plan could mean more than that?"

"I can't believe I'm hearing that from you."

Lillian took her time in replying. "I am trying hard to make myself worthy of your father."

"Pop is no saint."

"No, but he has been tested by the fires and come out stronger. I, on the other hand, melted and ran to the safety of my money every time the going got the least bit warm." Her smile turned bitter. "It was my parents' way of dealing with the world. Whenever things got bad, leave and let the lawyers clear away the mess. Pity I should have spent all these years doing what I disliked most about them. I thought so long as I didn't marry and put another child through what I had endured, everything would be just grand. In truth, all I did was construct a perfectly logical reason never to care, never to give, never to love."

"Don't be too hard on yourself."

"I am not being hard, I am being honest." She looked around the room, taking in the marble tiled floors and Persian carpets and beams and flagstone and paintings. "What a prison I made of my life."

"Not any more."

"No," Lillian agreed quietly. She surveyed Claire. "You look very nice. When is that man supposed to pick you up?"

"His name is Donovan," Claire corrected, but without heat. "He'll be here in about thirty minutes. He's going with me to Evelyn's for dinner."

The dark eyes were piercing. "Are you sure you did the right thing, inviting him to dine with you and your mother?"

"He was so insistent," Claire replied. "He always is. I have a lot of trouble saying no to him."

"Yes, that's one of the most unfortunate qualities of a man like that."

"But I've prayed about it," Claire went on. "And I feel at peace with the way things are going."

Lillian gave her a slow nod. "I never imagined I would come to the point where those words would carry such weight with me."

Claire hesitated, then asked, "Would you pray with me now?"

Lillian reached out, gave her a quick hug. "There is nothing on earth that would give me more joy."

Donovan came around to open her door. He had decided against using the studio limo. Claire did not seem the type to jump and shout over being driven around. He also wanted a chance at a little intimacy, and he was not ready to share that with a faceless driver.

Claire climbed from the rented Lexus, and warily examined her mom's '60s-style ranch house. As Donovan walked her towards the door, he commented, "It's small for Bel Air and too far back towards the reservoir. But it's still Bel Air."

"Well, look who's here!" Claire's mom looked like a lot of the older L.A. women he had met, immaculately groomed and dieted to the max. Donovan slowed to a halt, and watched as Claire accepted the quick embrace and tried to smile when her mother held her at arms' length and said, "Finally my little girl decides to come out and see how the real world lives!"

"Hello, Mom."

"And look at that dress, would you. A Fendi, isn't it? Imagine, my little girl standing here in designer fashion." She turned towards the man standing in the doorway and cried, "Just look at her, Ted. Whoever would have thought that a little girl raised in the back of beyond would have such marvelous dress sense?"

"Not so little," the man replied heartily. "She's almost a head taller than you."

"Mom, I'd like you to meet Donovan Stone. Donovan, this is Evelyn."

"How do you do."

"A pleasure, I'm sure." She took a proprietal grip on her daughter's arm and steered her towards the entrance. "You've not seen Ted since the wedding, have you? No, of course not. And my goodness, how long has it been since we were together? It must be almost a year."

"Three years," Claire corrected quietly. "I drove up from Ouray and we had a coffee at the Denver airport while you waited for your connection."

"Whenever. That's all behind us now." Evelyn guided her daughter into the house, ignoring Donovan entirely. "You've finally left that horrid little village behind you, and I'm going to show you a grand time."

Once they were all inside, Evelyn released her daughter so as to place her arm around her husband's waist. "Ted is dentist to a lot of the A-list stars."

"A-list, B-list, right through the alphabet. Love working with them. Love the tales. Love the hype. Love it all."

"And directors. And producers." Evelyn flashed her big smile. "It'll be such fun, making all the right connections for my lovely young daughter."

"Had Lenny Kravitz in the other day," Ted went on. "Guy

loves to gossip so much I had to charge him double-time." He patted down his greying pompadour. "Great guys. Great gals."

"We get so many invitations," her mother paused for a grand laugh. "It's like a card game, dealing out what we're going to be doing this week."

Ted looked fondly down at his wife. "Just look at those incredible teeth. And they didn't cost me a dime. Not that your mother let me off cheap. You ever seen her sweater drawer?"

"Ted, stop."

"She's a one-woman committee to keep all the goats in Tibet wearing crew cuts." When Claire did not laugh, he added, "That's where cashmere comes from. Chinese goats."

"Where are our manners," Evelyn exclaimed. "We haven't even asked your friend what he does. I'm sorry, I've forgotten your name."

"Donovan Stone," he answered smoothly. Taking it easy, glad he had come, knowing here was a way to open Claire up once and for all. One glance was enough to show she wasn't able to handle her mother alone. "I'm a consultant."

"How fascinating," Evelyn replied vaguely. "We have a lovely California chardonnay, can I get you both a glass?"

Claire replied with a shake of her head. Donovan covered for her with, "Chardonnay's fine with me." He paused, giving Evelyn time to turn away before adding, "We're neighbors, by the way. Temporarily, anyway."

That brought them both around. Ted asked, "You live around here?"

"When I'm in L.A., which is more and more these days." Another minor pause, relishing what was to come. "I keep a suite over at the Bel Air."

The bottle in Evelyn's hand was instantly forgotten   The Bel Air Hotel?"

"Great place," Donovan said. "Terrific staff. And I can get from there to the studio in no time flat."

A silence, then, "What studio is this?"

Another pause for effect, the tone kept casual. "I'm working with Roger Swindley."

Evelyn looked at her daughter, as though no longer sure who she was. "You work for Swindley Broadcasting?"

"No," Donovan said, drawing it out, "I work *with* Roger Swindley. I've been put in charge of his new venture in Denver."

"Denver, of course, that's where you live now, isn't it, Claire?" Ted offered. his eyes not leaving Donovan's face "I believe I've heard something about that venture Something to do with a movie."

"And a game. They're both called Babylon." Reveling in the attention, glad to see Claire's face registering surprise as well.

Claire demanded quietly, "You're going to work for Roger Swindley?"

"Signed the contract yesterday," he said proudly. Certain he had done the right thing, waiting until now to spring the news. "You're looking at the new president of the Swindley Airport Studios."

There was a long moment of silence before Evelyn glanced down and recognized the bottle in her hand. She took a glass from the cabinet, walked over, and handed it to Donovan. She gave him a smile that put all her others to shame. "We've never had an opportunity to meet Roger Swindley."

Claire spoke up, her voice far too quiet. "He's a monster."

The words were so startling that Donovan had no choice but to laugh, which allowed the others to cover their surprise by doing the same, and for Ted to say, "Hey, sure, it's a tough world out here. Got to have that killer instinct to make it in Hollywood." His glance was not to his wife, but rather to Donovan. "Isn't that right?"

Donovan nodded, still confused over Claire's attitude, but willing to let it slide. For the moment. "Here more than any-where."

Evelyn walked over and sat down, still at a loss as to what to say. Which was good, because as soon as she was settled, Claire spoke up. "I have something important to tell you."

"Oh, now let me guess," Evelyn interrupted, clapping her hands. "You and Donovan—"

"I asked Donovan to come with me tonight so he could hear this as well," Claire replied.

Though her tone remained quiet, there was a sense of gathering power. Donovan watched her, realizing he knew almost nothing about this strange young woman, not even enough to guess what she might be about to say.

But nothing could have prepared him for what came next. Claire leaned forward and said in that quiet yet strong voice, "I have accepted Jesus Christ into my life as Lord and Master. I want to share with you a little of what that means to me."

"The first time here, I was pretty much floundering," Donovan said, filling the car with chatter. Anything was better than sitting there and enduring more of the silence. "But I'm learning. The magic kingdom isn't what's down on the map as Hollywood. It's in this area called Westside. Beverly Hills, Bel Air, Westwood, those are the main parts. Santa Monica's not really Westside, but parts are sort of fringe dwellings, so is Malibu. West Hollywood forms the other borderland. And if there's a palace guesthouse, it has to be the Bel Air Hotel."

When Claire remained silent, he waved his hand to encompass the night and went on, "Hollywood isn't just a location, and the area is not where the filmmakers work. Hollywood is the place where dreams come true. Mine, anyway. But you've got to pay the price, learn the rules. The laws are totally different here. That's the cost of admittance."

He waited for a reaction. When none came, he pressed on, "It's all a game. All show. Long as you don't let it get to you, though, life out here is a constant high. After a few days you feel like the rest of the world doesn't ever really wake up. I tell you, this place cooks." He caught sight of her cowering against the side door. Well, not cowering, just leaning against it. Watching him with a steady gaze, as though nothing was hidden from her. Which left him tremendously unsteady. "What's the matter?"

"What did you think of what I said back there?"

He forced a laugh. "Too much too fast. I'll need some time to digest it." Which was a joke. He had known his reaction the instant she had started talking. She was going through a religious phase, nothing more. All that stuff she had ladled out, it was just the result of her wandering in from the mountains and getting hit by the big city, too much too fast. What she needed was to get away from it all, come out and have a little R&R with him. But he knew now was not the time to say it. Not just yet.

He was proud of himself, the way he was handling it. That pair they had left behind, they had been beyond stunned. Ted had frozen up hard, all that swell smile and glad-handing had vanished without a trace. Evelyn had almost come unglued, especially when Claire had walked over, embraced her mother, and said that she forgave her for everything, and wanted them to become true friends.

He turned down Rodeo Drive, where the Christmas lights had just gone up. All along the central strip the trees and bushes had been transformed into flickering outdoor chandeliers. The shop fronts were full of glitter and glamour. People swirled by in Porsches and Cadillacs and Rolls, or strolled along the broad sidewalks enjoying the balmy L.A. weather. "This place is like a giant movie set. Everybody's out to corner the spotlight."

"I don't belong here." The voice was calm, resolute.

He tried to laugh it off, but he was disappointed. He had hoped the place's charms would work on her as they had on him. "Only elves and fairies and princes of the magic kingdom ever feel at home on Rodeo Drive." He started to add, *And I'm one of the princes, or will be soon.* But something held him back. Instead he pulled into a vacant space across from where Via Rodeo climbed its little manmade hill. He cut the motor and reached into his side pocket. "I have something for you."

"Donovan, I can't—"

"Wait, just a second, okay?" He passed over the velvet box with the Fred logo stamped on the top. "A little something to say, I don't know, maybe just I'm glad you're here."

She hesitated, then accepted the box, opened the lid, and sat staring down at the earrings. He looked at her, then back to the box, proud of his choice. Alternating diamonds and rubies formed a heartshaped pattern set in twenty-one carat gold. Seven thousand bucks. His heart swelled at his own generosity, and the thanks that were sure to come.

Instead, she closed the box, set it on the dividing panel between them, and said quietly, "You're very sweet, Donovan. But I can't accept them."

He stared at the box, then back at her. "What?"

"Donovan," she said, and reached across, touched his arm, the mere grazing of her fingers leaving an electric tingle. But this calm of hers, it was eerie. He was the one who always knew the next step. Right now, though, he didn't have a clue. She leaned forward, and his heart leaped in anticipation of the old magic working its way in her again. Instead, she asked softly, "Would you like to pray with me?"

He was so stunned it took a long moment to croak out, "Here?"

She nodded slowly, rocking her whole upper body. Her face caught in the streetlight shone with gentle fervor. "Please. It would be the finest gift you could ever give me."

He swallowed back the laugh, though that was what he really wanted to do, laugh in her face. Roar with laughter. She was that weird. "What is it with you tonight?"

She withdrew her hand, leaned back against her door, and nodded once more. A single confirmation. She continued to gaze at him then, her eyes filling the same quiet resolve as her voice. "I made a mistake, that's all. And I kept making more mistakes every time I saw you."

"A mistake, with me?" He wasn't really hearing this. "Didn't you hear what I told your mother?"

"Every word."

"I'm on the way up. My path is finally set in place. You ought to give this religion stuff a rest, and hitch a ride to the stars while you've got a chance."

In reply, Claire opened her door. "My path is set as well, Donovan." She slid from the car and bent over to look at him. "And it's not the same as yours."

"Claire!" He found himself unable to let her go, the wrenching too sudden, too much out of his control. He was as shaken by the way she had gained the upper hand as he was by her leaving. But when she bent back down, he could not think of anything that might hold her, except possibly, "We still on for tomorrow's meeting with Swindley?"

"If you still want to take me."

"I'll pick you up at nine." He could feel it slowly slipping away, despite his maneuverings, his power. "Where are you going?"

"I thought I'd walk for a little while. I'll catch a cab back to Lillian's."

"Yeah, you do that," he grated, and in a tumble of anger and disappointment he realized that he had lost. Given it his best shot, and come out the loser.

BEVERLY HILLS

28

■ That night, Claire dreamed of the previous summer's final hike. At least, that was how the dream began.

It had been a gloomy day, the sky shrouded with the weight of a season's passage. Clouds hung heavy and low, the sun lost beyond the dark grey veil. She did not mind. She had never found gloom or rain to be a burden. On grey days, flowers shimmered with clearer colors. Muted tones within the rocks and trees and lichen revealed themselves, hues which were overpowered when the sun shone strongly.

She took the path up towards the Bridge of Heaven, a hogback ridge along the Amphitheater Range. It was an all-day hike, especially with her pace slowed by the fog. She was in no hurry. If the clouds delivered their load of snow, it would be her last highland walk of the year, and she wanted to linger just as long as possible.

She spent over an hour picking her way carefully through

heavy mist, unable to see more than a few feet in front of her, but knowing the path so well that it was enough. The silence was complete, even the birds quietened by the dark veil. Sheer cliffs dropped unseen off to her left, but it did not matter, not so long as she took it slow and cautiously.

Eventually the trail began to level off, announcing she was nearing the crest. At that moment, a brief puff of wind blew away the upper cover, and a blue-black void appeared overhead. The sudden shift from shrouded shadows to utter clarity drew a gasp from her lungs.

There came another puff of wind, and the cloud covering was pushed further down. A long winding trail stretched out before her, utterly flat, utterly straight, surrounded by a great billowing sea of white. Island pinnacles rose in the neighboring distance, the clouds sending frothy plumes up and over them with every breath of wind.

There came a sense of the world shifting, as an unseen and gentle wind drifted across her soul. She realized then that she was dreaming.

In the dream, she began to cry. Softly, quietly, unwilling even in her weeping to disturb the total glorious peace. Overhead blazed a sun, more brilliant and lustrous than any she had ever seen, or even imagined. And she knew that if she were to raise her eyes to it, she would not survive. Looking would be enough to consume her.

Her head remained bowed beneath that overwhelming light, and still she wept. Why should she ever go back down? Why not stay in this perfection forever? She wept because she had no answer, and because her heart melted with yearning to rest here eternally.

It was not a voice that answered her. It was a sense of guidance far beyond mere words. It was *knowledge,* a triumphant assurance that His peace would remain with her always. Wherever He called her to go. Whatever He called her to do. So long as she remained upon His path.

Claire woke up then, and rubbed a hand down a face wet with tears. She rolled from the bed, the action automatic, a movement brought with her from the dream, and slid down to her knees. The night's darkness was so illuminated with the unseen sun's brilliance that she could not help but bow her head.

DENVER AND LOS ANGELES

29

■ Harry spent the morning going through the motions, while his head and heart remained fastened upon Claire's absence. He missed her more than he thought possible, as though admitting his feelings to her had enlarged his own capacity to care.

He decided to leave an e-mail message for Troy, not so much because the kid needed to know Claire's whereabouts, but simply because he wanted to talk with someone about her.

Less than an hour later, his secretary came through with, "Call for you on one, somebody named Troy."

He grabbed the phone, said, "When are you coming in?"

"Never mind that," Troy snapped back. "Tell me you weren't serious."

"What are you talking about?"

"You didn't send her to Los Angeles. Not to meet with Skate's boss. Tell me it didn't happen."

"The guy's name is Swindley. And I didn't send her anywhere. She went because she felt she needed to talk with him."

"Oh, oh," Troy started moaning, which did nothing for Harry's own state of mind. "This is worse than bad."

"A number of questions came up in the course of our investigation," Harry said, trying to calm himself by convincing this kid from computerland. "They all pointed to Swindley. Some consultant to his organization offered to set up a meeting."

But Troy was having none of it. "You've got to stop her."

Harry had to smile. "It's not all that easy, stopping Claire from doing anything she's set her mind on."

"You've *got* to. These people are killers."

Despite himself, Harry felt the fear take hold, filling his chest with icy tendrils. "Do you have proof of that?"

"Enough to make me sure of what I'm saying. They destroy your mind. They eat your soul. I know. I've seen it happen."

Claire awoke not to a sense of lingering peace but rather to the feeling that she was still missing some essential key. She rolled from the bed, dressed, and started down the long hall, still searching. She walked into the sunlit kitchen and found Lillian on the phone. The older woman smiled, pointed to the coffee pot, and said into the receiver, "Your daughter just walked into the room, looking like a too-tall, redheaded angel. Wait, let her pour her first cup." She reached out with the phone. "Nathan wants to say hello."

Claire took a sip, then accepted the receiver. "Pop, I'm caught up in the feeling that I'm missing something important. It just won't let me go."

Nathan was clearly content to let her take the conversation where she wanted. "This has to do with why you're in Hollywood?"

"This story I'm working on," she agreed, pausing for another taste. She shook her head as Lillian lifted a piece of bread and pointed at the toaster. "I keep trying to push it away, but every time I do, it comes back stronger."

"From what I've heard," Nathan said, "this could be an important exposé of the entertainment industry."

"I'd like to think so." Claire smiled as Lillian came over with the pot and replenished her cup. "I just wish I knew what it is I'm not seeing."

Nathan was silent a long moment, then said, "The Bible is clear about our place and our role upon earth. We are stewards. Servants held responsible for our actions, for our talents, for our usage of God's creation. The Bible and entertainment are not contradictory. God does not condemn man's desire to relax and enjoy his amusements. But the Lord does stand opposed to any direction, whether in entertainment or in life, which is against the Scriptures' edicts. Those who have been granted such enormous powers and wealth, those who refuse to use them to exalt His glory and serve His kingdom, they shall have much to answer for."

Claire looked out over the sun-dappled garden, wondered at all the years she had refused to listen to such instruction.

"We are His hands, His voice, the bearers of His light and

His message." Nathan went on, "If you are seeking to do His will, then ask for both His blessing and His guidance. I am certain He will lead you."

It was there waiting for her when she went back upstairs. So clear and so vivid was the realization that she froze to the top step, unable to move.

Finally a voice from below called, "Claire?"

She turned around, very slowly, and softly said, "The drug."

Lillian peered worriedly up at her. "Are you all right?"

"I'm fine."

"You don't look fine. You look like you've been struck by lightning."

"It's been there in front of me all this time, and I haven't seen it."

"Harry's on the phone. Do you want me to tell him to call back?"

"No. I need to talk with him." She forced herself to start back down. "What a goof I've been."

Lillian watched her descend. "Did you finally figure out the answer?"

"No." She walked over and picked up the receiver. "But at least now I know the question."

"You've got to call this off." Harry's voice was as serious as she had ever heard. "I just talked to Troy. He thinks you're walking into the lion's den."

"He's right," Claire said. "You know how I kept feeling like there was something we were missing? Well, I know what it is."

"It's an editor's job to know when to cut and run. This story is ready."

"The drugs," she insisted. "I've got to confront Swindley over the drugs."

"You want to risk everything over a supposition? I'm telling you, Claire, I've got a bad feeling about all this. Stay away from that guy."

"Listen to me, Harry. It's the drug. That's the key. This isn't about money. Swindley's not out to addict more kids and sell another million copies of some game."

Harry huffed, "You could have fooled me."

"He's fooling everybody. Stop a minute and just think about those kids."

"They fried their brains to golden nuggets and wandered off to never-never land. What's so hard to figure out there?" He tried one more time. "Let it go, Claire. Please."

"Come on, Harry. This is major. I'm not talking about the ones who've vanished. Think for a second about the others. The ones Troy calls the Enforcers."

"What are you saying?"

"Think about all the trouble they went to, setting up those treasure troves, and then arranging to have the kids brain-washed once they arrived." Crazy how she could be so calm on the outside when her pulse was racing off the chart. "Why go to all that trouble to hook kids that are already hooked?"

Reluctantly Harry allowed her to pull him off his course. "I don't see—"

"The doors, the chambers, the Tower. All those subliminal messages, all that programming work. Why? If these kids are already so hooked that they're spending everything they've got and more on the game, why try to draw them in more tightly?"

Harry was silent a long moment. "I'm listening."

"I've felt like there's something else going on here. Right from the beginning. But I couldn't see what the point was, or how he was making it happen." The adrenaline rush was so strong she felt she could have lifted off the earth and flown on her own power. "But half of the puzzle was right there before us from the very beginning. The drug. He's using the drug to do something more than just hook the kids tighter to his little game."

"What do you think it is?"

"I don't know." She stretched and eased her back as much as her excitement would allow. "But I'm sure going to ask him to his face."

Harry thought it over, decided, "I'm coming out there."

"Really?" Delight lifted her voice an octave. "That would be great."

"Don't you do anything until I get there."

Lillian poked her head around the corner and said, "A car's just pulled up. Looks like your lad's early."

"He'll just have to wait, I'm not nearly ready," she said, then to Harry, "I have to go. Meet me at Lillian's."

"Claire—"

"I'll get back as soon as I can." With a smile, she set the receiver down on Harry's protests and raced for the bedroom.

After telling Donovan to wait, Lillian joined her in the bedroom. As Claire finished dressing, she told her what Harry had just said, trying to make light of his concern. Working to keep the confrontation from bothering her, now that the moment had arrived.

But Lillian was on Harry's side. "Hollywood has become a cauldron. In it churns the madness that threatens to engulf America. Letting those people dictate morals and politics and social issues in the name of entertainment is like giving the asylum keys to the inmates."

Claire checked her purse, made sure an extra notepad and her recorder were all there. "Are you telling me not to go?"

"I try to refrain from making futile gestures." Lillian stood in the doorway, her dark eyes flashing. "All I am saying is that the majority of people involved in the film trade are obsessed. About their profession, about their sports, their cars, their homes, their sex lives. They go in for extremes. They are ambitious to the point of viciousness. Such people make dangerous, unpredictable enemies."

Claire checked her hurried makeup in the mirror, decided it would have to do. "That doesn't help me a bit."

Lillian held her arms out. "You could not be dearer to me if you were my own child. Take care, my precious one. And watch your back."

Troy paced the room like a caged tiger. He knew what he had to do. But it meant taking care, and making plans. Everything had to be mapped out in advance. And he was going to need help.

Turning on his computer, Troy discovered that they had cut him out of the game. His warrior status had been revoked, his name erased from Babylon's rolls. He thought a long moment, then began typing at lightning speed.

He started making contacts with everyone he could, using an emergency net set in place from months and years of sharing games and drugs and addictions. They were not the most reliable of friends, but they were all he had.

Except for Claire.

He remained amazed by her and by her kindness. After taking her money for bail, then leaving her standing there at the jail, giving her every reason on earth to hate his guts, what does she do? She looked into the very depths of who he was, and offered him kindness. And answers. Words that shook him to the core, yet granted with such selfless concern that he felt like someone had finally found the key to his aching heart. That anybody could be so genuine and so caring for a gamer like him, that was just incredible.

Now she was in trouble. Or would be soon.

And he was just the guy to get her out.

Claire bounded down the steps and into Donovan's car. "Sorry to have held you up."

"I tried to call," Donovan replied glumly. "Maybe a dozen times. But the phone was always busy."

"Yeah, we were talking to Pop." She smiled at the memory. "It looks like he's getting serious with Lillian. Remember? You met her that day you came by the paper."

"Swell." He shot from the drive and sped down the boulevard. "Plans have changed. We're supposed to meet Roger at his new house. The one he's building out on the cliffs over Malibu."

Claire caught the tone, inspected his handsome features, recognized the look of a wounded victim. She resisted the urge to reach over, stroke the strawberry blond locks from his forehead. "Things haven't worked out like you wanted, have they?"

"What are you talking about?" His voice grated with well-stoked anger. "Things are *great.* I've got a great life ahead. Pity you don't want to come along for the ride."

"I can't." Strange how it was possible for her to sit beside him now, see the craggy handsome features, feel the magnetic pull, and know that it simply was not to be. Not now, not ever. And be content with the knowledge. "Our paths could not be further apart if they were on opposite sides of the globe."

"I'm talking power here," he countered. "Power and wealth and the good life. I deserved more than a put-down from you, lady."

"I have found my own power in faith," she replied, having no room for anger. "And the gift of Christ's salvation."

He took the turn onto Sunset and raced to catch the next light. "How did that religion thing creep in here?"

"Because it's important to me," she said, her voice steadying. "And it should be to you."

"Well, it's not."

"I understand," she said quietly, and she did. Truly understood. It was possible to accept, though it saddened her, not because it meant they could never be together; she already knew her chosen path was taking her towards another. No, she was saddened because of what he would never know. He had made his own choice, and had to live by it.

They traveled out to where sun-hardened hills took over from the city, continuing through rock-scrabble gullies to where the boulevard emptied onto the coastal road. Donovan turned right and headed north.

The road was six lanes and grimy and crowded with a melange of vehicles—trucks belching black fumes, fancy foreign racing cars, gawking tourists with out-of-state plates, rusted flatbeds driven by hard-bitten workers. Clusters of homes were crammed between the highway and the shore; beyond them lay the Pacific and its vast blue depths. Claire decided it would be good to come back and share this with Harry.

Harry. Strange that she should be sitting beside one man, enduring his cold aloofness, and yet feel so intimately connected with another. A good man, one she would need to work hard to deserve. The challenge left her breathless.

Donovan slowed and put on his turn signal as the road started up a steep slope. At its very crest rose a new home, one of steel and reflective glass. In the harsh sunlight it looked as stern and faceless as a skyscraper. Donovan turned through unfinished gates, the tall metal barriers leaning against the new rock wall, and sped up the drive. Palms lining the avenue were whipped to an enraged frenzy by a rising ocean wind.

Up close, the house looked even more impersonal. The house actually hung over the cliff's edge. Storm surf roared far below, sending up great spumes of spray over the gleaming structure. But the house remained proudly impervious to nature's wrath.

Donovan swung the car around so that Claire's side was adjacent to the entrance. Claire opened her door, and instantly felt as though the wind wanted to rip it from her grasp. When Donovan made no move to join her, she said, "Aren't you coming in?"

"Not my meeting." He looked at her and slowly shook his head. Decision hardened his features. "You know what they call an old dog who knows when to let go?"

She found herself sad, not because it was ending, but because it had ever been allowed to begin. "No, Donovan, I don't."

He revved the engine and snapped out a single word: "Smart."

The sunlight did not follow Claire inside. The interior was so vast, with so many windows and chandeliers and recessed spotlights, yet so dark. So enclosed. So ominous.

"Pretty reporter lady, hey, this is great." The guy called Skate glided across the marble-tiled foyer. "No, really."

"The name is Claire Kingsbury. I'm here to see . . ." She faltered at the sound of a car scrunching over gravel. Claire turned, watched through the open door as Donovan's car drove back down the drive.

She started back, wanting in sudden fear to go with him, but Skate's hand was already latched to her arm. "Claire, Clarity, reporter-lady, it's all the same to me. You gonna come easy? Your choice." A snicker. "Last one you'll ever have."

■ Roger Swindley's steel and glass citadel was air conditioned to the point of frigidity. Claire sat in a pinnacle room, perched like an eagle's lair far above the roaring sea. The storm had continued to gather ever since Claire had been literally dragged into the room and slammed into the leather settee.

Roger Swindley emerged after a time, settled down across from her, and declared, "Your meddlesome tactics have become an irritant, Miss Kingsbury."

"I demand that you let me go," she snapped, fighting to overcome the tremor in her voice.

"In time." His monotone was as flat as his gaze. "First we shall endeavor to supply all the answers you have been seeking so diligently."

"This is absurd." Claire glanced behind her. Skate and another muscle-bound hulk flanked the chamber's only exit. "Don't you realize that the paper knows where I am?"

Swindley paid her no mind whatsoever. "Let me share with you a simple fact, Miss Kingsbury. The public constantly want new sensations. More graphic violence. More sex. More foul language. More horrid dangers. More evil enemies. This is what sells. You know this, or at least your paper does. It constantly seeks out what is darkest and sourest about this world, and plasters it daily upon the front page. And why not, if this is what the people want to have, why not give it to them? We, all of us, continually expand the borders of entertainment." He jabbed the air between them with one rigid finger. "And it is only you, the deranged moralists, who object."

Despite herself, she could not help but rise to the accusation. "I object to everything you are and everything you do," Claire lashed back.

"Exactly. I am well aware of your predilection for the absurd crutch of religion, Miss Kingsbury. And you represent everything about our society that has become outdated. That is holding us back. It is time our civilization replaced the worn-out commands of a few desert wanderers." His monotone was as icy as the air. "We are talking about our society's direction. It is time to rise beyond body and space, beyond restrictions, beyond such nonsense as sin and wrongs. Rise to join with a true oversoul, one not just made for man, but *by* man. By the rulers set in place with the authority and power required to maintain order."

"Needless to say, you consider yourself one of these rulers." She found anger to be decent fuel against her fear and the glacial atmosphere. "I thought we were talking about a movie and game company."

Swindley offered her a complacent smile. "You know it to

be more than that. You must. Otherwise you would not have insisted upon this meeting."

"The drug." There was no need to fence about. "You have something planned for Nova."

"Beyond filling our coffers, the game was intended as a testing ground," Swindley confirmed. "A means of offering living proof to the rest of the world, indicating exactly what they might procure from me."

The realization hit her with the force of a body blow. "The Enforcers," she breathed. "They climb the Tower or enter the caves, and win the prize of damnation."

"Think what an advertiser would pay," Swindley intoned, "for a system that guaranteed that his product would receive a virtual monopoly from the public. Or a television company or a movie house or a presidential candidate."

"Mind control," Claire said. "You were developing a means of altering a person's thought processes."

"They are altered all the time," Swindley said, waving a blithe hand. "The masses are so gullible, they are sheep simply asking to be controlled. What I have done is to perfect a system. A drug so powerful it cannot be directly ingested except in minuscule quantities. One which could be sprayed in the atmosphere or attached to clothing or placed in drinking water. Add to that a usage of modern technology, delivering the message in a way so carefully monitored that those receiving it will afterwards never recall what they were told. They will simply obey."

"It doesn't seem so perfect to me," Claire countered. "What about all of those missing kids?"

Swindley showed irritation for the first time, a quick

flicker of emotion which came and went in a flash. "A few minor glitches. Any new system requires adjustments."

"What happened to them?"

"My associates here were alerted whenever one of the gamers arrived at the Tower or one of the other troves." His voice resumed its steel-hard monotone. "The game was made intentionally difficult. We had to limit the number of winners."

"That's what you call them?"

He chose to ignore her. "Monitoring was required, and we really did not need but so many test cases. A check was made of anyone who had arrived at the Tower. A simple call through the game itself was enough, merely to congratulate the new Enforcer. If any gamer had a negative reaction, which happened very seldom I hasten to add, then they were picked up, their computer systems erased, and the rejects were disposed of."

She stared at him in undisguised horror. "You killed them?"

"I had no need to." A particularly hard gust hammered rain against the window. "They were released on the streets of Los Angeles, there to gather with the other flotsam and jetsam of modern society."

"What was in the game that destroyed those kids?"

"Oh, I think it would be far easier to show you than try and explain," Swindley said, and waved his two men forward. "Take her."

Donovan drove back into Beverly Hills, reveling in the realization that the town was finally his. Even so, he could not overcome the heavy feeling to his heart.

Towards Claire he felt only anger. Even now, she blocked

him from feeling the joy and accomplishment he deserved. Every time the nagging sense of guilt attached itself to worry thoughts over having left her there with Swindley, he pushed it aside with the absolute conviction that she was only getting what she deserved. He did not know what Swindley had in mind, but no doubt he would scare her bad enough to have her back off. Which was fine, he told himself, despite the dull ache that resounded through his chest with every thump of his heart. She could not be allowed to get in the way of his dreams. Nobody could.

His thoughts turned to Trish, and the fact that she was arriving in two days. He felt his pulse quicken with anticipation. Now there was a lady who understood what it meant to go for the top. Donovan pressed down the accelerator and sped towards the city. Yes, she was definitely someone he should keep around, to help him enjoy the good life.

He deserved it all.

The upstairs corridor to Swindley's new house was still littered with the remnants of construction. As Claire was dragged up the stairs and onto the top landing, she managed to kick the stanchions out from under a painting platform, collapsing it onto the larger of her captives. But before she could pull free, the man called Skate grabbed her neck and rammed a knuckle into a pressure point below her chin. The pain was beyond awful. She cried out and would have collapsed, had he not supported her weight. Skate kept on the pressure as he half carried, half dragged her down the hall and into the chamber directly above where she had earlier been seated.

The room was built as a triangle. The two wedge-shaped

front walls were of glass. The clouds seemed to gather just outside, as though preparing to hurtle themselves against this bastion of modern pride. The room's only furniture was a pair of computers, a video camera on its tripod, a single stage, and a chair bolted to the floor.

"Skate and his companions have been up most of the night preparing for your arrival," Swindley said, watching as Skate tied her wrists, waist, and ankles to the metal-framed chair. "We have known for some time what the problem is within our little system, but we have lacked a willing subject with which to document our findings."

Her vision cleared in segments, the red hues of pain washing away gradually, finally allowing her the strength to whisper, "Donovan."

"What? Oh, yes, the gentleman shall not be coming back for you. He assumes you will be returning with the studio limo. Which of course will happen. But only after we have tested out our conclusions." Swindley glanced over to where Skate was slipping into a Second Skin, one of sheer matte black. "We are fairly certain that the problem lies within the dosage of Nova. If a subject enters into the Tower when the drug is beginning to wear off, his or her conscious mind struggles to regain control, and this battle is what causes the mental breakdown. We are therefore going to give you a very small dose, lead you to the Tower, and observe what happens."

Swindley stepped to one side as Skate slid the video camera's tripod up close to her and bent over to focus. "But you will not be allowed to suffer a full attack," he went on. "That might direct suspicion our way. Instead, you will be taken out before the breakdown is complete, given a larger dose, and then returned to the Tower." He gave her a deathmask of a smile. "There you will be given a full treatment, whereupon you will return to your paper, announce that you have discovered absolutely nothing of substance, and eventually return to that noxious little village from which you sprang."

Claire strained against her bonds. "You are a monster."

"And you are a most troublesome young lady. But not for much longer." He turned to where Skate waited. "Don't give yourself any more than is necessary to operate within the game. I want you to maintain full control and observe everything that happens."

"Right, Mr. S." Skate tore a Nova hologram into three bits. One segment he tossed aside. The second he attached to the tattoo beneath his right ear.

Swindley's toneless grey eyes turned back and watched as she struggled against the bindings. He observed as Skate walked over and jabbed the third star segment upon the wildly beating pulse of her neck.

"The essence of fear," Swindley said in his callous monotone, "is to be trapped in a situation from which there is no escape. There is nothing more terrifying than to watch helplessly as you are drawn closer and closer to your own doom."

Claire shook her head as much as the restraints permitted, but the star did not come loose. "You're insane."

"Is it insanity that drives a man to bend others to his will?" The voice was as dead as the eyes that gazed down at her. "If so, then most leaders of mankind down through the centuries have shared my dementia."

He turned away, saying to Skate as he did, "I'm due back

at the studio. Stay with her until it is completed."

"No problem," Skate said, and reached for the headgear. He fitted it over her eyes and ears, fastened a chinstrap into place, and plugged it in, utterly unmoved by her screams.

■ Claire did not even realize she was praying out loud until she heard Skate laughing. "Hey, no, don't stop. This is great. I mean, you're a little early with the last rites and all, but if you think it helps, be my guest."

"Just let me go," she pleaded. "You don't need to do anything."

"It's like this," he said, unfolding wings so dark they seemed to carve color from the sky. "The boss has said you need to go and meet the lady in the Tower. And what the boss says, goes."

They did not pass through the corridor or the staging area. Instead, there seemed to be a special path built in for Skate, one which permitted him instant access to any of the scenes. The different vistas passed to either side as he flew along, worlds that melded together, one with the next, like giant chambers within a madman's palace. Every one she looked at became as real as anything she had ever known, fleeting glimpses into impossible worlds. She knew it was the drug which guided her awareness. But knowing did not matter. As they flew down the tunnel, the game which surrounded her was *real.*

And at the tunnel's far end rose the Tower. Claire traveled pinned to Skate's chest, and watched as the silver tower grew from a speck in the distance until it dominated the entire horizon.

As they flew out of the tunnel's end, Skate pointed down and said, "That's the River Styx. It usually takes over a year of hard fighting before anybody gets this far. You've done it in what, about five minutes. All part of the service."

Although Skate's breathless squeak sounded exactly the same, his slender blond frame had been replaced by a flying parody. In place of warrior's gear, Skate wore a double-breasted suit with the padded shoulders of a comic-book gangster, topped by a mask grinning the most evil smile she had ever seen—except for that of Swindley himself.

Skate went on, "Just heard they've decided on a name for your friend Donovan's new company. Gonna call it Styx Enterprises, after the last barrier before a gamer reaches the Tower. Nice, don't you think?"

She bit off her response, wishing her addled mind would come up with something—anything—that could end this nightmare and free her. But like a nightmare, she was utterly caught up in it. Knowing that she had a drug coursing through her blood made no difference whatsoever. She had no control over what she saw. Closing her eyes only made it worse, for every time she did so a laser strobe started flashing, leaving her feeling as though her eyeballs were being fried, and an angry buzzing noise filled her head with the power of a billion dentist drills.

"My head hurts," she complained feebly.

"Yeah, it should, you keep trying to close your eyes like that. Little dingus in the helmet watches for too long a blink, then hits you with the sonic boom." Skate was enjoying himself thoroughly. "That's something new the boss thought up, had it fitted just for you. Glad to know it works."

They landed upon a broad avenue of golden brick. She tried to tell herself it was just an electronic image, just a cartoon drawing, but it did no good. To her, at that moment, she stood upon bricks of solid gold, before a pair of silver doors so huge she could barely make out their tops. Crests of jade green were hung upon them, depicting dragons circling a tower, upon which was seated a golden idol.

"Most people, they've got to fight their way up the steps," Skate said, indicating a staircase as broad as ten men that encircled the Tower. Claire looked up; from where she stood, the top was lost far up in the heavens. Skate continued with his verbal leer, "You, now, you get to take the elevator, open to VIPs only. Through those doors, one second of lift-off, and whoosh, you get to talk to the lady direct."

Skate stepped forward and rapped on the doors. With a booming rumble they began to open slowly, inch by inch, revealing a gaping maw of black within.

"Please, don't," she said, furious at the whimper in her voice, too frightened and too drained by the drug's force to do more.

"That's right, Skate," said a voice from behind them. "Don't do it."

Skate dropped her and she fell like a sack. Claire found herself utterly immobile, unable to even turn, as she wore no Second Skin. But she had fallen with her gaze pointed so that she could watch as Skate turned to peer at a warrior. There were very few weapons girded to his belt, and the shield was wooden instead of the golden one that she had seen her last time on the game. But the voice was unmistakable. She moaned out, "Troy."

Still, Skate's response was uncertain. "I know the voice, but not the guy."

"I tried to go online," Troy replied, "but my access was denied. I guessed you people decided to block me out."

"So you borrowed somebody else's gear." The grimace tightened, revealing rows of sharpened teeth. "Won't Swindley be pleased to learn I've got both his problems solved."

Troy seemed utterly unfazed by Skate. He stepped forward and said quietly, "Back off and let her go."

"Hey, I'd like to, really, but like I just told the lady here—" With the last word he whipped out a blazing orb, a fiery bundle of energy jutted with glowing spikes. It was connected to a long dangling chain, and that to a strap curled around Skate's wrist. He whirled it around his head, throwing a swath of blinding sparks over Troy, before sending it down in a swooping arc toward the warrior's head.

But Troy was ready, stepping under the sparks and catching the red-hot ball on his shield. The spikes imbedded themselves in the wood, so that when he did a whipping turn, the chain snapped and the ball came away.

Troy continued the turn, but as he swung back around, he unleashed his sword, a silver arc of razor-edge light that flashed in diamond brilliance as it curved towards Skate's head.

At the last instant Skate's shield appeared from nowhere, but almost too late. The blow was not stopped, only deflected, and it shattered the shield before wedging itself into what now were arched shoulders of chain-mail.

Skate shrugged off the remainder of his outer garments, revealing a battle costume of night-black steel. He crouched and shot lightning darts from pouches beneath his wrists, and followed them with small bombs slung about his waist. Troy dodged them with artistic fluidity, moving no more than was absolutely necessary, tiny motions that flickered so fast they were hard to follow and yet allowed him to retain his balance and be ready for the next.

Skate shouted a curse, reached behind him, and drew out a lance. But the instant of reaching was enough. Troy did not take the time to go for another weapon. Instead he leapt forward, smashing his shield and the globe imbedded on it directly into Skate's chest. Skate bellowed in rage as he was flung backwards. Before he could recover, Troy was upon him again, smashing down a second time and then a third, driving Skate further back with every blow, until Skate teetered on the brink of the Tower's entrance.

Only then did he become aware of what Troy intended. The realization brought a change to the mask, a loosening of the grimace, a flailing motion to grab the door, the frame, anything within reach. But it was too late.

A final slamming of Troy's shield sent him hurtling backwards into the darkness of the inner Tower of Babel.

Immediately the doors began to wheel back into place, slamming shut upon Skate's terror-stricken shrieks.

INTERIORITY AND MALIBU

32

■ "They were going to send me in there," Claire said, sobs coming in little gasps that sent tremors down her frame.

"I know," Troy said quietly. He stayed close, sitting there, patiently waiting for the worst to pass.

Behind them, the Tower stood cold and silent and implacable. Of Skate there had been no further sign.

"You have to move," Troy urged gently, when he thought she might be ready.

"I can't." Her voice was plaintive with how close she had come to her own end. "They've got me tied up, and they're going to come and do it again."

"You've got to try." Troy insisted. "How much Nova did they give you?"

"Just a little. They were trying an experiment," and at that the shudders started anew.

"Listen," Troy insisted. He thought a moment, trying to find something that would give her the strength to concentrate. "I've been thinking about everything you said."

Slowly, slowly, the words sank in, and as they did Claire focused fully upon him. "What?"

"Remember when we met in the game that last time? You talked to me about prayer and forgiveness and salvation." The absolute last words he would have ever thought of associating with this place. But even as he spoke them, he knew that their power had no bounds. "And God. And Jesus. I want to know more."

She was still now, her voice quiet but growing in strength. "You don't know how much it means to hear you say that."

"Will you teach me?"

"If I can," she replied simply. "It's all still really new to me as well."

"Maybe that's why I can understand you," he replied and rose to his feet. "But first we've got to get you out of here. Ready to try?"

And this time she replied, quietly but firmly, "Yes."

"Great. Here's what you do. Most of the top systems respond to voice commands. It keeps the overseers from having to work the keyboard while still gaming. There's a code word that activates the system, it's supposed to be secret, but I've been around enough Enforcers to know what they use. All we can do is hope that Skate operates on the same system."

"Okay. I'm ready."

"Wait. First tell me where you are in real time." He listened as Claire described the house and its location. "Okay.

I'm supposed to get a call from Harry soon as he lands in L.A., which should be about now. I'll relay the information."

"Harry," she repeated, and the word brought a thrill of hope to her voice. "Wait, you can also call Lillian Stockton Fletcher, she's in Beverly Hills." She repeated her number from memory.

"Great. Consider it done. Now listen. When you come out of it, you're going to feel like nothing's really what it is. That's the problem with the drug, it flashes in and out as you come down, leaving you wondering what's real and what's not. You have to *remember*. Use your memory to place reality in perspective."

"I understand."

"Okay. Here goes. The password is Gehenna."

Claire swallowed hard, took a shaky breath, and repeated, "Gehenna."

She heard a little ping in her right ear, then saw the glowing circle at the top right of her field of vision, and suddenly she was so excited she started to cry again.

She heard Troy say, "Shh, it's okay, stay straight now, we've got work to do."

"Okay, right, okay." Claire breathed deep, pushing aside the ache to her chest. "Go ahead."

"Just say, Close Game.

"Close Game," she repeated, and instantly there was another ping. "The red circle's been replaced by a question mark."

"It needs confirmation. Repeat the command. And good luck."

Claire took a breath and repeated, "Close Game."

Only when the images faded and closed, only when she was staring at a solid blank wall, did she realize that she had not even thanked Troy for her rescue.

The bindings did not prove as difficult as she had feared. While seeming to struggle against Skate's grip as they traveled through the game, she had in fact been pulling against the ropes. One wrist had loosened enough so that there was now some slack. Noises resounding from outside the room helped her focus as she tugged desperately, scarring her wrist and hand with rope-burns as she managed to draw one arm free. She fumbled with the chin-strap, pulled off the headgear, and slid it across the floor away from her.

Skate was sprawled across the padded rail, half in and half off the stage. His computer screen continued to send off swirling throngs of violent colors which frightened her every time she glanced over. Satisfied that he was not moving, she focused her attention on her other bonds.

The knots on her other hand proved extremely difficult, for it was hard to concentrate upon exactly what needed doing. Each frightened thought sent hordes of reptilian Skates and Swindleys crawling through sudden gaps in the walls. Instead of rain, the storm sent angry gremlins hurtling against the windows. Claire did as Troy had instructed and strived to remember. It helped. Not a lot, but enough.

With two hands free she was able to undo the ankles more easily. By the time she worked off the rope around her waist, her vision and mind were gradually beginning to clear.

She crept to the door and opened it a crack. Ignoring the

multicolored hues which scurried down the floor towards her, she craned and listened. All the sounds were coming from the floor below, echoing through the half-empty house like vacant memories.

As Claire struggled to throw off the last vestiges of the Nova drug, she spotted the coil of rope hanging from the painter's scaffolding. Her heart in her throat, she tiptoed out and hefted both rope and paint-spattered rags, then fled.

Back in the room, she tied one end of the rope to the doorknob, thus sealing the room shut. For added safety, she tied it firmly to the chair bolted to the floor. She then ripped the rags into long strips and began looping cloth back and forth around her wrist and then between thumb and forefingers, allowing just enough play for circulation and movement. She flexed her fingers, imagining at every moment that the door would turn, she would be caught in the act, they would burst through, and her fate would be sealed. Every once in a while she glanced over at Skate; the man did not move.

The two front windows were solid panes stretching from floor to ceiling and could not be opened. Outside, the darkness was gathering with frightening speed. The furious storm blanketed the sky, shutting out any hint of dusk. Frantically Claire searched the side windows and bit back a cry of relief when a panel slid back on its aluminum frame. The wind raged so hard that rain hurtling through the open window stung like needles. The window opening was only about eighteen inches wide, and she would have to crawl out without any ledge to lean on.

Claire offered a swift prayer, then slung one leg through the window, scrabbling for a hold on the wet outer glass. She

found that the rain was not all bad, for the cold and the sting-
ing pain helped sharpen her wits. She dropped one shoe off,
then the other, tossing them down to the unseen rocks below.
She slid further out, until her weight was balanced precariously
upon the windowframe. She looped the rope around her chest
and waist, then formed the slip knot at the base of her rib cage.
Her trembling hands made the movements difficult, and everything seemed to take ten times longer than it should, but
finally she succeeded.

Gripping the frame with the outer foot, taking a firm hold
upon the rope, she leaned out, straining against the wind that
strived to blow her away, further and further into the wild and
windy darkness.

Remember, Troy had told her. She thought of other times
when she had been forced to rappel under extreme condi-
tions. Times when smoke had swirled so thick she could hardly
breathe, and the distant base was lost in darkness. Like now.

What she had not been prepared for was the cold. The
side of her body turned towards the wind might as well have
been stripped bare. Her leg and ribs burned like they were
being scored with a white-hot fire. Her face was growing numb,
and her fingers were losing feeling.

There was a single instant of lowering wind, and Claire
rappelled down. She had no choice. To stay meant to die.

She pushed off the glass, relaxing her grip, and allowed
the rope to sing through her fingers and around her waist. She
caught and braked in as gradual a flow as she could manage.

She saw the window of the floor below rush up to meet
her. She aimed for the dark lining, which indicated a windowframe, and prayed that it would hold, for the interior

blazed with light. She rested only long enough to crouch and push and hurtle down. Despite the misery of trying to rappel down a wet glass wall, she was grateful for the storm, for no one would notice her unless they were to look directly at the window. The storm's noise masked every other sound.

The farther she fell, the louder grew the ocean's fury. It roared below her like a ravenous beast, crashing against the cliffside and throwing icy spumes up to join with the rain. Rappelling meant sliding downwards back first, normally something which did not bother her in the slightest, but the further she fell the more she feared crashing into the rocks below.

The wind picked up again, but she kept on, descending far too fast. Already she was losing feel of the rope. It was either fly or freeze. Her heart rate surged a notch higher with each landing upon the wall, which was not all bad, as it pushed more blood through her extremities and sharpened what senses she had left. On her next landing, she paused long enough to look down. The wind whipped spray all about her, a blinding lash that made the searching futile. She kept on.

But the fear had her ready to notice when the wall's smooth aluminum changed to rougher stone. She was no longer able to measure her descent by the rope passing through her hands, they were so numb. So she took a bite of the rope around her left arm. It would mean a raw wound tomorrow, but she might now survive the night.

The rope seared with the next descent, all her weight now passing through this curl of line around her arm. But it permitted her to walk downwards along the increasingly rough base of rock, little skips of a meter or so. She smelled the wool of her sweater sear with the friction. The ocean was now all that she could hear, so close that it drowned out the howling wind. She stopped, her breath gasping, and looked down once again. Nothing. Another few steps, then she saw it, the cliff rocks glistening like shadow-teeth. Slower now, then a gasping moan of relief when her backside touched the base.

She sat like that for a moment, her body too tense to even sprawl. Her breath pumped in and out like heaving bellows, a sigh to match the wind. Every crash from below sent up a shower of spray so heavy it seemed ready to claw her from the cliff. She had to move. She had to. But her body did not want to respond.

Slowly, her movements like those of an arthritic old woman, she rolled over, pressed down, pushed herself up. For a brief instant, Claire hoped the guards would realize she had escaped and come looking for her. At least the chamber was warm.

Her fingers searched desperately for holds as she took one careful side-step after another, on around the house's perimeter. When the corner shielded her from the worst of the wind, she picked up the pace a notch, then again when the front houselights splashed reassuringly just ahead.

She began running as fast as her exhausted limbs would carry her. She limped up the drive, through the unfinished gates, and down the side of the highway. She was sobbing with relief now and waving her hands over her head. In a voice that slurred the words so that not even she could understand what she was saying, she pleaded for every set of headlights to stop.

Suddenly brakes squealed, and a car careened across from the other side, doing a barely controlled four-wheel spin as it swooped down on her. Then the door opened and Harry spilled out into the rain, scooping her up into his arms, shout-ing against the rain and the blaring horns, demanding to know who did this to her, and begging for her to say that she was all right.

■ Trish watched him carefully the whole way from the airport to the Bel Air Hotel. When they arrived and the bellhops were scurrying about the car wishing them the warmest welcome money could buy, she just sat there until they were alone again. Then she said, "You've changed."

Donovan did not bother to deny it. Instead, he grimaced and said, "I've lost a couple of illusions."

"That's good," she said. "This close to the top, illusions can be costly."

"And morals," he murmured, thinking of Claire, wishing the ache would go away.

"You're learning. Good, I like that." She reached across to stroke his cheek. "It's the sure sign of a winner."

He could not help but respond to her caress. "I could pick up a lot from you."

"That's right, you could," she said, giving him a slow nod of approval. "So when do I meet the big man himself?"

"I'm not sure. Swindley's been a little hard to reach recently." In fact, Donovan had not heard from him since dropping Claire off at his Malibu home the week before. Donovan's calls had been taken by a secretary who had appeared as confused as he was.

"Well, there's time enough for that later." Trish gave him a quick smile of things to come, patted his arm, and purred, "Come on, lover boy. I need to show you how happy I am to see my winner again."

Donovan rose from the car and started across the little stone bridge after Trish. His steps felt leaden, as though he could not let go of the memories and the words and the look of Claire. Angrily Donovan slapped the bridge wall, shook his head, and struggled to clear his mind. There was nothing to be gained from this stupidity. He had everything going for him.

Everything.

■ Claire walked into the kitchen, gave the clock a sleepy inspection, and declared, "I can't believe I've slept this late."

"You were tired." Harry glanced up from the kitchen table, which was strewn with a half-dozen newspapers, and gave her a warm smile. "You won't believe what they're saying."

Claire held up a hand in self-defense. "Not before coffee. Please."

"I just made a fresh pot." He rose to his feet, guided her over to a chair, then went back to the counter. "Nathan left over an hour ago. He says to tell you not to be late."

"We're not due at the church for another five hours." She tried to avoid looking at the papers, but the headlines acted like magnets to her gaze. "Where did you find these?"

"I had the office express them here." He set down the steaming mug, swivelled the *Chicago Tribune* around, said, "Get a load of this one."

"I can't. Not yet," she protested weakly, but could not help reading. The banner headline took her breath away.

Denver Herald reporter uncovers mind-control plot

Links virtual reality game to drugs, disappearances

CHICAGO TRIBUNE NEWS SERVICES

DENVER—*Denver Herald* reporter Claire Kingsbury, who broke the story on the link between Babylon and the synthetic mind-control drug, Nova, described her own harrowing experience with the game at a news conference Tuesday.

"Babylon, despite how it is mar-keted, is not a game," Kingsbury said. "When paired with the drug, Nova, it becomes a nightmare for anyone daring or, in my case, forced to play. Even though I knew I was in a game, the drug so twisted my brain that I couldn't break free."

Harry walked to the kitchen window. "I've been up since dawn. The sunrise gradually transformed the mountains." He sipped from his own cup. "It was one of the most beautiful things I've ever seen. I almost woke you up."

"I've seen a highland dawn, Harry. I'm almost always up in time for them." Try as she might, she could not help but look at the next article, this one in the *Los Angeles Times*.

"Entertainment drugs" become even more menacing to society

LOS ANGELES TIMES NEWS SERVICES

DENVER—Recent investigations into illegal drug labs in the Colorado Rockies have revealed a new and startling narcotic trend developing in American culture.

One such new drug is called Nova and is so powerful that it is not taken orally but must be attached to the skin by way of a hologram, commonly referred to as a Starsign. According to the *Denver Herald . . .*

"I spoke to the office," Harry said to the window. "The phones have been going berserk. Calls from all over the place. They want you on the *Today* show. There's been an offer for you to write a book about this, with a six-figure advance. Management is having a field day. All of a sudden we're the brightest stars in the firmament, and all the Radley corporate executives want to fly down and shake our hands."

Claire pushed the paper away, only to see underneath a double-spaced photocopy of her next article, scheduled to be released the following day. The headline read, "Win the game and lose your life," and the article started, "His name is Buddy Wiggins, but he cannot tell us that himself. He has not spoken at all for over three weeks, not since reaching the ultimate prize of a game called Babylon . . ."

Claire turned around in her seat and protested, "I thought this was supposed to be a day off."

"Call it a busman's holiday," Harry said and pointed at the counter near where she stood. "A letter came from Troy this morning. He's joined our Bible study. Sounds like he's going to be all right."

"I'm glad." But she couldn't bring herself to pick up the envelope. It lay on that morning's *Denver Herald*, which was spread out to reveal two front-page articles.

New VR game linked to drugs, mind control

Babylon Players Used to Test Synthetic Drug

By Claire Kingsbury
DENVER HERALD STAFF WRITER

DENVER—Styx Enterprises, an interactive media company owned by Hollywood mogul Roger Swindley, has been linked to human testing of a synthetic mind-control drug and disappearances of several people, according to an investigative report conducted by the *Denver Herald*.

Babylon, the new virtual reality game that is sweeping the country . . .

and

FBI finds drug lab in Colorado highlands

DENVER (AP)—Federal officers uncovered a deserted laboratory Thursday on land owned by Roger Swindley, owner of Swindley Broadcasting and Styx Enterprises.

The FBI speculates that the facility was used recently in the manufacturing of the synthetic mind-control drug, Nova.

She looked at him in frantic appeal. "It's too much."

He smiled, shook his head. "It hasn't even begun."

"I don't know if I can handle it."

"Yes you can." His tone was strong, quiet, reassuring. "I'll help you."

But to Claire it felt as though the world had invaded the sanctuary of her mountain home. "Come skiing with me."

Harry laughed. "No chance. The only contact sport I go in for is parking my car."

"Not downhill. Cross country." Her tone was pleading. "A totally different experience."

He looked doubtful. "Does it involve moving faster than the speed of sound?"

"Not even close."

"Dropping off the side of mountains? Learning the value of a good scream? Becoming all too intimate with pine trees?"

"Silence, solitude, being one with nature." She moved away from the table and everything it contained. "Please, Harry."

He examined her face. "This is important to you?"

She nodded slowly. "Very."

The mid-December morning shone with shy glory, especially once they had left the town behind. Claire took it very slowly, sticking to empty paths so Harry would not feel self-conscious. In truth, he handled himself very well for a beginner. She avoided all the steeper inclines, let him set the pace, talked him gently through the awkward stage of becoming accustomed to feet almost six feet long.

"Don't try to walk. That's it. Slide and push, alternating pole and ski. Very good, Harry. You really are getting the hang of it."

He was puffing too hard to say much, but his face shown with genuine pleasure. "This is great."

Seeing that he was really enjoying himself twisted her heart with a sincere pain. "I can't thank you enough for doing this with me."

"No problem." He slid to a halt and gave her a flushed

smile. "You needed to get out of the house. I can understand that."

"It's more than that." She popped out of her skis, then jammed her pole into the catch at the back of Harry's binding. "Lift your heel up. That's it, now pull your toe free."

"Why? I don't want to stop yet."

"I want to show you something. Now free your other foot." She hefted their skis and jammed them into the snow. Then she took his hand and led him off the trail and into the forest.

Clear mornings in the highlands were dreams in the making. The world was still, fresh, totally new. Away from the brilliant sun, the sky darkened to almost midnight blue. Trees stood with branches outstretched, like shrouded penitents bearing white offerings to the new day. There was no room for worries, not even for all the clamor that surrounded her. Somehow the mountains filtered it all out.

Harry allowed her to lead them deeper into the woods. Around them spread a mountain world in a billion hues of grey. Through branches as stark as bones of charcoal they caught glimpses of rocky slopes left naked by drifting snow, and a lake flat and grey as polished steel.

Finally Claire stopped, and simply stood there, surrounded by winter and quiet. She looked around at a scene recreated out of ice and white and stillness. The world looked reborn, its fresh mantle untouched by eons or man. Claire sighed happily. The day was a gift.

Harry's voice was a scarce whisper. "It's like a church made by God's hand."

She nodded, licked dry lips, and whispered back, "God spoke to me out here. He showed me the mirror of who I was."

Harry was a long time in replying, "It must have been hard."

"Awful," she softly agreed. "But so very important."

He turned to her. "Thank you for sharing this with me."

She took off her glove, so as to touch his face. "I did it because I knew you would understand."

"Your next article is great, by the way," Harry said, walking with her towards the church. "Totally explosive. We're running it below the fold, page one."

"Harry, stop." But she was smiling. She couldn't help it. The day was just too grand. "Not now."

But he caught sight of her smile and used it as license to continue. "That'll give the other papers something more to chew over. Then the next day, boom. Another major barrage. Keep hitting them while everybody else in the trade is still trying to get over the shock of being caught totally flat-footed."

"Shhh. This isn't the time for business."

"You might as well get used to the idea of spending a lot of time in the courtroom. The Feds will use you against Swindley and his crowd and that company, whatever it is they're calling it."

"Styx," she supplied, so very glad that she could finally say the word without fear. Perhaps that was something else that had come from writing those articles, giving herself a way to work through everything that had happened.

Claire sighed happily as the church came into view. She slipped her hand into Harry's, an unconscious gesture, at least on her part. Harry glanced her way, then turned back, the smile on his face as tender an expression as he had ever worn.

Claire kept her face turned upwards as they walked, letting Harry share the hellos and excited chatter. In this snow-covered village she felt that she was a better person. More complete. Almost worthy of God and this man walking alongside her. There was such energy to this day that Claire felt ready to burst from her skin.

Together they paused before the church entrance. She stood beside Harry and watched happily as old friends filed into the church.

When there was a pause in the procession, she leaned over and kissed his cheek, not caring who saw it. But the words she whispered into his ear were for him and him alone. "I love you, Harry Mitchum. I loved you even before I knew it was true and real and meant to be."

He turned, stared into her eyes with a gaze that blazed with joy. Then he leaned forward and kissed her soundly. When he finally released her, he said quietly, "This is a miracle."

"It's more than that," she said. "It's perfect."

They tasted another kiss, but were interrupted by Miss Emma climbing the stairs. "Now that is just about enough," she said sharply. "You both can start learning some patience and wait until after the ceremony!"

Claire released him reluctantly. Harry smiled and said, "Looks like it's time to get started."

She nodded, stroked his face, then turned and took her place beside Lillian and Miss Emma. Harry hurried on through the entrance, leaving the three women standing out there alone, great swaths of white crinoline billowing in the soft breeze. As she waited for the organist to begin the bride's march, Claire reflected that she was happier than she had ever been in her entire life.

The music sounded and the pair of women staffing the doors ushered them through. Claire started down the church's central aisle, staring into each face as she went. She had never seen so many smiles. Or so many shining eyes. Never.

As they arrived at the front, Nathan stepped forward and took Lillian's arm. Claire moved over to one side and watched her friend. Lillian stood radiant and shimmering and so happy she could not keep one tear from escaping and coursing down her cheek.

Claire watched and listened as the marriage ceremony unfolded, and wondered at how Lillian could have kept hope alive for all those years. Through all the loneliness of living on an island of riches, cut off from human caring and genuine affection by a sea of wealth, Lillian had kept hold of her heart. It was an amazing feat. As Claire stood and heard the minister intone the vows, she knew in her heart that Lillian was a far stronger woman than she would ever be.

And her father. Standing straight and upright as always, unbent by the storms that had wreaked such havoc in his life. Claire turned and glanced back to where Harry stood; he watched not the wedding but her, his eyes saying all that his voice could not. Not then.

Claire turned back and gave silent thanks for the wonder of this man, her father, who in his own quiet way had reshaped the lives of those who came within reach, granting them a vision of what they yet did not know. She took a deep breath around her swollen heart and knew that if there was a hero to this saga, it was Nathan Kingsbury.

The minister intoned, "I now pronounce you man and wife," and a cheer erupted from the congregation.

Lillian pressed a hand to her chest and said simply, "Oh!" It was the sound of a thousand lonely nights escaping, vanishing into the well of remembrance, leaving her open and ready for all the tomorrows to come.

Nathan placed a gentle hand on her shoulder, his eyes quietly happy, ready and waiting for the minister to say, "You may now kiss the bride."

FEDERAL DISTRICT COURT FOR COLORADO

Docket Number: CF10284

United States v. Styx Enterprises, et al.

<u>Deposition of Claire Kingsbury: Day Three</u>
Offices of Mr. Josiah R. Holloway,
Attorney for the Defense

MR. HOLLOWAY: Are you aware, Miss Kingsbury, that other journalists and editors referred to you as part of the paper's Christian Mafia?

MISS KINGSBURY: I heard the term used, yes.

MR. HOLLOWAY: Would you not say, Miss Kingsbury, that this is fairly indicative of a hostility shared by numerous professionals towards both you and the quality of your work?

MISS KINGSBURY: Are you saved, Mr. Holloway?

MR. HOLLOWAY: Am I . . . Just answer the question, Miss Kingsbury.

MISS KINGSBURY: I ask only because those who

know the joy of salvation also know that many will turn against them for taking that step.

MR. HOLLOWAY: Miss Kingsbury, I must insist that you answer the question.

MISS KINGSBURY: I am trying to. There is still time to know the saving grace of Jesus Christ. Even for Donovan Stone. Even for Roger Swindley. Even for you.

ACKNOWLEDGMENTS

A book of this scope has drawn upon a very large number of people, all of whom have enriched my life and work with their unstinting patience and assistance. I am indeed grateful for their help.

Janet Thoma is my editor at Thomas Nelson Publishers. It has been a genuine delight to work with her. I am most grateful for the guidance and wisdom she has granted me. Todd Ross, the managing editor, and his wife, Molly, proved to be an amazing find; they previously both worked with newspapers in Florida, and helped tremendously in fashioning the newspaper stories included here.

Dr. George Hobson is both the Canon of the American Cathedral in Paris, an extremely talented poet, and a dear friend. He and his wife, Victoria, have assisted in a number of my books. When I decided that I wanted to take on the task of learning about the mountains well enough to write about them, George kindly shared with me some of his own writings.

I am indeed grateful for the deep and heartfelt insight which was gained through his work.

Richard Jones is a criminal lawyer based in Raleigh. He was kind enough to take time from a trial to walk me through how a defense attorney with a weak case might structure his opening depositions.

Our dear friend, Mara Papatheodorou, is an L.A.-based journalist with an astounding knowledge of the entertainment industry. She acted as tour guide and insider during our research into Hollywood and Beverly Hills.

Dr. Phil Robson is Drug Specialist at the Chiltern Clinic in Oxford, England. Sadly, he has come to know a very great deal about the effects of designer drugs on today's youth.

A number of people proved most helpful in coming to grips with the complexities of next-generation computers, interactive video games, internet gaming, and 3-D visualization. They include: Nigel Todd, Consultant with ICL; Max McMullin of Mesh Interactive; Ian Bird of Soho Computer Graphic Effects; and Andrew Bishop of Three-Dee Vision.

Pete Pierce is professor at the Toulouse Business School, and is a specialist in commercial applications of internet technology. He assisted mightily by pointing me in the right direction.

The lessons from the book of Mark came from a sermon by Pastor George Keller of the First Baptist Church in Merritt Island, Florida. This wonderful congregation has come to mean a great deal to my wife and me. We are indeed grateful for their teachings, and their strength of Spirit.

On my second of four research trips to Colorado, I met

the wonderful Sunderland family. Paul is an attorney living in Ouray; Jan formerly ran a specialist quilting shop in the town's center, but has given that up to home school her children. They and their fabulous kids did everything possible to give me a cram course on the Colorado Rockies. Throughout the time of both research and writing, they were always there to help in any way possible. I am indeed grateful both for their friendship and their guidance.

Henry Dubroof is the former Business Editor of a Denver newspaper. His intimate knowledge of the newspaper business was invaluable. His integrity and dedication have remained a true inspiration.

My wife, Isabella, has been a source of wisdom and guidance throughout this project. She has been alongside me from the beginning, making tremendously valuable suggestions, working as my partner and friend. Thank you, Sweetheart, for sharing in the work as well as the joy.